love your library

Rob B
writes
transla
of a
vibran

Buckinghamshire Libraries
0845 230 3232
www.buckscc.gov.uk/libraries

24 hour renewal line
0303 123 0035

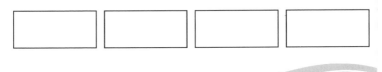

BIG FROG

Rob Badcock

Book Guild Publishing
Sussex, England

First published in Great Britain in 2011 by
The Book Guild Ltd
Pavilion View
19 New Road
Brighton, BN1 1UF

Typesetting in Meridien by
Norman Tilley Graphics Ltd, Northampton

Printed in Great Britain by
CPI Antony Rowe

A catalogue record for this book is available from
The British Library

ISBN 978 1 84624 832 0

For
Jean and James
and with thanks to
Liz and John

Prologue

When you go to post a letter in one of those red pillar boxes, something inside you hesitates. You pause. You check the address. You check the stamp. You check the collection time. These delaying tactics are no more than excuses. A deeper sense of unease holds you back from the inevitable. And when you do finally allow the envelope to slip from your fingertips into the gaping black slit, you pause again. You listen for the muffled thud as it lands on the mattress of mail inside. You listen. Just to check again. The finality of the act is almost enough to take your breath away. In fact, that's exactly what happens. You have been holding your breath. You have to make a conscious effort to exhale.

The last time the old woman had felt this way was over sixty years ago when she was a little girl of seven and the world was a different place. A very different place. When red pillar boxes really did stand on street corners …

As she now held out her lottery ticket to the long-haired boy with a slightly vacant expression, something deep inside her made her hesitate.

'Could you check this for me, please?' she said at last.

The boy nodded and fed her ticket into the terminal. He saw it nonchalantly register jackpot. 250 million dollars' worth of jackpot to be precise. No sirens, no fanfare, no ringing of bells. Just $250,000,000 on the screen before him. As pure and as simple as that.

'Any good?' she asked.

'No, sorry, better luck next time,' he said, hearing the echo of his words in disbelief. Why did he say that? He had never stolen anything in his life. Jesus Christ! 250 million dollars! What was he doing?

'I just had a funny sort of feeling that tonight would be my lucky night,' she sighed.

'No sorry,' he replied. He was suddenly the hit-and-run driver. The driver who didn't stop. The driver who couldn't stop. The driver who committed the crime and stepped on the gas. No turning back.

He wanted to.

But he couldn't.

'Look, would you like to check it for yourself?' he offered. Was this bluff or guilt? He had no idea. He was out of control.

'No, that's all right,' she sighed again. 'What will be, will be.'

'Do you want the ticket?' The boy held out the slip.

'No thanks, dearie,' she said. 'Put it where it belongs,' nodding towards the bin behind him.

The boy coolly screwed up the chit and threw it in the bin.

'Next, please,' he said, engaging eye contact with the customer waiting at the old woman's shoulder. The boy focused his every ounce of attention on the moustachioed man who ordered a packet of ten tequila-dipped liquorice cigarillos, with filter. He completed the transaction and searched for the old lady from the corner of his eye.

She was gone.

1

Rib Meskitoe.

Fourteen years, fair of hair, long of limb, ill at ease with himself and the world.

And homesick.

A number of things about the Wigan citidome had taken him by surprise. Firstly, that he was there at all. He was supposed to be in Kathmandu. Secondly, that he was stuck there. His ticket turned out to be one-way only.

How could things have gone so badly wrong? Just forty-eight hours earlier he had been leaning back in his seat on the lasercraft at Silbury Terminal waiting for his sleepwafer. The smiling stewardess had popped the thin blue disc in his mouth to melt on his tongue and immerse him in the deepest sleep lasting the 7 minutes 20 seconds it took the sleek ship *Sirius* to swoosh him to his destination.

The wrong destination.

He must have keyed in the wrong code on the easy-to-use self-service ticket machine. Mental note to queue next time.

OK, he had not been in the best frame of mind when he arrived at the terminal. Things had been getting worse by the day at home. Mum was on his case almost every waking moment.

OK, he knew she had problems, but he was doing his best. His best just never seemed to be good enough.

Things had come to a head when he'd forgotten to put Sunday's rubbish down the chute. She had gone ape. He had gone AWOL. For a whole four hours. Sloped off to skulk around Chaffron. When he'd cooled down enough to return home, he'd made his mind up. He was leaving home. Well, for a time at least …

The note left on the galley table had read 'Bye Mum. Off to earn some looty for us. Don't worry, love you. Rib x.' It had taken him three goes to compose the message in his best scratchy script.

OK, so he was all snarled up inside. OK, so he'd never been off the citidome in his life. But Wigan! Why Wigan? All had seemed well as the wake-up shot roused him from his flightsleep. As soon as he stepped into the arrivals hall, however, he knew something was wrong. The large sign of three pies on a skewer, the Wigan kebab, hanging heavy above the exit door told him that this was not Kathmandu, his rainbow's end.

Having had a good blub in the toilet, Rib came to terms with the fact that he would not be earning shed-loads of dollars preparing gourmet truffles harvested from the slopes of the Nepalese foothills after all. He registered, initially with a degree of caution, at the Operationsexchange bureau and started the same day on the afternoon shift at a food factory on 34th Street. It said 'Succulent Savoury Delights' above the door, but as soon as he stepped over the threshold Rib knew that he had entered the hardcore underworld of a meat-and-potato pie processing plant. He lasted for precisely twenty-seven minutes. It was like a vegetarian booking a day-cruise to the Isles of Scilly and ending up by mistake on a Japanese whaler in a force 10 sea in the Southern Ocean.

He was introduced to his co-workers, Reet and Petito, each weighing in at twenty-five stone. Reet looked him up and down and said, 'You're a young'un,' and belched full force in his face. She gave him a dirty grey cotton hat and an even dirtier grey overall. 'Come on, I'll show you where it's made,' she said and waddled along a steam-filled corridor. He followed her at a safe distance up a steel stairway onto a platform running round the perimeter of a massive stainless-steel vat, some 10 metres high.

'There!' Reet proudly pointed.

Rib peered over the rim at a sea of bubbling grey–brown sludge. The stench was overpowering. Something rose above the surface of the gloop. It was a whole sheep's head.

Rib retched into the vat. Several times, until there was nothing left and then once more for good measure. Reet observed with the distant air of someone who had seen it all before.

When he was finally done and able to stand upright, she said, 'Wipe yer gob on the front of yer overall.' He obeyed, without question. 'Health and Safety,' she explained knowingly, turning to waddle back down the stairs.

Rib followed her down the stairs, back along the steam-filled corridor and then took a sharp right straight out of the main door, shedding overall and hat in a skip beside the front gate.

And so, there he was, working on the lottery terminal at a supermarket. Having signed a contract for three months on a pod on the Dome's East Side, he knew that he had to be earning immediately.

The second visit of the day to the exchange offered a career move from manufacturing to retail. But this was no ordinary retail.

It was Waste-Rows.

A retro-outlet, more like a theme park than a shop, designed to replicate the extremes of how things used to be when people actually bought groceries. Of course, nobody shopped any more. Nobody needed to. Everything was automated. Production, delivery, you could even arrange for your food to be chewed for you. In a cunning feat of socio-leisure engineering, to stop large sections of the population slitting their wrists out of sheer boredom, the Protectorate invented Waste-Rows. The supermarket where you could quite legitimately, without fear of prosecution, indulge in the excesses of a shopping experience entirely based on waste. And pollution. And unacceptable behaviour.

So it was quite a risky place to work. Which explained the attractive hourly rate. And also explained the high staff turnover rate, but Rib didn't know that at the time.

A certain type of person shopped at Waste-Rows. A person who might: drag the whole family to the supermarket for the sole purpose of screaming at the kids and smacking them in front of the woman selling double-glazing; park in a disabled bay, car window wound down to blow smoke in the faces of passing wheelchair users; set up a twenty-minute road block at the Express Till by asking for cashback, redeeming thirty-seven vouchers and tokens, and returning various items of underwear worn only twice.

Another big pull was the freedom for customers to choose their own attire. To shed the monotone of the greysuit on entering the store and slip into something more … expressive. Survey results showed the most popular choice by far to be white stilettos, pink Lycra riding pants, fake fur top and Burberryesque scarf, topped off by a New York Yankees baseball cap. Women tended to go for something less loud.

The central in-store attraction was the big cardboard box at the end of Row Seven. No matter what rubbish you put in it, by the end of the day it was empty. Sold out. Waste-Rows used this refined merchandising model to do a roaring trade in ski suits, goggles, gloves and thermal long johns over twenty years after the last flake of snow had fallen on the planet. And how did they do that? They put a tacky advert with big red letters against a yellow background in the paper on a Friday night, filled the big cardboard box with ski gear, opened the doors on Saturday morning and stood clear of the stampede.

Waste-Rows. What a dump. Quite literally. The store proudly guaranteed that over 75 per cent of goods purchased would be shitcanned within twenty-four hours. And they were right ...

In spite of the raw energy of the place, it was quite lonely at first. Rib couldn't get along with the accent, the humour, the body scent. He was not accepted in the staffroom. Nothing hostile, just a thick impenetrable wall of antipathy. Except for Kaddie. Kevin Kadwallader, to give him his full name. A Welshman with a limp. So, quite naturally, Kaddie did all the things in the supermarket that a person with a disability really should not be doing. Like pushing a long serpent of trolleys around the car park in extremely adverse artificial weather conditions. For the greater part of the day and into the night. Indeed, Kaddie seemed to thrive on it. The longer the serpent the better, it seemed. Kaddie once confided that his world record was 97 trolleys pushed up and down the length of the car park for 4 hours 17 minutes without damaging a single vehicle.

'What's so clever about that?' asked Rib and immediately wished he hadn't.

'Well,' explained Kaddie, 'it's because my serpent is the longest. The secret is to keep it straight. If it starts to bend in the middle, then you've got a problem.'

Somehow Rib was half expecting an answer along these lines, but had allowed himself to be sucked into the Kadwallader psyche.

'And I like kites you know. You'll have to come and join us on Sunday morning. There's a whole load of us fly our kites out on East 10 at 7 o'clock.'

Yeah, right, thought Rib.

So next Sunday, there he was, out on the East 10 rim approaching a group of twenty or so enthusiasts playing all sorts of seriously impressive aerofoils on the wind. Blue fins, lilos, boxes ...

Rib stood and admired the aerobatics for a good few minutes before sighting a hunched figure, apart from the others, seated on a wicker basket with a winch in front of him. And reeled out from the winch was a line which went up and up and up. Shielding his eyes against the fierce sun, Rib thought he could make out a little dot. It didn't move, it just hung there, at the end of what must have been 400 metres of taut line.

Kaddie acknowledged Rib's arrival with a toothy grin.

'I knew you'd come. Isn't this just brill?'

'Mmm,' Rib replied.

'But what's your kite supposed to be doing, Kaddie? Isn't it supposed to be swooping and diving, looping the loops and all that?'

'No, you stupid boy, mine is simply the best. It's just perfect as it is.'

'Why?' asked Rib and immediately wished he hadn't.

'Well,' explained Kaddie. 'It's because mine is the longest. The secret is to keep it straight, if it starts to bend ...'

Mmm, thought Rib, sensing a theme.

'OK, OK.'

Every now and then the supermarket management invited Kaddie indoors to do some shelf-stacking. Kaddie would agree only if the sun was shining. If the weather machine lashed it down, he'd rather be out there with the trolleys. Part of the attraction was the outdoor uniform, the bright-orange anorak and green sou'wester. Indoors, Kaddie reverted to the grey overall with the yellow corporate chevron on the arm. Kaddie, though, objected violently to this total infringement against his favourite colour, grey, and took remedial action by shading in the yellow chevrons with grey shoe cleaner, which he also used for his grey shoes, which he wore over his grey socks, which he wore on his quite worryingly grey feet.

But, credit where credit's due, Kaddie was quite a good shelf-stacker. Until he reached Row Seventeen, that is, where he would always, without fail, manage to dislodge a two-kilo jar of pickled beetroot from the top shelf. On hearing the crash, people would rush to the aisle, only to find him giggling hysterically, standing in a spreading puddle of purple juice.

'Look at me,' he would say, in the Welshest of Welsh accents. 'I'm the only grey in the spillage!'

And people would laugh, without really knowing why.

Weird though he was, Kaddie was the closest Rib had as a friend in meat-and-potato pie land. Every now and then, one of the other lads would pick on Kaddie – he was easy meat and potato for that matter. And whilst Rib was not the bravest soul, he had stuck up for him on more than one occasion. The first time was when Kaddie was sitting in the corner of the empty staffroom. Dayno Spurg burst in and decided that he wanted to occupy the seat in which Kaddie was reclined, planning his next assault on Row Seventeen. When Rib entered, Dayno was raining a series of admittedly unconvincing blows around the Welshman's head, who by this stage was bleating incoherently from the corner of his mouth.

'Ey you, pack it in!' was Rib's highly original opening gambit. There then ensued a 45-second exchange of truly terrifying proportions along the lines of:

'Make me!'

'Yeah?'

'Yeah!'

'Yeah?'

and so on …

Neither Rib nor Dayno had the slightest intention of fighting each other, but face was saved, Kaddie came out of the corner more or less unscathed, and the bond between him and Rib grew that little bit stronger.

2

It took a lifetime for the outrageously retro digital clock on the supermarket wall to blink over to 20.00. Rib shut down the till, locked the cigarette cabinet and took the rubbish bin out to the back office just as he had done so day in day out for the past three weeks. Or at least that's how he hoped it looked. Beneath the surface of studied routine, his heart pounded, his knees trembled and his palms were so wet that when he bent down to pick up a discarded ticket from the floor it turned to papier-mâché in an instant.

Rib looked around. Everything was as it should be. The only time in the whole day that Waste-Rows' staff moved with a common purpose, a sense of teamwork, was when it was time to shut up shop. Each knew exactly what to do to minimise delay. Rib had to move fast. Normally, he would take the rubbish out to the back office, throw all the bags down the chute, and be back to join the rest of the gang by the front shutter within the minute. Once out of sight, he rummaged down into the bag for the winning ticket. He had memorised the number – 22, 7, 51, 5, 14, 9, 99 – and knew it would be about halfway down the bag. He began systematically by carefully taking out each piece of screwed-up paper, but then began to panic and just grabbed handfuls and opened them on the floor.

'And what do you think you're doing?' whispered Store Supervisor Svensson in his ear.

'Aargh!' shrieked Rib, wondering how the hell Svensson had snuck up on him. 'Er, I'm just looking for a … wibble,

wibble …' he went.

Later Rib couldn't recall what he had pretended to be looking for. Only that Svensson had told him to get the bag down the chute right now and be at the front door within thirty seconds, otherwise he needn't turn up the next day.

'OK, OK!' blurted Rib. 'Could you just check for me that the cigarette cabinet is locked please?' Svensson paused, ready to fire off a salvo at this kid asking him, the Store Supervisor, to help him lock up. But he needed to get away on time tonight. He was taking Susan from Sticky Buns to see *Police Academy 37* at the Kino in forty minutes.

So he cursed his way round to the counter, leaving Rib to stare at the bin, his mind racing. What were his options? Option number one – panic. No worries, in control. So far so good. Where next? Option number two – panic and hide contents of entire bin somewhere else in room. Quick scan of room reveals smooth, carbon-blue surfaces devoid of tables, chairs, boxes, containers, hidey-holes. Option number three – panic and stuff as many tickets from the bin into his pockets and any other suitable place, which he did.

Svensson reappeared just as Rib was forcing the half-empty bin liner down the chute.

'The bloody cabinet was already locked!' he spat out.

Rib nearly spat out thirteen screwed-up lottery tickets, two Mars bars wrappers and a liquorice allsort crammed into his gob. He managed to mumble an apology before being forced by Svensson out of the office and over towards the front door. They both dived under the shutter being lowered by Lombardi, the Assistant Store Supervisor. The Waste-Rows customer service consultants melted away into the night within moments. Rib emptied the contents of his mouth into his hand, then into his pocket.

Had he got the ticket?

Only one way to find out.

He headed towards what had become his local, Matzo's

Milk Bar. Matzo saw him enter, poured a pitcher of double-strength full-cream milk topped with honey-nut loop shavings and exchanged it for the thirty dollars offered by Rib. Rib took his drink to a table in the corner, made to go to the lavatory, then froze. He could feel Matzo's stare boring into his back. Rib went back to his table, took a long slug of his milk and nodded appreciatively towards Matzo. Matzo grunted in return and resumed to cleaning glasses with a tea towel which had seen distinctly better days.

Close call. There are some things in this world which you just don't do. Like fail to pay homage to a Matzo-poured milk pitcher. Really close call. After what seemed like a safe passage of time had passed, Rib strolled casually over to the door marked 'Men'. Once behind the locked door of the innermost cubicle, he emptied the contents of his pockets onto the floor. It took a full five minutes of panicky searching before he finally found the ticket. He pressed it against his damp forehead and closed his eyes, breathing deeply.

After flushing all other evidence of his theft down the pan (Hold on, was it really theft?), he put the seat down and sat on it just staring at the ticket. This would solve everything. Looty for Mum and then a sizeable wedge – let's say 10 million dollars – for Mr Rib Meskitoe, entrepreneur extraordinaire. Oh, and of course, a sizeable sum to the little old lady. A wave of guilt washed over him. He promised himself that he would find her and pay her back.

He gathered his breath and his ticket, regaining some sense of equilibrium and emerged from the lavatory back into the bar. Table 37 was cleared, wiped and clean. That was another thing about Matzo's. You leave your table, you leave your milk.

At first Rib had suspected other customers of minesweeping, but had soon come to realise that the establishment owner himself was the source of the disappearing pitchers. The formidable thickset Armenian had a strong sense of table manners tracing back to his peasant family roots. The dictum 'Do not leave the table until you've finished' was probably what was drummed into Matzo's forefathers. Matzo somehow turned this round to mean 'If you leave the table, then you've finished' and strictly applied it without fail. If any customer complained, he would fall victim to a vice-like headlock before being booted out onto the pavement. You didn't mess with Matzo. Locals would direct any unsuspecting incomers in need of refreshment to Matzo's just for a laugh.

Rib nodded his farewell to the stocky Armenian and noted the creamy state of his moustache, confirming where most of the thirty-dollars pitcher of full-cream milk with honey-nut loop shavings had ended up.

Rib left the bar, turned left and strode purposefully towards the Centre, his gaze directed downwards to avoid eye contact with passers-by. He failed to see a figure slip out from the shadows of the side alley next to Matzo's and tuck in behind him at twenty metres' distance.

Night had fallen, the stars dotting the roof of the Dome, a dazzling kaleidoscope caused by the screening filters in the glass carbon layers. Never failed to impress.

But tonight, this night, Rib did not afford the spectacle a second look. He had to get back to his pod. Blending into the pavement throng on the main drag, his sense of self-awareness was at fever pitch. Had he been seen? Had he been followed? What would happen to him if he were caught? Could he really expect to get away with it? Was he safe out here in the open, in full view of the streetscans? Why did he go and take the ticket in the first place? He still couldn't figure it out.

His angst had grown to such proportions by the time he reached the A1–Y27 intersect, that his i-shield had steamed up. He turned into his street half expecting his block to be surrounded by a cordon of polizzia. Not a soul to be seen.

Anywhere.

Quiet. Too damned quiet …

He headed down the street, now picking up the pace, keeping close to the wall. Approaching the entrance to his block, he fumbled for his key card. A figure shot out from the doorway and grabbed him by the shoulder. Rib instinctively struck out to land a blow bang on the nose of his assailant.

'Waargh!' shrieked the wounded Welshman as he crumpled to the floor. 'Waargh! Waargh! What did you do that for?' he managed to sob, trying to staunch the flow of blood with his sleeve.

'Kaddie! What the hell are you doing here?'

Kaddie continued with the waargh-waargh theme and was now attracting the interest of a couple of neighbours from the block opposite. The last thing Rib wanted at this stage of his life was the attention of others. He somehow bundled Kaddie through the door, into the lift, along the corridor and into Pod 512, also known as 'home' in the loosest sense of the word.

As the door closed behind them with a shoosh, Kaddie brightened up immediately.

'Ooh, you have made this nice,' he said, surveying the confined living space which was exactly the same as all the other twenty-odd thousand confined living spaces in the citidome.

'Never mind that!' snapped Rib. 'What the hell were you doing jumping out at me like that? Why were you here in the first place? Have you been following me?'

Kaddie shifted nervously from foot to foot. Rib approached him menacingly.

'Well, somebody's got to look after you, all the trouble you're in!'

This stopped Rib in his tracks. He swiftly went into total defence mode.

14

'What trouble? I'm not in any trouble, what do you mean?'

'Well,' went Kaddie. 'If you're not in trouble, then why are you acting as if you are? What were you doing in the back office at closing time? Why did you shoot off into Matzo's? Why didn't you drink your milk and why did you smack me on the nose and make me go waargh?'

Rib felt like smacking him on the nose and making him go waargh again. The last thing he needed in his way right now was an interfering halfwit. He needed to be strong, solid, resolute. He would sort this out on his own. I am a rock, I am an island, I'm telling no one anything ...

Two minutes later Rib had told Kaddie everything. His mum, the old woman, the ticket, his plans – or lack of them.

Kaddie sat quietly, contemplating the dried blood on his sleeve.

'Well,' he said, after a pause. 'I would say that you are, technically speaking, well and truly in the shite.'

'Thanks a bunch for the vote of confidence, mate. And how do you reach that conclusion? All I've got to do is cash in the ticket, get on the nearest laser back to MK, help Mum out and decide how I'm going to spend the rest of the looty.'

'Ha ha,' snorted Kaddie. 'Haven't we forgotten a little word there? Stolen ticket, stolen, stolen, stolen! What happens when your DNA doesn't match that of an old lady of seventy when you hand the ticket in?'

Now this, understandably, came rather as a blow to Rib's master plan. For Rib had never purchased a lottery ticket before. Therefore he had never won anything in the lottery before. Therefore he had never cashed a ticket in before. So he knew nothing about the DNA check.

Poop, thought Rib.

'And what's worse,' continued Kaddie, warming to this theme, 'is that the polizzia might be after you already.'

'What!' cried Rib.

'Well, yes. If the old lady did the same numbers every week, and knew them off by heart, she might have checked the winning line by now for herself and wondered, just wondered, why you failed to tell her that she had won a fortune!'

Poop, thought Rib again.

'But I could explain that it was all a mistake, the machine hadn't worked properly or something.'

'Well, the polizzia would check your story out of course. And while they were doing that, they'd slam you in the pokey straight away.'

Rib winced, he had no idea what the phrase meant but he didn't fancy being slammed in the pokey one little bit.

'And so, my little friend, that is why I consider you to be in the shite … well and truly … up to your neck and sinking fast. Unless …'

'Unless what?'

'Unless you let me help you.'

'You? Help me? Kaddie, I am appreciative and all that but you are, you know, special needs.' As soon as he'd said it he wished he hadn't.

'Ah, but you see,' Kaddie smiled a particularly wide toothless grin, 'special needs, special deeds. That's what's called for now, special deeds. Meet me at my place at five in the morning, no sooner, no later. In the meantime you get some sleep now. I'll work on a plan.'

Rib suddenly felt tired, too tired to argue. He saw Kaddie to the door, was about to close it when he remembered. 'Kaddie, I don't know where you live.'

'Next door, laddo, next door.'

The door closed behind the giggling Welshman.

He lives next door …?

Rib shook his head, set his alarm and climbed into bed. He immediately fell into a deep sleep. He dreamed of being chased along a rickety gantry, someone tying a long rubber rope to his legs before hurling him over the edge, down down down into a deep dark canyon. As he hit the water, a loud ringing filled his head. It was the alarm. It was five to five already. Rib jumped out of bed, rewound and fast-forwarded the events of the previous twelve hours, felt dizzy and sat down on the bed again.

Why was he entrusting his fate to someone he hardly knew, someone who was the butt of all jokes?

Why did he have to do anything anyway?

OK, he really did want to help Mum, but it could wait, couldn't it? He didn't have to cash in the ticket, he had up to three years to claim it. He could hang loose, save some looty, take a laser west. Or just stay put in meat-and-potato pie land. The laundry list of weak excuses grew by the second.

His thoughts were broken by the sound of his door binger. It was exactly five o'clock. He opened and Kaddie pushed past him, closing the door behind.

'Where were you? You were supposed to be at mine at five. It's now thirty seconds past – you're late! Now get all your little personal knick-knacks together in a small bag, it's time to leave.'

'I'm not going anywhere, I'm staying,' Rib said.

'No you're bloody not! You've got to leave the Dome now and I'm going to help you.'

'I said I'm not going anywhere and that's that, final, no discussion.'

'But last night you said you were going to use the looty to help your mum. What's happened, have you gone soft in the head or something?'

'Listen,' said Rib, gently crying. 'Leave me alone. I'm not going back to MK, I'm going to keep my head down,' and keeping his head down he sat on his bed and stared at a speck of dirt on the floor between his feet.

He felt Kaddie pace to the far wall, heard a rustle and then jumped up as a couple of handfuls of bright gold coins exploded around his feet. It looked uncannily like a couple of handfuls of 250 million dollars.

'Where did this come from?' asked Rib. Knowing the answer.

'I cashed in the lottery ticket,' was Kaddie's calm reply.

'You cashed in the lottery ticket! What do you mean you cashed in the lottery ticket?' Rib screamed.

'I mean I cashed in the lottery ticket.'

'What do you bloody mean you cashed in the lottery ticket! It was mine. How did you get it? You stole it!'

He stood up and flew at Kaddie. Kaddie didn't flinch. Didn't baulk. Didn't go waargh. But pushed Rib firmly in the chest so that he fell back on the bed.

'Now listen here, you ungrateful little shit. The ticket wasn't yours to begin with and I've put myself at great danger cashing it in. I had to use the … Welsh connection. I had to go to the Abergavenny Brothers.'

'You've told someone else!' cried Rib.

'Listen, there was no other way to get the cash, believe me. And I got a good deal. They only took 20 per cent.'

'Twenty per cent!' gurgled Rib feeling faint.

'Oh and I hope you don't mind but I took a slice too. To meet my expenses.'

'How much?'

'One hundred and fifty-one dollars. Don't worry, I took it out of their slice. I need a new kite. I think I'll get a grey one. Now get your knick-knacks together and let's go. We're late already and they'll be after us.'

'Who?'

'The polizzia, or even worse the Abergavenny Brothers. I'll see you outside in five minutes.'

Christ, breathed Rib, now suddenly compliant and packing a small bag as ordered. He'd heard somewhere that Matzo paid the Brothers protection. Which was worrying, because thus far in his young life Matzo was by far the most terrifying thing Rib had come across. Half out of fear, half out of instinct, Rib realised that he had to make safe the twenty shiny gold coins at his feet. He did so the only way he knew how. He opened the drawer next to his bunk, counted out twenty walnuts, and set to work. When he'd finished, he put the nuts into a small purple velvet bag, pulled the drawstring tight and carefully placed it at the bottom of his rucksack.

Ten minutes later he met Kaddie in the corridor. He was pulling a pink suitcase held together with a white leather belt. It had a faded triangular plastic sticker on it which read 'Colwyn Bay, Riviera of the North'.

'Come on, quick,' he urged.

Down the lift and out onto the street, they peeled left into the main Ailsa Craig drag. The whole city was empty save a few cleaning drones finishing off their drain duties.

The Wigan citidome. One of 666 distribution centres dotted across the globe supplying the departed human race with those nostalgic taste essentials from the life of yester-year, those delicacies for which people crave as soon as they venture a step beyond their own backyard. Marmite, Bombay mix, Cheesy Wotsits.

Mother Nature had been on the run since the 1970s and, since Watershed, the only human beings legitimately left on Planet Earth were employed in the network of citidomes, each servicing Mankind's new home with their own particular speciality food. Each citidome held a licence to produce and ship only one product, to avoid 'unhelpful competition' in the words of the Protectorate. Mind you, competition for the licences in the first place had been pretty fierce. Pistachio-flavoured ice cream had gone, against all the odds, to the Fartalone Brothers of Sirmione. Mass insurrection had ensued, the River Tiber flowed with blood and day trips to Venice were cancelled. But once scores were settled, and bribes were paid, the Sirmione citidome was built, covering the southern end of Lake Garda, and that was that.

19

Not all franchises were as keenly contested, though. Walsall earned the sole right to be the undisputed supplier of pork scratchings to the Universe. Unchallenged. Nor could anyone else be bothered to make mustard as deeply yellow and eye-wateringly strong as the citizens of Norwich. And Wigan, well, it was serious meat-and-potato pie country ...

The unlikely couple set out across the Main Plaza into the glass blue pillars of the trade zone, glinting in the sunrise. The eerily empty cobalt squares slipped past as Kaddie kept up a relentless place, his limp accentuated by the click-click of the case careering behind him on two wheels. Every hundred metres or so the coffer would lose its precarious equilibrium and bounce from side to side before turning turtle. Kaddie would stop, curse, twist the case back onto its wheels and set off again. Serious design flaw, thought Rib. Not the suitcase. The person pulling it.

At precisely 5.37 they reached the perimeter wall of the Dome. Rib noticed the streetscans paying attention to them as Kaddie hammered numbers into the keypad. The door opened and a wave of hot air hit them. It registered 36 degrees on Rib's i-shield. Rib stood in the doorway and watched Kaddie shuffle out onto the platform. Shit, thought Rib, 36 degrees and not even six yet.

'Come on,' screamed Kaddie. 'We've no time to lose. They will be here soon!'

Rib wanted to ask exactly who would be here soon but Kaddie was off and running again and thoughts of being slammed in the pokey returned. Rib raced after him.

Their frantic footfall echoed on the ribbed carbon steel of the platform. Rib sprinted up beside Kaddie, which wasn't particularly difficult. There were some things he had to understand. He had gone along with all this 'escape or be pokied' business without question, and now he needed some answers, like:

'Where the hell are we going? How are we going to get off

the Dome?'

'You want me to get you back to MK? OK, I'll get you back to MK,' wheezed the grey form beside him.

'But the laser terminal's in the centre.'

'Don't be daft. They'll already be there ready to grab you. There'll be a nice price on your head for sure.'

'So where are we going then?' panted Rib.

'Well, you've got to get off the Dome so that they can't follow you.'

Before Rib could reply Kaddie skidded to a halt.

'Here will do.'

Rib tumbled over the turtle-turned pink suitcase and his i-shield made contact with the platform with a resounding metallic thud.

'Don't help me up,' he muttered.

Kaddie was showing no signs of doing so. He was kneeling over the now-open suitcase from which he was unfolding a swathe of stretched turquoise fabric. It looked for all the world like a big kite.

'Kaddie, this is no time to be kite-flying. You said it yourself, I've got to get off the Dome.'

'This isn't a kite, it's a hang-glider. *Your* hang-glider.'

Rib's heart sank. No, it didn't sink; it hurtled to the soles of his feet and tried to force its way through the platform like a lift on the fifty-second floor with all its hawsers suddenly severed.

Where was the escape craft? Where was the sleek – preferably red – smart *Thunderbird 3* to lift off and transport him away from this godforsaken place?'

Rib picked up his i-shield and focused on the top right-hand corner of the fax-visor. He quickly found the definitions:

Hang: to kill by suspending someone by a rope around the neck.

21

Glider: an aeroplane without an engine.

Little comfort there. He walked to the rail edging the platform and looked out, took a deep breath and then looked down … How many evenings had he looked down on the rainforest canopy for those last few minutes before sunset and marvelled at the thousands of orange-flash lorikeets screeching their cacophonous goodnight concert to the world?

His thoughts snapped from memories of balmy evenings to a distant, disturbing sound. It came from behind them, along the platform.

It was the baying of hounds. And it sounded not just like hounds in the plural, but hounds as in lots of plurals. He stared back along the platform and could just make out a thin line of something in the haze. He squinted to focus his vision but all he could make out was two, maybe three indistinct verticals above a shimmering, bobbing line.

A thin, reedy horn blast rent the air.

Rib's i-shield told him it was 37 degrees but his blood ran cold. He had heard the horn and he now recognised the dogs. Foxhounds! He had only had contact with two types of dog in the refuge. A gentle pair of Dobermanns left outside the front gate one Sunday morning, and three foxhounds whose one mission in life had been to seduce him into a false sense of security with toilet-tissue puppy stuff only to tear chunks out of his calves at the slightest opportunity.

Rib stood transfixed. He could now hear the faint tink-tink of steel-capped boots on metal. The shimmer clarified into two figures and four dogs, now about 400 metres away.

'Quick!' shrieked Kaddie, 'Get out of your suit and put these on.'

Rib started to obey and unzipped his suit. He stopped, looked at Kaddie and then opened his mouth to protest. 'Take my suit off, in this heat? No way!' were his intended words.

Kaddie transfixed him with a look at one foreboding, menacing and downright scary.

'Get that suit off and put these on,' he hissed.

The staccato of steel heels on the platform became louder. Rib looked to his left. The figures were at 200 metres and closing. He could make out the red jackets, the black helmets, the dogs straining on long leashes. He took off his suit and put on the mottled brown-and-green shorts and jacket thrown at him by Kaddie.

'The i-shield. Take it off.'

Rib hesitated, knowing he would be naked and lost without it.

'Take the frigging thing off!' exploded Kaddie.

Rib stood motionless, transfixed by the approaching pack now at 150 metres.

Kaddie ripped Rib's i-shield off and hurled it over the side.

'Put your arms out.'

Rib obeyed and Kaddie started to strap the turquoise kite to him. His fingers moved swiftly and expertly over his back, snapping buckles, tying ties, tautening the fabric.

A hundred metres.

'OK, now listen,' Kaddie said, tugging hard on the last strap. He placed a wire in each of Rib's hands.

'You pull on the left wire to steer right and the right one to steer left.'

'All your instructions are in the bag and remember, do not land on the inside of the debris strip. Now go!' he screamed as he manhandled Rib over the platform rail.

He could smell the sweat of the men and see the froth dripping from the mouths of the dogs as he pushed himself out into space. The hot air rushed against his cheeks as he fought to control the glider. He jerked the left wire and swept into a smooth, wide arc. He looked up to see Kaddie leaning over the platform rail. One of the men had him in an arm lock. A second man raised his arm and smashed down a baton on the back of Kaddie's head.

'Kaddie!' cried Rib as his friend slumped from view.

Rib froze and, in doing so, kept a tight pull on the left wire, which held the glide in a tight arc that swooped him back towards the bulk of the Dome. He realised what he was doing and corrected his course with a tug on the right wire, exactly as the glider entered into dark shadow.

Three seconds later it smashed into one of the twenty-meter-diameter struts which held the Dome 400 metres aloft from the forest floor. Rib's head hit the structure, causing his nose to fracture just below the bridge, and his brow to split just above his left eye.

The unconscious frame of Rib Meskitoe bounced off the domestrut and, entwined in a turquoise shroud, spiralled in freefall into the darkness below.

3

It was 5 a.m., Monday 13 August 2042. Outside, the temperature was 32 degrees and rising. Inside the pod, a constant and comfortable 18 degrees. The man stood at the small smoke-glassed window and looked out over the rainforest canopy, noting the early steam shimmering from the tree-tops. He always rose at 4.30 and today was no exception. After drinking a half-cup of Russian Caravan tea, he rolled back the simple rough-weave rug on his living-room floor, stood it carefully on end in the corner and commenced his morning exercise routine.

As he did every morning.

After twenty-five minutes he took his pulse and took pleasure at the reading of 85, knowing with certainty that it would return to rest at 44 within minutes. He padded over to the i-view panel in the wall, keyed in his pulse rate and took a shower. The water temperature was programmed to reduce by three degrees every ten seconds until it reached freezing. The man, eyes closed, raised his face to the ice-cold stream for a further thirty seconds before stepping out of the shower. He dried himself and studied the slim, sinewy figure facing him in the mirror. A thin smile was allowed to form across his lips. Not bad for a man of sixty-two years, it read. The smile disappeared as soon as it had come. A long, well-manicured finger traced slowly along a scar above the left eye. He put on a robe, walked into the galley and made a second cup of tea.

He sipped slowly while he read through his programme for the day.

He finished his tea, put the cup in the washer and measured his pulse. It was forty-four.

The man returned to the living area and unfurled the rug in the middle of the floor. He adopted the lotus position, closed his eyes and allowed himself to sink, layer by layer, into a state of deep meditation. Moments later, the silence in the pod was shattered by a shrill, high-pitched alarm coming from the i-view panel, accompanied by a flashing blue light.

The man gave no outward sign of reaction. He allowed himself to surface, slowly, layer by layer, back to the room. Only when he was fully returned did he stand up, walk over to the panel and turn off the alarm.

He knew the alarm could mean only one thing. Breakout.

He tapped two terse instructions into the keypad, went to his bedroom and chose which clothes to wear. As he laid the black-edged grey zipsuit on his bed, Hesperus Besk felt a spasm of excitement course through his veins.

It was Dead or Alive time.

4

The red alert siren wailing in Pod 707 catapulted the occupier out of his bed onto the red shagpile-carpeted floor. He fumbled for his anachronistic spectacles before waddling over to the i-view panel. His glasses still not properly aligned, he pushed at the buttons until the siren stopped. He stared at the words flashing at him, rapid-blinking the sleep from his eyes.

A command followed by a question.

'Dead or Alive. You are assigned.

Do you accept?'

As his vacant stare surveyed the command and question, another command appeared.

'Respond within ten seconds.'

It then beeped down: '9 – 8 – 7 ...'

Molasses!! His brain screamed. What's my password? He slapped his right cheek hard.

'... 6 – 5 – 4' flashed the countdown.

What's my Dead or Alive password? his frontal lobe screamed in a frenzy.

Fox!!!

His plump fingers pummelled the three letters into the panel.

'Your quest is granted. The fugitive is intent on exiting the citidome at Port 13.'

So he's not even off the Dome yet? This really was too good to be true. If he could complete the quest without having to descend to the awfulness of the forest floor, easy meat, easy points. He opened a line to E-Prey, punched in instructions for four hounds and a handler to be at Port 13 in four minutes, and scurried into his bedroom to get dressed.

The red hunting jacket, blue waistcoat and black breeches stood waiting for him in the wardrobe. He squeezed into them (surely he hadn't put on that much weight?) and pulled on the shining black-leather boots. He grabbed the black riding hat, crop and horn from under his bed before entering the portloc. He hesitated as the door swished open. His teeth! He hadn't brushed his teeth!

To hell with it! the naughty demon on his left shoulder said. This is Dead or Alive, not Flossers Go to Yoga Classes.

'Tally-Ho' Blenkinsop lived next door to his ageing widowed mother. Biddy Blenkinsop had moved into Pod 708 some three years before, when she finally had to admit to herself that independence was no longer a realistic option. The everyday routines until then taken for granted – doing the shopping, keeping the pod clean, removing yoghurt cultures from the inside of the fridge door, going to the toilet unassisted – had become insurmountable obstacles. Of course, there was resistance, pride, stubbornness, humiliation. 'I can manage perfectly well on my own, thank you!' was a phrase which often came between mother and son. But in the end, both knew it had to happen.

Tony 'Tally-Ho' Blenkinsop just couldn't cope on his own any more. Biddy had hoped that he would meet up with some nice girl, maybe from the pie production depot, but no signs of progress there. The fact that her son was fifty-five, bald, fat and sweated copiously whenever remotely near a member of the opposite sex did not help.

So she moved next door into Pod 708.

Tally-Ho rationalised events differently. It was important, he had read, that older women left on their own had a purpose in life. If they lost their purpose in life, they could easily lose their marbles.

The fact that his mother already had several purposes in life in the form the presidency of the Wigan Citidome Furriers Guild, membership on a number of voluntary-sector committees, and not forgetting her evening class in hydrogen arc welding, seemed to conveniently escape him.

Nor was he in the slightest embarrassed at his mother having to sanitise Pod 707 on the occasions when he had failed to make it to the lavatory door in time. It was not as if it was a regular occurrence, was it? Although the combination of retsina and oysters, followed by lashings of baked beans washed down with Newcastle Brown, did seem to have that effect on him. Every Saturday night. Still, throwing out a carpet every week's no crime, is it? No chance for all those gruesome dust mites to establish themselves.

Two minutes later Tally-Ho rendezvoused at Port 13 with a sinewy man of advanced years going by the name of Sykes, struggling with the fervent forward antics of four foxhounds.

'Well?' barked Blenkinsop.

The sinewy Sykes flinched at the onslaught of ten-hour-old garlic-crusted anchovies marinated in Mongolian yak's cheese.

One of the hounds put its tail between its legs and crouched in a 'please don't beat me' mode. A second rolled over on its side and feigned dead.

'There would appear to be one fugitive with an accomplice. They appear to have come from the Ailsa Craig quarter, crossed the city district and entered the platform at Port 13 some two minutes ago,' said Sykes.

'Two minutes!' shrieked Blenkinsop. Then what are we waiting for?' He raised the hunting horn to his lips and blew hard. The blood-curdling sound caused the third hound to promptly evacuate its bowels over the left foot of Sykes.

It was 5.39 a.m. as the fat man, the thin man and the four hounds skidded out onto the platform and headed into the rising sun towards their quarry.

5

It was the slippery wet warmth of the giant slug sliding up the inside of his left thigh which woke him. The involuntary shudder sent a spasm through his whole body. His scream pierced the air as he grabbed at the slug but found himself twined up in the shreds of a turquoise material strapped to his arms and legs. He convulsed and rolled over, only to squash the slug between his knees.

Now he really screamed, sending a couple of hundred parakeets screeching into the air somewhere in the mid-distance.

He staggered to his feet and snatched at the slab of black slime on his leg, hurling it splat against Domestrut 64. Rib stood transfixed as the slug quivered its last against the cold carbon-steel surface before curling up and dropping to the ground before him.

A primeval shudder shook him again and he crumpled into a heap. He was in the Underdome. The ground was wet and cold. He was wet and cold. Very cold …

He touched his nose and immediately wished he hadn't. By now the local wildlife was becoming seriously hacked off at the wailing of this man child who had spiralled 400 metres down from the citidome platform, breaking its nose in the process. He felt the dried blood across the bridge of his nose and across his left brow.

Rib felt dizzy and faint. A slithering noise behind him jolted him to his senses and he struggled to his feet as a three-metre-long black snake with a yellow head coiled its way past to disappear into a hollow tree trunk.

He touched his nose again. The blood was hardened dry. How long had he been lying there? Minutes? Hours? He looked up at the massive underbelly of the Dome above him, all dark and ominous. As he disentangled himself from the turquoise kite fabric, he pieced together the flight along the platform, the pink suitcase, the sound of dogs, the horn, the launch into space, then Kaddie screaming at him.

Kaddie! The last thing he remembered was his thin frame leaning over the railing and a figure behind him smashing a cudgel down on his head. Rib held his head in his hands and sobbed. Pain now throbbed through the whole of his body. What was he supposed to do? He wanted to get back to MK, but not like this! If only Kaddie were down here with him, he'd tell him what to do. Strange how the balance of the relationship between them had shifted 180 degrees over the past few hours. He would have given anything to have Kaddie with him now.

Hold up, he remembered. Hadn't he said something about instructions? He took the rucksack off his back and wobbled over to the tree trunk, made to sit down on it, remembered the snake and decided not to sit down on it, but backed off to a safe distance where he emptied the contents of the bag onto the floor. Torch, Swiss Army knife, beanie hat, velvet bag, t-shirts, pair of shorts, first-aid kit, fli-wire and a piece of card. He unfolded the cardboard which turned out to be the front of a 500-gram carton of Cocowhatsits. Rib automatically started to absorb the text:

Sprogs and flicks just love the great chocolate taste in the crackly, twizzly twirls of Cocowhatsits cereal. But what they don't know is that cocowhatsits are actually packed with hidden wholegrain goodness!

'What? If it's so bloody good, why don't they just unhide it then?' Rib further noted that some settling of contents may have occurred during transit, which basically meant that the box was only a quarter full. He was about to dutifully read off the Recommended Daily Allowance for Riboflavin (B) and Folic Acid when he stopped mid-'30 gram serving'.

What the hell was he doing sitting here broken-nosed and scared poopless on the forest floor musing over the nutritional values of a chocolate wheat cereal?

Rib wasn't really sure what made him turn over the card to read the other side, maybe it was sixth sense. Maybe it was his feminine side coming to the fore.

No, it was definitely sixth sense, he decided.

The perfectly formed script gave him directions to the Slingshot Terminal, from where the token Sellotaped to the bottom of the card would buy him a one-way journey back to MK. He was to check in at Dick's Bar and wait for his flight to be called. A map drawn in red ink showed a dotted line, designating a trail leading from the Wigan citidome to Dick's Bar.

It showed a distance of 3 kilometres. That doesn't seem far, he thought. It showed that the trail led through the forest. A dense, dangerous, subtropical rainforest, thought Rib, and shivered …

Under the map, this time in green, were the following instructions:

- MAKE SURE YOU LAND OUTSIDE THE DEBRIS STRIP
- DO NOT ATTEMPT TO TAKE THE TRAIL AFTER DARK
- WHEN YOU REACH MK, FIND UNITY. THERE YOU WILL FIND THE KEY

Find Unity? he stared. He shook his head and decided to save that one until later. He reviewed the first two instructions. Maybe he should have read these earlier.

'Outside the debris strip.' What did that mean?

And 'after dark' …?

The screech of a thousand lorikeets suddenly became more than background noise. It was roosting time.

It was already late in the day. He must have been unconscious for hours. He stuffed the torch, the card, the knife and other contents back into the rucksack and started to run, stiffly at first, towards the forest edge. The sun, now low, flashed through the treetops bright in his eyes. As he looked up, he saw a glint of metal. A long glint of steel. Ahead of him. In a broad sweep between him and the forest. As he reduced to a half jog, Rib realised that he was staring at a wall. Some 4 metres high. Washing machines, turbo-driers, skate bikes, ironing boards and hundreds of other household items all pieced together to form a rusting rampart of rubbish stretching round the whole base of the citidome. So why had people done this, when every block was furnished with a recycling facility?

He stopped in his tracks.

The debris strip.

MAKE SURE YOU LAND OUTSIDE THE DEBRIS STRIP!

Poop …

He had to climb over this heap of metal and other waste just to get to the forest!

It was harder than it looked. He had to be careful. Each foothold gave a little with his weight and the edges were razor-sharp. And then, his eye caught something. Just in front of his left hand outstretched to take his next grip. It was a carcass, bleached white. And then he saw another, and another. And once he began to look for them he could see dozens of bodies of small animals. He recognised them as mostly bandicoots, one of the few creatures allowed as pets on a citidome, and by far the most popular.

He thought of his mum and the refuge. She spent her life

looking after mistreated animals. And now he knew why. People had disposed of these harmless little things just as they would an ice-lolly wrapper or a string of dental floss by just tossing them over the edge of the platform. Tears welled up in his eyes as he reached up to take his next hold, now desperate to move on from this awful place.

The Tommy Tipper toy dumper truck beneath his left foot gave way under his shifted weight. Rib fell against the tangle of metal and bone beneath him and felt a searing pain in his left shin. He looked down to see blood appearing, at first reluctantly and then with an oozing confidence, from a gash in his leg. He let out a gasp as the blood trickled down to the sock furled over the top of his boot. He decided to make it to the other side before he treated the wound.

This did not prove to be a wise move. It took him another ten minutes to negotiate the debris strip in the deepening gloom. By the time he touched terra firma on the forest side he was weak with the pain and had to take deep breaths to stop himself passing out. He felt inside the rucksack and found the tin with the label 'First Aid' on it. He unscrewed the antiseptic cream tube and smeared a big dollop on the end of his finger. He tenderly ran his finger down the length of the wound. Oh God, how it hurt. Another bout of deep breathing through the nostrils and he just about managed to wrap a strip of gauze round his leg and stem the flow of blood.

He spread the map open on the ground. He needed the torch too; it was getting darker by the minute. Once he had managed to throw light on the map, it seemed straight-forward. The trail from the citidome to his destination, Dick's Bar, ran beside a stream. It was the only stream that seemed to intersect the Dome perimeter, so all he had to do was follow the edge of the strip until he came to the stream and then chuck a right into the forest at ninety degrees.

But which way should he set off? Left was his instinct. If

he was lucky he would walk for five minutes, reach the stream and turn off right into the forest.

If he was unlucky, he would continue all the way round the edge of the citidome for 10 kilometres before hitting the stream.

He was lucky.

He found the stream after only two minutes, decided not to cross but turned into the forest and there it was, on his side of the water, a trail.

The forest canopy closed overhead to form a tunnel and Rib needed to use his torch straightaway, even though the sun's final rays for the day still burned from the west above the treetops. The slim, lank boy had been living on adrenaline ever since he left his pod some fifteen hours earlier that morning – apart from the fourteen or so hours he had lain unconscious underneath the citidome, that is. But now, as he entered this alien world, his cognitive powers started to kick in, and he wished they hadn't. He was fourteen years old. And every minute of those fourteen years had been spent on a citidome. Every day he had looked out over the forest and held it to be a wonderful, beautiful thing. As long as he was up there and it was down here.

The mythology of the rainforest was strong and pungent. Enormous venomous snakes, poisonous arrow vines, robber bands ... And here he was, in its midst. Its dark midst. He flashed the torch upwards and something moved crashing away from the beam across the canopy. He stood still. Save the babble of the black stream and the sound of his heart trying to fight its way out of his ribcage, the forest was again silent. He set off again along the track, having arrived at a very rough-and-ready calculation that he would reach Dick's Bar in 5,237 paces. He decided to cheat away a hundred to boost morale.

'5,137

'5,136

'5,135 ...' he whispered to himself, focusing on the beam of light cast by the torch on the trail before him.

He started to jog.

'4,932, 4,931, 4,930 ...'

He was scared. His leg hurt like coconut and he was still scared. He realised that the jog was increasing to a sprint.

'4,731, 4,730, 4,729, 4,728 ...'

And he slowed down, trying desperately to keep his torch and concentration fixed on the path ahead.

He had not expected the forest to be so still, so quiet. Save a few birds pillow-fighting off up to the right, silence reigned. But it was a silence full of power, full of menace, veiled only by the splash of dark water over wood and rock. In his imagination, the wall of forest on either side hid armies of gorillas, lions, tigers and bears ready to leap out and tear him limb from limb. And he knew he would offer no resistance. In fact, it would be a mercy killing. A blessed release.

He picked up the pace again.

'4,421, 4,420, 4,419 ...'

Shit, it was so hot and sticky.

He had moved from the cold, dank netherworld of the space inside the strip to the high humidity of a subtropical rainforest in a matter of minutes and he was soaked to the skin. If he had been wearing his i-shield, it would have told him that his heartbeat was 137, he was travelling at a speed of 7.24 kph, air temperature 33° and falling, humidity 98% and falling, and the likelihood of a tornado in the next 24 hours 0.72%.

But he wasn't wearing his i-shield. Kaddie had ripped it off and hurled it over the rail, hadn't he? Why?

Rib couldn't really rationalise and keep everything moving in one direction in a limb-coordinated way at the same time, so he tried to stop thinking and concentrate on the count.

'3,971, 3,970, 3,969 ...'

He fanned the torch ahead of him.

He was surprised how wide and clear the trail had been – a good 4 metres from the stream to the undergrowth all the way so far. Surely it wouldn't have taken long for it to be overgrown with suckers and vines and creepers? He stopped again to pause for breath. He could swim all night and day, but running was definitely not his fortissimo. He was about to set off when a long moaning sound made his blood run cold.

It came from somewhere in the trees just up to his right. Somewhere very close. He stood, frozen to the spot.

'Aaa-rk … Aaa-rk …' repeated the moaning followed by a soft trill.

Rib laughed and relaxed. He knew what it was. *Litoria chloris*. Red-eyed Green Tree-frog. Medium, tennis-ball-sized frog with smooth, bright-green back and white to bright-yellow grainy underside. Back of thigh: purple or brown. Digits end in large discs.

Rib smiled. When he was six, he'd helped his mum nurse one of these little beauties back to health in the refuge. He'd called it Freddie, rather unimaginatively.

But to come across one in its native habitat, that was really something, he thought, as he searched the lower branches of the palm with his torch beam. Couldn't wait to tell Mum. She'd be really impressed.

But of course, he thought, this isn't really its native habitat. Well, it is, and it isn't, he argued with himself. Well actually, it is now, although it used not to be, was the compromise agreement.

To think that only twenty years ago, *Litoria chloris* would be found in its tens of thousands mainly along the forested eastern seaboard of Australia. But no longer, thanks to Professor Clayton E Buzzard.

6

Buzzard, or 'Buzz' as he liked to be called (although no one ever did), had been the most brilliant, brainy scientist the world had ever known.

Dismissive of the works of Stephen Hawking by the age of six, the Alabama-born Buzzard flew over the Pond to become Trinity College, Cambridge's youngest ever Astronomy graduate. He stunned the world by discovering two black holes which had been playing hide-and-seek behind Mars for the past two million years and thrilled viewers with faultless performances on *Mastermind*, drawing widespread acclaim for his twenty-two correct and no passes specialist round on the 'Life and times of Pierre-Simon, marquis de Laplace, French mathematician and astronomer, 1749–1827'. His mother, Rayleen, brought his run of wins to a halt when she declared that three Caithness crystal-cut glass decanters were enough to dust on her Alabama mantelpiece and that was that.

By way of relaxation, Buzzard became a prolific inventor. He spent his two years at Cambridge residing in the Gonville Hotel, overlooking Parker's Piece. On his first night in Executive Suite 3, he set about remodelling a piece of equipment that had commanded centre stage in hotel rooms since time immemorial. By 7.30 a.m. the next morning, his people back in the States were busy patenting the Buzzard Trouser-shirt-and-wetsuit Press. By the end of the month, the Corgi Trouser Press Corporation had folded.

He grew into a quiet, studious man who avoided publicity.

He was, however, a constant subject of speculation in the marital stakes. After all, he was widely held to be the most intelligent man ever to have existed. And he was worth billions, seriously loaded.

He finally fell for the charms of Jenny Lind, an actress who spellbound him with a breathtaking Lady Macbeth at the Kongelige Teater, Copenhagen. He met her backstage after the performance and proposed there and then. On hearing the news, mother Rayleen declared, 'Over my dead body!' She died the next day in an unfortunate crop-spraying accident and Clayton married Jenny in the fall of that year.

Ten months later Jenny gave birth to a baby boy. He was named Tycho, after the Danish astronomer Brahe and he was the apple of Clayton's eye. On the other hand, Jenny was not the maternal type and insisted that she play no part in bringing up baby. As soon as her svelte figure was restored, she was back on the boards in London, Paris, Rome.

Actually Clayton didn't mind. Preparing and administering Tycho's bottle feeds four times a day gave a calming symmetry to his existence. Tycho, on the other hand, proved to be less than happy with the arrangement. He grizzled constantly, evacuated his bowels irregularly and cried all night.

Every night.

For three whole months.

Jenny was seldom home anyway, but when she was, she slept in the guest suite on the third floor with earplugs firmly pressed in. Doctors and nurses puzzled at little Tycho's condition. They were concerned at his growth, which was not as it should be, and suggested he spend a period in the Half-Moon Bay Clinic.

The most intelligent man in the world would hear nothing of this, however. He would continue to care for his son and all would be well.

It took another eight weeks for Tycho to improve, coinciding with the time he moved on to solids. He started to sleep, he stopped crying and his evacuations became more solid and regular. But he remained a weedy little runt of a child and grew into a sickly specimen of boyhood.

While all of this was going on in the Buzzard household, the world was not a well place either. Global warming was reaching alarming proportions. The ice caps were melting, most of the Third World was showing signs of being too hot to sustain human life and sea levels were rising at a menacing rate.

Holiday patterns were also changing rapidly. Travel agents offered escorted tours to the balmy shores of Spitzbergen rather than to the Med, and the Arctic Basin became home to the planet's most desirable real estate.

One day, so the story goes, Professor Clayton E Buzzard received an invitation to the White House from the President of the United States. The invitation did not come as a card with gold-lettered RSVP at the bottom, but in the form of two angular-jawed men wearing black suits and dark sunglasses, who allowed him five minutes to brush his teeth before ushering him into the spacious rear suite of the black Oldsmobile WD40.

Of course, Buzzard could have refused. He was, however, intrigued at the prospect of meeting the most powerful woman in the world, so he went along with it.

'Good morning, Professor Buzzard. So good of you to come at such short notice.'

Consuela Sweetcorn addressed him whilst looking out of the Oval Office window at the thin line of protesters on the other side of the razor wire. She took a long draw on the Havana Corona stuck in the corner of her mouth as she turned to face him.

'Please, take a seat,' she offered with the upturned palm of her left hand and sat down herself behind the huge desk.

'Thank you, Ma'am,' nodded Buzzard as he sat down. 'How can I be of assistance?'

'Well, cutting right to the chase, Professor, it's about global warming. I'm aware that previous administrations have not always, ahem, placed the issue at the top of the cherry tree ...'

Professor Buzzard raised his eyebrows.

'... But I want to let you know that I intend personally to take a strong leadership stance on this issue.'

The Professor's eyebrows flexed again.

'Professor,' she said, now engaging him in meaningful eye contact. 'My people say that, on current prognosis, we may have no longer than a hundred years.'

'Four,' Buzzard corrected.

The Havana dropped from the President's lips and landed in her lap, where it started to smoulder. Buzzard stood up, leaned forward, delicately removed the cigar from a place where no man had boldly gone for the past seven years and stubbed it out on the antique Disney Wilderness Lodge ashtray on the desk.

'Four years?' she coughed. 'Are you telling me that we only have four years before the planet goes ape?'

Buzzard struggled with the phraseology but pressed on regardless.

'And seven months, give or take a few days,' he added helpfully.

'Shit,' said the President.

'Mmm, shit indeed,' said the Professor.

The two shared this common ground in respectful silence for some thirty seconds before the President snapped to, and looked Buzzard in the eye.

'Four years! What the hell can we do? What the hell is there to do, Professor?'

'The only solution is to evacuate, Madam President.'

'Evacuate?' she scoffed. 'Shit! Listen, Professor, we ain't got enough bomb bunkers to house the world's population. Not that everybody would receive an invitation, mind you.'

'No, Madam President, you misunderstood. I mean evacuate to Planet Tycho.'

'Planet what?' Consuela Sweetcorn quickly flicked through her understanding of all the planets in the Solar System and was sure that Planet Tycho was not one of them.

'And where, Professor, is exactly this Planet Tycho?'

'It's in the Alfalfa-Beta System. About 12,000 million miles away.'

'So how come I haven't heard of it?'

'Nobody has.'

'Except you of course.'

'That's right, except me. I discovered it three years ago,' he said, trying to sound as modest as possible.

'So you've discovered a new planet and you haven't told anybody about it?' She stood up.

'Yes, that's right.'

'Why not?'

'Because nobody's asked me.'

The President made as if to say something, but no sound came out of her mouth.

She stood up and then sat down heavily, staring at the man in the chair opposite.

'Would you like a glass of water, Madam President?' Buzzard offered.

'Yes, thank you.' She took a sip and tried to collect her thoughts.

Buzzard sensed the President's scepticism and put on his i-shield.

'May I show you?' he offered. 'Your shield, Ma'am?'

The President took her i-shield from the third desk drawer down on the right and put it on, rather hesitantly. He deftly manipulated Tycho onto her screen, where it slowly turned on its axis.

'Do you have it, Madam President?'

'Yes, I do,' she murmured, transfixed.

'If I may just give you a swift guided tour?'

She nodded

'Tycho is the largest of the inner planets in the Alfalfa-Beta System. The lower atmosphere consists mainly of nitrogen and oxygen. Ozone in the upper layers protects the planet from its sun's harmful radiation. And, Madam President, the layer is 100 per cent intact. The special thing about Tycho is that its surface is largely covered by water, approximately 70 per cent, the remainder by continental land masses. It has an equilateral diameter of 1,275 kilometres, an orbit period of 366 days, it ...'

'Hold it just there, please.'

'Madam President?'

'I'm no expert at these things but haven't you just reeled off the vital statistics of Earth?'

'Precisely, Madam President, precisely. Tycho is an exact replica of Earth. A twin, if you like!'

'Let's just get this right, so you are suggesting that the only solution is for mankind to up sticks and move house from Earth to, er ...'

'Tycho,' assisted Buzzard.

'Tycho,' repeated the President.

'In essence, yes, Ma'am. Global warming is irreversible. Well, not exactly irreversible but it would take Earth about 20,000 years to repair itself.'

'But how, Professor, do you propose that we ship out the whole of the world's population to this new planet?'

'I'm glad you asked that, Madam President, because this challenge has greatly occupied my mind of late. I estimate that we would need to build, over the course of the next three years, 5,700 new spacecraft, each with a capacity of 32,400 passengers ...'

'Thirty two thousand four hundred!' spat the President. 'Are you out of your tiny mind? The largest spacecraft currently in commission holds 120. We do not possess a single spacecraft that carries anywhere near 32,400 passengers, let alone ... how many?'

'Five thousand seven hundred.'

'Yes, five thousand seven hundred. And anyway, a craft that big hasn't been invented yet.'

Buzzard's right eyebrow arched in modest pride.

'Hold on, wait a minute, are you saying that you ...'

The Professor allowed himself to direct a disarming smile at the most powerful person on Earth.

Sweetcorn was already seeing the headlines in her head. She would be creating history. She would go down as the greatest President, no, the greatest world leader of all time. Sweetcorn, Saviour of Mankind ...

'But there's just one problem, Madam President.'

'Problem?' Sweetcorn did not take to this word. She had stood proud and tall on this pedestal of immortality for only, how long, some twelve seconds before it was being rocked from side to side by this word, 'problem'.

'Even according to my best-case scenario estimates, there would be a shortfall, a gap.'

'A gap?'

'Yes, a gap of some five years.'

'Five years?' the President parroted.

'Yes, five years, which would mean we would consign at least three billion people to certain death.'

The President became dizzy. A moment ago, she was Florence Nightingale, Mother Teresa and Bob Geldof all rolled into one, and now she was facing a rap of mass genocide.

'Whoa now! Whouch! Hold on! What's all this "We would consign" stuff? I haven't committed myself to a cotton-pickin' thing. You come into my office, tell me the world's burning, you come up with some dagnabbit story about a new planet that we're all gonna move to, and then you say it's our fault, *my* fault that three billion people are going to be wasted.'

44

'Madam President, may I remind you that you invited me here. And I use the word "invited" in its broadest sense.'

She made as if to protest but Buzzard raised his hand.

'And, if I may continue, there is a solution.'

'A solution?'

'Yes, the three billion gap can be closed if we effect a scientific intervention.'

'A scientific intervention?'

'Yes,' said Buzzard, unable to conceal a growing weariness in his tone. 'A scientific intervention. If we can stall the warming process by five years then we could evacuate the whole world's population in its entirety.'

Sweetcorn picked herself up, adjusted her clothing and began to remount the pedestal of immortality. 'How?'

'We delay the melting process at the ice caps by reducing the seawater temperature by a single degree Celsius.'

Buzzard knew a thing or two about melting permafrost: He was also a dab hand at retreating glaciers, fracturing ice shelves and decreasing sea ice area. He was at his happiest conducting an imaginary debate with himself on links between climate, snow and ice cover, ocean thermosaline circulation and atmospheric carbon dioxide.

Buzzard's bedside table had no place for Joanne Harris, William Shakespeare or Haruki Murakami. All available space was occupied by *Hydrological Observations Reported by Frederick Chapman, Palaeontologist to the National Museum, Melbourne*. Chapman had sailed on the Australasian Antarctic Expedition in 1911–14 under the leadership of Sir Douglas Mawson. Buzzard would spend hours poring over seawater temperature and density observations precisely tabulated by date, hour, latitude, longitude, depth of sea floor and corrected temperatures.

Buzzard was obsessed with bottom soundings. Not the giggle-inducing rude noises made by students in a lift, but the corrected temperature readings taken at 4,280 metres below sea level off the Antarctic Shelf in November 1913. Compared to the readings taken in the same place 112 years on, they were different. Very different.

He knew his climate change, did Clayton E Buzzard.

'But isn't the water temperature really cold there already?'

'Yes, Madam President, of course it is. And a further reduction will provide a benefactory and benevolent buffer of time which will retard the melt.'

'Retard the melt?' the President exclaimed.

'Yes, Madam President, retard the melt.'

'And save the three billion?'

'Yes, Madam President, save the three billion. You're getting the picture.' He made as if to answer the next question before it came. He was too late.

'But how?'

'By adding retro-agent B313 to the Arctic and Antarctic Oceans, within 500 metres of each ice pack.

The President sat silent for a while, in deep thought.

'Dropped by ship?'

'Helicopter.'

'How many?'

'Two hundred and seventeen. It's critical that the agent hits the water at exactly the same time.'

'Two hundred and seventeen choppers,' she repeated. She picked up a blue phone, one of four on her desk. 'Get me Commander Kenyon,' she barked.

'Kenyon? And a good day to you. Kenyon, do we have more than 217 choppers readily available? Good!' And with that she slammed down the phone, leaving Kenyon with a question about choppers dangling in mid-air.

'OK, we have the capability. What next?' she asked, warming to the task.

'Well, far from it to be for me to suggest, but should one not perhaps organise a summit to share this course of action with all nations of the world? I could come as guest speaker, with a little PowerPoint presentation. No more than twelve slides, nice colour graphics – yes, the deep blue of the Arctic Ocean would form a great backdrop to yellow text …'

'Now hold your horses, Buzzard!' the President interrupted with a certain glint in her eye. 'I think at this stage we'll keep the lid on this one. Now who better to take the leadership in saving the world than the United States of America?'

'But Madam President …'

'Buzzard!'

He jumped, alarmed at the ferocity of her outburst. This woman's cuckoo, he thought, completely cuckoo.

'OK, Professor, now here's what we do. Do you have a production capability for this retro thingy 517?'

'Retro-agent B313'

'Mmmm, whatever, well do you?'

'Yes, I can make it myself. That's how I invented it.'

'But you'll need thousands of gallons of the stuff to spray over the whole ocean?'

'No,' he laughed, 'not a bit. Just a few drops really. Fifty mil from each of the helicopters should do the trick.'

'Fifty mil?'

'About three tablespoonfuls.'

'Shit,' swore the President. 'That's some powerful shit.'

'Powerful shit indeed, Madam President,' corroborated Buzzard.

'OK, let's do it. It's Clayton, isn't it?'

'Yes, Ma'am, it is.'

'OK Clayton, let's do it. Let's go save the planet.'

'As you wish, Ma'am,' said Buzzard, wanting to just get the hell out of there.

'Now how long will it take to get the agent produced and ready?'

'Well I could, I suppose, set my lab team on it Monday

morning and then ... It shouldn't take any more than 24 hours.'

'Monday's no good. Can't you make it sooner?'

President Sweetcorn stood up and walked slowly round her desk, behind the Professor's chair and placed her hands on his shoulders.

'Now, Clayton, we are mature adults ...'

Buzzard blanched.

'And we both have needs. Urgent needs ... Now, are you sure there's no way we can do it right now?'

Clayton E Buzzard nearly farted but managed to clench it in.

'I have ambitions to be the greatest President of all time. And you, Professor Buzzard ...' She started to gently massage his shoulders.

'... You, I'm sure, want to be the greatest professor of all time. So I reckon you can set to and make up those little phials all on your own tonight, don't you think?'

She whispered in his left ear. 'And I think we'll keep this little secret to ourselves, won't we?'

Her fingers dug deep into his flesh and he yelped a 'yes' in shrill response.

'That's good,' she said, smoothing the crumpled shoulder line of his jacket. 'So, Clayton, I'll get the boys to drive you back to your lab and I want you to make those 217 little phials or doses or whatever you call them ready for tomorrow noon. I'll ask the boys to stay with you for company.'

'I'm sure there's no need, Madam Pre ...'

'No, I insist,' she insisted.

So Buzzard returned under full escort to his lab in Milwaukee, personally prepared the 217 capsules of retro-agent B313, communicated the coordinates for the drop to Commander Kenyon, sat back and waited.

7

It was 1.32 in the morning. Charlie Kumala was on the nightshift and was seriously late. Not surprising really, he thought as he pedalled furiously the wrong way up Catharine Street. The number of times the rosters had been changed this month already, Charlie wasn't sure whether he was on days or nights from one week to the next. He cut the corner over the pavement at the Mill Road intersect, safe in the knowledge that he would meet neither foot nor road traffic at this early hour. He approached the railway bridge. He remembered, when he was a boy, that the bridge had appeared fearsomely steep, a first-gear up-on-the-pedals lung-searing job. Now, a flick of the gear switch and over in seconds.

He sped downhill, taking the broken lines in the middle of the road, clocking 50 kph, the speed thrill tempered by the knowledge that he was already 34 minutes late for work. The night-time peace of Parker's Piece was rent by the squeal of Kumala's rear tyre as he took the ninety-degree left at full pelt into Gonville and headed down and through Cathedral Interchange into Lensfield. Two hundred yards, touch on the back brake, dismount and wheel left into the entrance of the Scott Polar Research Institute. He chained his machine to the railing, just next to the faded sign which had probably been there for tens if not hundreds of years: 'Bicycles are not be chained to this railing, by order of the Dean.'

He strode up the broad, flat steps and through the doors which hissed open by way of a greeting. He walked into the reception lobby of the Institute expecting to meet the sarcastic barb of the night porter, Colin. 'Morning, Kumala, nest too warm, was it?' should have been one of his better-crafted compositions. But toothless Colin wasn't there. And he should have been.

Charlie moved on, down the marbled corridor to Room 107, his place of work. He walked in to find Colin sitting at his, Charlie's, workplace transfixed to the high-glo plasma on the wall.

'Colin, what the hell are you …'

'Mr Kumala, sir, take a look at this.' Very unusual for the sarky Colin to be addressing him as 'sir'. In fact he had never addressed him so.

'Look here, sir, this can't be right, can it?' He pointed at the reading to the bottom right of the screen. Minus 1.7 degrees it read. It took a couple of seconds to sink in.

'Minus 1.7 degrees. That can't be right,' he murmured.

'No, that's what I thought, sir. That *can't* be right.'

They shared a minute's silence staring intently at the gauge, thinking, That can't be right. During this time, the temperature steadily rose by another quarter of a degree. And it continued to climb.

Charlie Kumala was employed to sit in front of this screen every night and monitor every temperature variation of the water off the Antarctic Shelf to the thousandth of a degree. He could hardly believe what he was seeing now. The reading must be wrong, the sensors faulty, the machine malfunctioning.

He got straight on the phone to Professor Allan Cockburn who did little to mask his annoyance at being called out in the middle of the night. By the time he reached the Institute, rubbed his eyes firstly to remove the sleep from the corners and then to try to remove the disbelief, the temperature had risen to minus 1.2 degrees. And by 7.30 when all the sensors had been checked, the machinery checked and readings from other centres had flooded into the Institute, Cockburn, Kumala, Colin and the rest of the world knew one thing. The Arctic and Antarctic Oceans were warming by the minute, which meant only one thing.

The ice caps were melting by the minute.

8

Rib stopped. He thought he saw something on the ground in front of him. Tyre tracks! Could be a six-by-six Toyota. He knelt down gingerly and fingered the tread marks in the mud. He was mesmerised by the sensation of the warm, wet, sticky substance that squeezed oozy gloop between his fingers. Yep, Toyota Taipan, 20-litre hybrid, CO_2 emission 1.4, kpg 192, 0–90 3.4 seconds, a serious beast of a machine with an impressive throb of an engine.

The impressive throb of the engine powering the V512 hybrid Toyota Taipan along the trail insinuated itself into his consciousness as he let the watery remains of the mud drip from his fingertips. Yep, again, definitely a Toyota Taipan, he thought. He saw lights flash in the foliage to his left. The flash of headlights.

The headlights of a Toyota Taipan, churning and sliding towards him from back down the trail.

Rib hurled himself off the track into the undergrowth, scrambling on all fours over a rotting tree trunk and flattening himself to the ground behind it. The Taipan slowed and came to a standstill some 5 metres further on from his hiding place. The headlights shone fierce against the fronds and ferns of the forest, dimming and brightening faintly in tandem with the guttural throb of the powerful twenty-litre engine.

The temptation to stand up, walk over to the driver's door and ask for a lift was strong. He was hurting, he was tired and he was frightened. He resisted the urge but raised his head slightly to gain a better view of the truck. He thought he could make out the shape of a figure in the driver's seat. At that instant the figure turned its face towards him and Rib felt its stare aim directly at him. He ducked down immediately, pressing his right cheek into the damp earth. He could feel the pulse of the engine reverberate through the mud against his face. And then, three throaty roars of the motor, and the wagon lurched forward again, sliding and slithering off down the track, its headlights casting an eerie light against the black wall of the forest.

Rib lay flat against the earth for a full two minutes after he had seen the last red flash of the brake lights disappear into the darkness. He raised himself gingerly to his feet and immediately felt the throbbing pain in his left shin as he limped from the undergrowth back onto the trail. He bit his lip and picked up the count again.

'3,521, 3,520, 3,519 …'

He continued for what seemed like hours, now and then slipping on the increasingly waterlogged trail. He promised himself a drink and a rest at two thousand paces to go but cheated, taking it two hundred steps early. He slumped to the ground bang slap in the middle of the track – if the Toyota had chosen to come back to meet him, he would have just sat there and let it hit him. A touch of his leg told him he was still losing blood. He wanted to lie down and sleep there, in the middle of this dark and hostile nature. For ever …

He knew if he closed his eyes for one second he wouldn't open them again. Forcing himself to his feet, he took a deep breath and staggered a few steps forward. He tried to focus on the ellipse of the torch beam swaying alarmingly from side to side before him. Got to stabilise it! he thought, gritting his teeth. Got to steady it! And he did, more or less. By concentrating every fibre of his body and soul on keeping the beam straight down the track he moved, step by step, closer to Slingshot Inn, aka Dick's Bar. With less than 500 metres to

ROB BADCOCK

go, Rib stumbled and fell. The torch flew from his hand and smashed against a rock. Rib sprawled in slow motion forward into the mud, rolled once and came to rest on his back, his arms and legs starfished, his eyes closed. Or at least he thought they were closed. But they weren't, he blinked to check the closure status.

Closed. Blackness.

Open. Blackness.

He wanted to sleep to ten past eternity, with the alarm clock turned to snooze mode to allow another couple of eons or so. But something gritty in his core gnawed at his brain, telling him to keep his eyes open. Strangely, it spoke in Welsh tongue, sounding unnervingly like Kaddie.

'Look, you arse, only a few hundred metres to go. Come on! You owe it to your mum! You owe it to yourself!'

His eyes were now wide open, straining to focus on the emerging variations of pitch blackness to less than pitch blackness above him. The more his eyes became acclimatised, the more he could define a faint degree of lightness above him, through the forest canopy. He struggled to his feet, wincing as he did so, and set off tentatively down what he hoped to be the track, using the thin sliver of less dark above him as his guide. He had now lost count of his steps but surely no more than 300 metres left? He was right. At that stage, 282 metres to be precise. 282 metres which would take over forty minutes to negotiate. If he fell once, Rib fell twenty times. If he gave up once, he gave up thirty times.

And then at 10.27 p.m. at a distance of only 62 metres from his destination, Rib Meskitoe went into regression. He sat down on the track, curled into a ball with his head on his knees, his hands clasped tightly across his lower shinbones and began to rock gently. The warm rain now increased in ferocity and formed a stream down the furrow of his forehead, mixing with his salty tears before dripping from the end of his nose. Rocking to and fro, he half sang, half sobbed the words to a song which had become his personal angst anthem at times of crisis. Words of broken love, slammed doors, drunken tears burning the garden green.

He had first come across the piece one Saturday afternoon when trawling for chess intelligence. He had been searching for end-game strategies using castles as the primary weapon, when he stumbled across 'Castles Made of Sand'. Intrigued, he scrolled further to discover that it was a song on the second album of a trio called the Jimi Hendrix Experience. He listened to the music and liked it at once. Not one of his mates, not even the Deccaheads, shared his passion for The Experience, which made it even better. The guitarist, Hendrix, was the top. Sheer brilliance, sheer music. It had read on the album sleeve: 'Jimi Hendrix writes his own music and almost sings it. He also plays guitar.'

He also plays guitar!

Rib could still raise a smile, as he rocked back and forth in the mud of a subtropical rainforest, at this outrageous understatement. But the music also had its flipside. Blue Despair. When Rib had encountered the most crushing moment of his short life in the Ice Room, he had sought solace in Hendrix. He returned time and time again to that one track, 'Castles Made of Sand'. Everything connected to him, related to him, was bound up in that sad, sad lyric.

Whenever he felt good, things went bad. Whenever he felt strong, his confidence crumbled.

'Castles Made of Sand'. A song written for him.

A self-fulfilling prophecy. 'Even the good times are bad' could be his epitaph. He could hear the insistent drumbeat of Mitch Mitchell at the end of the track.

Insistent. The end of the track.

Rib uncoiled and listened. He was sure he could hear, somewhere ahead in the wet darkness, the sound of a drum solo. At the end of the track.

He was now on full alert. 'Castles Made of Sand' didn't end with a drum solo ...

He stood up and lurched forward. The rain intensified and the noise intensified. A further 50 metres and suddenly to his immediate left stood a single-storey building. With a corrugated-tin roof, on which the rain hammered a frenetic drumbeat.

There was a sign outside.

A red neon sign.

Which flickered 'Dick's Bar'.

The rain now poured down in lake-loads, splashing mud up onto the hubcaps of the four vehicles standing in the car park.

9

'What do you mean, you must have made a mistake?' screamed the President into Buzzard's left ear. He started to stammer, something which he did only when under duress. And he was certainly under duress, sitting in the Oval Office at two in the morning, dressed only in his Winnie the Pooh pyjamas.

The men in dark suits and dark glasses had not been so friendly in plucking him from his Milwaukee slumber.

'I, I, I, I,' Buzzard vowelled.

'Do you realise what you've done!' Sweetcorn shrieked. 'You've created a climate catastrophe situation which will make the 2004 tsunami phenomenon look like a fart bubble in a spa tub.'

'You realise that millions, no billions of people will die, most of the Earth as we know it will be under water. And all because of your stupid scientific intervention.'

'B ... but I don't understand what can have gone wrong. The formula was scientifically tested and proven, the co-ordinates were clear. I can't explain ...' and he broke down sobbing with his head in his hands. He broke off to fix the President with a fierce stare.

'And your part in this, Madam President? Your unbridled ambition for greatness, the covert operation, the 217 helicopters? You pushed the button!'

His left cheek was stung by the flat of her hand. The force of the blow knocked him off the chair and he lay on the carpet, in foetus position, doing a very good impression of a gibbering wreck.

'You pathetic little fool. And as for the choppers …' she laughed. 'What choppers are you speaking of, Professor? It is true that last night 217 of our finest crews were sent out on a secret mission to engage terrorist forces in the Upper Volta, but,' she held her hand to her brow in mock sorrow, 'not one of them returned. All killed in action, every man jack of them. Heroes every one …'

This stimulated a further sobbing fit from the prostrate Professor. He didn't remain prostrate and sobbing on the floor of the Oval Office for long, however. He was soon prostrate and sobbing on the floor of a police cell floor in downtown Washington, on a charge of first-degree homicide on a mass-genocide scale.

The great flood which covered over a third of the land mass of the world became known as the Watershed. It was a defining moment in the history of mankind, the point at which man turned his back on Planet Earth and looked to the stars, or Planet Tycho to be more precise.

It hadn't taken President Consuela Sweetcorn long to realise that she could stand on an even higher pedestal if she were to be the saviour of mankind, the leader to inspire and engineer Exodus, the evacuation of Earth's remaining population to the stars. And it hadn't taken President Consuela Sweetcorn long to realise that she couldn't do this without one man.

Buzzard …

So Buzzard was plucked by the men in black suits, this time from his downtown Washington cell, and put to work on designing and constructing the 5,700 spacecraft needed to shuttle the surviving billions to their new home in the Alfalfa-Beta System.

At first, he protested, refused to cooperate. He finally saw reason in a blinding moment of revelation when the President offered to go to the press with the story. 'Mad scientist experiment puts Big Apple under 20 metres of water.' And, of course, the Big Apple didn't bob, it drowned. As did

Christchurch, Sydney, Tokyo, London and Hull.

Hull first.

Buzzard finally succumbed and was put to work in a secret location somewhere in the High Nevadas surrounded by the finest minds a silver dollar could buy. What drove him on over the coming years was not the constant threat of the President, but the hope of redemption for his catastrophic miscalculation. If he could successfully implement Exodus, then the cup half-full would be sweet nectar to his lips and his terrible guilt could be absolved.

Buzzard worked tirelessly to this end. Day in, day out. All the time at the back of his mind needled, however, the nagging question. How had he got it so wrong? So disastrously wrong.

The answer was quite simple.

Professor Clayton E Buzzard was arguably the most brilliant scientific intellect in the whole wide world. But he was crap at basic arithmetic. He was, well, above that sort of thing. He couldn't add up. He couldn't take away. He would become disoriented at the dizzy heights of eight sevens are fifty-six. And decimal points were not his forte. Which was why Jenny Lind should never have entrusted Clayton E with the thrice-daily measuring of powdered milk into little Tycho's baby food bottles.

Which was why President Sweetcorn should definitely not have allowed him to put together retro-agent B313 without the support of his lab team.

Both with disastrous consequences.

Tycho barely made his first birthday, his only source of nourishment being baby milk, served at one-tenth strength by his doting father.

And as for Planet Earth, well, the rest was history ...

Watershed.

Exodus.

Citidomes.

10

The slim figure walked over towards the primitive, single-storey wooden building, took in the mesh on the single window, the rain streaming from a broken gutter, the small red plastic barrel hanging over the entrance. He took a deep breath and entered Dick's Bar aka The Slingshot Inn.

Cigarette smoke attacked the lungs as soon as he entered the room. He coughed involuntarily.

The seven eyes of the bar's occupants – one barman and three customers – turned towards him. He had no way of knowing whether the icy silence had prevailed prior to his entrance. Icy as in 32 degrees. Silence as in deafening barrage of rain on the tin roof. He suspected not.

A first scan of the single-room bar told him this much.

Barman: Height 2.18. Weight 150k. Big. Very big.

Distinguishing characteristics: forked red beard and an overwhelming first impression of small green piggy eyes and extreme body size.

And, seated on the orange plastic banquette against the far wall:

Customer Number One: Male, height 1.90, medium build, matted, dirty shoulder-length black hair. Seated next to him, **Customer Number Two:** Male, height 1.90, medium build, matted, dirty shoulder-length brown hair. Both were dressed in combat fatigues.

The seventh eye belonged to **Customer Number Three**, a woman slouched in the far right corner of the bar. Height 1.80. Buxom build, matted dirty shoulder-length blonde hair and wearing a bright-blue neoprene bodysuit ripped at the right shoulder and the left knee. Her good eye followed the new customer as he walked to the bar. Her false eye, a yellow marble with crimson swirls, didn't …

'Good evening, sir, and what be your poison?'

'Just a beer, please.'

'An excellent choice, sir. What we wants is Watneys.'

He took a glass from the shelf behind him, wiped it on the edge of his smock whilst he shuffled out of sight to what presumably was the store at the back. He returned holding a large red and yellow canister which he proceeded to shake vigorously. The words 'Party Can' emerged from the blur of the frenzied activity.

'If you could just step aside, sir,' he requested before inserting an evil-looking horn-handled tin opener into the can. The stream of foam exploded against the wall just above the head of the two men, totally soaking them.

'There you go, boys, beer shampoo,' he laughed.

'You're a twat you are, Tiny!' Customer Number One grinned from a mouth boasting a single brown tooth. 'What is he?'

'A twat,' concurred Customer Number Two.

The one-eyed Lady in Blue said nothing.

'Hee hee, lively little number,' said Tiny, as he poured what remained of the contents of the half-gallon can into the glass. It barely reached halfway.

'That will be twenty dollars please, sir.' It came as a challenge. Twenty dollars for half a glass of beer. But now was not the time to respond … he must remain focused.

He handed over a twenty-dollar coin and Tiny Dick the barman doffed an imaginary cap.

'Thank you, kind sir.' The two men giggled. 'And would sir like some nibbles?' He pointed to three packets of stork scratchings, stapled to the picture of an attractive young woman of oriental extraction. 'Perhaps this one, sir,' the barman suggested, touching the packet which covered the woman's right breast.

An expectant hush came over the bar. The two men on the banquette held their breadth.

'Only one dollar fifty, sir,' Tiny tempted, stroking the packet with his stubby forefinger.

'No thanks, the beer will suffice.' A groan of disappointment escaped from the lips of Customer Number Two.

How long had those last three packets of stork scratchings covering the private parts of some probably long-since-dead woman entranced the regulars of Dick's Bar? He took his beer and went over to the far left corner, sat down on the sticky orange plastic seat and raised the glass to his lips.

Python piss! Thank the Lord that most of it had failed to reach his glass.

The rain rattled on the tin roof as the storm seemed to grow in strength.

The Lady in Blue rose from her chair and tottered to the jukebox, inserted a coin and returned to her seat.

A haunting melody struggled to impose itself against the storm. 'Summertime' by Gershwin and Heyward. The jukebox tried in vain to convince the bar that the living was easy. Even less convincing was the claim that her momma was good-looking.

Tiny Dick unleashed an outburst of wind more ferocious than the storm above. The two men collapsed in a fit of laughter. The Lady in Blue slurred an insult in their general direction.

'Arsewipes!'

A thunderclap broke immediately overhead, threatening to rip the roof off. At the same time, the door opened. A thin figure stood in the entrance, blinked and coughed. It was a boy, wearing a khaki beanie hat, a muddy brown shirt and shorts. He had a wound running the length of his left shin, bandage hanging loose. He looked in a bad way. The bar went quiet. 'Summertime' came to an end. The barman and two men eyed the boy as wolves would a Bambi.

A Bambi, smiled Besk to himself. Thin-legged, wide-eyed.. Vulnerable to attack, as he had been on the forest track. One could have taken him there and then, reflected Besk. But too soon, too easy. He had picked him up clearly on the night scan, a figure, hiding behind the log ... Easy dispatch, quick reward. And again here, in this primitive environment, here for the taking.

The last time Hesperus Besk had entered Dead or Alive, the mission had been completed effectively and swiftly in less than eight hours. The prey stuck like a squealing pig on the end of a javelin at twenty metres' distance. He had promised himself then that next time he would extend the experience. Savour the moment.

The boy had gone to the bar and ordered a glass of water which he took back to the table next to the jukebox. Besk could clearly see how his hand trembled as he raised the drink up to his lips. He finished it in one and then sat upright breathing deeply, his back pressed against the wall.

The Lady in Blue put 'Summertime' on again and performed a slow, gyrating dance to the great amusement of the two men on the bench. As she danced, swaying from side to side on steep yellow stilettos, she looked at Besk and smiled. Not a full-mouth, cheek-creasing smile. More of a wince. More of a grimace. One thing, however, was certain ...

She was giving him the eye.

She had only the one.

She tottered back to the jukebox and ordered 'Summertime' again.

As the haunting lyric took her back to the middle of the beer-stained floor, she raised her right eyebrow at Besk.

He found the coloured marble in the socket strangely erotic. He had not planned for an experience this trip, but why not? It was four long months since he had last … expressed himself.

The song played out and she returned to her seat in the corner having decided that three 'Summertimes' were enough for one evening.

'34.8,' remarked Customer Number One.

Everybody then looked at the red neon digital thermometer. It read 34.8 degrees. What else would it read? Why did they all have to check?

'34.9,' said Customer Number Two.

The temperature was rising, even though it was getting later. The storm was abating, reasoned Besk. There would be immediate but short-lived increase in temperature before the night cooled again.

The rain stopped. Besk noted that the boy had fallen asleep, the blond mop of hair spreading over his folded arms onto the tabletop.

'33.9,' said Customer Number One. Then the sound of footsteps approaching, boots squelching in the mud.

A man in a dark-brown leather sheep rancher's cape and broad-rimmed leather hat entered, walked over to the bar and addressed the barman with a nod and a single word.

'Dick.'

Tiny Dick nodded back and went to open a party can (the two customers ducked instinctively).

'No thanks, mate, I'll just have a hotshot.'

Tiny Dick headed beneath the bar and produced a dented pewter hip flask. He poured a milky-brown liquid into a shot glass. The Australian downed it in one, shuddered, shook the rain off his shoulders and extracted a manifest from inside the cape.

'One passenger for MK,' he offered the room, then looked at Besk.

Besk shook his head and nodded towards the boy on the far wall, now asleep

'Cheers, mate,' the Australian responded, went over to the boy and shook him gently by the arm.

'MK, mate?'

The boy woke with a start, tried to take in his surroundings with a wide-eyed sense of total incomprehension, as if awaking from a deep faint. His body reacted by jerking him to his feet where he stood swaying and blinking.

'No worries, mate, no worries. Sorry to wake you, but we leave in twenty minutes.'

'The Slingshot?' the boy asked.

'Yep that's right. Beaut of a beast and straight as a die. Token?'

'Sure,' said the boy and fumbled the token from his rucksack.

'Looks good.' Cairns cleared his throat.

'How many items of hand luggage do you have?'

'One,' replied Rib, pointing to his rucksack.

'Did you pack this bag yourself?'

'Er ... yes,' lied Rib.

'Has anybody asked you to put anything in your bag?'

'Er ... no.'

'Do you have any sharp implements in your bag?'

'Er ... no.' Rib thought he wouldn't mention the Swiss Army penknife.

'OK, mate, when you're ready. Will all passengers for the 23.24 for MK please proceed to Gate 1, where the Beast is now boarding.'

And with that, he opened the door for his cargo of one, ushered him through, turned to nod ta-ta to the bar, and, with a laugh, repeated, 'The Beast is now boarding.' And with that they left.

Twenty minutes to departure, considered Besk. Time to put right the python piss on his palate.

Besk stood up and walked to the bar, sensing a heightened tension in the room as he did so.

Tiny Dick reached for a new party can. 'And what would sir like?'

'Sir would like a Tiger Gold Medal Lager Beer, please.'

Tiny Dick chuckled. 'We don't do Tiger beer here, sir. What we wants is Watneys.'

He reached for the can opener. 'Oh, but I think you do,' said Besk, unzipping his suit and taking out his ID strobe. Tiny Dick looked at the strobe and stiffened. His hand never made contact with the can opener.

'Er … Tiger Beer it is then, sir.' Beads of perspiration appeared on his already sweaty brow.

'Thank you, and if you would be so kind, an accompanying glass of Absolut Vodka.'

'Er, yes, sir,' whispered Dick as he disappeared from behind the bar into the backroom.

He reappeared within the minute with a bottle of golden ale crested with a foil wrap bearing the emblem of a tiger and a palm tree.

'Tiger beer, sir, the genuine article.'

Besk nodded appreciatively as the barman poured it into a glass.

'And your vodka, sir.'

Tiny Dick placed an iced glass next to the Tiger.

'What we usually wants is Watneys, sir, but on occasions such as this, sir, *noblesse oblige*.'

He reached beneath the bar, produced a 70-centilitre bottle of ice-cold Absolut and poured into the frosted glass to a meniscus perfection. He looked down on his work of art, spread both hands flat on the bar either side of the glasses, and raised an eyebrow.

'To your satisfaction, sir?'

The flap of skin between thumb and forefinger is seldom exposed. A clenched fist, a karate chop protects the thin tissue from harm.

The downward stab of the scalpel which pinned the flap of

Tiny Dick's left hand to the wooden surface of the bar was as quick as it was unequivocal.

Besk let his hand slide down the shaft of the scalpel to cover Dick's hand. He could feel the warm blood rising up from the fleshy wound.

A movement from Customer Number One.

Besk addressed him without turning his head.

'And you?'

Besk hissed into the face of the barman.

'Do I look like a man who would partake of Absolut vodka from a blue Australia Zoo shot glass with a pewter emblem of a wombat welded to it? Do I? Do I!!!' he screamed.

'No sir, no sir,' gasped Tiny Dick, increasingly aware of the increasing flow of blood trickling onto the floor drip-drip from the surface of the bar, *his* bar.

Besk took a piece of Sanigauze from his trouser pocket, tugged the scalpel from the wood and flesh, and wiped the blade carefully before returning it to the sheath in his inside breast pocket.

'Now,' he said, fixing Tiny Dick with a cold stare. 'An appropriate shot glass. I suggest a Muurla Ratia. Bring the drinks over to my table … You will get it right this time, won't you?'

'Yes, yes, sir,' whispered Tiny, desperately trying to stem the flow of blood with the corner of his apron. Three minutes later Besk sipped at the ice-cold glass served on a small silver tray by the quaking barman. The bar's five eyes strained for his reaction. He nodded his approval at Tiny Dick, who laughed nervously and backed off to the relative safety of his bar.

Besk finished his drinks without interruption, save for a longing look from the Lady in Blue, still half reclined in the seat in the corner. He checked his watch, stood up and strode swiftly over to the door. On leaving, he left the occupants with one final comment.

'31.2.'

Tiny Dick, Customers One and Two and the Lady in Blue all looked up at the flickering red neon thermometer. It said 31.2.

When they looked to the door again, the slim figure in the greysuit with a scalpel in the breast pocket was gone.

11

Brisbane Cairns was not a bad man. His business certainly brought him into contact with bad men and bad women on a daily basis. But on the whole he was all right, which is why he chose not to take advantage of his single passenger, now slumped asleep as the 6 x 6 bumped along the track towards the terminal. Cairns had built the Slingshot five years previously, using his training as an engineer and his experience as a fairground operator in Eumundi. The Beast, as he fondly called it, was one in a network which Cairns ran as a franchise business. His partners changed on a regular basis, usually through swift and immediate termination of contract. By Cairns, without notice.

The Slingshot operated out of ten terminals: Wigan, Norwich, Edinburgh, Sheffield, Cardiff, Walsall, Exeter, Haltwhistle and MK. Well, it didn't actually operate out of the ten citidomes, of course, because it was totally illegal. The terminals were all sited in impenetrable rainforest between 5 and 10 kilometres from the main centres and were patronised by those who frequented ground level. Hence the daily contact with bad men and bad women. A bit like a no-frills airline, really.

This sprog did not fit the normal customer profile. He was too young, too clean-looking, too *innocent*-looking to be on ground level. Cairns felt almost paternal as he gently shook the boy's shoulder.

'Sorry to wake you again, mate, but we're here.'

They got out of the truck and Cairns guided the boy up a

double flight of metal stairs which had in a previous life been the fire escape of the Birmingham and Midshires Building Society, Bold Street, Liverpool.

The top of the stairs opened out onto a platform. At the end, a hut with the words 'Ticket Office' painted in red over the door. The boy stood on the platform and looked up at the masterpiece of civil engineering cum Ferris wheel that was the Slingshot.

'Wow!' was all he could gasp.

'She is rather impressive, isn't she? I told you she was a beaut. Now, mate, have you ever flown with us before?' He knew as he asked that the answer would be no.

'No.'

'OK, no worries. We'll just get you nice and comfy in the pod, give you a little jab in the arm. You'll wake up in MK in no time.' He failed to mention that the boy had a 78 per cent chance of landing safety in the 500-square-metres Villoprene net stretched across the former pitch of Stony Stratford football club. The 'Wheel of Misfortune' was what his enemies called the Beast.

'Jab?' said the boy, visibly paling. 'Not a wafer?'

'Naah, a jab's scientifically proven to be much safer than a wafer.'

Safer than a wafer, Brisbane thought. Must write that down.

'And though I say so myself, I'm a dab hand with the jab. So no worries, my little mate.'

He led the boy to the pod at the bottom of the huge wheel. He strapped the kid into the rough leather bucket seat and pulled hard on the buckle.

From a white box with a red cross on the lid fixed to a post beside the wheel, he took out a long hypodermic syringe and loaded it from a bottle with a pink liquid. The boy's eyes stared wildly like a cow's before the slaughter and he began to struggle.

'It's OK, mate, it's OK,' soothed Cairns as he held the boy down and plunged the rusty needle into his arm.

The kid went limp in a matter of seconds. Cairns tested the harness again, closed the pod canopy and walked back to the ticket office. The rain started to mallet the tin roof, the storm returning with a vengeance. A crack of lightning lit up the clearing, throwing the giant wheel into sharp relief against the thrashing forest wall. The thunderclap that followed seconds later confirmed that the storm was almost over-head. Cairns sat down at the console and started the flight sequence.

Destination coordinates entered. Liquid hydrogen feed engaged. He was reaching out to press the green ignition button to send the Slingshot wheeling into launch mode when a second crack of lightning ripped the hot air directly above the hut. The flash lit up the platform, only for a split second. But in that slice of time, he looked up and saw a slim figure in a greysuit, standing only 10 metres in front of the open window of the office.

One elbow was raised. The lightning flashed against the steel shaft of a weapon.

A crossbow.

As the thunderclap smashed down on the corrugated-iron roof of the hut, he instinctively threw himself to his right. Too late. Brisbane Cairns crashed face down onto the floor, the red feathered flight of a ten-centimetre-long steel bolt sticking out of his left ear.

Besk darted across the platform and flattened himself against the wall of the ticket office before satisfying himself that there was no sound of life inside. He knelt and peered round the door jamb to seek affirmation of the terminal act – the body of a large man sprawled across the floor, his head resting in a pool of darkening blood.

He took no closer order.

He didn't need to.

Besk padded back over the platform in a half-stooping run. Ever vigilant. Covering the shadows in case the man had an assistant. No sign of any.

He moved to the Slingshot and the pod housing the night's only passenger. He looked through the scorched and scarred cockpit and made out the wan figure, his life seemingly strangled out of him by the bucket-seat harness.

Besk pressed the release button and pulled the lever to open the cockpit. It yielded with a distinct degree of resistance. Some seventy or so flights had rendered the former open swoosh into a grudging grate.

But Besk insisted and pulled back the canopy with a wrench of his right hand and stood, leaning over the boy. He could barely discern his breathing. He felt for a pulse and, after a second, found it. Slow, say forty, but steady. Besk's finger traced down the boy's jaw line and back up to the cheek bone before taking reluctant leave. He was there for the taking. For the third time. On the trail. At the inn. And now, most tempting. Here in his hands.

The quarry.

Cornered.

He noticed a bag half hidden under the seat. No doubt the 200 million dollars sat deviously secreted somewhere therein.

So easy.

Yet somehow so … *unsatisfactory*.

Too easy, maybe.

Besk breathed out long and hard through his nostrils and stepped away from the pod.

The rain had ceased. A calm had descended over the rainforest, punctuated only by a few indeterminable grunts from the undergrowth and scuffles in the canopy. He then slammed the cockpit shut and made sure the locking mechanism was engaged by pulling the handle hard. It was locked. He walked briskly back to the ticket office, stepped over the body of Cairns and changed the flight coordinates. To a set of digits familiar to him. One thing was certain. The boy would land nowhere near MK. Another thing was certain. The pod would not land in a Slingshot net at all. One thing was uncertain. That the boy would land safely. The Beast was too crude to be certain, which was why Besk had taken a tracer chip from his belt and attached it to the roof of the pod.

Besk initiated the launch sequence, sending the Slingshot gently into motion. The huge wheel circled slowly into idle phase, sending the pod high up towards treetop level. The index finger of Besk's left hand was poised above the green launch button. As he looked up to see the capsule reach the top of the arc, he paused momentarily to sense check his course of action.

Why had he spared the boy? He could kill him and cash in the Dead or Alive credits now. He knew the answer. He craved stimulus. The thrill of the chase. The drug of a five-day hunt was something which his body, his soul screamed out for. Since the last round, he had spent a seeming eternity in courtroom corridors, in the apartments of high-ranking polizzia officials, in the dark corners of the citidome frequented by shady characters. All moving his agenda relentlessly forward. All requiring his powers of persuasion, subterfuge and deception to the full. Now he needed the rush.

The Beast, as if sensing the loss of its master, hissed and whirred into slingmode in brute response to Besk hitting the green button. The roar of the wheel now spinning into a blur was deafening. Besk strained to see the pod hurled high into the night air, high above the trees thrashing to the music of the Beast, now King Kong like in its fury.

'Bon voyage, mon petit,' whispered Besk.

The die was cast.

The hunt was on.

He would now follow a strictly defined routine which had brought him unchallenged success as the ultimate Dead or Alive player. He would return to his truck, ascertain location of the pod, plot the route, take a light supper of omelette and kiwi fruit, choose his apparel and equipment for the next day, and finally descend into meditative state for thirty-five minutes before returning to his bunk.

His 6 x 6 stood where he had left it, at the corner of the flattened area of mud loosely constituting the Slingshot Inn car park. To his surprise, but no more than that, he noted four new arrivals, all vehicles of mongrel origin, lined up close to the front of the inn.

He beamed open the lock on his truck at eighteen paces' distance.

Then, in the middle of a quagmire of a car park in the middle of a rainforest, Hesperus Besk stopped stock still and looked over to the door of Dick's Bar. He breathed deeply. He had a new plan. He would break the mould, unwrap the regime, take the routine to a new plane …

… Of excitement.

For he realised that he had unfinished business to which he must attend.

A woman wearing a ripped blue jumpsuit and yellow high heels with a coloured marble for a right eye.

The Lady in Blue.

He quickly formulated his plan. How he would take her to a place she had never experienced before.

As he started to walk towards the entrance of the inn, the forefinger of his left hand moved to his right chest and stroked the length of the steel shaft of the scalpel resting in his inside pocket.

'Hush, little baby, don't you cry,' he whispered.

12

Before he opened his eyes, Rib heard the sound of running water echoing somewhere in the distance. Not too far away. Below and to his right. He then heard splashing and laughter. Two, maybe three voices. Female voices.

Before he opened his eyes, he felt the pain. Not only in his left leg. Although that was still bad. But his head, his left shoulder and his right wrist, which seemed to be strapped up against his chest. And his nose still hurt, too.

Before he opened his eyes, he smelt scent. Lavender, he thought, and he felt the crispness of the single sheet lightly covering his body.

He opened his eyes.

He was lying in what looked like a large circular room with a well in the middle from where the laughter and the splashing came. He tried to call out, but all he could do was groan. Before he slipped back into unconsciousness, he heard the sound of footsteps coming up a stairwell to his left. Over the next two days, he drifted in and out of sleep, registering small changes in his state. Change of dressings, water being gently poured into his mouth, an extra-thick fluffy white pillow.

Lavender.

Jasmine.

Lavender again.

So when he finally came to, he felt almost acclimatised, at ease with his environment, without fully understanding why.

'Back in the land of the living, are we?' came a voice from behind him. It belonged to a young woman, blonde, in her mid-twenties Rib guessed, dressed in a white shift and wearing white clogs. She was spick, seriously spick.

'Yeah, I suppose so,' said Rib, giving her his best smile under the circumstances, a smile which changed to an even better wince as he tried to shift position. He suddenly remembered the lottery, the looty. 'Where are my things?' he asked.

'Take it easy now,' she said, now standing beside him. 'They're safely locked away for you. How's your leg? You've had a close call. You've got to rest now. I'll come and see you again in an hour. Just press the alarm if you need anything before,' she said, pointing at the red button on his bedhead. As she took the first step down the stairs, she turned and said, 'My name's Ruth.'

Rib said, 'Hi. My name's Rib.'

'Yes, I know,' she smiled.

'Wait a minute, Ruth, where am I? Am I in MK?'

'In MK?' she laughed. 'No, this isn't MK. Now you get some rest. You've had a shock to your system. Jonathan will explain everything to you when you're fit and ready and that won't be for a couple of days yet. See you later.' She waved as she descended the stairs out of view.

Rib made to protest but didn't have the energy. He slipped back into a deep sleep and dreamed of pushing a long line of trolleys stacked with orange-coloured beer crates down a muddy path in the rainforest, circled by screeching parakeets.

Step by step, Ruth nursed him back to something approaching fitness. His leg had responded well to the large blue pills she forced him to take three times a day, and the dressing was replaced regularly, revealing the makings of a rather excellent scar running parallel to his shin bone. It still hurt like hell but, in front of Ruth, Rib was a brave boy. His nose felt different of course, because it was different, on account of the crunching encounter with Domestrut 47.

The food she served him was incredible. It tasted, well … real. The meat was marbled with fat and tasted wonderful, the vegetables fresh and full of flavour and the fish was sublime. Coming from meat-and-potato pie land, he thought he was in heaven. Good though it was, Rib was sure that he wasn't in heaven. And every time he asked where he was, he was always referred to the upcoming meeting with Jonathan.

Ruth was happy to tell him about his immediate surroundings. He had been nursed in the Aqua Basta, which she explained was a place for quiet meditation and healing. When he was finally steady on his legs, she gave him a guided tour. He had been convalescing on the first floor and she took him down to the ground floor, where the central feature was a pool, shaped like a Roman bath. In fact, the whole décor, heavy on terracotta tiles and intricate blue mosaics, had a strong Italian feel about it. Surrounding the pool was a whole series of spa rooms, and that was where the Italian connection stopped: Indian Blossom Steam Room, Turkish Hammam, Japanese Salt Steam, Swedish Sauna, Finnish Bastu and another one that was so hot Rib didn't make it past the door but he was sure he could taste vindaloo on his lips as he showered.

Back alongside the white marbled corridor was the Conservatory Café where Rib took all his meals, clad in the obligatory white towelling robe. Now here the whole ambience was pure Italian. Paninis, bruschettas, pasta, cappuccinos, lattes, espressos. Not a bacon sandwich in sight. Not that he was complaining; he could get used to this.

During one visit to the Turkish Hammam he sat and pieced together how he had got to this place, wherever it was. The misdirected trip to Wigan citidome, the old lady, the lottery ticket, the dawn flight to the platform, the hang-glider crash, the nightmare trek through the rainforest, the Slingshot Inn, and then, the Slingshot itself. All he could remember was the prick of the needle, and then waking up in the Aqua Basta. His reveries were broken by Ruth entering the café and seeking him out. She sat down beside him.

'Hey, Rib,' she said.

He smiled by way of a response.

'Jonathan's ready to see you now.'

Excellent, thought Rib, now I finally find out where I am.

A tall, slim, bronzed figure with cropped light hair, deep-blue eyes, a designer-cut stubble of a beard came over to the table. Rib stood, knowing this to be Jonathan.

The man grasped Rib's outstretched hand with both of his and held it there for a tad too long.

'Rib, we've been worried about you. But, hey, it's good to see you're back on the mend. I'm sure we've got Ruth to thank for that.' His nod in her direction was clearly a signal that she should leave. She smiled and left the café with no farewell, no look over her shoulder.

Jonathan's arms were brown and covered with blond hairs. He wore a simple knotted leather band on his left wrist matching his chunky leather sandals. Rib couldn't help noticing that his fingernails and toenails were perfectly manicured. Jonathan released his grip and sat down beside Rib.

'Yes, young man, you have had an amazing escape, but you're in safe hands now and in a safe place. Safe and sound.'

'Where am I? Am I far from MK?' Rib went straight to the point. He had been building up to this for days now.

Jonathan laughed. 'I'll take your second question first. No, I'm afraid you're nowhere near MK. I'd say you were about a hundred miles away.' Rib's heart sank. 'But look on the bright side, you've landed in the best possible place. In Middlemedes.'

'Middlemedes? Never heard of it and how the hell did I get here?'

'Now hold on, steady now, Rib, we haven't looked after you badly so far now, have we?'

'No, I'm sorry,' Rib said, feeling foolish. 'I really am grateful, it's just that I've got to get to MK and I don't understand how I've ended up here. And every time I've asked, people have fobbed me off with the "Jonathan will explain" routine.'

'Well, here I am. I'll tell you everything you want to know about Middlemedes and I'll show you how you got here. Tell you what, let's get you changed into some outdoor clothes and we'll take a walk. I'll explain on the way.'

Ten minutes later Rib met Jonathan in the circular reception area which had a large marble desk and a number of pedestals with Roman-looking busts on them. Rib felt somewhat self-conscious in the yellow jogging suit which had been supplied for him, but less so when they walked out of the building: everybody passing by was wearing a jogging suit. Admittedly mostly green, but some in other colours. The first thing that struck Rib was the temperature. It felt about 19 degrees. The same temperature as inside the Dome, even though they were outdoors. That couldn't be right …

They set off along a walkway. A bell sounded behind them and a family passed them on bicycles.

Rib started. 'Wow, they're dink,' he said. He'd never seen a real bicycle before, only in games.

'It's the only way to get around,' said Jonathan. 'No fuel needed, keeps you fit and it's fun too.' As they turned into what looked like a square, he noticed an area with literally hundreds of bicycles parked up.

They walked past a shop which gave an impression of a seriously upmarket Waste-Rows. It was called the Mede Mart. 'This is where you can buy all the food you need. That's if you're into cooking?' Jonathan asked.

'Yeah, sure,' replied Rib, meaning, 'No, I don't do cooking but I'm not going to admit that to you.'

Jonathan stopped at the crest of a small bridge which crossed a small stream connecting two small ponds. Jonathan swept his arm 180 degrees around him.

'Life at Middlemedes revolves around the Village Square, with whitewashed walls, pantiled roofs and leafy terraces. There's an inviting cluster of eating places here, including our lovely contemporary Italian restaurant, Pacino's.'

Italian. Surprise, surprise, thought Rib.

Jonathan continued: 'Easy informality is the hallmark of Middlemedes, imaginatively designed to create a real village feel. You can steep yourself, Rib, in the al fresco style of the Mediterranean, all in harmony with the Englishness of Middle England.' These words, English and Middle England sounded like something out of a tourist brochure for old people. The sort of olde-worlde travel destination you'd read about on a Trawlsite for really old people. The Deccahead granddad was a member of a club called Sago, presumably because that was all its subscribers could eat. They'd all go off together, monopolise the hotel and complain about the price of Viagra and haemorrhoid cream. But this place wasn't just for old people, there were families here too. Mums and dads with babies, all making quite a lot of noise. Jonathan pressed on with studied enthusiasm.

'As you can see, Rib, the contoured Village Square is an inspiration, with terraces at upper as well as ground level and viewpoints in all kinds of unexpected places. There, on one side of the meandering stream, is the exquisitely planted Piazza – pure Italian chic,' he added, looking to Rib for a reaction.

'Well, yeah, it really is … pure Italian chic,' was all he could offer in return without really understanding what it meant.

'And just over there,' Jonathan pointed, 'is the leisure

bowl and the subtropical swimming paradise. We've just extended this already fabulous facility to include a new hundred-metre laned swimming pool.'

Now this really did catch Rib's attention. Until his departure to Wigan, he had swum regularly, three times a week, at the Sports Garden. Everyone had access for a maximum of five sessions per week and Rib chose four ninety-minute stints in the pool plus a half-hour on the kayak machine of a Tuesday evening. He was pretty good at front crawl and on occasion, yielding to the constant pressure of the coach, had entered a gala. He acquitted himself reasonably well but never really enjoyed it. This competition thing wasn't really his cup of coffee.

'So how deep is the pool then?' he enquired.

'1.5 metres all the way. Twenty lanes, anti-washback damper. If you're a Speedo guy, you'll be seriously impressed, believe me.'

'Yeah, I'd like to give that a go.'

'Well, you'll have every opportunity, Rib. All in good time.'

Jonathan took Rib by the arm and directed him up a path to their left. The village was alive, full of bright energy, babbling voices and water. So different from the soft, subdued hum of dome life. He was beginning to like it, although the dull pain in his leg reminded him that he had come from one place and should have been at another. His thought train was interrupted by Jonathan, pointing to his right. 'Just look at that. One big and beautiful orangery. Here you can chill out amongst the citrus trees and terracotta pots. You see, Rib, everything combines here to make for a simply stunning village.'

Rib had to admit that it did look great. No greys, no carbon steel, no cobalt blues. 'So what is Middlemedes then, Jonathan, is it some sort of holiday centre?'

Rib thought he saw a tautening of Jonathan's jaw line.

Then after a slight pause Jonathan stopped and smiled.

'There's something for everyone here at Middlemedes, Rib, and that includes you. You can do whatever you like; there's absolutely no pressure. Wherever you're at, there's a whole range of things you can tap into at your level. Stress just melts away as you abandon yourself to some of the most sublime multi-sensory experiences.'

Rib opened his mouth to say, 'But hold on, is it a holiday centre or isn't it?' but Jonathan held up his hand. 'We have more ways to relax than you could ever imagine. You take life at your own pace and freedom comes with the territory, a beautiful, natural setting that induces relaxation from the moment you arrive. Although,' Jonathan paused, 'it has to be admitted, Rib, that your particular mode of arrival was somewhat irregular. I said I'd show you, didn't I? We found you down in the forest ... Well, not exactly *down* in the forest.' He chuckled to himself. 'Do you want to see?'

'Sure.'

'OK, it's only about fifteen minutes' walk from here and I can show more of the Mede on the way.' He strode off purposefully up a winding path beside the stream. Past the restaurants, coffee houses, sweet shop – have to go back there, Rib noted – up through a chicane of bamboo screens and then, suddenly, they were out of the village.

Jonathan switched into tourist guide mode.

'The Mede covers some 500 acres and in the thirteenth century was part of the hunting forest of Sherwood. The forest at that time was an intricate mixture of woodland pasture containing mature oaks, heather and grassland. Of course, we all know what's happened to our climate since then, and our principal landscape goal is to return the present coniferous woodland to the glory days of yesteryear. To do this, we have an ongoing replanting programme for indigenous trees and shrubs.

'We have created 30 acres of lakes, streams and ponds as

well as a rich mosaic of woodland clearings for heathland and grassland regeneration. As you know, Rib, our environment has been subject to savage attack in our recent past and the defence of our natural wildlife is down to the skill and dedication of our biodiversity landscape teams.' He stopped and looked into the middle distance wistfully.

Rib stopped to take in the scene before him. A lake, a big lake, about a kilometre long, broken by a number of small inlets and islets. He could see figures moving, some walking, some cycling on a path which seemed to go all the way round. Trees came down to the water's edge in places, but not the trees which he had encountered at close quarters in his rainforest flight from the Dome. These were darker, with spiky leaves, almost needle-like. And on the lake, waterfowl of differing kinds. Not the screeching horde of a thousand lorikeets here, but dozens of birds quietly paddling about their own business, seeming to mix quite happily in each other's company. Most of an indistinguishable brown colour. Rib didn't recognise any of these species.

'I don't recognise any of these species,' Rib said.

Jonathan laughed. 'No reason why you should. These are all native waterfowl. Teal, mallard, coot, merganser,' he pointed. 'Not to be found everywhere. It's rather special, isn't it?'

Rib nodded. So what is this place, a holiday camp, a zoo? he asked himself. This time he thought better of posing the question again to Jonathan. He would find out soon enough anyway.

At the same time Rib was trying to figure out what was different about the scene set before him. OK, the birds were different. OK the trees were different. But there was something else. The whole picture was wrong. It was like looking at the world through a filter. The only comparison being offered by his brain was the paint finishes you could choose from in the Vespa showroom – azure-blue shine, blue gloss or blue matt. And this was matt, definitely matt. No sparkle, no reflection, no edge.

His thought process was broken by an overhead screech. Rib looked up to see a large, thin bird with white underbelly, long beak and long legs being dive-bombed by two smaller but bulky-looking black attackers. As the three zigzagged their way past the headland to his right, Rib's eyes did not follow the birds but remained focused straight above. Above the lake, above the whole forest was suspended a thin, finely meshed net, hardly visible. It was a bluey-green colour and yes, it was this that must be giving everything a dull, muted appearance.

Jonathan followed Rib's thought. 'Ah, I see you're interested in our net. The net, of course, enables us to sustain a great rural outdoor experience, totally in harmony with nature. It provides our community with the necessary protection from the sun's rays.

'And it keeps all these native birds in ...'

'And the other birds out.' Rib wished he hadn't finished Jonathan's sentence for him. His eyes narrowed and he took a sharp intake of breath before his features resumed normal service with a broad smile.

'And of course the net saved your smoky...'

'My smoky?'

'Bacon,' finished Jonathan.

Bacon be arsed, thought Rib as he followed the thin, tanned figure who had set off along the path which skirted the lake. And how did he get than tan anyway? If this filter-net thingy protected Middlemedes from the sun's rays, why was he so brown? Why did he care? His leg was starting to hurt again and he reached down to touch the dressing on his left shin. It was sore to the touch and he flinched. Ruth had changed the dressing conscientiously for him every morning and he thought it was getting better, but this morning ...

'Are you OK?'

'Yeah it's just the leg; it doesn't feel too good today.'

'It will take time to heal, and it will probably get worse before it gets better and remember, you had a close call.' The path opened out to a wide area, open to the shore; it looked for all the world like a beach. Rib ran forward a few paces, knelt down and grabbed a handful of sand and let it trickle through his fingers. He did it again, and again …

He looked back at Jonathan who was observing him quietly.

'Hey, this is a beach, an actual beach. How did this get here?' For Rib, a beach was something from a film, a disc, a wafer. He'd never seen one in real life, never felt the smooth but at the same time gritty sensation of sand under his feet.

'You mean our sandy beach beside our breezy water-sports lake? Well, we put it here. It takes a lot of cleaning,' Jonathan said, nodding at three large rakes propped up against a ranch-style fence, 'but it's just one of the great jobs we have here, raking the sand.'

Raking the sand? A job? thought Rib. Why not? If it's here, someone's got to do it I suppose.

Two girls were busy washing out a brightly painted yellow kayak at the water's edge. 'Hey!' they said and waved.

Rib half lifted his arm and ventured, 'Hiya!'

'Um, we prefer "hey" as the form of address here on the Mede, Rib.'

'Not "hiya"?'

'No, not really, "hey" is so much more friendly, more inter-national, don't you think?'

'OK then, "hey" it is,' said Rib, although actually, no, I don't think it's more friendly and as far as the international bit, the duck population's hardly international is it? But who cares? All the more reason to get back to MK where he could hiya to his heart's content to his mates, the Deccaheads, when he next saw them.

Jonathan strode on, past something which looked like a

restaurant. Rib followed, slowing to note the name above the door of the restaurant. Friggya's Fondue House. Rib couldn't even begin to imagine what lay behind those walls. They followed a surfaced road which ran about 20 metres from the edge of the lake from the road. Rib took in the emerging make-up of the landscape. On the far shore, in amongst the dense trees, stood rows of houses, the white-painted ones standing out in the half-light. Jonathan touched his arm and pointed to a row of timber buildings coming up on their right.

'I see you've spotted our comfortably furnished forest lodges over there, but just look at these. Our latest two-storey houses with a distinctly Scandinavian feel. And of course we also have penthouse suites, lakeside apartments and VIP lodges. In fact, that's where you'll be staying, in one of our VIP lodges.'

'Me, staying in a what's it called? VIP? What's that stand for?'

'Well, the term is rather embarrassingly historic and means "Very Important Person", although today's connotation is something of the highest quality. Don't get hung up on the term; all it means is a really good suite. We don't, of course, differentiate between Medemates in terms of importance.'

'Medemates?' thought Rib.

They came to a sandy gravel track, long and straight. It dipped into a hollow and went up the other side. At the far end, probably about 800 metres away, Rib thought he could see a high fence of some sort. They walked down the path. To their right was dense forest, mainly made up of what Rib was later to learn were conifers of various types. It was noticeably cooler here. Nicely so. Right at the bottom of the slope Jonathan veered off into the forest. Rib followed him along a steeply descending narrow track, through the trees. Thick, fronded vegetation brushed waist high against him as he half stumbled. He joined Jonathan in a small clearing. The sun's rays shafted through the forest below them making bright sliverscreens of light on which midges played. All the sounds, the bird calls, human voices, running water now gently faded into the distance. Just like the sounds of the outside world seconds before you drift away to sleep on a sunny afternoon. It was beautiful ...

For once Jonathan didn't say a word; he didn't tell Rib that the forest and woodland were a wildlife haven which sustained a rich diversity of flora and fauna and was home to the only remaining colony of red squirrels in Europe. He just stood there with Rib, breathing in the cool, shifting currents of air that slowly, seductively, circulated across the forest floor. The silence was shattered by a screeching green flash overhead. Rib instinctively ducked, even though the green woodpecker had passed 10 metres above his head.

'Four pairs in this section,' Jonathan stated proudly as if he had somehow fathered them himself. 'And if you look right to the top of the Norwegian pine, no, the one just over there, to the right, see? With the snapped branch near the top? That's where we found you.'

'You mean, that's where I landed?' said Rib falteringly, craning his neck up almost at right angles.

'Crashed more like! The combination of the net and the tree canopy saved you. You actually partially ripped through the net, but it took most of the force of your craft. Somehow, and this is where you were really lucky, you smashed into the top section of the spruce which snapped over to the pine and that's where you came to rest – balanced precariously on a bridge of timber no wider than a grown man's thigh.'

Rib felt dizzy at the thought. 'How did I get down from there?'

'With a degree of difficulty. We had a team of four guys getting you out of the craft, onto a stretcher and gently lowering you with winches and pulleys to the forest floor. At that stage you were unconscious, your pulse barely there to be taken. Believe you me Rib, you were in a bad way.'

'Well, I suppose I owe somebody a big thank-you,' Rib said.

'That would be a nice gesture. You'll find Harry, Charlie, Benz and Eno at the Bike Centre.'

'Where's that?'

'Don't worry, no need to rush things, you'll get to see that tomorrow. Now, let's get you to your lodge.'

They turned and made their way back up the track. It seemed steeper than before. There was no longer movement in the air; it felt close, stifling.

Rib stopped. Sweat poured from his scalp and formed into beads, rolling down his forehead.

'Jonathan,' he gasped. 'I'm not feeling so good.'

He felt Jonathan's tight grip on his wrist and, in one movement, Rib was being carried over Jonathan's shoulder the remaining 20 or so metres up to the gravel path.

Rib felt faint, not helped by the fact that his head was upside down. What he remembered afterwards was an upside-down yellow buggy waiting for them on the road with an upside-down trailer-type arrangement in tow with a stretcher on it. In the driver's seat was an upside-down man whom he didn't recognise. In the passenger seat sat an upside-down Ruth. This was the last thing Rib remembered before he passed out. The buggy moved off unevenly up the track towards the perimeter fence, turned left to bump its way beside the driving range, turned right at the Rural Retreat and entered Conifer Quarter, where all the direction signs and lodge numbers were bright green.

The buggy stopped at Lodge 707. Careful hands lifted the stretcher from the trailer and carried Rib in. Within four minutes, he was lying in his usual sleeping position. On his right-hand side, his right hand under the pillow, his left outside the blanket. His breathing now deep, now even. He drifted in and out of half-sleep, half-consciousness. At one time he saw two figures standing at the foot of his bed. He spoke to them.

'What are you doing at the foot of my bed?' he asked with little challenge or conviction. They didn't answer. How could they? It was a dream. He could see the room, a wardrobe with a mirror, a table beside his bed with a lamp, red curtains, the two figures. But it was all a dream.

The red curtains were partly open. It was blowing outside. He caught the silhouette of branches waving in the wind. He drifted off into a deep sleep.

The next moment it was morning. He blinked, took in his surroundings, blinked again. The room seemed vaguely familiar. The crisp white sheets, the soft mattress, the gentle play of light through the window onto the opposite wall all told his body to stay put. He stretched, yawned.

Something was wrong. He was wearing someone else's clothes. He raised the sheets, he was wearing PJs. He never wore pyjamas. And now he was wearing pyjamas, a green baggy T-shirt with the Middlemedes motif on the sleeve and green baggy shorts. His dressing was also clean. In other words it had been changed since yesterday. Yesterday. What had happened yesterday? How had he got here?

He remembered the walk with Jonathan. The lake, the ducks, the net above the treetops. The girls cleaning the canoes, the coolness of the woodland, the wetness of the bracken, the steepness of the slope, but no more.

Rib felt good. He felt rested. He sat up, swinging his legs gingerly to the floor. He needn't have worried. He felt OK. He felt good – for the first time since he clocked on the morning shift however many days it was ago at Waste-Rows.

He wriggled his toes in the shaggy carpet pile of the bedroom and thought of the smooth coldness of his living-room floor back at his pod in the citidome. Hungry to explore his new surroundings and, well, hungry, he stood up, arched his back and stretched his arms up to the ceiling just a fingertip away and went out of the bedroom. He stepped into a small passageway and looked out to an open-plan living area. This must be one of the forest lodges which Jonathan pointed out, he thought. The walls were white throughout, the floor covered with a rough-spun carpet, deep red in colour. And there was a seat which ran along two walls in an L-shape like a sort of bench, with cushions on it, again red. In the corner was an open fireplace with a chimney. As his eyes followed the contours of the room around, they came to a large window-door at which a large brown duck was standing. It fixed him with his eye and quacked. It quacked again.

'He'll stand there all day if you don't feed him,' came a voice from behind him.

Rib jumped out of his skin. He jolted round to face a woman standing in the doorway of the room which had bathroom written on the door. The woman had wet hair, combed long and straight. She wore a towel. Just a towel. It was Ruth. Rib tried not to stare.

'Oh hiya – sorry, hey,' he said.

'Hey,' she said, 'now are you going to feed that duck?' She padded into a little kitchenette area and came out with a bag. 'I'd got these for breakfast,' she said, taking a bread roll from the bag, 'but I guess it's OK if we share?'

'Yep, of course' said Rib, trying not to look at her brown shoulders, her *bare* shoulders.

She brushed past him and opened the door. The duck made to waddle in but a gentle push from her foot persuaded him otherwise. Her toenails were painted a deep red, almost brown. Rib could not take his eyes from them. It was a big, sliding door and she pushed it wide open. She sat down on the door sill and tore off a piece of the roll and threw it towards the duck, who gratefully snapped and gulped it as if it were his last. Rib remained rooted to the spot, staring, not at the duck but now at the line of wet blonde hair snaking across her right shoulder blade.

A thought suddenly struck him. Ruth had obviously stayed the night in his lodge. He had to ask the question.

'Ruth, who undressed me and put me in these pyjamas?'

She half turned and smiled at him. 'Ah now, Master Rib, now there's a question ...' So it had been her. Rib knew it and the thought that he had been undressed by Ruth came back to occupy his mind at Middlemedes throughout the days to come.

Approximately once every four seconds. He couldn't wait to tell the Deccahead twins.

13

The Deccaheads …

Rib's mind wandered back to the night before he left MK. He had fixed to meet his college mates, Dick and Donny Deccahead, at half past seven at their local, the New Pitz. Rib was running late. Overdue assignments. He finally scootered off campus at eight thirty. All done.

Five minutes later, he was walking into the vestibule and through to the bar. Well, he would have been, had it not been for the gorilla in the black tie who grabbed him by the collar and requested legitimation.

'Legitimation?' Rib choked. 'I come here every night! You know that.'

'Uh-uh? Do you now? Then show me, I still love to see it,' he hissed, smiling at his fellow Level 2 Door Supervisor.

Rib released himself and flashed his entrance code onto his i-shield. They let him in. He brushed himself down, dusted himself off and entered the Milky Bar. Walking through the glass panel swing door he looked over to the far-left corner where he knew his mates would be sitting.

And sure enough, there they were.

White-suited.

Frilly-shirted.

Spangly high-heel booted.

Blond-fringed.

Dick and Donny as Benny and Björn.

The Deccaheads were twins, but no ordinary twins. Every three months they would adopt a new joint persona. This time round it was the male half of Abba. Total immersion. They had just emerged from an incredibly funny Laurel and Hardy phase which had gone some way towards making good the testing Adolf and Eva period in the eyes of their detractors.

But there was something even more remarkable about Dick and Donny. They spoke only in rhyme. Simultaneous stereo sound. Non-believers maintained that they practised and practised behind closed doors for hours on end, planning for every likely scenario and eventuality. Rib preferred to believe that they were genuinely telepathic. Whatever the case, he found them good to be around.

'Hiya,' he greeted them.

They responded with their version of 'Fernando':

'If I had to drink the same again,

I would, my friend, Meskitoe.'

Which was Benny and Björn's way of saying it was his round. He smiled and went to get the drinks. That was the trouble being late; they were a few drinks ahead of him already. Still, plenty of time to catch up. There was a fair crowd in tonight and while he waited to be served, he pondered over his friends' explanation as to why they communicated only in rhyme.

The Deccahead boys maintained that the rhyme pronome had been imprinted on their psyche by their father reading Rupert Bear bedtime stories to them every night for the best part of eight years. Not the wordy bit at the bottom, but the rhyming bit under the pictures, of course. And not content with one story, their father insisted on reading a whole annual every night. Poor sods, thought Rib, mental torture of the highest order. At first, Rib hadn't believed a word, not having even heard of this Rupert Bear character. So he checked it out on the Trawl and to his surprise discovered this whole world of rather sinister characters played out in excellent cartoons but less than excellent rhyme.

What amazed him most in reading some of the stories was that a little bear would travel in time in an upside-down umbrella, would take off in a plane with a Lapp girl to another planet (Rib wasn't totally sure what a Lapp girl was), and yet the only thing that concerned Mr and Mrs Bear was whether he would be home in time for tea or not. No wonder the Deccaheads were weird. Fancy having that for two and a half hours every night!

'Do you want a drink or not?' asked the barman.

'Oh sorry, I was miles away,' said Rib. 'Yes please, two halves of semi-skimmed with a giggle top on each and I'll have a pint of full-fat with a double giggle top.' After all he had some catching up to do.

Having paid for the drinks he joined Benny and Björn back at the table and several giggle tops later he was well in the mood and on the way.

The New Pitz had been recently refurbished and reopened aspiring to be 'the latest in urbochic, with the ultimate thrill of fusion.' Nobody had the faintest idea what fusion was. All it did was put five dollars on a plate of special noodles but no one seemed to complain.

The real transformation in the place had been the addition of the Cool Room, the Chill Room and the Ice Room. All to accommodate the theme of the year: Chess. Chess was in. Chess was it. Chess was the only thing to do and be seen doing. People went to see chess films, read chess books, wore chess T-shirts, cut hedges in the shape of knights and castles.

They even *played* chess.

Much of this was to do with the fact that last year's fashion had been large round cheeses. Then people had just gone through the motions, but you could sense that whatever followed would be a roaring success.

So the three rooms were all chess themed and interlinked. The ultimate was to play in the Ice Room where the champion defended the crown against all challengers. To get to

94

the Ice Room, you had to emerge triumphant from the Chill Room and to get to the Chill Room you had to qualify from the Cool Room. Now, of course, nobody had actually played sitting across the other side of a board to their opponent for ages.

This was where the New Pitz had stolen a march over all the other clubs. It had radically re-invented chess as a face-to-face, eyeball-to-eyeball game. And it was in the Ice Room, and only the Ice Room that this highest level of engagement took place. The setting was breathtaking. The two combatants each sat on an ice-sculpted throne either side of an ice table, a frozen block 2 metres square by a half metre thick. The seats were covered with mock reindeer skin, and thick sealskin gloves lay on the table at the ready. Fibre-optic rays flooded the room with a controlled brightness which, from whichever angle you looked, drew your eye to one point – the board.

The board was formed out of an uneven slab of ice into which was inlaid a square. As Rib sat in the bar pouring giggle-milk down his neck like there was no tomorrow, he knew exactly how it was to be in the Ice Room, exactly how it felt to be seated on one of the ice thrones, exactly how it felt to take a first tingling hold on one of those magnificent chessmen.

Because he had played there.

On the first night of opening, he had taken control of his console in the Chill Room with sixty-three other players. At the sound of the buzzer the round robin commenced. Playing in a set of eight simultaneously Rib progressed to the next round with ease, winning seven and drawing one. Forty minutes later he walked through to the Chill Room with three other would-be masters. Twenty-seven minutes on he sat in a small anteroom sipping on a straight fat-free goat's, having disposed of his opponents with incisive, attacking, three-dimensional play.

At precisely 2200 hours he was ushered into the Ice Room with formality and deference. The Champion already seated, the pieces standing ready, their still yet powerful presence almost overwhelming. He walked the seven steps to the table at just the right speed. Not too hurried, but not too slowly cocky-like. After all, this was respect of the highest order.

Emilie Tramontana-Hulot stood up and smiled. They shook hands. Grown men would have melted away there and then at her open smile. Rib knew her from college. Well, he didn't actually know her, and she certainly didn't know him. She was in fifth grade studying a combined major in Thermo-nano-dynamics and Indian Head Massage.

She was quite simply, stunningly beautiful. Her grey shirt was unzipped ten teeth to reveal a flash of crimson silk. The only other sign of adornment was a thick black-leather bracelet studded with three square topaz stones. Her eyes somewhere between green and grey.

Rib ran his hand through his hair nervously. His fingers got stuck and he tried to remember when he'd last shampooed.

He forced his mind to lock back onto the game, the reason why he was there … to play a game of chess.

Rib loved chess and he was good. Very good. As a sprog he'd played his mates from the seclusion of his bedroom for fun on the Trawl. They'd set up a ladder, and more often than not he'd feature in the top two or three at the end of the month.

But the turning point had been his tenth birthday. He had rushed downstairs at some unearthly hour and into the kitchen where his mum was cooking coffee. She embraced him with a 'Happy Birthday, honey'. He liked it when she called him 'honey', though not in front of his maties. She rocked him from side to side in a big hug and he managed to steal a glance under her arm at the kitchen table upon which his presents, by tradition, would be heaped. But there was no heap, just a single flat package wrapped in plain silver paper.

'Hope you like it, honey,' she said, releasing him.

He found it difficult to hide his disappointment at only having one present. His mum had expected this reaction.

'I think you'll like it, hun,' she said encouragingly. 'Go on, open it.'

Which he did. And what he saw was nothing like anything he'd seen before.

It was a simulated chessboard made in some sort of pre-carbonate material. The squares were set out, and numbered A1 across to H8 in vertical columns. To the right of the board was a set of chessmen and instructions – go/stop, non auto, new game and some others. Above the symbols was a small screen with the words Animated Display. And above that seven rows of six tiny holes. Rib took these to be some sort of speaker.

And above the speaker, in bright-blue letters, was written:

KASPAROV ALCHEMIST CHESS COMPUTER.

Rib had taken three point seven seconds to scan and assimilate his new possession. He looked up and his eyes met his mum's smile.

'What?' she asked. He got up and hugged her.

'It's great, Mum. Where did you get it? I've never seen anything like it.'

'It's a long story,' she replied. 'Let's just say that it's a bit special. You can be sure that none of your mates will have one. So be very, very careful with it. Absolutely no trading, OK!'

'Of course not,' said Rib and gave her an extra squeeze before returning to the computer. He had learned later that it was a genuine antique, over fifty years old and had cost his mum the best part of three thousand dollars. Three thousand dollars she didn't have.

The playing surface was bordered by a thin blue square. He ran his finger along the line. Starting at A8, moving slowly along to H8, down to H1, along to A1 and back up to A8. It was slightly rough to the touch. The sensation was electric. He held the tip of his finger on the A8 square for a second, before pressing the go/stop button. The display screen came alive with a loud beep which made Rib jump. It showed a digital clock registering zero. And beside the read-out was a little chubby cartoon face, looking very anxious indeed. Over the coming days Rib was to get to know this amusing character as Alec, The Little Alchemist. His goal in life was to be Rib's constant companion, ready and willing to play whenever he wanted. But there was something missing.

'Mum, where are the pieces?'

'Turn it over,' she replied.

As soon as he lifted the board the pieces rattled against each other within the body of the set. He pushed open the compartment lid with two pawn symbols on it and just stared. He eye was held by the fixed gaze of a white knight on its side, amidst friends and foes. It was beautiful. After a long pause, he carefully extracted the piece from the attention of the black king and black castle and held him between thumb and forefinger. Chessmen had been at best a 3D virtual on his i-shield but to hold one! … this was different, entirely different. He turned the piece over to reveal a green-felt base. Inviting him to slide the piece across the surface of the back of the board. It felt … good. Very good. He took the pieces out carefully one by one and lined them up in formation on the table. In turn, he picked up each of them and took the men through their moves before returning them to their original position. Who knows how long he would have continued to play this mesmerising courtship. The spell was broken by his mum.

'Oh and you'll need this too,' she said, handing him the instruction manual.

Rib turned his attention to the forty-eight-page instruction booklet, took it over to the seat by the window, taking the white knight with him in his left hand for company. His mum went out to feed the animals at 8.15. When she returned at 9.50 he was still sat there, deep in the text, now reading it for the third time.

He was particularly taken by 'Alec's many moods' which showed on the display after each move. Of the eleven expressions, his favourite was a precocious pout, which was supposed to mean 'Yes, I'd say that mate is right around the corner'.

So yes, Rib Meskitoe was well equipped to challenge Emilie Tramontana-Hulot. He not only had the experience, the intelligence, the tactics ...

... He knew how to handle chessmen.

They both approached the game in open, offensive mood. They moved quickly and confidently, exchanging early sacrifices to gain position. The end game was reached in less than seventeen minutes. But Rib was growing increasingly uncomfortable. He had the white queen marked down against a pawn, and had attacking options with either his bishop or castle, but all was not well with him. He froze. After two minutes' pause the sweat was pouring out of him. Emilie asked him if he was all right. He assured her that he was and then advanced his knight to exert further pressure on her queen. This duly opened the door and rolled out the red carpet for the champion to destroy him in three easy moves. He could picture Alec's tear-stained face.

'I can't believe I really lost this game ...'

'Won't you please give me another chance?' he would have said.

She stood and offered her hand. He held it briefly and mumbled 'I'm sorry about the finish. I was hopeless.'

'No, no, you were great. I liked your style. We'll have to play again sometime,' she said.

'Yeah,' he muttered, turning away. 'Sometime. Thanks ...'

He walked out of the Ice Room, past the anteroom where the next challenger was seated waiting. Through the Chill Room, Cool Room and out into the bar of the New Pitz.

He had ignored Dick and Donny's shouts and headed straight out, taken the first shuttle home, run straight upstairs, taken his Kasparov Alchemist from his desk, placed it at the bottom of the pile of discarded, out-of-fashion possessions and artefacts on top of his wardrobe and sworn never to play chess again.

He'd often wondered how he'd fouled up. She had been there for the taking. So near, and yet so far away. When the chips were down, his fat wasn't hot enough.

He put it down to one thing. He didn't have the stomach for battle. He couldn't take the intense, unbearable pressure of face-to-face combat. He had felt weak, exposed and vulnerable, like never before.

And that was why, instead of taking part in one of the most exciting strategy games invented by mankind, Rib preferred to sip milk stimulants with two deviants.

Singing tortured and twisted versions of Abba songs.

'Super stupor,
Booze is gonna blind me,
Feel like having fun,
Farting like a nun,
And spewing over everyone.'

14

Ruth had returned to the bathroom, presumably to get dressed. She emerged five minutes later.

'OK, time to show you around. First let's see what's on your screen.' She took a remote control from the low table in the centre of the room, pointed it at the black box with a screen next to the fireplace, and pressed the red button.

A white dot appeared in the centre of the screen. A couple of horizontal lines flickered for a second or two before the screen went green and a message started to appear, ticker-taping from left to right, letter by letter.

'W-e-l-c-o-m-e to L-o-d-g-e 707, Rib,' it clicked. 'We hope you had a good night's sleep. Your account stands at,' and then flashing in blue, '1000 credits.'

'Wow, a thousand credits!' whistled Rib. 'That sounds a lot. What can I get for that?' he asked.

'Well, it's quite simple, you take this card,' she said, reaching down beside the television, 'and you present it whenever you buy something – food, drink or any of the dozens of great activities we have here. Everyday your account is totalled up and the balance is shown on your screen. A thousand credits should last you about a weekend.'

'A whole weekend?' Rib cried. 'Well, I'll have to give them to you, Ruth, because I'm not planning to stay here. I've got to get back to MK.'

'You're not fit enough to go anywhere yet. You're still too weak to travel. That leg of yours will take some time to heal.' She turned and brushed past him, her sleeve touching the hair on his forearm. 'Why don't you just relax and enjoy yourself?'

Mmm, I suppose it wouldn't harm to hang around a couple of days, he thought.

'Your clothes are in the wardrobe, see you outside the front in five minutes,' she said as she disappeared through the door. In a 100–1 against sort of way Rib had rather hoped that Ruth would be helping him back into his clothes, but this clearly not being on the agenda, he visited the bathroom, had a quick wash and donned the bright-yellow jogging suit and trainers. She was waiting in the road outside for him when he emerged from the lodge. As he neared her, she sniffed, frowned and then raised her eyebrows. 'What on earth have you got on?'

'A bright-yellow jogging suit,' snapped Rib. 'I would have thought that was obvious.'

'No I mean, cologne, what have you got on?'

'Oh I see,' blushed Rib. 'Well, in the bathroom,' he explained, 'there was a green bottle which said on the label that it had a great smell in it – and it said splash it all over, so I did.'

'Ah, now I see. Well, the fact is that it's rather a powerful scent. Indeed overpowering, if not used wisely. How much did you use?' she said, backing off as Rib took a step nearer.

'The whole bottle,' he said.

'The whole bottle!' she gasped, 'a whole bottle on your face?'

'No, I splashed it all over, stupid.'

'All over?'

'Yes, all over, that's what it said on the bottle, so that's what I did,' Rib said, getting angry.

'I hate to have to say this, Rib, but I think you've overdone it slightly. Just the slightest dab behind each ear would have been more than enough. I think you'd better go shower it off.'

Rib stomped back into the lodge, showered and rejoined Ruth on the road.

As they walked down the road, she tried to engage him in conversation but to little avail.

For Rib was in a sulk.

And could he sulk.

He could sulk for Britain.

In fact, Rib was a regular Sulkmaster General, when he put his mind to it.

And of course, he had every right, being made a fool of.

And looking like a bleeding banana.

After they crossed a bridge over a stream, stopped to look at a swan protecting its eggs on a huge twig-and-stick nest and walked down to the lake, Rib had de-sulked a bit. This was really quite a nice place, he had to admit. Everybody they encountered seemed friendly and said 'hey'. Nobody seemed stressed or in a hurry. There were lots of people on bicycles. Every time they approached, they rang their bell. To start with this got on Rib's paps but every single passing cyclist gave a cheery thanks as they rode past, so Rib had no real cause for complaint.

They followed the gravel path round the edge of the lake. On the other side, at about 300 metres' distance, Rib could pick out the bright red-and-yellow canoes on the beach. So, he thought, letting his eyes follow the far shore to the left to the dense clump of deep green, that's where I was yesterday, that's where I landed.

Within minutes Rib found himself back amongst the terracotta in the Village Square. He had expected, even hoped that they would be stopping off for something to eat and drink at one of the many outlets but Ruth strode purposefully on over the square, past the Mede Mart and through a wooden gate which seemed to be the exit from the village.

'Where are we going?' asked Rib, jogging up beside her.

'How about breakfast?'

'You'll have time for that later and I'm afraid you'll be dining alone. I've got to get back to my shift at ten. But first I just need to show you how your credits work. Follow me.'

They threaded their way through an open area where hundreds of bikes were parked.

Ruth patted the saddle of one of the bikes as she strode past. 'You'll need one of these. Might as well get one today.'

Where? How? Why? thought Rib but Ruth was off again before he could say anything. Where had the friendly, smiling Ruth gone? All of a sudden she seemed distant, business-like, focused on matters elsewhere.

They crossed two roads, took a sharp left along a tree-lined bike path and then came to an open space banked on each side by tennis courts. Straight ahead lay a large warehouse-type building with an enormous blue racquet with red strings riveted to the wall. As they approached, Rib made out the words 'Leisure Allotment' over the front entrance.

'Allotment? What is this place?' asked Rib as they went through the sliding doors.

'It's quite clever, isn't it? said Ruth. 'This is where we allot the various leisure and play activities in exchange for credits. And allotment also means a small portion of land let out for allotivations. It's a sort of play on words.'

Rib genuinely didn't get it and he said so.

'Well,' explained Ruth, 'allotments are a perfect communal hub of harmony. And that's what we have here at Middle-medes. Our self-sustaining economy and spiritual well-being are based on every Medemate trading for leisure.'

Ruth's ready explanation did nothing for Rib. Clear as mud, he thought, but couldn't be bothered to disagree. And at that instant, as they went through a second set of doors, his jaw dropped. They were standing at the end of an enormous hangar, in which almost every sport ever invented seemed to be going on at the same time. Tennis, badminton, basketball, cricket, football, skating, hockey. There must have been over a thousand people playing.

'Wow,' was all he could say.

'Impressive, isn't it? And it's all there for you, Rib. Over here is where you book.'

'Hold on,' Rib interjected, 'I can't actually play any of these games, I've only seen them on the screen! The only sports I can do are swimming and ...'

'And what?'

He was going to say chess but stopped himself.

'Just swimming.'

'OK, OK, but that's no problem. We have ace instructors here, you'll pick a new sport up in no time. Anyway, let me show you how to book.'

Rib grudgingly went along with her explaining how many credits a game of squash cost, what the cancellation fees were, where to get changed.

'Now I really must get going, I'm late already. Have a good afternoon.'

'But, Ruth,' Rib protested, 'I still don't understand how this credit business works.'

'I'll go over it when you come in to the Aqua Basta to get your dressing changed. Be there at 6 p.m.' And she left.

'Fine,' said Rib to himself. 'I'll see you then. Six o'clock it is.' He felt his shin. If Ruth hadn't mentioned the dressing, he wouldn't have thought about his injury. Won't need any more treatment after tonight, he thought.

Feels 100 per cent now.

Rib turned round to take in the sea of bubbling activity in the hangar and decided to enter the spirit. He started on safe ground by booking forty minutes in the fitness suite, where he burned 500 calories on the rowing machine and another 400, less comfortably, on the treadmill. Suitably warmed up, he returned to the booking station to see if he could buy a game of badminton with someone. The attendant put out a search and a young man by the name of Hal duly presented himself five minutes later. Unfortunately it proved to be Hal by name and Hal by nature so Rib tried to keep at least 5 metres between him and his opponent's fetid breath. When the game demanded closer contact, Rib's only strategy was to hold his breath. The problem was this soon rendered him dizzy and Rib lost critical set points in succession, finally culminating in victory for Hal, whereupon his opponent embraced him and asked when they could next have a game. Rib could only wave his arms around and raise his eyes to the heavens before he stumbled off the court and into an untainted block of fresh air.

He spent the rest of the afternoon as a spectator, taking in most of the other racquet sports, pausing only to partake of an excellent club sandwich and a milk in the bar.

The time sped past and it was half five before he knew it. Having asked for directions at the booking desk, he found his way to Aqua Basta quite easily. The coloured direction signs actually worked and he was beginning to get a mental picture of the layout of the place.

He walked between the two ornamental bay trees at the spa entrance with a sense of anticipation. There was no doubt about it: this place was the height of luxury, way beyond anything Rib had experienced before. And then, of course, he was looking forward to seeing Ruth.

Having changed into a white towelling robe, he sat swinging his legs on the treatment bench in Room 17 when Ruth came in. She looked more relaxed than when she left him earlier in the day, much more like her old self.

'Hey, how was the rest of your day?' she asked.

'It was great, I really enjoyed it, although I met a guy there whose dog breath nearly blew my head off.'

'Ah,' said Ruth, 'that must have been Halitosis Hal. I forgot to mention that, sorry … Now let's have a look at that leg of yours.'

He obeyed by lifting his leg up onto the bench and

watched with keen interest as she carefully removed the dressing. The wound seemed dry, the pink tissue still raw and taut but holding.

'Good, good,' Ruth murmured, almost to herself. 'I'm really pleased with that. It looks pretty much healed already.'

'And it's not hurting any more.'

Ruth walked over to the window, paused a second or two and then with her back turned to him and said, 'But we mustn't rush things, we need to keep you clean.' Her voice seemed somehow strained. She turned to face him.

'Are you thinking of going swimming over the next couple of days?'

'Well, yes, I suppose so,' said Rib, although he hadn't really planned to be hanging around.

'What I think we should do is keep it covered. I don't want any waterborne infections taking hold.'

'OK, whatever you say,' Rib said compliantly as she administered a turquoise salve before applying a bandage.

'A hundred per cent waterproof so you can swim as much as you want.'

'Thanks,' said Rib. 'I think I'll give it a go tomorrow. And now, are you going to explain this credits business to me? I still don't really get it.'

'Sure,' she said. 'Get changed, meet me in the conservatory in ten minutes time. Oh, and mine's a latte,' she added as she left the room.

'As I said, Rib, it's a simple trade economy,' Ruth started once she'd taken a first sip of her drink. They were seated at a table in the far corner the café, half beneath a large hibiscus. Rib knew that it was a hibiscus because it said so on the copper label tied to its trunk. 'Thanks, I needed that. Now where was I? Oh yes, at the end of each working day, you get paid in credits and your account balance is shown on the screen in your lodge. You can then use your balance to pay for leisure, food, sport, everything you need. This coffee will have cost four credits, your water two credits. That would amount to about half an hour's work.'

'Surely that would depend on what sort of work,' Rib threw in.

'No, everyone gets paid the same for every job. All jobs have equal value, everyone works for twenty hours a week, no more, no less. Everyone has to spend all their credits by the end of each month otherwise they're forfeited.'

'So you can't save? That doesn't seem fair.'

'What would you save for?' asked Ruth. 'All you need is here and if each Medemate didn't spend their allocation each month, the economy would not balance. The harmony would be compromised.'

The harmony would be compromised, thought Rib. Strange combination of words. A soft word and a hard word. Sweet with the bitter. Smooth with the rough. Ruth was suddenly serious again. 'Well,' laughed Rib, 'we can't be compromising any harmony now, can we? ... But I haven't worked, have I?'

'No,' Ruth said, 'you're a guest and I'm sure that you're going to enjoy your stay here. Now I've taken the liberty of planning a schedule for you over the next two days. The activities will total your balance exactly, so if you stick to the plan you won't overspend.'

She handed Rib a folded sheet of brown paper. He unfolded it and read:

Day 1	Day 2
Breakfast	Breakfast
Hire bicycle	Cycle to Subtropical Paradise
Cycle to Archery Range	Swim in Subtropical Paradise
Archery lesson	
Lunch at Beeno's	Lunch at Beeno's
Cycle to Lake	Cycle to Lake
Kayak lesson	Kayak on Lake

Cycle back to lodge	Cycle back to lodge
Dinner at The Forresters	Dinner at Luigi's
Lakeside walk home	Lakeside walk home

'Looks good,' he said. 'Thanks, but how do I find these places?'

'Map on the other side,' said Ruth. 'And on your way home tonight, you need to buy in your breakfast from the Mede Mart. I can recommend the maple waffles.' She made to leave. 'Oh nearly forgot, I'll meet you every day here at six for the first week to check out your dressing, OK?' as she dashed off.

Yeah, OK replied Rib to himself. So I just go off and enjoy myself, not knowing anyone, not being able even to play these stupid sports.

He was still grumbling when he returned to Lodge 707, ate an absolutely acceptable lasagne verdi, watched the vintage classic *Red Dwarf 32* on teevee, before he retired to his bedroom, sank his head into the warm deep pillow and drifted off into a deep, contented sleep, dreaming of boyhood memories of marbles, goldfish and hamster wheels with a recollection of the time when he had tried to combine the three.

The next few days were amongst the happiest of his life. He followed Ruth's schedule, made friends, learned how to play squash, bowls and pool, ate the most delicious Italian food – several times a day – and became aware of how to tell the difference between a tree creeper and a nuthatch. The only minor setback was the bike. He duly checked in at the Bike Hire Station, conveyed his thanks to Harry, Charlie, Benz and Eno for rescuing him and took instructions.

'It's as easy as falling off a log,' was the perverse encouragement offered by Benz. Well, Rib found that indeed it was as easy as falling off a log, which he managed to do with monotonous regularity. And when he finally fell off the bike after it had careered down a slope and into the lake, he compromised by lowering the saddle as far down as it would go and sort of scooted along the paths, filling his trainers with gravel in the process. But it worked. Sort of.

He looked forward to his appointments with Ruth and he would pour out the experiences of the day while she applied the turquoise balm and re-dressed his wound.

'You're certainly looking better and enjoying life by the sound of things,' she said.

She was right, he really was enjoying himself. For the first time in his life, he was beginning to feel at ease with his environment, at ease with himself.

That night he parked up his bike outside Lodge 707 and looked up at the filtered moon. The shadows of two large birds flew across the face of the dead planet. He shivered.

Because it suddenly came to him that he had not given a single thought to his mum, to the refuge, to the fact that he was supposed to be finding his way back to MK. Pangs of guilt revisited him regularly through a supper of coco-pips and swamp mallows and haunted him through a fitful night's sleep.

15

The refuge was how Alice Meskitoe had coped with life after the death of her man, Mike. Not a single night passed without her looking at his picture on her bedside table, wishing him goodnight with a kiss and then rocking herself to sleep with a pillow in her arms.

It wasn't the best address in the Dome. It was in the part designated as an 'Employment Zone'. In other words, this was the production area. Not that Employment Zone was a true description, because most of the processes were 100 per cent mechanised and robot-aided. Someone, somewhere, had once told her that Employment Zone was an old term arrived at in the 1970s when the original city was built. And the term had stuck.

Through thick and thin. Through Watershed and Exodus, H1-222 was right on the easternmost rim of the MK citidome and had views out over the edge of the platform. But it could hardly be termed as prime real estate. It was a converted industrial unit, due for demolition twenty years ago, but leased out to her by a benign bureaucrat in a moment of inspired non-compliance for 'community purposes'. At least that was what she had put in the planning application. And ever since she had converted the unit to part living quarters, part animal refuge, it had been MK citidome versus Alice Meskitoe.

She threw all of her energy into the refuge, into caring for the animals and birds discarded by dome dwellers and Tycho travellers. A mix of breeds from Mother Earth and the New

Planet was rescued, cared for and loved at 222. She became a local celebrity, ever on the ASKMK TV site. She was asked to become a board member of the Community Foundation and she had loved every minute of her two terms of office there.

She had a strong network of friends and supporters. Maggie at the Fellowship, Hazel at the Foundation, Alf at the University. And she needed them.

For every day, the system was out to get her. The Citi-council wanted the refuge closed down. As simple as that.

16

'Waaargh, waaargh, waaargh!'

Rib sat bolt upright, scared poopless, a deafening siren sound pulverising his senses. He half jumped, half fell out of bed and staggered into the hall. A red light was flashing on and off in synch with the siren. It was the teevee. On the screen flashed in red the words:

'Alarm! Alarm!

Credit expired!'

Rib shot over to the unit and pressed the off switch. Nothing happened.

'Waaargh, waaargh!' persisted the siren. Rib pressed every button on the box. Still nothing happened.

He ripped the cable out of the wall and stood in the middle of the room, returned to silence, save the pounding of his heartbeat. Racing at about 137, he reckoned. He went back to bed but couldn't sleep. He worried over his overspend. There he was trying to get 200 million dollars to MK and he'd got into debt problems.

Aaah, he twigged. Idiot. I am rich beyond belief. I can afford to pay, ergo, there is no problem. This comforting logic moved Rib to drift back into a fitful sleep until he was wakened by the wan light of daybreak seeping through the bedroom curtains.

He got washed and dressed, went into the living room and tuned in to Loopy Toons on the cartoon web. After about ten seconds of *Bandicoots Are Go!* he realised that something was up. He looked around the room, sensing that something, somewhere has been moved. His gaze returned to the teevee and he sussed it. Last night he had torn the wire out of the wall. It had been the only way he could stop the siren.

And here he sat, watching Buddy Bandicoot tying his sister to the train line, the teevee switched on, the plug in the socket. This could mean only one thing, Rib deduced. Someone had fixed the wire back into the wall while he had been asleep.

A rap on the door startled him. He opened the door to be faced by two guidos he hadn't seen before. They were big, looked like they bench-pressed for Britain.

'Jonathan wants to see you,' said the one on the left.

'Hey,' offered Rib to defuse the distinct display of testosterone.

'Now,' said the one on the right.

'Okey-doke,' replied Rib. 'I'll just get my shoes.' As he put his trainers on in the hall, his mind raced. This must be about the debt. Are these guys going to beat me up? Surely not here in Middlemedes. It was all peace and love and cosmic cornflakes, wasn't it? They guided him to the green buggy parked outside and set off towards the village at a velocity a little too high for Rib's liking.

'Am I in trouble?' he asked.

'No,' answered the one on the right who was now sitting on the left. 'Jonathan just wants to see you, that's all.'

Rib kept his counsel for the rest of the bumpy trip. He recognised the road they were taking as they sped towards the Village Square, no surprise there. But the buggy continued straight past the entrance to the Mede Mart. It sped between a couple of cyclists who had wisely stopped to let it pass and veered left at a crossroads. From being totally disoriented, Rib suddenly realised where they were. The buggy was now approaching the beach with the volleyball net and the canoes.

So what's going to happen? thought Rib. Are they going to

pedalo me out to the middle of the lake, tie a lump of concrete to my feet and throw me overboard? They never reached the pedalos. The buggy screeched to a halt outside the single-storey restaurant which was Friggya's Fondue House, the water of the lake lapping against the wooden jetty which formed part of the outside dining area. It looked safe enough.

Rib walked towards the door, however, with a sense of foreboding. Partly because his two companions had gently, but with a sense of purpose, taken him by each arm and guided him out of the buggy and towards the restaurant. No sound could be heard as Rib took the final few steps to the entrance. No splash of paddles, no singing of birds. Even the subtropical paradise seemed to be holding its breath as the door swung open. A huge creature, with what looked like a bun attached to each side of her head, opened the door and beckoned him in. She wore white clogs and a red-and-white checked smock, beneath which moved the woman mountain that was Friggya. Her folded forearms resembled two hams. Bristly hams.

Rib decided there and then that he was going to be nice to Friggya.

'Hey,' he said with a smile.

'Your table awaits,' she said without a smile.

He walked into her House of Fondue. The whirring of the buggy into movement told him that he was now alone. Apart from the maîtresse d', of course. How could he fail to notice her presence.

'You are on Table 1,' she said, pointing him to the far corner. It was dark inside, the windows covered by shutters. The only light given off was from red candles on each table and a sharper light on the table in the far corner to which he was ushered. And as he neared, he could see the figure of a man seated at table one. A figure waiting for him. Jonathan waiting for him.

'Ah Rib, good to see you. Come and sit down. I hope you haven't eaten.' Rib sat down and surveyed the table before him. Centre stage were two small cauldrons bubbling over a kind of small brazier. 'Have you ever tried fondue?' Jonathan asked. 'It really is fun.'

'Look, Jonathan,' began Rib. 'If it's about the credit limit, I'm really sorry, I ...' Jonathan raised his hand to interrupt.

'In one pot you have melted cheese, in the other the finest triple-pressed oil. It really is all the rage. Now, shall I begin?'

He took a long-pronged fork and speared a mushroom which, until then, had been happily coexisting with twenty-two other fungi on a blue ceramic platter. Jonathan then impaled a baby courgette on the same fork, and finally returned to the blue platter for a final go at the mushrooms. He then carefully placed the fork in the cauldron with the oil. The mushrooms and courgettes begun to sizzle immediately.

The oil must be really hot, thought Rib.

Jonathan then loaded another fork in studied silence. This time with strips of steak and chicken. Finally he took a chunk of bread from a wicker basket and let that fry on a fork in the cheese cauldron.

'There,' he said with some satisfaction. 'Now it's your turn. Help yourself. You take the forks with the red spot on the end. You'll see that I've got the blue spots. This stops us taking each other's food. I told you it was fun.'

Rib sensed that it would be wise to follow this fun-filled ceremony of the fondue and let Jonathan broach the subject of the expired credit. Because Rib was sure that was why he had been summoned.

There followed an ordeal of hot oil splashing on his arm, pieces of uncooked food falling off the end of the fork and losing about three layers of skin from the roof of his mouth. Rib went through about three and a half litres of carrot juice in an attempt to cool his palate. All while Jonathan happily prattled on about how the oil has to be at exactly the right temperature to form a perfect seal, thereby keeping all the natural goodness in. Finally, he pushed his plate to the centre of the table, leaned back in his chair and put his hands behind his head.

'Now, young Rib, about your debt ...'

Debt sounded bad. Best offer to pay. In full. Now. 'It's OK, Jonathan, I can pay. I do have the looty.'

An amused look walked across Jonathan's face and then disappeared somewhere behind his left ear.

'Pay? How can you pay? You have no credit.'

'But I've got looty, real money, not some Minnie Mouse bohemian token system.'

'Ah, but, Rib, your money counts for nothing here. It is valueless. It has no currency. But no problem, young man.' The smile reappeared. 'You can easily work your way back into credit.'

'Well, I wasn't actually planning to stay here for long. I've got to get back to MK.'

'Of course, of course, and all in good time. Ruth tells me you still have some way to go before you're really fit. So why not work a few hours a day, enjoy yourself and build up your reserves. What do you say?'

Rib didn't feel that he was in a position to protest. After all, they had saved his life, really. And he could do with a rest. The memories of the flight from Wigandome, the night in the rainforest and Dick's Bar flooded back. It was scarcely believable that he had survived. And his mum wasn't expecting anything of him. She never did ... So a few more days wouldn't harm ... After all, as long as his looty was safety stashed, which it was ...

'OK then, it's a deal. Now where do I go to get work?'

Jonathan reached across the table and took Rib by the hand. Looking him straight in the eye he said, 'Rib, welcome.'

He held Rib's hand for just that little too long before breaking off. 'Friggya, the note please!'

Friggya brought over the bill and Jonathan paid. 'Next meal's on you. Once you've built up your credit.'

Friggya awaited them at the door. 'Did you like fondue?' she asked.

By this time, Rib's scorched tongue, incinerated palate and burnt lips formed to enounce two words which came out like 'esh fanksh'. More carrot juice required. Mental note. Steer clear of fondue.

Jonathan waved Rib goodbye having given him directions to the Jobmart. Rib decided to return to his lodge before entering the world of work. Ten minutes later he was back in his kitchen, swishing round mouthfuls of water to soothe his blistered gob.

Time for a quick nap, he thought.

He walked into the bedroom and froze. Neatly arranged on his bed was a green jogging suit. The colour all the other Medemates wore. Still, he lightened up (Goodbye, human banana) and he changed into the new suit, condemning the yellow monstrosity to the washing basket.

He duly reported at the Jobmart at two in the afternoon and at four clocked on his first shift as a fully fledged Medemate. His job was to clean all the ball marks from the wall of Squash Courts 3 and 4. It was OK, mainly because he knew it would only last for two hours. Two shifts a day would give you credit for all you need, he remembered Ruth telling him. And it was encouraging when passers-by stopped and observed him at work and then burst into applause. 'Good job,' they cried. Weird …

His second shift was replenishing the bird feeders at the hide and he really liked that. He went back into the hide after his job was done and watched with fascination the flurry of feeding activity that followed. Over the weeks to come, this would be his favourite shift and he quickly realised that he had to stay one step ahead of the squirrels if the birds were to get fed. Rib spent much of his spare time designing squirrel-proof feeders which involved elaborate constructions of metal, string and wood. With the occasional jet of water for the persistent offenders.

Days passed, weeks slipped by, as Rib settled easily into the soothing work–life balance that was Middlemedes. What he liked most about it was the variety. He could and did choose to try a range of different jobs, so that there was never any danger of getting bored. At the same time, he developed a routine for his free time. Most evenings he would find his way to the Metro Bar, where he would sit beside the floor-to-ceiling plate-glass window and watch Medemates descend down the final chute of the rapids into the plunge pool. Increasingly, because it was good credit value, he also played the motion simulator in the corner of the bar.

This was bright yellow, had a black screen and windows, and stood perched on four scissor-like legs. From the outside, it looked ridiculous, lurching and tilting backwards and for-wards, a small red light flashing above the door. From the inside, it wasn't much better. You strapped yourself in a bucket seat, pressed one of the five options – this time Jurassic Terror Ride – and steered the craft through a series of adventures whilst it did its level best to separate you from the contents of your stomach.

So incredibly low-tech. So incredibly primitive.

And yet, such a good laugh. Rib played it most evenings, improving his score from 13,715 to 32,920, ranking number three on the all-comers' list.

On the way home he'd take the narrow gravel road which Jonathan had walked him down on the day of his first tour. And he'd follow the steep track down through the wet bracken. Through the cool of the wood. All the way down to the bottom where he came to a perimeter fence.

About 4 metres high.

Made of a metal mesh of sorts. And rusty.

And every time he would leave the track to take a closer look at the fence, a jogger would appear.

Or a cyclist.

Or two.

Every time.

And every time they'd say, 'Hey, how are you doing? Getting late.'

And Rib would return to the track and work his way up the slope, along the gravel road, around the tennis courts and back to Lodge 707.

Before checking in for work, he soon adopted a routine of working out in the hundred-metre pool which Jonathan had so proudly shown him on his introductory tour. Being an early riser, Rib usually had the pool to himself and by eight he would be well into his fourth set of 400-metres freestyles. From his first week's pay he had bought a pair of cool blue trunks and, extravagantly, a top-of-the-range pair of Speedo goggles.

He swam effortlessly, his long sinewy pull generating a deceptive turn of speed. He was devouring the lengths at a clockwork sixty seconds. Consistently and easily. And once he was through the initial 500 metres' grind, he was on autopilot. His endorphins kicking in and taking him back to MK … his home, his mum's refuge, the college, the New Pitz. All good, warm feelings.

A loud underwater squeak interrupted his thoughtflow. Three weeks back, when he had first heard it, he had wondered what on earth was going on. Dolphins in the pool? But it was just another Medemate entering the pool. A very heavy Medemate. Totally bald, mid-fifties, seriously old and overweight. Around 200 kilos was Rib's guess.

Which was where the underwater squeak came from. Clear as a bell. Caused by the metal steps being forced into friction against the tiled surface of the pool walls by the downward pressure of the fat man's bulk. His descent into the pool was agonisingly slow. Step by step. Squeak by squeak. Rib counted that he covered five full lengths by the time the man completed his journey down the steps. He then swam two lengths of slow breaststroke, his body mass hanging almost perpendicular to the surface, his mouth and nose only one inch above the water before he began the long ascent of the steps. Rib reckoned he spent ten minutes in the pool and ten minutes getting in and out. And probably burned up more calories on the steps.

Rib named him the Unhappy Hippo. Hippo because of the resemblance and unhappy because, although he shared the pool with Rib every day, day in day out, he never once acknowledged his presence. Which was quite unusual for a Medemate.

Swimming was Rib's escape, his space, his time to think. After each session he felt good, really good, physically and mentally.

So when he saw one Tuesday a shift advertisement in the Jobmart for an assistant swimming instructor, he signed up.

He reported in at six in the evening later that day to a certain Helen, tracksuited and standing poolside at the far end of the subtropical paradise. A section had been roped off for the lessons.

All kids living at Middlemedes were taught to swim. And that made total sense because of all the fun chutes, rapids, lake activities that were on offer. A non-swimming sprog would be a seriously deprived sprog in such surroundings.

Kids would sign up to lessons according to their ability and progress up the chain. From tadpoles to frogs to seahorses to sharks to killer whales.

Helen's group was for the absolute beginners. They had never been in the water before. It was their first lesson.

They were called pebbles.

Most of them were three or four years of age. They stood shivering in a line at the edge of the pool. They were not shivering because of the air temperature, it was a balmy 25 degrees. It was the fear which caused their chubby little knees to knock. Some were tearful, having been plucked from their mothers' embraces by the businesslike Helen.

Some of the mothers were tearful too, watching from the spectator balcony. Others sat there solving a su-doku and not seeming to give a flying fortress whether their little one swam or sank.

The eight little pebbles were standing on the edge of the pool in a line. Helen, having introduced herself to Rib, told him to go to the store locker and bring out the box of floats.

Rib dragged the big box over to the side of the pool. It contained all sorts of brightly coloured floats, cubes, serpents, balls, all made of a squeaky polystyrene material.

Helen addressed the pebbles. 'OK, children, now today is going to be real fun. I'm going to teach you that water is safe, water is fun, water is so you. And we've got lots of wacky floats for you to play with – crocodiles, snakes, hippos.' She turned away from the pool, pulling her red tracksuit top over her head. 'OK, Rib,' she shouted. 'Throw them all in, as far as you can.'

Rib paused. Radical, he thought. Mine is not to reason why, and he picked up the first unsuspecting pebble by the name of Benny and hurled him in a perfect arc to enter the pool with a splash some 5 metres from the side.

Benny was not a good little pebble, for he floated quickly to the surface, which was rather unfortunate because at the very moment his little body clawed its way to the surface and his little mouth opened to take his first desperate gulp of air, the second pebble, named Vivienne, landed smack on his head. Screams from the balcony told Helen that all was not as it should be. She turned to see Rib chasing the third pebble who had run behind a potted palm and was now writhing hysterically on the floor.

'Rib, stop! I meant the floats, you fool,' cried Helen as she dived towards the two pebbles in the pool who, it must be said, were now very pebble-like, lying motionless on the bottom.

Sirens, screams, alarms, mouth to mouth, more screams followed. Rib sought shelter by avoiding eye contact and throwing all the floats in the pool and taking a long time to collect them. Helen, having successfully revived the two little pebbles, and less than successfully sought to calm down two incandescent mothers, was less than Medematey in her personal development and appraisal feedback to Rib poolside after the session had closed.

'You total bumwipe! Never, ever, and I mean *ever*, come near me again or I'll shove the polystyrene banana where the sun don't shine.'

Fine, Rib thought. If you'd spent more time on your lesson plan, this wouldn't have happened.

Rib brewed up a sulky storm and sought to relieve the high pressure by walking down through the wood where he'd landed weeks before. As he neared the fence at the bottom of the slope, he was passed by the customary couple out for a bike ride. Instead of the usual friendly greeting, he was met with a full-force fart from the flick on the trail bike as they pedalled past. Not your everyday sort of fart, but a tin of baked beans, demi-litre of Newcastle Brown, topped off with rhubarb crumble sort of fart.

Rib strode back up the slope, at first angered but then amused by the fact that the fart attack was clearly orchestrated.

If, as he suspected, the female fart aimed at him – all the more poignant and pungent for being female – was an expression of the Middlemede community's dissatisfaction with him, then how had they planned it?

Had they phoned round all the women in the Mede and

asked whether anyone was expecting to pass wind at precisely 7.45?

Or, more sinisterly, had they pounced upon an unsuspecting cyclist up on the path and force-fed her a fart capsule due to erupt in forty-five seconds?

Either way it was *both* ridiculous and sinister. He headed back to the village, checked in at the Metro Bar, moved his score up another 137 on the simulator and then saw off two litres of goat's milk.

As he walked back to Lodge 707 he wondered what colour kite Kaddie would be flying tonight, and felt a pang of guilt about his mum and the plight of the refuge.

He slept badly dreaming of large green crocodiles slithering through a putrid swamp full of gas bubbles. Next morning, after a quick, cold, power shower, Rib cycled into the Jobmart to seek alternative employment. Strangely there seemed little open to him when he pressed the select button on the screen.

No bird feeder filler.

No squash court cleaner.

No assistant swimming instructor …

Only, and each time Rib reset the selector, the same reading came out, 'Volkswagen Golf Sweeper', again, and again, and again.

Rib called over a Jobmart advisor. 'How come I normally choose from 40–50 jobsearch options and now I've only got one option coming up?'

'Must be the only one left,' was the shrugged response. 'Do you want it or not?'

Rib's swift mental calculation told him that he needed to up his credit tally or a very unwelcome return to the fondue table might be in the offing.

So he trudged out past the beached yellow canoes, past the luxury detached lakeside villas with en-suite jacuzzi and reported at the driving range dead on ten. To a guy called

Percy. His name could easily have been Pringle. He was labelled Pringle on every item of clothing visible to the eye, sweater, cap, gloves, eyeshades. Percy was clearly an upper-crust Medemate, hence his stewardship of the Middlemedes driving range.

Golf. Now that was one sport that Rib didn't get. Where was the competition? If you had a second player defending the hole, all well and good. But walking around a field for three hours, knocking balls into holes, the only excitement being how to keep the crease in your trousers perfect by the picking-the-ball-out-of-the-hole-with-the-straight-leg tech-nique. Where was the fun in that? Why not be allowed to chuck your opponent's ball on the lake? That's competition.

The utter futility of the sport was magnified manifold by the driving range. No walks, no fields, no crease-keeping challenge. Just buying a bucket of balls and smacking them into the middle distance, to rest somewhere near a flag, intended or not.

And this was where the Volkswagen Golf ball collector came in to play. It was a scaled-down version of the VW Golf Classic, about half-size, with the rear seat removed to house a large stiff bottle-brush which operated a bit like a water wheel, sweeping golf balls up from the ground as the car moved over them.

Percy the Pringle had fully briefed him for a good fifteen seconds on what to do.

'Drive it like a car. Right pedal accelerates, left pedal brakes. Sweep the balls up like you'd mow a lawn with prime stripes. You have eight minutes to sweep the whole field so get a move on!'

Rib had never driven a car, let alone mown a lawn. And what the hell were prime stripes? And what was a lawn? But as one of the model students of the year at MK College, he was a bright star and was soon striping his way up the course, away from the bays towards the 200-metre flag.

As he systematically criss-crossed his way up the driving range, his mind drifted back to the events of the past four weeks. Or was it five?

What had happened to Kaddie? He vaguely remembered the struggling figure on the Wigandome platform being struck across the back of the head before he himself had plummeted down to the forest below. And how had he survived the nightmarish trek through the rainforest?

And how was Mum at the refuge? The rush of guilt returned. The whole reason for him leaving MK was to make it right for her. And here he was collecting golf balls just to tot up another twenty credits to spend on a couple of litres of goat's milk and another couple of simulator rides.

Rib's thoughts were shattered by the smash of a golf ball pinging off the side window of the Golf. It pinged off the window instead of shattering it only by grace of the weld mesh which armoured the car, protecting it against any accidental wayward shot.

"Whoa!' screamed Rib, swerving the Golf reactively. 'What the shit?' Nobody should be here in the driving bays and certainly no one should have been teeing off when he was collecting. He turned the nose of the vehicle towards the thirteen bays some 75 metres distant, to try to spot the perpetrator. What he saw was the second ball coming straight at him but only a split second before it embedded itself in the mesh with a smack a matter of centimetres before his eyes.

He hammered on the brake and sat stock still, his heart thumping. This was no wayward shot. This was no accident. His fear turned to anger as he pushed open the driver's door, intent on sprinting to the driving bay to sort out the lunatic with a driver. His anger turned quickly back to fear as the third ball smacked against the half-open door.

'Whoa!' Whatever the rights or wrongs, this tonk could certainly twat a golf ball.

Rib rolled across to the passenger door, pushed it open and somersaulted out of the cabin, ending up some 5 metres away from the car, flat on his front, facing the bays.

No fourth ball, so he got up and broke into a crouched run towards the range. He saw the glint of sunlight on the shaft of an iron and instinctively threw himself to the ground.

Still no fourth ball. Looking up, he saw a figure break out into the open from behind the bays, out onto the track towards the tennis courts. Rib's legs started to move before his brain clicked in to gear. His overriding instinct was to get hold of this arsewipe, drag him out onto the fairway, stake him to the ground with the fifty-metre flag and then run over him with the Golf.

A number of times, four would do.

Probably.

He set off on a diagonal run towards the gate easing into a deceptively speedy loping stride. As the paths of the pursued and the pursuer converged, the pursuer noted that the pursued was short, stocky and … incredibly fast. So fast that instead of heading him off at the gate, Rib found himself some 20 metres behind as he negotiated the five bar.

The 20 metres stretched to twenty-five as he sprinted behind his assailant, now approaching the double doors of the Rural Retreat, the highly recommended family eat-and-play zone. Just 5 metres from the door, the figure swerved to avoid a toddler toddling with no particular place to go and parted company with his baseball cap, revealing a shock of dark red hair as he darted through the door.

Rib hurdled the toddler to enter the Rural Retreat, to be met with a wall of sound. Mostly, although not exclusively from adults: a few fathers were the worse for wear. The place was packed. Far from being a luxurious retreat, this particular feature of Middlemedes was a hell on earth. Buggies, nappies, food trodden into the carpet, a compilation of England World Cup penalty shoot-out misses on the plasma.

From the moment he entered, Rib knew that he had absolutely no chance of finding the mysterious driver who had seriously upset his equilibrium. He conducted a perfunctory search of the three dining rooms, the snooker hall and the bar before heading back to the entrance. Once outside, he noticed something which revived his interest, the baseball cap lost by his attacker. He stopped to pick it up out of the hedge. It was a black cap with the logo 'Ummagumma's Noodle Factory' in light blue above the peak. The cap was a size seven. Rib folded it, stuck it in his pocket and headed thoughtfully back to Lodge 707. Had he turned to look through the window into the ball pool, he would have seen sixteen kids throwing themselves all over the place. And a seventeenth figure, he might have made out, if he were totally lucky, fully submerged, save an eye, a black eyebrow and a tuft of deep-red hair watching his departure with intent interest.

At six thirty precisely, Rib was forming a queue of one outside Ummagumma's. He'd already been there for fifteen minutes, which had given him more than ample time to study the menu on the board outside the front door. It was entirely varied, as long as you liked noodles. Which Rib didn't, particularly. But he was not there for the noodles. He was there for the owner of the noodle baseball cap.

At precisely 18.34 the doors were flung open by the Ummagumma's Noodles Factory maître d', predictably decked in a black suit topped by a black cap with light-blue lettering.

'Hi there, my name's Dee and I'm your Maître Dee.' He peeled off into a staccato giggle, shortened somewhat by Rib's deadpan response. 'You like noodles?'

Rib remained unresponsive.

'Well, you're at the right place, oh and have we got oodles of noodles, just for you.' And with the 'you' he thwacked a wooden menu board across Rib's chest, clearly deciding not to invest more customer service in this callow youth at his door.

Rib ignored this fit of pique and moved in to the main hall. To the right, a row of plain wooden benches, some fifteen in number, each with vases of flowers at precise intervals. To the left an array of shining metal surfaces, shining cooking utensils, shiny bowls and plates, all gleaming … shining. And heavily staffed. At least ten cooks chopping, slicing, searing, juggling, whooping and at least a dozen waiting on. But Rib was looking for a 'cast member' with flaming-red hair but without a cap. A bit like a 'minister without a portfolio', although Rib didn't actually know what that meant.

Everybody seemed too busy to pay him attention, so he chose a spot in the middle of the middle bench. From there he would have a good view not only of the kitchen but of the restaurant entrance.

A short girl with short flaming-red hair came over to serve him.

'Hey, something to drink?' she asked.

He looked up at her with his mouth wide open. She had flaming-red hair, she was not wearing a cap. She was not a he.

'Where is your cap?' Rib asked.

'Where is your cap, now I'm sorry but that is not a cock-tail which I am familiar with. How do you make it? Whisky?' She spoke in a monotone, no pitch, no variation. She spoke in a long straight line. But not a straight line along the surface. A straight line some two octaves below the surface. And full of Ks and Ts and Us. So cocktail was Kkuuukktail. 'If you don't close your mouth you will swallow a fly,' she said as her eyes flashed him a laugh.

'I mean where is your cap? Your baseball cap? The black one with the light-blue lettering?' Rib persisted.

'Oh, lost this afternoon, when some idiot chased after me.'

'That was me!' said Rib as calmly as he could, rising now

129

to his full height and glowering down at the girl.

'Oh, so you're an idiot?' she asked wide-eyed.

'Now look here,' Rib shouted and banged his fist down on the table.

A short Japanese-looking guy had appeared from nowhere and was now standing tight next to the girl, twiddling in his grip a particularly sharp-looking meat cleaver.

'Hey, Rika, you OK?'

'Sure, everything's fine,' she smiled. He melted away leaving them standing. Rib shifted from foot to foot, embarrassed before he sat down.

'Now,' she said, 'let's start again. What would you like to drink?'

'Err, I'll have a demi goat's milk with a coffee melt top.'

'OK,' she said, turning away 'one demi goat's coming up.'

'Wait,' he said. 'Why did you attack me today? That was totally off-limits, it was dangerous.'

'Attack!' she snorted. A different flash from her eyes this time. And not so friendly.

'Listen, my little Medemate, if you thought that was an attack, you've led a sheltered life. One demi goat's milk coming up,' she repeated as she turned towards the kitchen.

Rib's fury was bridled only by the thought of the twiddling meat cleaver. The sheer attitude! He was livid. And here she was again.

'One goat's milk, as ordered, kind sir.'

She was being deliberately provocative.

'Thanks,' he grunted. 'Now are you going to tell me about the cap and the driving range?'

'No,' she smiled. 'I'm not, now, what would you like to eat?'

'So, you're not denying it was you who peppered me this afternoon with golf balls.'

'No, I'm not. But I'm working now and that is not a work conversation and therefore I am not having it. Now, what would you like to eat?' The last sentence was uttered in a rather firm way.

Rib, lost for words, quickly scanned the menu. It all seemed the same. Noodles. 'It all seems the same to me, what would you recommend?'

'Well,' she faltered. 'It *is* actually all the same. Big bowl of noodles drowned in a hot spicy soup with lots of cabbage strips.'

'What, all of them?' Rib asked.

'More or less. Listen, I've got other customers to serve, just choose any number between one and seventy-two.'

Rib thought long and hard. 'Thirty-three,' declared Rib as if he had just announced to the world that he had discovered the secret of eternal life.

She wrote down thirty-three intently on her pad. 'What have I ordered?' he asked.

She turned towards the kitchen and shouted over her shoulder. 'Big bowl of noodles drowned in hot spicy soup.'

He heard the 'with cabbage strips' screamed in his direction as she tanked her way through the door to the kitchen.

Rib sat there staring blankly at the incomprehensible menu. He was suddenly tired. Very tired.

It was almost as if the past six weeks at Middlemedes had cocooned and protected him from the natural edge and aggression of the human race and now this girl had opened it all up for him again – like a nasty ugly sore.

She brought his dish minutes later. He muttered thanks without looking up because he didn't mean it.

The next fifteen or so minutes he spent pushing two dough balls around a swamp of noodle and cabbage. His only mouthful of the soupy stock had confirmed that the soup was indeed hot and spicy. What he hadn't been prepared for was the utter tastelessness of it all. He got the note and signed it, all without looking up.

When the receipt was thrown back on the table, it said:

131

'I told you the food was crap. Meet me tonight at 7 p.m. at Chez Claude, Village Square. Rika.'

Rib looked up and his eyes were caught in the headlights of her unwavering gaze. She uttered just three words. 'You be there.' Very deeply. Before powering off to the kitchen area.

I should cocoa! he fumed as he pushed his way out of the now-busy Ummagummas. Who the hell does she thinks she is? What makes her think I'd be interested in meeting up with her? After all, what does she look like? Built like a pocket battleship. Red hair! No attempt at smink. Asking him, Rib Meskitoe, out! I should cocoa ... Never in a month of Mondays.

*

By two minutes past seven he was nervous. By ten past seven he was agitated. By fifteen over he was about to leave Chez Claude's in a state of serious dudgeon.

Then she arrived. 'Sorry I'm late,' she said before he had a chance to say anything. 'Look,' she said softly, taking the menu from his hand. 'Let me order for you. The food here is good. I work here too.' She duly ordered and the food was every bit as good as she had promised.

She ordered an array of dishes that he'd never heard of. She took a long time to choose the wine. She selected one called Médoc.

Rib had never drunk wine before. It was initially sharp to the palate but was having the very upfront effect of a double-litre goat's with a triple giggle top. She asked where he came from. He said MK and was surprised that she knew quite a lot about it.

He studied her carefully as they somehow small talked through the entrees. 'Rika, I've come across that name before somewhere. But Latukartta. Where on earth is your surname from?'

'Mr Meskitoe, you disappoint me. As a pure-bred MK boy you surely should know your Lappish connexions. Remember all the boat race victories? Remember the line of great rowers from the Arctic Circle? Latukartta,' she repeated. 'Literally, it means "cross-country skiing route".'

17

Rib couldn't help but smile at her reference to the Boat Race. Milton Keynes had grown steadily to become one of the largest cities in the country, yet still suffered jibes and sneers about concrete cows, roundabouts and its franchised football club.

But that all changed in 2020.

The year the city's university won the Boat Race.

The then Vice-Chancellor, Bertil Koch, had ambitions to put his institution well and truly on the map. So he took a strategic decision all on his own one Wednesday night in the bath that the university, *his* university, would gate-crash that most hallowed of old-school parties played out between Putney and Mortlake each spring.

Much to the amusement and disdain of the Establishment, he tried to enter a crew through formal channels. Without a flicker of success. Then, one defining summer's evening at an Open University reception to celebrate Bringing Beagle Home, the worm turned. Having downed one port too many, Sir Sorely Fitzgibberish, Vice-Chancellor of an eminent Oxford college, dealt Bertil Koch a thinly veiled insult. 'It will take you 700 years to build a real university. And it will take you even longer to build a real eight.' The surrounding sycophants squealed with mirth at the wittiness of the remark. Koch nodded politely, excused himself and left the reception.

As he strode down to the car park he made a pact with himself. He would win the Boat Race. No holds barred. Winner take all. Make my day, punk. At any cost.

Koch hurled all his energies into his new obsession. At precisely 5.45 on the morning of Sunday 13 October, ten brown envelopes plopped onto the mats of the Minister of State for Sport, eight high-ranking academics, and the Director General of the BBC. Each envelope contained compromising photographs involving the recipient, a call girl called Kylie, a llama named Rod and a yellow plastic turkey baster. By the following Friday, the University of Milton Keynes were in the Boat Race.

Koch now focused his every fibre on creating the best crew the world had ever seen. He invested millions of the university's hard-won reserves. His formula was simple. He found the best physical specimens on the planet and, in the finest Oxbridge tradition, made them an offer they couldn't refuse. First-class honours degrees, comfy digs, all the spotted dick a boy could eat, and the ultimate in state-of-the-art training facilities.

And this was where the Lapland connection came in. Having trawled the best CVs from rowing clubs throughout the world, Koch kept coming back to one place.

Akas Lompolo, a small Lappish village 100 kilometres north of the Arctic Circle. Building a natural body strength forged from kayaking up and down Lake Akas all summer and Nordic skiing up and down the frozen Lake Akas all winter, the people of the village were pretty fit. What made the difference, however, was their diet. All good healthy stuff in the summer. As many berries as you could eat. All fresh from the forest. Cloudberries, bilberries, raspberries, wild strawberries …

And in the winters, the good citizens of Akas Lompolo could choose between no fewer than three pizza houses, all located on the main drag. Tradition had it that every Saturday night the young men of the village would gather at Julli's to devour a supersize Good King Wenceslas. Deep-pan, crisp and even. Topped with ground reindeer horn, grated elk hoof and a plop of brown bear bile.

All guaranteed not only to put lead in the pencil, but to propel the young men of the village over Lake Akas at a pace unparalleled elsewhere in the world.

So, scholarships were put in place, the elite squad was shaped, modelled and formed by fair means and foul. By fair means at the university's state-of-the-art Rowing Excellence Academy. By foul means at the performance-enhancing chemical spa hidden in a rented warehouse behind Lidl's in Oldbrook.

Koch was the proudest man in the world when his boat lined up against the might of the light and dark blues that historic blustery March afternoon of 2019. A matter of twenty minutes later he was the most disappointed man in the world when the MK University boat crossed the line in second place, only a canvas down on the powerful Oxford eight.

The public loved it. BBC viewing figures went through the roof. The *Daily Telegraph* described the race as 'A shot in the arm for a fading tradition.' If only they knew, mused Koch. The Vice-Chancellor appeared on *Oprah*, was asked to write a weekly column in the *Citizen*, inhaled more heady oxygen of publicity than he had ever breathed in his life. Yet he was not a man at ease with himself. They had not won. This rowing lark was harder than it seemed ... In his heart of hearts, Bertil Koch realised that his crew needed that extra edge from somewhere. But where?

That extra edge arrived on his desk two months later in the form of a business card. A simple message printed in Times New Roman: 'Budge Dobson, Sports Psychologist, 01223 672006'. Koch recognised the code as a Cambridge number. He turned the card. Written in a neat italic script were the words 'I can bring you the boat race. BD.'

Koch's heart missed a beat. He had tried to immerse himself in matters academic, return to some sense of normality. It had not worked. He had become even more irritable of late, if that were possible. Made less frequent visits to the gym, more frequent visits to the off-licence. These seven words on a piece of plain white card restored his faith in humankind, gave him the naive rush of optimism of a pauper placing his last dollar on the 20–1 outsider.

He arranged to meet Dobson that same Friday in Cambridge in the back bar of The Eagle. Koch had arrived early and installed himself in the far corner, from where he could see the entrance. They had agreed to meet at six. Six came and went. Koch was just finishing his second pint of Adnam's Broadside when a bearded, barrel-chested man entered the bar and walked straight over to his table, hand outstretched. 'Dobson. Apologies for the tardiness. Same again?'

Koch nodded, trying not to show how much the hand-shake had hurt.

The man named Dobson headed for the bar, now crowded in a two-deep throng of students, late shoppers and office out-spill. He returned thirty seconds later with a foaming pint in each fist.

'Fine brew, Adnam's,' was his opening salvo.

'Yes, cheers,' responded Koch, rather weakly, he thought. He was so used to calling the shots in his world, so used to people jumping at his every turn of phrase. Yet this man before him, already finishing off the glass of Suffolk bitter before he had taken a sip, was clearly made of stern stuff.

'So you got my card then?' he said, wiping the beer foam from his walrus moustache. Yorkshire, registered Koch, definitely Yorkshire.

'Listen,' continued the man named Dobson. 'I don't piss people about, and I don't like being pissed about.' Leeds, smiled Koch to himself. Unmistakeably Leeds.

'No, absolutely,' responded the Vice-Chancellor. 'I don't like being pissed about either,' he added and wished he hadn't. It sounded stupid when he said it.

'So let's talk business then,' said Dobson, slamming his empty glass down on the table.

Koch jumped and spilled beer down his Lacoste fleece. 'Yes, sure,' he braved. 'Let's talk business!'

'Important things first, mind. Another pint.' It was not a question. Koch looked at his three-quarters-full glass and said yes thank you. No other reply was possible. And while the stocky Yorkshire man parted the crowd at the bar like a Moses on the shore of the Red Sea, the Vice-Chancellor nearly choked in an attempt to down his ale in one.

Dobson returned to the table in a trice and wasted no time in dispatching the greater part of his Adnam's in one gulp.

Koch ventured a sip, suddenly realising that he was starting his fourth pint in less then thirty minutes. What the hell, he thought. Why not? He couldn't remember the last time he had sat in a bar knocking back the beers.

Before he had chance to savour the moment, Dobson struck. 'Hundred grand,' he said.

'Sorry?' choked Koch.

'My fee. Hundred grand. For the boat race.'

'A hundred thousand pounds? That's preposterous,' retorted Koch.

'Listen, Vice-Chancellor, I said I was not a man to piss people about. And I'm sure you're not a man who would want to piss me about.' Koch shook his head immediately.

'The way I see it, you have to ask yourself this question. How much is winning the Boat Race worth to me? How much, Vice-Chancellor, how much? Now, whilst you're milling that over, I'll get the drinks in.' And off he went to the bar, for what would be Koch's pint number five.

How much was it worth to him? You couldn't really put a price on it, was his answer. He would happily sign a cheque for a million if it guaranteed victory, immortality. But how could he be sure that this testy northerner could deliver? It was about time, he told himself, that he took the upper hand in the negotiations.

Dobson returned and put the two Broadsides on the table.

'Now, Mr Dobson. Give me one good reason why I should believe that you could win the Boat Race for me. And as for your proposed fee, it's out of the question.'

Dobson fixed him with a stare and drank long and deep from his glass. 'I am a man of my word, Vice-Chancellor. If I say I can win the Boat Race for you, then you can tek it as gospel. Hundred grand, tek it or leave it.'

Koch looked at the man seated opposite. He watched him down his pint. He watched him use his sleeve to wipe the beer from his straw-like moustache. He watched him get up and walk out of the back bar of The Eagle.

Koch smiled to himself. That showed him. Think he could come to the table and go three rounds with one of higher education's heavyweights? Huh! Hundred grand indeed! Testosterone surged through the veins of the Vice-Chancellor with such force that his cufflinks rattled. He celebrated this show of machismo by downing a double Dubonnet at the bar before leaving. The blinding brightness of the low evening sun caught him unawares and he tripped arse over head on a baby buggy parked outside the door. He stumbled to his feet, fists raised to take on all-comers but thankfully listened to an inner voice of reason which whispered, 'Bertil, you are the Vice-Chancellor of the University of Milton Keynes. It is five minutes to seven in the evening. People are looking at you. You are pissed as a fart. Go home.'

Somehow, Koch managed to find his way back to his hotel and was fast asleep by seven thirty, fully clothed, on the bathroom floor. He shouldn't have had the Dubonnet …

The following afternoon found him pacing the floor of his sumptuous suite overlooking Bouverie Square back in MK. He had barked instructions to his long-suffering secretary that he was not to be disturbed. Under any circumstances.

Unless a certain Mr Dobson were to call.

He didn't.

Koch knew deep down that he had made a serious mistake. He knew deep down that the man named Dobson was the only one who could deliver him the prize. And he, one of the country's most eminent academics, had passed the chance by.

He tried phoning. Only to hear the same answer phone message. 'I'm out, piss off.'

Then two weeks later and totally out of the blue, a business card mysteriously found its way under the Vice-Chancellor's office door.

Koch put down his collector's copy of the *Beano*, walked over to the door and picked up the card. It read 'Budge Dobson, Sports Psychologist, 01223 67200.' He turned the card. Written in a neat italic script were the words 'One hundred and fifty grand. Final offer. Tek it or leave it. BD.'

Koch did not dare leave it a second time. Terms were agreed, this time not in the back bar of The Eagle. The man named Dobson seemed utterly relaxed about almost every clause and condition of the contract drawn up by Koch. All bar one. He insisted that he, and he alone, be responsible for choosing the cox. He wanted nothing to do with the oarsmen, wanted nothing to do with their training regime, wanted nothing to do with the boat. He just needed to select the cox.

This not only puzzled but exasperated Koch. 'So, Mr Dobson, are you telling me that I am paying you the sum of one hundred and fifty thousand just to appoint the small person who points the hull in the right direction?'

'No,' Dobson replied. 'You are paying me one hundred and fifty thousand to win the fookin' Boat Race for you. And if you're thinking of pissing me about, Vice-Chancellor ...'

'No, no,' relented Koch and they shook on the deal.

The University of Milton Keynes proceeded to win the

Boat Race for the next five years. Koch became a hero. MK became the place to be. Blue-chip companies competed for scarce city centre plots. Student enrolments quadrupled. People came on holiday from Barcelona.

Throughout what became known as the Golden Age of British rowing, Koch often sat at the end of the day on the Senior Balcony of 200 Silbury, overlooking the leafy Bouverie Square, and pondered over a dry Martini or two how Dobson had done it. Whenever he had broached the question directly, however, the dour Tyke would bristle and threaten to walk away. And Koch would always back down. After all, whatever he was doing was working. And that was all that mattered.

The icing on the cake was that the five victories won by the University of Milton Keynes 2020 to 2025 proved to be the closest, most exciting finishes in the history of the race. Every single one an absolute thriller. The photo-finish of 2022 against Oxford. The canvas win against Cambridge the following year, when the MK crew were an unbelievable ten lengths down with a hundred metres to go. All of which served to elevate the Boat Race to being the most popular event on the sporting calendar. The Superbowl, the FA Cup Final and Wimbledon paled into insignificance beside the born-again national treasure.

How the bloody hell did he do it? Koch asked himself. How did he do it?

The answer was quite simple.

For all his outward roughness, Budge Dobson was what used to be known as a people person. He knew how to make people laugh, how to make people cry. He knew what made people happy, what made them sad.

He knew what made people tick.

He had first realised that he was the Special One – the one person in the whole universe who could make a raw, unknown university eight into the best the world had ever

141

seen – on that blustery March afternoon of 2019, the day when the MK crew lost narrowly to Oxford on its Thames debut.

Dobson had stationed himself in the crowd awaiting the crews at the boat house after the finish. He watched intently as the three slender hulls drifted sideways into the shore. The body language of the crews couldn't have been more contrasting. The men of Oxford smacked the water with the flat of their hands, whooped war cries of triumph, smiled and waved at their girlfriends and boyfriends. The Cambridge crew looked more sheepish than anything else. They had not expected to win – Oxford had been odds-on favourites. They hadn't quite expected to be turned over by a set of no-marks from the concrete-cow country but who cared? They were already looking forward to the photo-shoot and post-race party at the Beefeater Astoria sponsored by *Hello!* magazine. Anybody who was anybody would be parading at this high-light of the social calendar.

As for the MK eight, not a flicker of emotion was to be seen. No trace of a laugh, nor a tear. No sign of a grimace nor a smile. The ice-cool crew from the Arctic came ashore, carried the good ship *Silbury* into the boathouse and returned to stand in a line on the foreshore to watch proceedings with a detached deference. BBC's water-sports anchorman, Johnny West, tried to elicit comment from the men from MK. The best he got was from the stroke, Pekka Nurmi, and that was 'No comment.' They stood stock still in a silent line seemingly deep in reflection.

Dobson had watched this unusual scene unfold before him with increasing interest. What was going on here? They should be waving at the crowds, they should be celebrating their incredible achievement. Dobson took out a pair of mini-binoculars from an inside pocket and focused on the faces of the crew, one by one. Something strange was going on. He didn't know what, but he was hell as like going to leave until he understood. And then in flash everything changed.

The Oxford crew performed the time-honoured tradition of throwing the cox of the winning boat into the river. One-two-three ... splash. The crowd cheered raucously. Dobson did not join in. His eyes were still fixed firmly on the MK crew.

The reaction in their eyes was instant. He saw a spark of fire, a flash of spirit. Nurmi whispered something in Juskelainen's ear and they both laughed. Budge Dobson carefully placed his binoculars back in his pocket and left the cheering throng on the riverbank to head back to the Underground.

Dobson knew he was on to something. Dobson did not do excitement. But as the Cambridge train pulled out from Platform 2 at King's Cross, he was so excited he could scarcely breathe. He popped a Fisherman's Friend in his mouth to calm down. It didn't work. It wasn't until he was pedalling his trusty Raleigh down Gwydir Street that he was back on an even keel.

Once inside number forty-four, he installed himself by the Baxi in the back parlour, filled a pipeful of Old Holborn and settled in for a full night's work. By the time the first sparrow had celebrated the coming of a new day by evacuating its bowels down the kitchen window at 6.07, Budge Dobson leaned back and clasped his rough skinned hands behind his head.

Job done.

By way of celebration, he pan-frizzled a generous slice of lard swiftly joined by six Irish pork sausages and fried them on high gas until crispy black on the outside. He cut four doorsteps of crusty white bloomer bread then trowelled on a liberal coating of Stork margarine. The sausage sandwiches were topped off by a dollop each of Hammond's Chop Sauce, 2011 vintage. The early-bird breakfast was washed down by a can of Tetley's Mild. Swiftly followed by a second.

Ten minutes later, Budge Dobson, Sports Psychologist par extraordinaire, was tucked up snug as a bug in a rug under his 250-tog Leeds Rhinos duvet snoring the defiant message to the world of a satisfied man.

For he knew exactly how he would win the Boat Race for the University of Milton Keynes. His strategy was, indeed, not only simple but stunningly ingenious.

Dobson took pride in his mastery of algebra, his favourite formula being:

$$a + b + c + d = xy$$

where

a = The boys from Finland were good at rowing, but lacked the real deep down desire to win the race.

b = They needed that one extra level of motivation to ignite as a winning eight.

c = The one thing that sparked their interest was the winning crew chucking their cox into the water.

d = Finns hate Swedes.

xy = Recruit a Swedish cox.

Simple.

Budge Dobson found the answer to his prayers in the form of a certain Karl-Johann Gyllenhammar, an obnoxious, self-opinionated runt studying Botany at the University of Uppsala. He came from a long line of Gyllenhammars enjoying the privileges of an aristocratic class still hanging on quite nicely thank you to the good life.

When the Akas crew met their new cox for the first time in November 2019, the chemistry was immediate. The words 'hatred', 'abhorrence' and 'hostility' didn't come close.

As soon as Gyllenhammar barked out his first call, the men from Lapland focused every ounce of preparation, every sinew of pure brute strength on winning the right to throw the Swede as far into the cold dark waters of the river as possible. For the MK University crew, indeed for the whole Finnish nation, the Boat Race itself became a sideshow. The real money changed hands on the length of coxhurl expressed in metres from the shore. The record grew impressively from 15 metres in 2020 through to 32 metres in 2023. Each year the men of Akas did the minimum necessary to win the race, hence the close finishes. They saved all their energy for the finale played out in front of the boathouse. Gyllenhammar went along with it, taking the cheering from the bank to be acclaim of his expert coxmanship. And, after all, he was the most successful cox of all time. His reign came to an end in unfortunate circumstances in 2025 when he crash-landed on top of the referee's launch positioned 55 metres from the shore. Two broken legs, shattered pelvis, ruptured spleen, cracked sunglasses. The crowd went wild.

And then, of course, came Watershed.

18

Watershed …

Billions lost their lives as the first wave of tsunamis obliterated coastal communities around the world. The greatest natural disaster in the history of mankind. Although, of course, it wasn't a natural disaster in the strictest sense of the term. More like a man-made natural disaster.

The tidal waves were followed by the most ferocious weather systems ever seen on the planet. Hurricanes raged across plains and steppes, seeking out and snuffing out those who had run to the hills and mountains for refuge. In the course of the first few days of Watershed, the human race had been decimated.

Military rule came into force, initially under each nation state but soon under a worldwide coalition government – the Protectorate – when it became clear that a global solution was needed for a global crisis.

Consuela Sweetcorn landed the job as Secretary General of the Protectorate. On the strength of holding the strongest single bargaining chip in her hand. In her sweaty, podgy palm she held the one thing that could save mankind: Buzzard and his new planet and his giant spacecraft.

It wasn't long before Buzzard's fleet of megatonne spaceships started to roll off the production line and the shuttle service to the new planet, Tycho, became operational. The first major policy challenge facing the new coalition government was how to allocate seats. Demand far outstripped supply, of course, and things were starting to get ugly at the terminals. Bureaucrats went to work on devising a scorecard which rated and weighted an individual's body mass, credit rating, academic attainment and personality profile. And the beauty was that it would take an army of public servants to administer the scheme.

Sweetcorn kicked it into the long grass at first sight. 'I've never seen such a heap of hogshit in all my days,' she declared. 'Do you realise how many claims for discrimination this would leave me personally exposed to? I ain't havin' it. If this is all you can come up with, I'll think of a system myself!'

And so it came to pass that people were allocated tickets to Tycho in alphabetical order. It was party time for the Allans and Augars of the world. For the Zappas and Zimmermans, however, it felt as if the world had fallen out of their bottom. Annabelle Wonderwall cried for twenty-four hours non-stop, having divorced her husband Arnie Ankle the previous week for being boring and poor.

The second big problem for the new government was the rainforest. Within a matter of weeks it had sprouted up at an alarming rate in habitats which had previously hosted pastures and meadows. And it was growing fast. Real fast.

Having again dismissed the suggestions of her civil servants as hogshit of the highest order, she consulted her Chief of Staff, Commander Boseman. 'Napalm,' was his short reply. Sensing Sweetcorn's scepticism, he added, 'Or failing that, nuke the bastard!'

The Secretary General was struggling with this. What the hell should she do? She hesitated for a moment, before picking up the phone.

To Buzzard.

Where else could she go?

The professor's reply was immediate and precise. Build cities on stilts. 400 metres high. With their own micro-climates. Domes.

Sweetcorn trusted his judgement on this one and ordered the construction of citidomes on a massive scale across the world. After all, she reflected, the old Buzzard had really made only the one mistake.

Once the mass evacuation of the surviving members of the human race to the new planet had happened, most of the citidomes were de-commissioned, leaving just a few to operate as food distribution centres to Tycho. Whilst most people did everything within their power to get on the first flight available, some chose to stay behind. For different reasons. Fear of spaceflight. Too old to embrace a new life. And for some, an uneasy feeling about the whole thing. Rumours had filtered back about crash landings, spacecraft spinning out of control. These stories were never verified, of course. Tycho was shrouded in a cloak of secrecy …

19

Now fortified by the truly excellent wine, Rib decided to tackle the events of the afternoon with Rika again.

'So why all the aggression today at the golf range? What sort of behaviour was that?'

She smiled. 'I was helping you.'

'And how do you figure that one out?'

'Well, you were becoming a seriously laid-back totally compliant Medemate and I thought I'd shake you up a bit.'

'How come you know so much about me?' Rib could feel himself getting angry. 'And what's wrong with chilling out here? People have been good to me here. There's no aggression, no demands, there's a sense of, what's it called, community. How can that be bad?'

'Well, it's not bad at all. If that's how you want to be for the rest of your life.'

Rib put his glass down. 'What do you mean, for the rest of my life? I'm only passing through. I'm on my way to MK.'

She looked long and hard at him while she chewed on a chicken leg. 'And what makes you think they'd let you go?' she asked slowly, before taking a sip of her wine.

The fork on the way to Rib's mouth stopped mid-air, hovered for a couple of seconds, before slowly returning to rest beside his plate.

'You are seriously gone,' he said. 'People have called me a nutter all my life, but you are different intertoto cup. How sick are you? First you attack me with golf balls, then you go all nicey-nicey on me, then you call me some kind of prisoner. What's going to happen next? Is a big white ball twice the size of a bus going to roll through the Village Square. You are sick,' he snarled.

'OK,' Rika said, wiping the corner of her mouth with the sky-blue serviette. 'I got you wrong. I saw something different in you but you're really how you are, aren't you, Rib? You're just a kid. I thought the chase after me was a parody. I thought for one moment it was a cleverly disguised statement of interest. But it wasn't, was it? You're just a kid who's going to be here for a long, long time.'

'Listen you,' Rib snapped. 'I can walk out of this place anytime I like. It's some kind of leisure retreat. It's not a prison for goodness sake.'

'OK. It's not then. Fine. And what, by the way, will Ruth's prognosis be tomorrow?'

Rib flushed. 'Ruth? What do you mean? What's Ruth got to do with anything? She's going to take a look at the wound on my leg, it's a routine thing. I just check in and she checks it out. Every two or three days or so. And what's that to you?'

Rika leaned over the table and gripped his wrist vice-like. 'Oh nothing, Ruth's very good at that sort of thing. Did it not occur to you that four weeks is one hell of a long time for a cut to heal? But, of course, Ruth's touch is very special, isn't it?'

'Piss off!' Rib ripped his arm free and jumped up. People on neighbouring tables went silent and stared. Rib rushed out of the restaurant, down the steps, over the bridge and out into the cycle park.

The cold fresh air and the wine hit him at the same time. He rapped his shins against the pedal of a toddler's bike, knocking it over as he did so. It brought tears to his eyes, adding to the tears already there. He felt angry, hurt and foolish. He ran all the way back to Lodge 707.

Rika Latukartta leaned over to capture and consume the

emaining fries left on Rib's plate, having returned with compound interest the stares of the couple on the adjacent able. She paid the note, strolled over to the pool bar and after a couple of drinks walked back to her quarters where she spent the next two hours putting final touches to her prep-arations for the next day. She went to bed at ten thirty and enjoyed an undisturbed sleep.

Unlike Rib.

Strange – in such an idyllic, easy-going, fresh-air, healthy-living sort of place – how many really bad thought nights he had. The girl was off her trolley. 'How can you be sure they'd let you go,' and what she'd said, or implied about Ruth! Clearly a case of jealousy there.

He fermented for a couple of hours more before finally surrendering to the power of nod at 2.45 in the morning. He tried to dream but couldn't. He didn't even allow himself a nightmare.

The next day happened to be his appointment at the clinic to check his wound. As he walked down to the lake, he could feel the fresh air cleansing his anger and anxieties with each step he took. By the time he had strolled through the village square, he felt positively optimistic.

He was looking forward to seeing Ruth, if the truth be known.

Following the usual protocols, he checked into Aqua Basta, went through to the men's locker room and changed into a beautifully warm white towelling robe. Then into Treatment Room 4 to wait for Ruth. She arrived at ten on the dot with her customary smile and gentle conversation. 'Where have you eaten? How have you slept? Have you met many new people?'

They small-talked like this for a couple of minutes as Ruth took the contents of her blue canvas bag and put them on the table beside the treatment couch. Bandage, scissors, lint, bottle of lotion.

151

'So you're settling in really well then,' she confirmed.

'Sure, but I'm not here for the duration you know. It's been really good but I guess it's time to make tracks. How do I check out by the way? Pay all my bills, obviously, but what about taking the sheets off my bed? And where is the front gate exactly?'

As he posed these questions, she undid his bandage. He was momentarily mesmerised by the reflected light from the pool through the window playing on the blonde hairs on her fake tanned forearm.

'Now which question do you want me to answer first?' she laughed after a pause. 'Look,' she said, revealing his wound, which seemed pretty well healed until he saw a small section in the middle of the scar which still oozed. 'You're in no fit state to leave just yet. You're well on the mend and you'll soon be fine.'

Ruth then turned and put the bottle which she had taken out of the blue canvas bag back into her blue canvas bag. She replaced it with another bottle, this one containing a pink lotion instead of the usual turquoise.

As she turned back, their eyes met. Rib, never one for holding eye contact, looked at her long and hard, before asking her the question he promised himself he wouldn't ask.

'Ruth, can you tell me something?'

'Sure,' she said, undoing the top on the bottle. 'Fire away.'

'Wouldn't it be better to leave the wound open to heal rather than keeping it lotioned and covered?'

She laughed as if relieved. 'What, and expose it to the airborne bacteria? Listen, Rib, this is no sanitised dome. This is nature. No, I would not want to risk that.' And she carefully applied a gobbet of pink ointment to his wound with the tip of her right index finger and gently rubbed it in.

Time slowed to a standstill. Each soft touch spanned a life-time.

Rib would look back on this as a defining moment in his life. Ruth then cut a strip of lint, laid it precisely over the centre of his scar, applied a clean bandage and patted him on the shoulder.

When she'd done and they'd said goodbye, he walked slowly back to the male locker room. It was empty. He stood in front of the full-length mirror and studied his reflection. Beads of sweat appeared on his forehead. They formed into a single rivulet which somehow found a course down the bridge of his nose, right to the tip, where it gathered final strength before dripping to make a tiny splash between his feet.

Soon to be followed by another.

And another.

Why was he not satisfied with Ruth's answer to his question? And why had she changed the bottle?

A nagging, tearing doubt had entered his mind. It was that she-devil's fault. She's jealous of Ruth and would say anything to turn him against her. She was wrong, so wrong.

But the doubt did not recede. It grew in proportion to the drips from his nose. Now hitting the floor at seven second intervals, sauna-style.

He snapped to, took a cool shower, dressed and left the building. He had to think. He had to get this straight. 50 metres down the path, his heartbeat told him he was walking far too fast and he slowed his pace.

A couple passed him on bikes.

'Hey,' waved the girl.

'Hey,' he waved back.

He slowed to a stop, watching them as they disappeared round the corner of the building with the sign 'House of Harmony' over the front door.

He counted to ten, fully expecting to see them reappear. His paranoia was taking command. Stop it! He heard himself say aloud as he started off again towards the Village Square.

He came to the House of Harmony. He'd walked or cycled past it dozens of times without really seeing it. It was a single-storey, whitewashed building made out of some kind of brick, with a corrugated-tin roof. Looking at it now for the first time, he noted that it had only one small window on the elevation facing him, and that showed nothing but dark-red curtains in closed mode.

As Rib came to the front of the building, he saw that the heavy wooden door was ajar. He slowed, looked up and down the path. No one in sight. He walked over to the door and peered inside. There was a dark entrance lobby, with a single light shining onto a sign on the far wall. Rib looked up and down the path again. Still no one. He stepped in.

He could hear the hum of voices from within the hall, from behind a blue door which stood slightly ajar. The sign beneath the single light read 'Middlemedemates Induction Meet'. The hum gave way to a single voice. A voice which Rib recognised.

Rib peeked through the crack in the door and saw the hall filled with Medemates in their green tracksuits, all kneeling on the floor, with a single figure dressed in a simple white smock, arms spread wide, standing before them.

'For it is written in the brochure,' he chanted in a nasal, high-pitched tone, 'that you can enjoy food and wine in our relaxed and informal Continental pavement café.' The pitch went down on the 'ca' and up on 'fé'.

'Continental Pavement Ca-fé,' murmured the Medemates in unison.

'The footpaths are illuminated, although you may find a torch useful in pla-ces,' he droned.

'Useful in pla-ces,' echoed the floor.

'Enjoy a Sunday jazz brunch and savour the mellow sounds of the Buster Babcock Combo.'

'Cock Com-bo!' repeated the kneeling Medemates.

Rib froze.

Induction? This was not induction, it was more like indoctrination! This was … surreal. This was … I've got to get out of here.

He thought he'd been rumbled when a young sprog, not much older than him, cast a searching look from his kneeling position on the back row. Rib stepped back sharply. Had he been spotted?

No, the sprog faced forwards again and continued his responses without wavering. Rib backed slowly towards the front door on tiptoe. He stole a last furtive look at the board. 'Middlemedemate Induction Meet' and there and then decided that he had to leave.

Now.

Back onto the pathway, he retraced his steps to Aqua Basta to fetch his bag from the locker. From the very first day when he had come, his precious belongings had been sitting in Locker Number 22, placed there by Ruth. He had taken the key from her that day over six weeks ago.

Not once had he opened the locker. Not once had he checked the contents of his bag.

Because he had trusted her.

Totally.

As his pace quickened, his thoughts raced. What if they'd opened it? What if they'd found the looty? Who were 'they' anyway? What was this place? Jonathan was the leader, no doubting that. But was he good? Was he bad? And what part did the red-haired flick play in all this? He hated to admit it, but her words gathered strength the more he analysed the situation. He tried to push them to the back of his mind but he couldn't. He refused to believe that Ruth was involved. She couldn't be. She … just wouldn't have done anything to hurt him. Not after she'd spent so much time nursing him back to health.

He was now at the Aqua Basta entrance. He slowed to a stroll. Mustn't attract attention to myself. As soon as he walked into reception, the girl looked up.

'Hey, Rib,' she smiled. 'Can't get enough of us, eh?' she started to tap into her screen. 'But what are you booked in for? I don't recall you being down for any other sessions today.'

'Oh no, it's OK. I'm not. I just think I ... er, left something behind me in the locker room. I've just come back to ... er ... see.'

'Fine,' she said. 'If you can't find whatever it is you've mislaid, I'll put out a search for it.'

'Thanks, that's great,' said Rib, heading off down the passage. He entered the locker room, saw that he was alone and closed the door behind him. He leaned back against the door and breathed deeply. He had to move fast, but carefully. If his suspicions about this place were right, there would be eyes everywhere. He quickly scanned the room for cameras. To his relief he saw none.

Three long strides took him to the far wall where the storage lockers were banked. He unzipped the lowest pocket of his jogging suit and took out the key to Locker 22.

He opened it.

The crumpled khaki bag sat there like a long-lost friend. Where have you been? It seemed to ask. Why did you leave me here on my own for so long? 'Shut up,' said Rib to the silent bag. Now think carefully, do I check it out here or do I take it back to the lodge? Back to the lodge! screamed the voice of reason and the bag. So Rib obeyed.

He slung the bag across his back, closed the locker and turned the key.

Rib walked out of the locker room, back down the passage and into the atrium with an air of studied nonchalance, then immediately caught the eye of the receptionist.

'Hey, Rib, see you found what you were looking for, then,' she said, nodding towards the bag on his back.

Rib laughed, a little too hard and a little too long. 'Oh the bag, yeah, the bag!' he joked. 'Yep, left it under the bench. What a total twonk, huh?'

She smiled.

He strolled out through the door, turned and gave a wave to her just before the doors hissed together.

His heart was about to jump out of his throat. His pulse must be up to 200. Still, he reflected as he sauntered back down the path. I think I handled that rather well. Mission accomplished.

It seemed to Rib as if every cyclist, every jogger, every baby in their buggy fixed him with their enquiring stare on his walk back to Lodge 707.

When he finally reached his destination after a couple of cunning detours, designed to throw any pursuers off the scent, he went straight to the fridge, poured a half-litre of goat's milk, delved deep into his backpack and took out the sachet of giggle which he had stashed away for emergency use. He held it in his palm, which was not the best idea because his hand was shaking so much that the sachet slid from his grasp onto the galley floor. Rib picked it up, opened it and stirred the contents into his goat's milk. He let it mash for the required eleven seconds and then pulled long and hard. His draft dispatched half the glass. He was about to down the remainder when there was a sharp tap on the patio door. Rib nearly dropped the drink. He ducked down below the galley worktop and spread himself on the floor. The tapping became more urgent.

Tap tap tap.

Rib needed to understand the opposition. How many of them were there? He crawled across the cold galley floor and moved snake-like over the living-room floor towards the door. The curtain was half pulled across. If he could just peek underneath …

The tapping resumed.

Insistent.

Rib was now at the curtain. He slowly lifted it up, centimetre by centimetre so that he could check out his unwelcome caller. His right cheek pressed against the wooden floor, lifted the curtain just enough for his right eye to focus on …

A beak.

Of a duck.

'Duck!' screamed Rib, jumping and knocking over a standard lamp. 'Duck! A bloody duck!'

The duck responded, quite predictably with a quack as if to say, 'Yes I am a duck, always have been, always will be. What's the problem with that? Where's the bread?' Rib closed the curtains, laughed to himself, half in anger, half in embarrassment and another half in sheer relief. He walked round the galley bar and finished off the goat's. He then played disc one of *The Who Live at Leeds* until his pulse rate returned to its normal forty-four. All the while staring at his bag, still unopened, which sat on the red rug in the middle of the room.

The music stopped.

Rib took a deep breath, walked over to the bag, picked it up and undid the two toggles.

He opened the flap and examined the contents carefully. Taking them out one by one and laying them in a line on the coffee table:

Walnuts.

All there. Every single one.

Map of route to Slingshot.

Knife with fifteen types of blade.

1 shirt – starched, folded and lavender-scented.

1 pair of shorts, likewise.

1 fli-wire

4 T-shirts

2 pairs of underpants – unrecognisably fragrant and presentable.

So, the contents of his bag had been through someone else's hands. Ruth's? came the irresistible question.

Rib returned to the walnut shells. Examined each of the twenty for any sign of tampering.

None.

Every seal intact. Therefore, looty safe and secure. Rib breathed deeply, partly with relief but partly in fearful anticipation of what he now had to do.

Plan B.

The accumulation of bitter experience in his short life had taught him one thing. Plan A seldom, if ever, works. Whereas Plan B ...

He looked at the screen. It registered sixteen credits. He still had time to spend them on some food. Yeah, he'd need that. The digital time reading 14.17 on the screen snapped some sense back into him. He estimated that the best time of departure would be 2.00 in the morning. When would be the next time he would get any sleep? Who knows? So, head down for serious zeds.

Rib was still awake at 19.30 on account of a barbeque being held in the lodge two doors down. He'd managed to doze off a couple of times, but for no more than twenty minutes.

So it was hardly surprising that when he finally found the land of nod, it held him there for some time. Until 3.45, to be precise.

'Shit!' hissed Rib as he hurled himself out of bed. It would be light in two and half hours. 'Shit! Shit! Shit!' he cursed as he threw on his khakis, checked his bag for the umpteenth time and took a supply of carefully selected provisions from the fridge.

His passage to the Village Square was uneventful, although slightly longer than he had estimated. The absence of the illuminated dome of the Subtropical Paradise, the now-extinguished floodlights of the five-a-side football pitches served to make the lakeside walk a little more perilous than usual.

He slipped through the Village Square, keeping to the high borders of shrubbery. He felt exposed as he crept over the wooden bridge but had no need to. The square was as still as the grave.

It was eerily quiet. Back in the MK Dome, there would have been some level of activity on the street, whatever the time. But not here at Middlemedes.

Thankfully …

Rib darted up the short flight of steps to the Pool Bar door. He reached into a side pocket of his bag and pulled out the Swiss Army penknife. According to Kaddie's written instructions, Blade 14 was the universal lock-picker. Blade 14 would get him into the Pool Bar. Rib levered out Blade 14 with his thumbnail. Even though the night air was chill, he realised that he was sweating profusely. He'd never done this sort of thing before.

He took the knife in his right hand and took hold of the left door handle with his left hand. Without knowing why, he gave it a gentle push.

It yielded.

It wasn't locked.

Rib panicked and dived into the shrubbery wondering whether someone was inside working late – or working early. He peered through the window into the bar. No lights on. He retraced the three steps to the entrance and slipped through the door. Having frequented the bar every evening for the past three weeks, he quickly found his bearings. From the far glass wall, he could make out the light-blue shimmer of the pool. To the left, the bar. To the right, the bowling alley lanes. And in the far corner, Venturer.

Rib felt his way over to the simulator. The red lettering on the plinth to the left of the handrail gave a stern warning to anybody who had a bad back, suffered from motion sickness, was pregnant, had a glass eye or any combination of the above.

Rib set to work with a will. He had calculated that he had three hours tops to convert this ten-dollar-a-go amusement ride into a sophisticated piece of transportation that would get him out of here and back to MK. He worked feverishly on the engine, stripping out the quaint mechanism, placing each piece carefully on the hand towel which he had brought with him. It was not without a degree of guilt that he dismantled Venturer's innards. They just didn't make them like this any more, he thought, as he snapped into place the hydrocell chip. He worked confidently over the next forty minutes, pausing only to wipe the sweat from his brow with his sleeve. Riley, Head of the School of Nano-zoomology at MK College, would have been proud of him.

20

Rib smiled when he recalled his first encounter with Riley, as he was known. Not Professor Riley, not Mr Riley, and certainly not Richard.

Just Riley.

Rib had turned up for interview at college for a place on the course and had been directed to Room 49b, the waiting room of the School of Nanozoomology. He took a seat and began to leaf through the periodicals and magazines piled untidily on a coffee table in the middle of the room. He was just in danger of becoming engrossed in *What Space Caravan?* when an old man in a brown overall scurried into the room. He had a broom. No dustpan. Just a broom and an extremely old-looking broom it looked too, with a number of nasty-looking bent nails sticking out of the broom head.

He started to sweep the floor vigorously, at the same time wheezing out the theme tune of *The Godfather* through pursed lips.

'Lift up your feet please, young sir,' he requested as he swept the pile of crumbs, dust and lollipop sticks from one side of the room to the other.

Rib duly obliged.

The janitor paused and leaned on his broom. Rib sensed that this signalled the opener of a conversation and looked up from his magazine.

'So what brings you to this particular school, then, if I might enquire?' wheezed the old man.

'Well, I want to graduate in Nanozoomology and I hear

this is the best place to do it.'

The old man scratched his head. 'Are you sure?' He gave Rib a cheeky grin.

'How do you mean?'

'Well, you must know for a fact that there is a ... erm, pseudo-coded added-value over-representation of young women on this programme of learning. At least I think that's what they call it. In other words, if you come here you'll be up to your neck in members of the opposite ... er ... sex, 32:1.'

'Sounds a good reason for joining up,' laughed Rib.

The old man cleared his throat noisily and resumed his sweeping with an energy that threatened to snap the broom head from its stick.

Rib returned to *What Space Caravan?* and the janitor harrumphed something indescribable as he swept out of the room, leaving a heap of debris in the doorway as he did so.

A silence, albeit a dusty silence, descended on the waiting room. Rib put down the magazine and rehearsed the answers to the questions that he knew he would be asked in the interview.

'Tell me, Mr Meskitoe, why do you want to study at the School of Nanozoomology?'

'Well, sir, MK College is recognised as a world leader in the field and I want to be part of a school which has the highest standards, a rock-solid set of eco-values and a marvellous mission statement.'

'And what is our mission statement?'

'We zoom to conquer?'

'Yes, well done, and now would you like to tell me ...?'

His thoughts were interrupted by the arrival of a rather stern-looking woman with horn-rimmed spectacles. She wore broguishly sensible shoes, a tweed skirt, a tartan-patterned blouse and a dark-blue Barbour bodywarmer, even though it was an ambient 19.6 degrees. Her high-pitched, squeaky Scouse accent came as something of a surprise.

'Would Mr Meskitoe be so kind as to walk this way, please?' Without waiting for an answer, she turned and strode back down the corridor. Rib followed, desperately trying not to mimic her stride pattern.

She stopped at the door at the end of the corridor. It looked solid, made of mahogany, Rib guessed. On a brass plate fixed to the door, at eye level, he read a single word.

'Riley.'

The woman from Fazakerly (Rib later learned) opened the door and ushered him in. He faced three people behind a large wooden desk, again, mahogany, Rib gauged. The rest of the room was white.

White ceiling.

White walls.

White shagpile carpet.

Deep shagpile carpet.

So deep he could feel it tickle his ankles. And disconcertingly, on the desk, an antique long-playing vinyl record.

The White Album.

This was not what he had expected. This was not good, not good at all. He wrenched his eyes way from the record to face his three interviewers. Front left, a middle-aged man, grey-suited, dark-blue MK College lanyard round his neck. Front right, a middle-aged woman, grey-suited, dark-blue MK College lanyard round her neck. And between them, an old man wearing faded denims, a 'Blodwyn Pig' T-shirt and no dark-blue MK College lanyard within sight.

Shit.

It was the janitor.

Riley, alias the janitor, invited him to take a seat, which was a problem because the only three chairs in the room were already occupied. He nodded at the floor in front of the desk. He hesitated, then sat down, at first cross-legged, then shifting uncomfortably to take up the pose of a flick on the bonnet of a car at a motor show, then back to the security of crossed legs. From where he was sitting, he could just make out the tops of their heads over the front of the desk. They helped him by leaning forward, synchronised, to grant him the honour of eye contact. This was the only help he would get.

'So you've come here to be up to your neck in young women then, have you, Master Meskitoe?' came the opening gambit of Riley, Head of the School of Nanozoomology.

Checkmate in one.

To this day, Rib did not know how he had been accepted onto the course. The Professor fired a seemingly random series of questions at him. The best he could do was fend them off.

'Why is the sky blue?'

'Because … because blue is the colour.'

What was the name of the evil matron in *One Flew over the Cuckoo's Nest*?'

'Nurse … er, Cratchit.'

'Close. Ratched.'

'And finally, what is the cyclic variable on the Z drive of a Worlizter Nanodrome?'

At last, something he knew. '.0075 per cent, sir.'

The Professor paused.

'Hmm. Good!' he stood up, leaned forward and extended a scrawny, freckled hand.

'Congratulations, Master Meskitoe, you are now a student of MK College. Your first module commences next Thursday. You will now enrol in Room 13, second floor. They will tell you all you need to know.'

Rib stood up, rather unsteadily, a touch of cramp in his left calf. He went to shake hands with the panel.

The Professor, still standing, dismissed this move with the wave of a hand. 'That's it for now. Playtime over. There's work to be done. Off you pop.'

Riley was arguably the best teacher in the world. He was a

Yoda, a joker, a Svengali, all rolled into one. But with a ruthless, Presbyterian, disciplinarian streak added to the mix.

And a passion for the Old Norse sagas.

For some totally unfathomable reason, Riley insisted on weaving into his lectures and tutorials tales of Scandinavian mythology.

The students humoured him and went along with it. Some even took interest in the heroics of the Vikings and their predecessors because they knew they had the best teacher in the world.

Except Danny Dorvic, of course.

During one Nanozoometrics A–Z tutorial, Riley was in full flow when Dorvic interrupted him.

'Excuse me, sir.'

A deathly hush fell on the group – for no one interrupted Riley.

'Am I in the wrong tutorial? My logbook has it down for Nanozoometrics A–Z, not Noggin, King of the Nogs!' He looked around for the supporting giggles and chuckles. There were none.

Allen, Augar and Barker stared at the floor, Bailey and Barraclough stared intently out of the window, and Carling looked as if he'd cacked himself and was hoping nobody could smell it.

Dorvic wavered, now unsure of his ground. But in a moment of insane defiance, like the last desperate act of the blindfolded man at the end of the plank who flicks a V at Captain Cut-Throat, he pressed on.

'With respect, sir.'

Sharp intake of breath from all present. And Carling definitely had cacked himself.

'I thought I had come to college to study space science, not silly stories of fat men with long beards getting pissed and slicing hunks out of each other … Sir … with respect …' he tailed off.

166

Dorvic sat down.

Carling stood up, about to ask for permission to leave the room. A warm sensation trickled down the inside of his left thigh. He sat down again.

All eyes were now focused on Riley.

Riley drew a deep breath before fixing Dorvic with a stare that would freeze hell over a thousand times.

'So, Master Dorvic, you rate the study of space science more highly than the study of Old Icelandic, do you?'

Dorvic responded with an effort at a wan smile.

'Tell me, Master Dorvic, who would you say is the greatest traveller ever?'

Dorvic thought before he answered. 'Neil Armstrong, sir.'

'Ah, an understandable but nonetheless predictable response. First man on the moon, Apollo 12. And what were his words, Dorvic, when he first set foot on the moon?'

'One small step for man, one great leap for mankind, sir.'

'Exactly. A scripted, rehearsed, sound bite for the head-lines, the newsreels, the politicians. And people bought it. Even you, Master Dorvic, bought it two generations after the event. Compare this putrid piece of tabloid prose with the words of the great explorer Bjarni Herjolfsson when he discovered America.' Quizzical looks around the group. 'No, it wasn't Columbus, it wasn't Vespucci; it was Bjarni Herjolfsson who set off from Iceland in a small boat in hostile seas.

'And what did he say when he saw the shores of the vast New World for the first time? Did he say "One small paddle for me, one great paddle for the Vikings"? No, did he bollocks! He turned round from the bow, looked at his men on the oars and said 'Boys, I don't think this is Greenland ...'

The Professor paused, then said softly. 'Sirs, the art of stoic understatement, in its most heroic form. "Boys, I don't think this is Greenland,"' he repeated softly, savouring each word.

'Class finished!' he snapped, picking up his files, discs and stilo. In the doorway he turned, put his right hand to his forehead, scratched his head, Columbo-like, and said, 'Master Dorvic, do you wish to proceed with your studies, King of the Nogs and all?'

'Yes, sir.'

'Then you will present a resume of *Hrafnkel's Saga* to the group next week, no more than 500 words. Spoken, not PowerPointed. Agreed?'

'Agreed, sir,' said Dorvic.

And sure enough he did. They had all left the room slowly that day, some a little bemused, some intrigued, some inspired. All except Carling, that is, who had remained seated.

Rib had really enjoyed the course and he had done rather well. Graduated with flying colours. And won the Student of the Year Award.

All down to Riley.

21

And he really would have been proud if he could see him now, making the final connection into the T-drive in pre-test mode.

'There, that should do it,' he muttered to himself as he clicked the final chip in. 'Now let's see if it works.'

He climbed into the cabin and pressed the single big square button on the dashboard. It lit up green.

'Bongo,' he said to himself.

A quick glance at his timepiece told him that he had just over fifty minutes to finish the job. Now for the hydraulics. Transforming the motor was the easy bit. After all, his Year 2 practical core project had been the conversion of an antique Postman Pat supermarket ride into a lethal machine which won silver medal in the All-College Robowars Tournament. The reason why it didn't win gold was a controversial ruling by the match referee against the blasting of *Postman Pat's* theme tune from a large speaker on the roof of the vehicle.

'In contravention of the spirit of the rules' was the verdict. 'Ballsdash!' had been Rib's reaction at the time and still was. The all-pervasive musical reference to a black-and-white cat had been central to his game plan. And the strategy had worked. Once the tune insinuated its way into your senses, you just couldn't concentrate. And it would stay there. Rib realised too late that the very recall of the tune would now mean that he would have endure 'each and every morning' for the next two hours or so.

The next bit was going to be tricky. Not exactly uncharted

waters but choppy nonetheless. He had to convert the *Venturer II*'s four scissor legs, two on each side – their existing function as pitch-and-roll mechanisms designed to persuade the contents of the rider's stomach to part company with its body – to being four real legs able to carry the cabin at speeds of up to 50 kph at infinitely variable height.

Tricky indeed.

On his regular previous visits to the Pool Bar, he'd reccied out the raw materials available and had identified the heavy-duty rubber castor cups under the legs of the two pool tables as fit for purpose. He removed them one by one and was tempted to just go for the four, so heavy were the tables to lift. But he decided to take all eight and have the luxury of four spares.

Twenty minutes later, *Venturer II* was ready for her maiden voyage. No waving of flags, no smashing of champagne bottle against her hull, just a deft decoupling of the six-step steel staircase from the yellow cabin.

There she was, liberated at last. Ready for lift-off. And not a moment too soon. The first search lights of the dawn sun started to creep across the carpet. Rib climbed into the cockpit and pressed the green for Go button. It lit immediately and *Venturer II* rose up smoothly into travel mode.

Rib strapped himself in.

'Shit,' he cursed and strapped himself out.

The Pool Bar door.

It was shut.

He had not installed a park mode. Just three gears: forward, fast forward, and hold on to your nollocks. Could he leave it in uncontrolled neutral while he opened the door? Should he smash his way through and suffer the consequences? Too risky. Far too risky.

He opened the door, climbed out and sprinted the twelve steps over to the door, opened it and sprinted back.

Venturer II was waiting for him as if to say 'Where did you think I was going? Oh ye of little faith!'

He strapped himself in again and pushed the joystick forward. *Venturer II* leapt forward in three adventurous gleeful bounds and embedded herself in the bar.

'Shit, shit, shit!' Rib swore.

Five seconds into the journey and crashed already, with soapy spumes of Carlsberg Special spraying from the ruptured pumps all over the windscreen.

'Shit!'

And no reverse gear.

'Shit!!'

And now flashing alarms going off all over the place.

'Shit!!!'

Without engaging his brain, Rib instinctively engaged hold-on-to-your-nollocks mode. *Venturer II* ripped through the bar, careered off the wall taking out all the mounted spirit bottles, including the intriguingly seductive Jamaican Navy Rum, before setting off round the circumference of the bar at a firm but steady 20 kph. In one way, it was fortunate that the Pool Bar was circular. Insofar as *Venturer II* passed the exit. Twenty times. In another way, it wasn't. Insofar as *Venturer II* was being driven by a fourteen-year-old who didn't even know what L-plates stood for.

Luckily, *Venturer II* had been built to last and suffered no more than near-terminal friction in reducing the wallpaper of the Pool Bar to a gooey papier-mâché. Getting nowhere fast, Rib hit the red button marked stop.

Venturer II stopped.

Rib didn't. His body tested to the full the safety harness designed to hold a bobbing swaying human torso going gently up and down, backwards and forwards. The harness held, sort of. He ended up face splayed against the windscreen with the joystick pressed firmly against the less-than-joyful nether region of his body.

At the third attempt, he managed to steer *Venturer II*

ROB BADCOCK

through the doorway. She lurched down the steps, taking no
prisoners in knocking four large terracotta urns containing
pink pelargoniums onto the floor where they smithereened
into orange shards of sharp clay.

Up and over the bridge without too much difficulty and
then a sharp right past the noodle place.

Suddenly before him was a line of bobbling lights. Torches.
Sounds of men shouting.

'Left, left!' screamed a voice into his left ear.

'Aaargh!' was Rib's considered reaction, jumping out of his
skin. Someone was in the cabin with him! 'Left!' the voice
shrieked, in an unmistakeably guttural tone.

Rib yanked the stick hard left and *Venturer II* responded
well, veering off into the entrance of the road, signed Pine
Lodges 121–229.

'What the hell are you doing here?' he hissed, not taking
his eyes off the road for a moment.

Rika climbed over the back of the bench to join him.

'Saving your bacon is what it looks like,' she laughed.
'Now take a right. Here, just past the lamp post.'

Rib obeyed and, again, *Venturer II* responded well to his
touch. That was a better turn. Will need to sort out the
hydraulics though. His thoughts returned to his unwelcome
passenger.

'I asked you a question. What the hell are you doing
here?'

Torches flashing and shouts ahead to the right. And the
baying of hounds.

'Dogs!' Rib swore. 'Where the hell have dogs come from?
And big ones by the sounds of it. Shepherds or Dobermanns.'

'Down here, coming up on the left. Take the track just by
the firebeater … See it?'

'Yep!' he answered through gritted teeth as he swung
the craft ninety degrees down a narrow track leading into
the forest. Rib recognised the place. It was where he had

172

crashed. Jonathan had brought him here. He reached down to the bandage on his leg. It was still sore to the touch.

The track was steep. Too steep. *Venturer II* plunged into the bracken nose first, sending Rib and Rika smashing into the front screen. Luckily, the craft stayed upright. If it had rolled, it would have been as helpless as a beetle on its back.

Rib's blood froze. He was staring eye to eye with a hell-hound. Rib's right cheek pressed against the screen was a matter of a centimetre away from the slavering jaws of a Dobermann. A Dobermann who was behaving as if hadn't tasted raw meat for some time. In a frenzy it snarled and tried to bite into the screen, its teeth scraping across the rein-forced glass. Rib smacked the Go button and the motor engaged. *Venturer II* tottered to her feet and set off unsteadily down the track. The dog had now been joined by two others and all three were running between the craft's legs, jumping up and snapping at the underbelly of the cabin.

They came to the bottom of the slope, reaching the wider path which followed the perimeter fence. Something broke with a crack. The piercing yelp told them that one of the dogs had got too close to *Venturer II*'s scissor legs and had parted company with a tail or a leg. Normally Rib would be distraught at such pain suffered by an animal but in this case he rationalised that it was one less dog ready to rip his throat apart.

'OK, look for two silver birches coming up on the right,' said Rika. 'Slow down a little ... Here they are. Point us between them and give it full power.'

'But that will take us straight into the fence!'

'Don't worry, trust me. Do it now!'

The two remaining dogs had now been joined by a handler who started to bang on the side of the cabin. He was scream-ing something which Rib couldn't make out.

'Do it now!' shrieked Rika.

Rib smacked it into third and pressed the throttle. *Venturer II* hurtled forwards smacking one of the dogs aside as if swatting a fly. As they hit the fence between the two trees, Rib flinched to take the impact. It never came.

The wire parted from the centre like a curtain. It had been pre-cut. They scrambled through and out into the field beyond and crossed the field unhindered hearing the shouts and cries fading into distance behind them.

It was 6.20 a.m. The temperature 37 degrees with a slight early-morning breeze drifting in from the west.

22

The bright yellow simulator ride branded *Venturer II* revelled in her new-found freedom. Her scissor legs crossed the open field until her headlights shone big and bright against the wall which was the rainforest. She veered left and followed the line of the trees, saxing a course over fallen trunks, threshing through low-lying bush, springing over swollen streams.

There was no pursuit. The clinical ease with which the machine had dismembered their leader dissuaded the pack of hounds from further chase. The men with torches had dared go no further than the fence. They had stood mesmerised by the sight of the alien-looking craft teetering above the early mist covering the field. *Venturer II* followed the line of the forest until she ran out of open country. She slowed to a walking speed, as if unsure of her route, before turning ninety degrees right though a gap in the trees and plunged into the dark heart of the rainforest.

The whirring clatter of the large yellow beast crashing into their lives sent a wave of frogs, skunks, rats and other small mammals rushing away from the track into the understorey. Hundreds of small birds screeched their escape up to the canopy, where in turn a flock of brightly coloured lorikeets took noisy flight from the intruder.

The normally persuasive tendrilled hooks of wait-a-while had no hold on the metal monster as it cut a swathe through their tangle.

They travelled for two hours, stopping every now and

then to listen for signs of pursuit. There was none.

They were making good progress through a gap between the trees when the track suddenly plunged away to the left in a deep descent. *Venturer II* followed blindly, bouncing off the buttress of a fig palm, her hull then scraping against an outcrop of rock on the other side of the path. She pinballed downwards for a further 20 metres before totally losing control and turning turtle, slithering down a bed of mud on her back, her four scissor legs clicking helplessly in the air.

She hit the water at 30 kph, sending a plume of spray some 20 metres around her. The impact catapulted the craft head over heels so that it landed right way up, calmly bobbing on the surface of the lake as if it were the most natural thing for it to be doing.

Silence.

Silence, as if the whole rainforest held its breath to see what strange trick this new animal would perform next.

Total silence.

Broken by screams from inside.

'Shit! We're floating, we're on water! Aarggh, we're leak-ing – do something!'

'Hold on, don't keep screaming! I said *stop screaming*! Extend the legs to full height. We'll then be able to walk on the bottom!'

Click. Whirr.

Pause.

'Shit. They won't reach! We're out of our depth! And we're leaking!'

'I know. My feet are wet too. Open the doors!'

'What?'

'Open the doors or I'll break your legs.'

The doors slid open. Rib sulked as Rika successfully steered them to the other side of the lake with the help of a piece of driftwood and an impressive demonstration of oarsmanship, though he wouldn't have admitted it.

As *Venturer II*'s motor was re-engaged, her legs tested, and the mud washed off the windscreen, peace momentarily reigned between them. Since breaking through the perimeter fence, they had fought like cat and dog. She barking incessant directions, he spitting and cursing in response, especially when she tried to grab the joystick, which she did on at least five occasions.

'OK, we've got to move on now,' she said.

'Why, do you think they're following? From Middle-medes?'

'No, I don't mean them. I mean we can hardly travel in this heap throughout the whole day, can we?'

Rib felt himself tense at the word 'heap'. 'Why not? The conversion's good enough to take it. It has the design, it has the power, it has the capacity.'

'It also has the colour, my little friend. Bright, screamingly loud yellow. Hello, everybody! Here we are! Estimated time of arrival, whenever you want us. And the noise it makes. It's like Edward Scissorhands on acid, this thing, when it gets going.'

The reference was lost on Rib, who felt slighted that his creation was coming under so much criticism from an unwanted stowaway. 'If it's so crap, hitch a ride with any other wagon that happens to be passing then.'

'Touchy, touchy. Don't be so sensitive. The wagon works well. It's just the colour that I have a problem with.'

'So what was I supposed to do? Motorise the pool table because it was green? That would have been ideal, chugging along in the jungle sitting cross-legged on top of a pool table. Especially in the rain. But that would have been just fine by you, wouldn't it, because the colour was right!'

Rika took a deep breath and paused before she asked, 'You have so much anger in you, Rib. Is there something you want to tell me?'

'You!?' he exploded. 'You're not even supposed to be here

in the first place. If I needed a travelling companion, the last person on earth I'd pick would be you! I mean, have you looked at yourself lately?' He eased off the speed. He was going too fast. He was getting really wound up. He'd be no good to Mum smashed to bits in a simulator ride on the forest floor. They travelled for the next half-hour in silence, save her occasional directions in words of one or two syllables.

Left.

Straight on.

Slow down.

Another ten minutes passed. You could slice the silence with a knife. He could bear it no longer.

'Look, what I said back there. Maybe I was a little …'

'Forget it, it's fine,' she said.

'I mean, what I said about you being …'

'I said, it's fine,' she said. 'Final say on the matter, end of story, *punkt sloot*.' Then suddenly she jabbed a finger at the windscreen. 'Pull over here. You see the old gate post? Just here.'

Rib manoeuvred *Venturer II* off the track into a small clearing in the forest. He switched off the motor and turned to look at her, about to retry the apology line.

'Lunch,' she said, with a broad smile which in an instant melted all the frost away.

'Great,' he replied, feeling hungry all of a sudden, trying to think back to when he last ate.

'What have we got?' he asked.

'Well, I know what I've got. Just some basic survival rations. I'm really more interested in what you've brought along.'

He leaned back and grabbed his rucksack from behind the seat.

Rib produced a packet of brown biscuits and placed it proudly on the dashboard shelf.

'What's that?'

'A packet of biscuits.'

'I can see that. What kind of biscuits?'

'Bourbon.'

Pause.

'I cannot stand Bourbon biscuits. Just like I cannot stand the taste of Marmite, Bovril, Twiglets and elk testicles.'

Pause.

'Nor can I,' agreed Rib.

'You don't like Bourbon biscuits either?'

Pause.

'Then why did you bring them?'

'Because I was in a hurry. I just grabbed the first thing I saw.'

'OK, no problem. What else have you got?'

Pause. A longer one this time.

'Nothing.'

'Nothing? That's it?'

'Yep.'

'One packet of Bourbon biscuits, about as appetising as a mouthful of elk testicles.'

'They're a bit better if you dunk them in strawberry-flavoured goat's milk,' he added with an apologetic little grin.

'Elks bollocks?'

'No, Bourbon biscuits.'

'Excellent! Well, it's just as well that I've brought something.' She laughed as she grabbed a leather bag from behind the seat. 'Let's get outside and stretch our legs.'

Rib obliged by opening the door and gestured for her to go first. The heat hit them both as they stepped out. It had been hot in the cabin but out here the humidity was overwhelming.

'Over here,' she pointed and padded off into the undergrowth, her bag clacking against her back. They followed a narrow animal track for some 20 metres before the forest floor opened out.

'Here will do,' she said, stopping by a huge buttress of an even larger tree. The buttress must have been a good 10 metres high. And as for the tree, Rib thought as he looked up into the canopy, he had no idea how high it went.

'Here will do nicely,' she said as she squatted down and carefully emptied her bag. Strange-looking cooking utensils, all with a well-worn thick black coating. And then a number of packs, presumably dried food, labelled with long unrecognisable words, presumably Finnish. She went though them one by one.

'*Mustikkapiirakka* – bilberry pie.

'*Mansikka* – strawberries.

'*Peruna sose* – mashed potato.

'*Munkki* …'

'Monkey? You're going to eat monkey!' Rib asked.

'It means doughnut, you doughnut,' she laughed and leapt at him, pinning him down on his back. She grabbed his wrists and sat on top of him.

'Get off!' he swore as he struggled to break free.

Rib swam an average 8,000 metres a week and was in pretty good nick. Try as he might, he couldn't throw her off.

'Will you get off!' he grunted, still straining to twist her over.

'All right, all right, you little munkki, you.' She released her grip and made to climb off. As a parting gesture she tickled him under his right arm.

He lashed out at her with his left food, missing narrowly as she danced away, laughing.

'That's not funny. Piss off!'

She picked out a pot from amongst the collection of utensils and headed away through the trees.

'I'm going to get some water. Be back in ten minutes.' She disappeared from sight round a buttress of a tree, giggling as she went.

Don't hurry, he thought as he picked himself up and brushed off the damp mat of soil, dead leaves and twigs which stuck to the back of his arms and legs. He took his packet of Bourbon biscuits and went back to *Venturer II*, where he sat and sulked.

He was deep in thought, weighing up the pros and cons of pressing the Go button and pressing on without her, when he heard sounds of her return.

Crackling of twigs and branches. The smell of smoke. Pots clinking. The smell of cooking. It smelled good.

Some fifteen minutes later, she came out of the forest towards him. She was carrying something. A tin plate and a tin cup.

'Here you are. Reindeer, mashed potato, lingonberry sauce and some water to wash it down.'

'No thanks,' he said, looking away.

She turned and walked back into the rainforest without a word.

The smell of the reindeer dinner had wafted into *Venturer II*, preying on his senses, to the point where he just had to open the Bourbons. He kicked the empty packet under the seat as Rika made her way, billycans now clinking from a strap on her belt, out of the trees back towards him.

'Ready to go?' she queried as she climbed into the cabin. 'Budge up.' Her heel made contact with something crinkly and she reached down between her legs to feel under the bench.

'Ooh, what's this then?' she asked in feigned surprise.

'A whole packet?' she said, holding the offending item between thumb and forefinger. 'Impressive. Totally nuts, but impressive.'

Rib did not rise to the bait, but closed the door, pressed the Go button and steered *Venturer II* back on to the trail.

Few words passed between them as they journeyed south for the rest of the day. She would offer to drive, saying that he needed the break, that he was looking tired. He would say no thank you; he was fine.

Mostly, they followed the course of small roads, which formed firebreak-thin passages through the towering forest. Rib wondered on more than one occasion how the roads didn't grow over. Someone must be using them regularly. Just as well, he thought.

At precisely 2.33 he felt faint. He wasn't sure whether it was a build-up of the heat in the cockpit, the effects of eating nothing but a pack of Bourbons in the past twenty-four hours, or a combination of the two. He slowed *Venturer II* to 5 kph before slumping over the dashboard.

'Hey, are you all right?' Rika asked.

'No, I'm not feeling so good. It's all right, I'll be fine in a minute.'

Rika took hold of the joystick. This time there was no sign of protest from Rib. She steered the craft deftly off the road and brought it to a halt under the shade of a giant cedar.

She turned the motor off.

'Come on, let's take a look at you,' she said as she gently raised him to a sitting position. He tried to smile but couldn't. Beads of perspiration popped from his brow by the second. His head was banging. His shin was throbbing.

'Boy, you don't look good,' she said. She felt his forehead. Temperature. She felt his pulse. Fever. Infection, maybe.

'Where does it hurt?'

'My head, my leg …' he whispered.

She looked down at the gauze dressing on his left shin.

'What's this?' She shook him gently. 'Rib, what's this bandage?'

'Special lotion. Make it better. Ruth.'

'Ruth?' Rika hissed under her breath. 'Ruth put this on? To make your leg better? Rib answer me. Did she put the bandage on your leg to make it better?'

Rib nodded drowsily.

She worked quickly, snapping open a blade drawn from a sheath on her belt. She slipped the tip of the knife under the gauze and sliced it open from the bottom, like a surgeon opening up an abdomen.

'Oooh!' said Rib, wincing, his eyes closed.

'Oooh!' said Rika, grimacing at the mess of a wound now revealed.

'Oooh!' he groaned again. 'I don't feel good.'

He went to stand up and fell over in a deep faint.

She caught him just as his head was about to smash into the windscreen. She lay him on his side on the bench, took a first-aid pack from her bag and set about cleaning the wound.

As she did so, a muttered curse, an occasional insult escaped her lips. Mostly aimed at her patient's former nurse.

Ruth.

23

Before he opened his eyes, Rib heard the sound of fire crackling somewhere in the distance. Not too far away. Somewhere to his right. He heard the sound of a voice singing. Soft and gentle, like a lullaby.

Before he opened his eyes, he felt pain. In his left leg, though not as bad as before. But his head ... his head was throbbing.

Before he opened his eyes, he smelt cooking. Meat, he thought, onions and gravy.

He opened his eyes.

He was lying on a rough canvas sheet spread over a bed of dry leaves, which rustled and crackled as he shifted weight. Above and around him, a shelter of branches and larger leaves trussed together with twine and vine to make a tent. He remembered. The escape. The crash, the water, the heat. He leaned over, raised a flap of the shelter and looked out in the direction of the singing.

Rika was kneeling over a fire some 10 metres away, rocking gently back and forwards on her heels.

'That smells good,' he said.

Startled, she dropped the spoon she was holding into the pot and let out a few words which sounded more oath than lullaby.

'Hey,' she said, retrieving the spoon and wiping it on her sleeve. 'And how is the English patient?'

'OK thanks but my head still hurts.'

'It will do, you had a nasty little infection. How's the leg?'

'Well,' he said, gingerly emerging from the shelter. 'It still hurts but it doesn't feel too bad really.'

'Good, I just knew you'd start feeling better the moment I took that bandage off.'

'How do you mean?' said Rib as he stood up, stretching both arms over his head. 'If it wasn't for that bandage, I would have been in much worse shape.'

Rika laughed.

Rib stiffened.

'Why the laugh?'

'Work it out for yourself,' she said as she stirred the stew. 'How long does a wound normally take to heal? One week? Two weeks? How long did yours take? Not to heal, I mean.' She looked over her shoulder at Rib, who stared at her impassively without answering. 'Over twice as long,' she continued.

He didn't have the energy to challenge her. He felt drowsy again. He lay down on the sheet and closed his eyes. 'You will feel better right away,' he heard her say from some distant place. 'I promise.'

He slipped into a dream sleep where he lay on his back on a roughly hewn board floating in the middle of a black lake. It was night-time. He looked up at thick clouds racing across the moon. The heavens screamed storm with all their might, against the still of the deep dark lake. Still, except for the occasional splash against his cold cheek. He could not move a muscle, stretched out on the board as if pinned. The moon looked as if it were moving. But it couldn't be. It must be the clouds. The moon can't move that fast. But it did. He couldn't move his head. His eyes followed the moon as far as they could until it disappeared from sight into the lake. And then total blackness. As if the moon had been switched off. He felt drops of water on his cheek. He didn't know whether his eyes were open or closed, it was so black. Something wet and oozy slimed across his face, covering his forehead. It felt thick and sinewy. A giant sea slug had slithered from the water. Onto the board, then onto his face. To slurp out his eyes.

'Aaargh! Aaargh!' he screamed as he tore the creature away and hurled it with all his might into the lake.

He sat bolt upright. The lake was gone.

The darkness was gone. He didn't know where he was. He didn't know who he was. He blinked and looked around. He was sitting on a bed made of branches and leaves in a clearing in a jungle, being stared at by a girl with a distinct look of annoyance on her face.

'Go and pick that up now!' she said.

'But, but, it was a long black squishy thing. Sluggy. Going to suck …'

'Not it wasn't. It was a wet towel lovingly placed on your fevered brow by the resident nursey here. Now go and fetch it!'

Rib tried to stand up but couldn't. Rika sighed before stomping off into the vegetation. The thrashing of under-growth and breaking of branches indicated the increased frustration of the searcher as the seconds ticked by. She finally emerged holding a dirty towel between thumb and forefinger.

'I walk through the forest to the creek, wash my one and only towel in the water, walk back and place it lovingly on your forehead to make you feel better, and what do you do? You chuck it as far as you can into the undergrowth. Now look at it! Covered in all sorts of shit!'

The bottom lip of the little boy Rib trembled as a tear formed in his right eye, rolled slowly down his cheek before bursting into a dozen droplets as it fell upon a dead leaf between his feet. Everything welled up inside him. The pain, the anger, the hurt, the fear. All into that one tear.

'Oh come on,' she said. 'Sorry, I didn't mean it.' She sat down beside him and put her arm round his shoulder. He swallowed hard, looking away from her, not wishing to show his weakness.

She leaned forward and peered round into his face. 'Fancy a drink?'

He nodded, still trying not to look at her.

'OK, a special Lappish pick-me-up for you, my little English patient,' she said as she jumped up and walked over the pot bubbling over the fire. He wished she wouldn't call him that.

She soon returned with two cups of warm blue liquid, placing one carefully in his right hand.

'Cloudberry,' she explained. 'Drink. It will do you good.'

He sipped and it felt as if it would do him good. It reminded him of the drink his mum used to make him when he was off school with the 'enza.

'Rich in vitamins, antioxidants and universal life-fizz.'

He managed a smile.

'How are you feeling?'

He pondered a second, took a second sip and nodded. 'OK.'

'Your leg?'

He looked down. The wound was dry. 'Wow,' he said. 'That's amazing. How come it's healed all of a sudden?'

Rika took a slug of her cloudberry before smiling wryly.

'Well, I tried to explain before, but you wouldn't listen.'

'Go on then.'

'The blue balm and the bandage faithfully administered by Ruth stopped your wound from healing.'

Rib went through the mental motions of outrage, indignation, scorn and protest but expressed none of these because deep down he knew she was right.

He thought long and hard. 'So you're saying that Ruth didn't want me to get better.'

'No, I'm not saying that. She, or rather they, did not want you to leave Middlemede.'

'Why? I thought they were a peace-loving hippy-happy community. Why would they want to do that to me?'

'Think about it. Two reasons. First, they like to keep themselves to themselves. No intruders. So they get very nervous about letting people tell the outside world about them. And secondly, they saw you as a welcome addition to their gene pool.'

'What do you mean?'

'A fit young sprog like you. Do I have to paint pictures?'

He reddened and she laughed. 'More cloudberry?'

'No thanks, but thanks, it was really good. And I do feel a lot better now. So … thanks.'

'Wow, three thanks in a sentence. Sounds like a good line for a song. This calls for something a little stronger to celebrate the return to health of Master Rib Meskitoe.' She reached down to one of the many zip pockets on her trousers and produced two miniature plastic bottles. 'Koskenkorva,' she whispered as if in awe.

'Eh?'

'I might have known,' she sighed. 'You don't drink, do you?'

'Of course, double goats with a …'

'Oh please, do me a favour,' she interrupted. 'I don't mean that designer piss. I mean real alcohol. And you don't get more real than Koskenkorva.'

She ripped the tops off the two bottles and handed one to him.

'Cheers,' she said.

'I'm not sure what there is to celebrate,' he answered. 'We're on the run, Planet Earth's dead and buried. Good health.'

'Hey, listen, you,' she said with a stern glint in her eye. 'Look around you. Does this rainforest look unhealthy to you? Unpredictable, yes. Dangerous, even, yes. But unhealthy? No. And do you know why? Because it doesn't have man by the millions tramping all over it set on making money by the millions by despoiling and abusing it. Fragile – OK, I'll give you that. But don't you tell me it's not going to survive. Now, where were we? Up your bottom,' she toasted.

He laughed and took a sip.

'No, no, nooo! Down in one like this,' she cried, duly hurling the vodka down her throat. Rib followed suit and then wished he hadn't. As if the searing effect of the strong hot spirit on his throat wasn't enough, its effect on the pool of lukewarm cloudberry happily settling down for the night in his stomach was as dramatic as it was immediate.

(Whilst Rib had slept, Rika had set about the domestic necessities of camp life with a will. She collected wood, lit a fire and selected the evening's meal from her pack. While that was bubbling away, she put on a pan of berry juice. Rika always travelled light, her whole wardrobe comprising two pairs of black trousers, two black tops, two pairs of black socks and two pairs of bright red knickers. All cheapo stuff, apart from the knicks, which she'd really splashed out on. The ultimate in crease-resistant underwear, engineered by Daughter of Rohan. Wear for a week, soak in a stream, hang on a branch, seduce a passing prince. That sort of thing.

Feeling really domesticated, she went one better than a branch and set up a washing line in the clearing, just downwind of the fire. Weighed up the pros and cons of getting the clothes dried more quickly against the contamination of smoke and cooking. She went for the quick dry. The passing prince would have to take the scent of reindeer and parsnip stew on her underwear as part of the exciting voyage of discovery that was Rika.)

So when the stream of bluey cream projectile vomit left Rib's mouth and formed a perfect arc before hitting the washing line, Rika was less than pleased. Not the trousers, not the tops, not the socks. No, it had to be her knickers. Her red knicks took the brunt.

'Holy Odin!' she exclaimed. 'Why the frigg did you have to do that? And why the knicks? They're the only thing of worth I have. Why the frigging knicks?'

'Sorry, sorry,' blurted Rib, wiping his mouth on his sleeve. He made as if to stand, but still couldn't.

'Leave it, I'll do it,' she said, walking over to the line. The mutterings and cursings followed her into the forest, the oaths echoing off the buttresses of the giant cedars.

Rib held his head in his hands. He strained to hear what she was shouting. He managed to extract words and phrases from the raging rant.

'Tried to be nice … covered my towel in shit … cooked him a meal … shared best vodka … sicked all over my knicks!'

He could hear the sounds of sizeable shrubs being uprooted, branches of significant girth being snapped in two. Creatures of the rainforest stampeding in retreat.

Then silence. Did he detect a sob?

She emerged from the fronds, strode over and stood before him, hands on hips. The forest waited with bated breath. Not a flicker of expression on her face. Her grey eyes … grey? I thought they were green before … fixed him in a vice-like vice.

Without releasing him, she reached down to unzip a pocket on her left thigh and produced two more stay-freeze Koskenkorva minis.

'OK, this time you sip,' she instructed, cracking off both tops and handing him a bottle.

'Look,' he said. 'I really didn't mean …'

'Sip!' she said and raised the miniature in toast.

Spirits were raised, fences mended, bridges crossed. Long after the last birds had nested noisily for the night, long after the first frog calls had roared from the dark of the forest, the two still sat deep in conversation before the flickering embers of the fire. They talked as if for the first time about their hopes, their fears, their loves, their hates, their lives, them-selves ... All the time staring into the glow of the fire. Punc-tuated only by the occasional opening of another zip pocket and the cracking open of another Koskenkorva couplet. Each time he would say, 'How much more have you got?' Each time she would reply, 'I have as much as you want.'

He somehow summoned up the courage to touch her knee. She didn't move his hand away, so he thought he might as well give it a little stroke. A strange noise came from the base of her throat. She started to breath deeply and rhythmically. She then jabbed her elbow in his ribs, making him gasp with pain.

'Listen, monkey, lesson number one. Never mistake asthma for passion,' she said as she went off in search of her inhaler.

'Sorry,' he slurred to himself.

The pile of empties soon tallied twelve. She suddenly stood up and said, 'Time for bed.'

He giggled and said, 'Zebedeee,' without really knowing why. It was all he could think of.

He said it again.

It sounded just as stupid as the first time.

A tree frog croaked a signal from deep in the forest. And all of a sudden it didn't sound so stupid after all ...

24

It was 5.15 a.m. Besk looked at himself in the shaving mirror. He had completed his morning ritual and now sat on the rear sill of his cruiserwagon studying his face. His razor applying the final touches. For once, he studied not the clean line of his jaw, the tautness of the fake-tanned skin over the high cheekbones, the small round scar above his left eye.

This time it was the eyes. The blue–grey stare came back at him without expression. Had he always been like this? Surely not. He blinked and looked into the half-distance letting his mind replay to the time when Isobel was alive. She had taken him from studious cadet to Deputy Chief of Police, ever at his side. When he was elevated to the highest level of office, placed in charge of coordinating Exodus for the region, she called it his finest hour. And she had been right. As long as she stood with him, he was untouchable. Commendations, awards, special invitations to special places, from the rich and famous and sometimes the infamous.

As a good policeman, Besk grew to acknowledge and understand the psyche of those who straddled the boundary of what was within the law and what was beyond it. He moved back and forth with increasing skill and confidence across the shady badlands between right and wrong. Whenever Isobel grew anxious and counselled caution, he would apply the brake, pause and reassess his position. She was usually right.

And then she was taken from him. He found her unconscious on the floor of the galley when he returned home late one night after a particularly arduous audit committee. He was deputising for the Chief, who had an important rendezvous.

For three long weeks he sat at her bedside in a private annexe to Ward 17. A stroke, they had said. He held her hand, recited poetry, recounted places they had visited, or just sat looking at her, hoping upon hope that she would return. On Wednesday 14 June he walked into her room and there she was, awake and sitting up.

'Isobel,' he gasped. 'Isobel, my love!' He took the three strides from the door to the bed and they embraced.

'Easy, easy,' she said. 'I'm not quite ready to wrestle yet.' He sat beside the bed, filled her glass with water and they talked. Seemingly for hours. She then asked him a favour.

'Darling, could you possibly get me some cosmetics. I feel a bit of a mess.'

'But you look just fine,' he protested.

'Please,' she implored.

'OK, OK!' he laughed. 'But you know they won't stock Chanel here!'

'No matter, get whatever you can.'

He tripped down the travelator to the Plaza, where he bought a basket of perfumes, oils and glosses, as best he could.

He walked back to the ward thinking of the summer cottage on Tycho. They would go there. He would redecorate, order new curtains, a new bedspread. Lavender-and-white stripes. Marimekko ...

He strode through the ward doors, raised his left knee to balance the basket while he disinfected his hands and moved off down the corridor, a smile on his face.

'Mr Besk, could I have a word please?' intercepted a nurse. 'Nurse Gilda Gotobed' her badge said. She shepherded him into a side room and told him to sit down. It was a small room. Two chairs, a sink, a box of detergent wedged behind the open pipework. They sat, facing each other, both hunched, their knees almost touching. She took the basket of smink from his lap gently and put it on the floor. And in that one movement, that one action, that one gesture of reaching out … the conversation was had. They both knew what was to be.

'I'm really sorry, Mr Besk, I've got bad news.'

A single tear brimmed the lower lid of his left eye. He focused his whole being on keeping it there, hardly hearing the words of the woman before him, herself in tears.

'It was so sudden … She seemed so much brighter … Did all we could … So, so sorry …'

He took it hard.

Very hard.

Mourned without mourning.

Grieved without grieving.

Refused the compassionate leave offered by the Authority.

Drove himself into his work with a fierce, steely determination which worried his colleagues and, finally, caused the Chief to move him.

Move him upstairs.

To the elevated position of Praecox Magister.

'It's for your own good, ' he had said. 'Believe me, it's for the best.'

He had not believed him then, and didn't believe him now. It was almost five years to the day and here he was, seeking cheap stimulus chasing a petty criminal cross-country.

A tear formed in his left eye.

This time he didn't resist. He let it roll down his cheek and break into a dozen droplets on a dry leaf between his feet. It was the first time he had cried since her death.

It was the very tear that he had suppressed five years ago. It had stayed with him, within him. Until now.

He took the shaving mirror from its clip holder on the rear door of the wagon, tumbled and turned it in his hand, like a trickster cardsharp would the ace of spades.

And squeezed.

The only sign of movement was the vein in his left fore-arm. Besk looked up at the thick rays of light shafting through the canopy. A dragonfly traversed his sightline and he followed it. Bright-blue wings, slender fire-red body, dancing in and out of the sunray.

Besk was transported by its beauty. Into a different time, into a different place. A time of blues and greens and silvers. Of tinkling laughter and deep love.

The crack of the mirror snapped his senses back to the here and now. A thin stream of blood snaked its way down his wrist. A perfunctory glance told him that the glass had sliced the flesh just below the thumb. He walked round to the half-open door of the cruiser, leaned into the cabin and took out the first-aid box from the glove compartment. He walked over to an outcrop of rock some 10 metres away from the vehicle. It took him a full five minutes to tweezer out the six sliver-thin shards of glass from his hand. When he was satisfied that the wound was clean, he swabbed it and walked back to the wagon. As he did so, he looked up in search of the dragonfly.

It was gone.

The tear was gone.

He had grieved.

He returned to his grooming ritual, reaching for the bottle of cologne from the crocodile-skin shaving bag. He could feel by the weight of the bottle that it was less than half-full. He held it up to the light to check exactly how much there was remaining, absent-mindedly scanning the ingredients as he did so: purified water, fragrance, i-butyl alcohol, denatonium benzonate, tocopherol, essence of potoroo, whiptail wallaby, quokka. Any other man's after-shave would declare 'NO ANIMAL TESTING', but not his. The sought-after essence extracted from the glands of rare marsupials was like gold dust, a single bottle costing more than the average man's annual salary. The thought lightened his sombre mood as he felt the soothing splash of cologne against his skin.

Besk climbed into the cabin, strapped himself into the safety harness, hit the ignition and smacked the Toyota into a slithering scream down the track.

He reached the main road after some five minutes and set off south. He looked in the mirror and saw the faint line of tear-trace down his cheek. The tear was gone.

Besk allowed himself a smile. He was going to enjoy the day.

For today he would kill ...

25

Half past seven in the morning, somewhere south of Sherwood Rainforest, temperature 31 degrees, humidity 98 per
cent.

Venturer II bucked stiffly into life and teetered out of the
forest. Steam rose from the track. Screeches stretched down
from the canopy, singly first then gathering in strength until
the crescendo of a thousand parrots announced a new day as
glorious as the day gone by.

'Steady, steady!' Rib cried as Rika accelerated a little too
hard, narrowly missing an outcrop of rock to the right.

'Take it easy, don't go spare, Rib,' she laughed. 'This is as
easy as skinning a bear.'

They drove for half an hour before reaching a wide road
with a metal barrier down the middle. Rib's head hurt. Goat's
milk never left him with a hangover like this.

He looked across at her, her face set in a mask of con-
centrated determination as she wrestled with the controls.
The very idea of her driving *Venturer II* would have seemed
preposterous until today.

Today he felt differently about the world.

He was letting her drive his machine. He was letting her
fire off stupid puns on his name. He'd suffered Rib-eye,
Rib-tickler, Rib cage and now, spare Rib. But somehow it was
OK.

He had absolutely no memory of what had happened the
previous night. When he woke, she was in the final stages
of breaking camp, pausing only to bring over a breakfast of

meatballs and juice. He had declined, and she had shrugged before polishing it off herself.

All he knew was that it was different.

One of the occupational hazards of hanging out with the Deccaheads was lack of activity on the flick front. Every now and then, a flick would turn his eye – and Ruth certainly had – but it had never translated into anything more than an embarrassed smile and staying awake all night.

Venturer II veered left onto the highway, flanked by the towering rainforest. He wanted to ask about last night, but couldn't summon up the courage.

They drove on in silence.

26

Tally-Ho Blenkinsop was having the time of his life. Window wound down, right forearm resting on the sill, safe in the knowledge that he was protected from the sun's rays by a liberal application of factor 90 Ambre Solaire to his arm. Nowhere else, just his right arm. He always bought Ambre Solaire. He just loved their advertising jingles. 'Wo-oh-ho-ho-ho! Bodyform, Bodyform, for you!' he sang lustily at the top of his voice, something inside him telling him that it wasn't quite right …

But he didn't care. He was heading towards the Deep South on the old highway known as the M1, travelling at a steady 40 kph, the wagon's autopilot deftly steering a course between the potholes, fallen branches and other debris strewn across the motorway. On either side of the road, the rainforest towered, sometimes up to 40 metres to the tree-tops.

A flock of brightly coloured birds, parrots he thought they were, took off from the canopy at his noisy approach. He slowed down to take a better look at the rusty sign coming up. 'Keep two chevrons apart,' it said. Tally-Ho was having trouble with the road signs. Some of them didn't make any sense at all. What were chevrons? And why should they be kept apart? Were they a type of little super-monkey which had to be prevented from breeding at all costs, otherwise they would conquer the world? He scratched his head. He really couldn't fathom it out.

Only yesterday he'd come across another equally mysterious sign. It had said 'Beware. Hidden Dip.' This had greatly alarmed Blenkinsop, so much so that he pulled over to the side of the road and called his mother. It took her over half an hour to assure her son that he was not about to be attacked by a tub of taramasalata lurking in the undergrowth.

She had finally persuaded him that it was safe to continue his journey and off he went. Should he call her and check out the credentials of these chevrons? Can't be too careful. So many questions. Tally-Ho's brain started to hurt, so he switched on the surround sound and hit the random play button.

'Life in the fast lane,' sang the Eagles. 'Sure to make you lose your mind. Life in the fast …'

'Hey! That's me all right!' he laughed.

Life in the fast lane.

He overrode the autopilot and took the wheel, checked mirror, indicated right and moved smoothly into the outside lane. 'Life in the fast lane!' he bellowed.

Tally-Ho wasn't the only one bellowing. A specifically climactic aspect of life was being enacted in the fast lane, right in front of him. He slowed to a crawl, to take in the scene. An enormous bull-elephant, and oh my God, was it enormous, had mounted a lady elephant and was thundering into her so that the very ground shook. On the outside carriageway of the M1. Just north of the Kegworth turn-off. If he'd had a glass of water in his cup holder, it would have trembled like the one in *Jurassic Park*, when the *T. rex* came to get the kids. No, it was worse than that. The water would have spilled all over the edge. Thud, thud, thud, it went. Punctuated by a loud roar.

Tally-Ho sort of knew that rogue bull-elephants were dangerous. What he should also have sort of known was that a bull-elephant is likely to be less than amused if his first hump for four years is in any way in danger of being disturbed.

So Tally-Ho's decision to try and get a closer look was not the wisest move he'd ever made.

He slipped the chevvy into first, moved over to the middle lane and crawled up until he was level with the two elephants. The racket was deafening. All of it coming from the big male on top. The lady elephant seemed totally uninterested, wafting her trunk slowly between two identical tufts of grass growing out of the broken tarmac, clearly in two minds as to which she should pull out. The male meanwhile seemed increasingly frantic as he pounded away. He then caught sight of the grey chevvy out of the corner of his eye.

Now, Bluto, as he was called, had not seen a wagon before. To him, Tally-Ho's 6 x 6 looked a bit like a lady elephant. A petite elephant. Well, maybe more of a rhino. But who cares, he was desperate. Bloody typical though, thought Bluto, now slowing to a steadier rhythm. Not a sign of a screw for four years, and now two of them turn up at once. Just outside Kegworth, of all places.

Bluto came from a line of thousands of animals liberated by a loose network of animal rights activists at the time of the Watershed. The zoo authorities around the world had decreed that, at precisely 10 a.m. on the morning of the 22 January, all animals should be humanely destroyed to save them from a terrible death by drowning in the floods. A trifle unfair on the penguins, otters and polar bears, but the resolution had been passed, so that was that.

A brilliantly executed plan by the activists opened all cages, compounds and bat tunnels at precisely midnight. The operation was a resounding success with only a couple of minor exceptions. The chimps at Dudley Zoo staged a sit-in. 'There's no bloody way we're going anywhere until we've had our breakfast,' was the stance.

What had not been foreseen, however, was the effect that Clayton E Buzzard's retro-agent B313 was to have on the flora and fauna of Planet Earth. A by-product of the cooling retardant was an agent which, when brought into contact with fresh water, emitted a growth hormone. Any plant or animal which used a contaminated water source grew twice as rapidly and up to twice its normal size. (Man, of course largely escaped such alarming effects by being totally reliant on small plastic bottles of fakespa water which had been sold at extortionate prices for the previous twenty years.)

The net result being that most of England was now covered by dense rainforest and roamed by a wide variety of extremely large, non-native wild animals and plants.

Which was why the hard shoulder of the M1 at Kegworth was lined by cathedral fig, curtain fig and giant red cedar trees.

And why the surface of the outside lane southbound of the M1 at Kegworth was beginning to crumble under the massive weight of Bluto thrusting into his indifferent mate.

Bluto's dilemma was hornful. He had invested much energy on the seemingly unwilling cow beneath him and was loathe to dismount. I mean, it had been four years … A bird in the hand is worth two in the bush. But he wanted the two in the bush. And he was strangely attracted to the rhythmic throb of the 6 x 6's powerful V6 engine. Its sleek, smooth lines.

What was really catching his eye, however, was the red-oxide-coated exhaust pipe, bobbing ever so slightly in cadence with the engine. It was driving him wild. What should he do? This just wasn't fair.

Far away Biddy Blenkinsop was adjusting her spectacles for the umpteenth time. She nervously unfolded the piece of paper before her and read through her lines again. However many times she'd done it, she was never entirely at ease in delivering her speech at the Wigan Citidome Furriers Guild Annual Awards lunch. And today was no exception. A discreet nod from the Toastmaster and she was on.

She got to her feet.

'Pray, be silent for the Right Worshipful President of the Wigan Citidome Furriers Guild.'

A tinkle of polite applause. A spoon dropped onto a side plate. An uncontrolled fart from the far end of the table.

'Lady members, honorary guests, Privy Lord Magistrates, it gives me great pleasure to present tonight's awards for out-standing achievement towards the Guild's objectives. I have prepared a little audiovisual presentation to highlight the tremendous good works carried out by our winners.'

Another slight ripple of applause from the gathered ranks of octogenarians. 'Ooh, isn't she a one for all the latest tech-nology.' 'How does she do it, year after year?' 'Not another fucking PowerPoint, surely!'

The Toastmaster discreetly assisted Biddy to connect up her laptop to the screen. All systems go.

'Our first award goes to …' A *Hawaii-Five-O* ringtone filled the room. It was Biddy's *Hawaii-Five-O* ringtone.

Being in her eighty-ninth year, she was a little hard of hearing and her eyesight had seen better days. So she always used her laptop for calls, texts and vidicoms. What with all the nerviness about the speech, she had forgotten to turn it off.

'Hey, Mother, it's me Tony.'

'Hello, Tony, this isn't the best of times. Is it important?'

'Yes Mother. I'm on the motorway and I'm really wound up about something.'

'This isn't about hidden dips again, is it?'

Raised eyebrows and a couple of giggles around the table.

'No, Mother, this is serious.' Tony Tally-Ho Blenkinsop then pressed 'send' from his webcam.

Pointed at Bluto and Partner.

The business end.

From a distance of five metres.

Tally-Ho knew little about women and absolutely nothing

203

about sex. It was all a mystery to him. He had only one place to go for an explanation.

'Mother, what are they doing?'

Biddy took in the images on her laptop nearly swooned. She pressed to delete.

Missed it by a mile.

And transported the live connection directly onto the big screen …

5 metres wide.

Which was just as well because Bluto had reached a policy decision. He was clearly getting nowhere with frigid Brigid, so he started to carefully disengage from her.

Ready to couple with the perky little new animal purring by his side.

Tally-Ho was proud how he zoomed in to capture this disengagement of Bluto from his partner.

Inch by inch.

Foot by foot.

The Toastmaster moved to turn off the screen. He received a sharp crack on the shinbone from Rose Zeilwegger's walking cane.

'Leave it or I'll break your fucking leg!' she snarled.

The room fell silent save for the occasional clatter of dentures falling onto dessert plates.

Bluto finally managed to extricate himself and started to move towards the camera.

'Get out of there!' screamed Biddy at her son, who duly obliged. He left the camera running as he hit the accelerator. So there followed a series of jerky shots of the sky, a raging bull elephant rearing up on its hind legs, and a pool of liquid of a pale straw colour sloshing around the footwell of the wagon.

Everyone present agreed that it was the best awards evening ever in the long history of the Furriers Guild. Biddy had sold forty-two copies of the film by noon the following day.

As befits someone with the memory span of a gnat, Tally-Ho soon recovered from the Narrow Escape at Kegworth and continued on his journey south. By his very rough-and-ready reckoning, he should reach a place called Lutterworth by lunchtime. Lutterworth at lunchtime, he savoured. His mind drifted to the prospect of a sumptuous feast al fresco. After all, that was what Dead or Alive was all about for him. He'd long lost the scent of the prey on the scanner, which was a blessing. The last thing he wanted was to be caught up in any violence. His mother had mistakenly bought him an annual subscription as a birthday present in the hope that it would 'get him out a little more'.

Well, he sure was getting out now. For the past few weeks he'd poodled around the highways and byways of the country with no real idea of where he was going or why he was going there. The one constant of each day being ... luncheon.

Being born and bred on the Wigan citidome, Tally-Ho was enchanted by the names of former settlements which unfurled before him – Zouch, Merry Lees, Newton Unthank – conjuring up images of jolly yeomen quaffing tankards of foaming ale by a village cricket green.

Blenkinsop grew in confidence. Even the road signs seemed less threatening. A slight relapse at the stern warning 'Tiredness Kills' soon remedied by a pinch on his fleshy arm and a couple of slaps around the cheeks. He didn't know tiredness killed. How come Mother hadn't told him that? In fact, how come she'd spent so much time trying to rock him to sleep when he was a baby? Mmmm ...

Junction 20 sailed by on his left. 'Whoa!' Tally-Ho screamed as he switched to manual, shifted into reverse and bumped his way back to the exit slip road. Having checked his rear-view mirror, of course. It didn't take him long to find the perfect place to pitch camp. A thinly-wooded clearing with good, all round visibility. He got out of the cabin, stretched his arms in the air and belched. Feeling a lot better for that, he walked round to the other side of the wagon.

Biddy Blenkinsop had spared no expense in buying for her son a fully automated customised camperwagon. It had to be fully automated because he couldn't do anything for himself. So when Tally-Ho pressed the 'camp' button, the side of the wagon opened and a full-sized awning unfolded. Down dropped a teak table and two chairs, down fluttered a check-patterned tablecloth.

Tally-Ho rummaged in the glove compartment and produced his bible, his favourite book. In fact, it was his only book, entitled *Groovy Cocktails: Shake It, Daddio!*

He knew it from cover to cover. If he'd read it once he'd read it a thousand times.

He'd quickly graduated from the classic Singapore Sling and Harvey Wallbanger to the more adventurous Sidecar through to the lethal Zombie. Now what would he have today?

He had to come back to his old faithful, a Bazooka Joe Shooter. He placed his order at the Robobar by barking an instruction into the funnel at the top.

'Two Bazooka Joe Shooters, please.'

He watched as a shot glass came into view on the Robobar's carousel. First blue curaçao then crème de banane poured into the glass. A spoon then appeared and the Irish cream liqueur flowed smoothly over it to form a perfect float on the top. And then, this was the best bit. It never ceased to thrill and amaze him. The yellow crème de banane sunk slowly to the bottom and mixed with the curaçao to create a luminous green layer beneath the Irish cream. Wow! How funky is that? He took a sip of the cocktail, smacked his lips in appreciation while the second was being poured, making sure he caught the yellow-to-green bit again.

He then climbed into the bedroom at the back of the wagon to change for lunch. Whoops? That reminded him, he hadn't even ordered his lunch yet. He called up the menu on the Robochef screen and decided on the following: Starters – tuna fish steaks on bitter red-wine onions; Main course – roast turkey ballotine with a ham and Armagnac stuffing, and to finish – a Morrisons supasava low-fat chocolate mousse. Have to watch those calories. Tally-Ho then slowly and deliberately articulated every vowel and syllable of his order into the Robochef funnel. He still recalled the time he'd had a few too many scoops before placing a dessert order for a 'fresh fruits-of-the-forest tart' and put in one too many fs, with disastrous consequences, he remembered as he got changed in the bedroom. When he reappeared some ten minutes later, fully togged up in his finest fox-hunting gear, he carefully laid the table for two. He then took the second Bazooka Joe Shooter, at the same time asking Robobar to uncork the Châteauneuf-du-Pape.

'Aren't you going to have your cocktail, Martin?' he asked. Martin did not reply.

Because he couldn't.

For Martin was his imaginary friend.

'I'd better have it then, before it gets too warm,' said Tally-Ho taking it over to the table. He loved these moments, when they could share the events of the day over a drink.

'I don't mind saying, there was a time there when it was getting a bit scary. That elephant, oh my God, he was enormous! But you, calm port in a storm and all that, you're always the quiet one …'

His mother had long since stopped worrying about her son's friend. At first, when she heard him talking to himself in his bedroom or in the bathroom, she thought he'd signed up for drama class and was rehearsing his lines. If only. And anyway, it was something kids grew out of … But when Martin was the only invitee to Tony's fiftieth birthday party, she reconciled herself to the reality that this particular kid was not going to grow out of it. But whatever. It was harmless. As long as he was happy.

And Tony Tally-Ho Blenkinsop was happy. He stood by Martin's side, looked up at the clear blue cloudless sky above the trees, felt the whisper of a soft warm breeze against his cheek and sighed. 'If the good Lord were to take me now, Martin, I'd die a happy man!'

He poured the wine.

It was 1.35 p.m. Temperature 34.7 degrees. Wind speed 1.3 kph.

27

Venturer II reached the highway known as the M1 just before noon. 'OK, now I know where we are,' said Rika, accelerating left onto the road.

'You mean you didn't know before?' asked Rib.

'Well, sort of,' she shrugged.

'Wow,' he said, looking at the towering guard of giant trees standing to attention either side of the highway as far as the eye could see.

They'll soon be touching, he said to himself. How many years or even months would it take before the road became a tunnel, darker and darker by the day?

A flock of brightly coloured birds, which he now easily recognised as parakeets, took off from the rainforest canopy at *Venturer II*'s noisy approach.

Rika skilfully steered a careful course between potholes and fallen branches. Tarmac erupted in still life where tree roots had broken through. They drove for an hour until she pulled to the hard shoulder.

'What's up. Why are we stopping?'

She didn't answer, but turned off the motor, pressed door release and climbed out of the cabin. Rib watched her walk over to the outside lane, kneel down and examine something on the road surface. Whatever it was, she poked at it, raised a finger to her nose, pulled a face and wiped her finger on the back of her pants. He jumped out onto the highway and walked over to her.

'What is it?'

'What's grey and comes in buckets?' she answered without looking round.

'I don't know, what is grey and comes in buckets?'

'An elephant.'

'Ha bloody ha. Now are you going to tell me what is attracting your attention so.'

'Elephant semen.'

'What!'

'Look, a whole pile of it. Still steaming. Not so long ago, an elephant has shot his bolt right here in the fast lane of the M1.' She turned to look at Rib.

'Now why would he want to do that?'

Rib searched for an answer. It was certainly a good question. Better than 'Why did the chicken cross the road?' Why did the elephant ejaculate in the outside lane of the motorway? Because he fancied a fast fuck, he thought. He kept it to himself …

'Erm, erm,' he wavered. He gazed into the semi-distance in mock concentration. His eyes locked on to the solution. White letters on blue background.

'Kegworth,' he asserted.

'Kegworth? What do you mean, Kegworth?'

'I'm trying to change the subject.'

She stood up, walked over to him and smacked him on the arse.

'Ow!' he said, half in pain, half in pleasure, without really knowing which. 'Why did you do that?'

'Because you deserved it!' she laughed.

Was it the pain I deserved or the pleasure? he asked himself, rubbing his rump.

'African or Indian elephant?' he asked as he joined her back in the cabin.

Inexplicably, she went into a sulk, forced a reluctant *Venturer II* into gear, put her foot down and hunched over the gear stick, her body language screaming out against him.

He thought better of enquiring further, instead staring vacantly at the wall of the rainforest rushing past. He thought of Kaddie, he thought of the twenty walnuts and their contents – he instinctively reached down to touch his bag on the cabin floor between his feet. He thought of Ruth massaging the back of his neck as he lay on a white plastic recliner in the spa. He drifted into a deep sleep.

Rika glanced at him and snorted.

African or Indian! How the hell should she know the difference just from an ejaculation? What kind of girl did he think she was? She calmed down as the names of former settlements unfurled before her – Zouch, Merry Lees, Newton Unthank – conjuring up images of jolly yeomen quaffing tankards of foaming ale by a village cricket green.

They were approaching a large motorway sign. At about 70 metres, Rika could pick out the wording. Junction 20. Time to eat, her stomach told her. There was no real reason to pull off. They had not met a soul all morning. But something told her that their bright-yellow craft should best stay hidden from view. They didn't want any unwelcome attention at this stage. As *Venturer II* climbed the slip road, Rib awoke with a start.

'Have I been asleep?' he asked.

'Either that or you had another reason for closing your eyes for half an hour and dribbling from the side of your mouth.'

'Oh, sorry,' he said, wiping his mouth with his sleeve. 'Where are we?'

'Junction 20. I thought we'd stop off for a bite to eat.'

'Sounds good,' he said, relieved that her mood seemed to have lightened. She followed a side road that had narrowed to little more than a vehicle's width with the irresistible onset of the rainforest. She saw a gap in the undergrowth to the left, brought *Venturer II* to a halt and turned off the motor.

'I'll just go and find some water,' she said as she reached

211

behind the seat for a billycan.

'I'll come with you,' Rib said as he climbed out of his side of the cabin, careful to take his bag with him.

As he walked a few paces behind her, it surprised him how spacious and open the forest was. The paths were often bordered by a mass of vines and trees that created the impression of an impenetrable jungle, but the cavernous understorey behind was quite easy to walk through.

He looked up at the climbing plants hanging like tangled ropes, knotting the treetops together. Vines creeping up the trunks and over shrubs. Orchids, ferns and mosses sprouting from the branches.

He paused a second to marvel at the columns of strangler figs which had grown downwards to envelop and suffocate their hosts in a lattice of aerial roots. They looked like something out of a bakery shop window. He thought back to the dense stands of proud conifers at Middlemedes and wondered how long they could hold out.

All of a sudden the figure before him stopped dead and half stumbled into a crouch.

'Get down,' she hissed.

Rib nearly fell on top of her.

'What's up?' he started to say, and then took in the scene before them.

They had come to clearing where there stood a cruiser-wagon with a sort of awning coming out from its side. Beneath the chequered awning was a fully laid table, the sun's rays reflecting off the cutlery. Two large wine glasses stood untouched at the side of two empty plates. Beside the table lay the figure of a man.

They stayed motionless for some twenty seconds surveying the scene before Rika crept out into the clearing. Rib followed. Rika went over to the man on the ground and knelt beside him.

'He's dead.'

'Dead?' cried Rib. 'Jesus Christ, how?'

'He's been shot,' she replied in a matter-of-fact voice.

'Shot! Jesus Christ!'

She stood up and walked over to the Robochef.

'Mmm, smells good. This will save us a job. Smells very good indeed.'

'Are you joking!' Rib screamed. 'There's a bloody corpse here and you're thinking about food!' He went to walk over to the body but caught sight of the wound in the back of the man's head and thought better of it.

Rika took the bottle of red wine from the table and examined the label.

'Châteauneuf-du-Pape. Mmm, classy ...' She then stifled a cry. 'Oh no! Oh my God, run, Rib, run!!'

'What's up?' he called as she sprinted away from the wagon.

'Run, for God's sake! Run!' she screamed as she tore over the forest floor like a tornado, hurdling logs and crashing through bushes. Rib followed, casting anxious looks over his shoulder. She reached *Venturer II* some 30 metres ahead of him and had already started the motor before he got to the passenger door. The machine reared unsteadily into life as he climbed through the door.

'Whoa! Easy! Are you going to tell me what's up?'

'We've got to get as far away from this place as possible,' she snarled as she smashed the side of the hull against a tree in her haste to get back onto the slip road.

She was shaking. Rib had never seen her like this. Always brash, ever in your face. But now she was scared. Really scared. He decided to let her concentrate on her driving.

After they'd passed Junction 18, he ventured contact. 'Now are you going to tell me what happened back there?'

'We're in trouble.'

'Why? I know it was terrible. That man lying there dead ...'

'No, you don't understand. The wine. The glasses of red wine.'

'Now you've lost me again.'

'The wine was clear. Don't you get it?' she screamed at him. 'Leave any drink with sugar in it standing out in a rainforest for more than a minute and what do you get?'

Rib's continued blank expression only served to heighten her level of exasperation.

'Midges, flies, mozzies, insects. Dozens of them.'

The fog in Rib's brain started to clear. 'So the fact that there weren't any insects in the wine …'

'Meant that it had just been poured.'

'And dead men don't pour wine …'

'Well done. Dead men don't pour wine. Indeed they do not.'

'Then the man lying on the ground must have been killed just before we came across him.'

'Less than sixty seconds before, I would say.'

Rib paused. Logic was sometimes a struggle. 'Which means that the man's killer was probably still there watching us …'

'Yes, which was why we had to get out of there.'

'Shit.'

'Deep pile shit.'

And the worse thing was, she had a pretty good idea who the killer was.

'Deep pile shit,' she whispered to herself as *Venturer II* scissored her way south.

28

The further south they travelled, the more difficult the terrain became. In places, the forest had joined together to close the highway completely. In others, the road was flooded and *Venturer II* could only make slow progress by extending its scissor legs to their full height.

All the way, Rika steered the craft with a grim determination, unwilling to engage in conversation. The more he tried to talk to her about the scene they had left behind them, the more tense and subdued she became.

'Listen, for once and for all, I'm telling you that we're in great danger. Now stop asking me stupid questions!'

Some thirty minutes later the road plunged down what was once a hill. Now it was a lake, a deep one.

'OK, this is as far as we go,' said Rika as she turned off the motor.

'What do you mean, as far as we go? I'm going to MK. I haven't gone through everything I've gone through to turn back now.'

'No, you don't get me. What I mean is that this piece of yellow scrap metal can't take us any further. I can paddle it for a couple of hundred metres, but no more. Look at the road ahead!'

'Can't we head cross-country? There's got to be higher ground. A ridge, maybe?'

'Yep, I'm sure there is. And where would you hang out if you were a cut-throat low-life waiting for some passing travellers to molest?'

'On the ridge?' Rib thought for a moment. 'If you can just pull us over, onto a flattish piece of ground, then I may be able to make some changes to the motor.'

She look at him quizzically but, for once, did as she was asked. She manoeuvred the craft gently through the undergrowth so as not to leave a trail.

'What exactly do you have in mind?' she asked as *Venturer II* lowered to standstill.

'Well, I think I could make her go amphibian with a bit of luck. Yeah, across water and then on land again. Amphibian …'

'How long would it take you? Enough time for me to cook some coffee? Set up camp, maybe?'

'Sure, I'd need a good couple of hours, at least.'

They both set about their business in silence. The smell of red meat, onions and something else wafted over to Rib as he knelt intently over the power unit. She had clearly finished her task well ahead of schedule, and it smelt good. She walked over to him.

'How's it going?'

'OK, I think I can do it, but I'm not quite there yet.'

'Look, while I'm waiting I'll get some washing on.'

'Are you sure we shouldn't be pressing on? Not so long ago you were saying we were in serious danger.'

'Er, I think we're probably all right now. Maybe I'm paranoid. The existence of the sea means the existence of pirates,' she added meaningfully.

'Yeah, right' was all Rib could muster.

'I'm going to chuck a few clothes in the creek and give them a rinse. I seem to recall that my red knicks need doing again.'

Rib buried his head further into the bowels of the *Venturer II* to avoid eye contact. 'Can I wash any of your stuff? I'll get it from your bag, shall I?' she asked as she reached into the cabin.

'Whoa! I mean thanks, let me get it for you,' said Rib,

jumping up and pushing past her. He grabbed his bag from behind the seat and produced three screwed-up T-shirts.

'Here … er, thanks,' he said.

'My pleasure,' she smiled, taking them. 'You must have something very precious in the bottom of that little bag of yours,' she said as she turned away.

Rib chose not to respond, returning to the re-assembly of the drive unit, having satisfied himself that the twenty nuts were still safely occupying the bottom of the bag. It wasn't that he didn't trust her; there was just something holding him back from telling her about the coins.

Forty minutes later and the world seemed a good place. He had successfully converted his trusty machine and they were both wiping the last morsels of a very tasty stew indeed from their plates. The light was fading fast and sparks shot up from the fire's embers at their feet. They both stared into the depth of the fire, entranced by its ever-changing face and form.

'Nutter,' she said. 'Why do all your T-shirts have "Nutter" written on the front?'

Rib looked over at his shirts hanging from a line stretched between two bushes and laughed.

'Oh, it's my nickname. It means "idiot", "lunatic", "madman".'

'Idiot, yes, lunatic, maybe, madman, no,' was her verdict.

'That's very kind of you. Thank you. I'll take that as a compliment.'

'There must be more to it than that,' she said.

'Well, there is actually,' he paused, 'but it's a bit silly really.'

'Go on,' she urged, her eyes locking with his.

'Promise you won't take the piddle …'

'Promise.'

'Well, OK then. It all began when I was little. We all used to go round my Uncle Fred's and Auntie Ethel's on Boxing

Day. They were great traditionalists and followed all the Christmas protocols to the letter. Roast turkey, Christmas pudding, dates and ... nuts'

'Nuts?'

'Yeah, normally a whole net of mixed nuts which Uncle Fred, as head of the household, would ceremoniously crack open for each of this guests. Whether they wanted them or not. And each year, as he grew older and his strength waned, he would strain at the nutcracker as if he was about to blow a gasket. He'd start to go blue in the face, his hand would tremble and shake, either until he gave the nut up as a bad job, or it exploded in his palm.'

Rika laughed.

'But the worst was, he somehow had got it into his head that I liked walnuts. So every time he crushed a walnut into smithereens, he gave it to me.'

'"There you go, Rib me lad, cracked to perfection." Cracked to buggery. So as not to offend, I had to somehow separate out the flesh of the nut from the shell inside my mouth before he gave me another one.'

'All very interesting, but surely he was the nutter, not you.'

'Ah well, I became somewhat obsessive about nuts, particularly walnuts.'

'Obsessive?'

'Yeah, I practised cracking nuts for hours on end in my room.'

'I bet your mum had fun cleaning the carpet.'

'No, that was the point. I took cracking nuts to an art form. Perfect, clean crack every time. No crushed or splintered flesh. Each nut perfectly whole and sound. And all without nutcrackers.'

'Without nutcrackers? I don't get it. How did you crack them?'

'Between finger and thumb.'

'I don't believe you.'

'But it's true. It comes with practice. Just the right amount of pressure in the right place across the seam. And out she comes, sweet as a nut.'

She looked at him, still not sure she believed what he was telling her.

'And that is why people called me "The Nutter". Now I wouldn't make that up, would I?'

'No, I suppose not.'

Her smile was cut short by a cracking sound in the forest. Like someone stepping on a branch.

'Hush,' she said. 'Come on, we're moving!' She gathered up the pots and plates and set off in a crouched run towards *Venturer II*. 'You grab the clothes,' she hissed. 'Quick!!'

When he climbed into the cabin, he budged her over from the driver's position. He cut her short when she started to protest.

'Listen, I've fixed her, so I'm driving her to start with.'

He edged *Venturer II* back on to the highway, took her down to the first expanse of water standing before them, waded the vehicle in, retracted the legs and engaged the new jet-flow drive. Nothing happened and *Venturer II* gently bobbed round until it faced the way they came.

They both looked at each other. A gurgling, whirring sound came from the back of the cabin and before Rib could react *Venturer II* roared, reared up and skidded like a skimmingdish across the surface of the water to come to a grinding crash onto the tarmacadam of the M1.

'Shit!' they both screamed in unison before they hit the screen. The motor stalled.

'Bit on the lively side!' Rib laughed. 'Are you all right?'

'Yes, no thanks to you. Move over, I'm driving.'

'Let me just check for any damage first,' said Rib as he opened the door. Luckily, the only bruising was to his ego and *Venturer II* took like a frog to water under Rika's skilful steer. He had to admit, she was a lot better at driving than he was. What was it that made Finns such good drivers?

He took the wheel an hour later when she complained of feeling tired. He had driven no more than a couple of hundred metres when he felt her head on his left shoulder. He looked down at her face. Her eyes were closed and she looked drained.

'What's this place we're heading for?' she said softly, keeping her eyes closed.

'MK. My home.'

'MK. Strange name. How come?'

'It stands for Milton Keynes.'

'Milton Keynes? How do you spell that?'

'M-I-L-T-O-N K-E-Y-N-E-S.'

The cabin went silent apart from the click of the legs or the whirr of the jet. The headlight fanned a bright beam on the road ahead. The whole thing was surreal, like a French art-house black-and-white film, thought Rib.

'Listen, monkey,' she said.

'God, you made me jump. I thought you were asleep. What do you want?'

'No,' she murmured, scarcely audible, her eyes still closed. 'Listen, Monkey. Throw Milton Keynes high into the sky and see how the letters fall back to earth. Listen, Monkey ...'

Rib laughed. That can't be right. He checked and it was right. Listen, Monkey. A perfect anagram.

Her deep breathing against his shoulder told him that she now really was asleep.

He felt so close to her. And yet what was making him uneasy?

They had pushed on that night to put as much distance as they could between them and the scene of carnage in the clearing. When Rika woke in the cabin, she was stiff of limb and dry in the mouth. Rib was hunched over the joystick staring hollow-eyed at the beam on the road ahead. Her yawn startled him.

'I thought you'd sleep right through,' he said. And talk about snore! And what was all that whimpering and yelping about? You were like a little puppy having a nightmare!'

'More like a big bitch. But you're right about the dream. It was weird. Now scissor down, big boy. I want a widdle.'

Rib duly obliged and *Venturer II* saxed to a faltering halt at the side of the road. She jumped out, ran round the back of the machine and squatted. Steam rose from the still hot tarmac. In clouds.

'By Friggja, that's better, I needed …' She cut short as she climbed back into the cabin. He was fast asleep, his head resting at an awkward angle on the back of the bench. She grabbed a blanket from behind the seat, folded it and gently lifted his head to allow her to slide it under his cheek.

She looked at him and smiled, noting the strong muscle definition of his forearm. With the back of her hand, she lightly brushed the blond hairs on his arm against the grain, so that they stood up in tousled disarray. She then smoothed them back flat and they lay to rest in perfect lines. She repeated the process three times over and thought to herself, Another time, another place …

A bubble of dribble started to form from the corner of his mouth. She watched with fascination as a mini-glacier of saliva started to slide down his chin, the proud little bubble of spit forming a terminal moraine at the end.

The bubble burst.

She scratched her nose and heaved a sigh. The moment had gone. She looked at her watch. It was 23.11. She felt refreshed from her sleep and decided to drive on. Too late to set up camp and no sense in waking him. If only she could cough the yellow monster into life as quietly as possible. Which, of course, she did with consummate ease. As she gently guided *Venturer II* between and over fallen branches and other debris strewn across the motorway, she tried to analyse the dream she had had earlier.

29

Rika Latukartta always remembered her dreams.

Vividly.

Without fail.

Which was sometimes very good.

And sometimes very bad …

This one was neither, merely weird.

It took place in a different time zone. Before 2007 she somehow sensed. She stood in a galley which, by her standards, was super-spacious. You could have held a small party in it. The appliances were all white, one of them noisily whirring away. It was a Bosch Exxcel dishwasher and it showed nineteen minutes remaining of the Eco Cycle. (Huh! Fat use that turned out to be!) The kitchen units were a bluey-green colour with fake grain fronts. She stood before a double sink, washing some drinking glasses in a bowl full of suds. She finished rinsing the glasses and left them to dry on the draining board. She dried her hands on a red-and-white checked towel folded over a radiator. Against the back wall of the galley stood a table with a set of open shelving standing on it. Cream and brown. It was filled with glasses, special ones collected from holidays past – Orlando, Dublin, Tokyo …

Places which no longer existed.

There were also books stacked in the bottom left corner of the shelving. Cook books. *Linda's Kitchen*. Falling to bits from overuse. *Delia Smith's Winter Collection*. Good at Christmas. And extremely useful as a bookend.

Rika wore faded-blue trousers in thick material, a plain white T-shirt and a pair of white clogs.

Clogs! Much to her surprise, she could actually walk in them.

Something caught her eye through the galley window. It was Rib, walking across a grassed area carrying what looked like a small table. Her gaze absorbed the scene outside for a moment. She saw a fenced area, with plants and shrubs, washing line with bright-coloured pegs on it but no washing, and their British blue cat, Lilla, drinking filthy water out of a brown plastic flowerpot tray.

(Their cat? Him and her? Rika and Rib? Their cat?)

It was only a dream, she told herself as she furrowed back further.

They were living in a house. A brick house surrounded by dozens of other brick houses. All with red-tiled roofs. All the same, yet different. Different trees growing in their areas, different antennae. Some round, stuck on the side of the house. Some tubular attached to the roof.

Rib came into the galley via a smaller side chamber which had a wooden door opening out onto the fenced area. He was sweating profusely.

'What are you doing?' she asked as he struggled in with the table.

He did not answer but walked into the dining room. Rika followed him through the galley and into the living room at the front of the house.

There she found her Mamma and Pappa sitting on a long grey sofa in the window recess. They were watching a television programme where actors who couldn't sing were being judged by no-marks who couldn't judge. A lovely big cuddly orange-and-white cat named Raj lay curled up between them, seemingly at total peace, love and cosmic karma with the world apart from one ear keenly pricked to take in the slightest change in the environment. If an air hostess had passed wind on the Ryanair flight from Stansted to Dublin some three thousand feet above their heads, Raj would have picked it up. And enjoyed ...

Rib carefully stacked the wooden table on top of a pile of other furniture in the middle of the room. Four white plastic chairs, a three-seater bench and a wicker chest of drawers. Against the far wall of the room were propped a fusty rolled-up carpet, a furled parasol and a pair of skis.

'What the hell are you doing?' Rika hissed as she followed Rib back out to the galley. He showed no sign of answering until she grabbed him by the shoulder and turned him round to face him.

'It's all right, I'm just emptying the summerhouse.'

'I can bloody see that!' she snapped.

(Bloody? That's not a word she used.)

'*Why* are you emptying the summerhouse?'

'I've got to clear it out so that I can get at the snake.' And with that, he went out onto the grassed area again. She saw him enter the small blue-painted wooden building and close the door behind him.

What did he mean, the snake? What snake? She'd never seen a snake near the house before. They'd once seen a grass snake in the park when they were on the way back from feeding the swans. Maybe one had hibernated behind the stove.

She shrugged and went back into the living room to join her parents.

A half-hour later, Rib reappeared in the hall, where he stood flushed of face and shifting uneasily from one foot to the other.

'Honey,' he said.

(Honey?)

'Fancy going for a drink?'

Rika turned to her Mamma and Pappa. 'Is it OK if we go out for a quick drink? Won't be long. Is there anything you need from Morrisons?'

(Why was she speaking to them in English? They couldn't understand a word.)

They smiled their consent.

'Don't bleedin' bother to ask me,' scowled the big ginger cat Raj. 'And I wouldn't mind some Duck and Turkey Kit-e-Kat for a change instead of that dried crap you get by the sackful from the vet's.'

On the television screen, a chubby judge of indeterminate gender tried to look serious as he told a soap star, in a tight purple miniskirt and white boots, that it wasn't her best song but she had persona and presence, and he hoped she would be there tomorrow because she was a winner.

Rika shouted goodbye as she hustled Rib out of the front door to the car. It wasn't until they had pulled out from Langerstone on to Tattenhoe Street that she spoke.

'Did you get it?'

'Yeah.' He winced as he spoke.

'Are you OK?' she asked.

'Yeah, sort of. I think I might have been bitten!' He felt his chest gingerly.

'Bitten? I didn't think grass snakes could bite.'

He didn't answer. They turned left at the roundabout, took the first right and then two lefts into the pub car park. It seemed quite empty, save the obligatory two white vans parked in the disabled spaces.

As he climbed out of the car, Rika heard him gasp.

'Are you sure you're OK?' she asked.

'Yeah, I'm fine. Nothing that a beer won't cure.'

They walked through the doors of the Nut & Squirrel, their local. No queue at the bar, so Rib strode over and ordered the usual large glass of Long Shadow red and a pint of Deuchars while Rika went through to the non-smoking lounge to grab a table. (The smell of smoke. The non-smoking lounge. That's how she'd known the dream was set sometime before 2007. That was when the ban on smoking in public places was introduced in England, wasn't it?)

She sat down on the mock-leather sofa in the alcove at the far right end of the lounge. He soon joined her. She noticed that his glass was already half empty. That was unusual. Ever since they'd been together, the procedure was a clink of the glass and a 'Cheers!' before the first sip was taken.

'Are you sure you're OK?' she asked again.

'Well, not really. I think it bit me. Here.' He pointed to his chest and then, calm as you like, pulled up his T-shirt to reveal not the expected pin-point punctures of a small snake but the hand's-width rip of a larger maw. She could clearly see where the fangs had sunken into his flesh, leaving trails of blood-mixed venom down his torso.

She screamed.

That was when she had woken up.

30

They drove on the next day for a good 50 kilometres without incident. Dead on noon they both agreed without argument that it was high time for something to eat and drink. They pulled off the main highway and covered their bright-yellow craft, now wearing the battle wounds of two days' hard travel, with giant fronds tied down with creepers. Rika started to set camp under the shade of a cathedral palm, just by the road so that they had a good vantage point both up and down the road.

'Sshh,' she said suddenly.

'What is it?'

She knelt down and put her ear to the ground. 'Someone's coming. A lot of them. Quick, get under cover.'

They sprinted back into the undergrowth and lay flat against the earth behind a fallen branch of a fig palm. As he pressed his cheek against the moist peat, Rib remembered how he had been here before. On the track to the Slingshot Inn, when he had heard the cruiser coming. How long ago was that? Three, four months? A wave of guilt washed over him as he thought of his mum, and what she must be going through. He had 200 million dollars in his bag, but they were of absolutely no use to her down here on the floor of the rainforest.

He could now hear the noise of tramping, or was it the vibration coming up through the twiggy leaf mould to his cheek.

It was both.

'Don't look,' she whispered.

But he did. He couldn't help it. He lay watching through a gap in the fronds shielding the log.

A whole army marched past. Some two, three hundred strong. Leather boots strapped on with thongs or belts. Bearded men, their scorched faces almost blackened with sunburn, eyes fixed on the road ahead. Tramping in step, causing the earth to shudder against Rib's body. His body suddenly soaked in sweat. Pouring from every pore. He was terrified.

They wore a uniform. It was a deep-red bandana tied around the head with the knot over the right ear. No more, no less.

They wore a common strip of coloured cloth. They also carried to a man a metre's length of pipe with a daub of paint halfway up, again deep red. Was it paint or dried blood? The pipes were threaded with chains which had every imaginable instrument of violence and pain attached to the other end. A sphere of razor wire, an orb of rusting nails.

They clanked and rattled past, like the army of Uruk-hai on the move towards Helm's Deep. Although this was far more frightening. Their fixed stares of silence turned Rib's blood to ice. These were not celluloid monsters. These were for real.

They were followed by a train of carts, and boats on wheels, piled with plunder, dragged along by emaciated boys with whip-cracked backs. And finally, three carts with cages with women inside. Some with child. All naked,

The tramping eased into the distance, the earth against Rib's cheek became still again. He made to raise himself.

'Stay where you are,' Rika hissed as she pressed down firmly on his left shoulder blade. 'There may be a rear guard.'

Minutes passed, stretching into some sixteen before she gave the all clear.

'Come on,' she urged. 'Back to the craft.' They found

228

Venturer II as they had left her, removed the camouflage and climbed in. Rib made as to start the motor.

'What are you doing?' she said, grabbing his wrist.

'Getting as far away from here as possible. Did you see them? What the hell were they anyway?'

'You don't want to know,' she said and looked away.

'But did you see those boys? And those women? What the hell had they been through? Who were those men?'

She paused before saying, 'They call themselves the Slakterghast.'

They sat in silence, he asking a thousand unspoken questions, she answering not a single one. He wanted to ask her how she knew of them. Maybe later ...

She snapped into decisive mode. 'We can't take the M1 highway. They'll be camped a few K to the south and they'll take anything on the road.'

'But we've got to take the M1, haven't we? MK is on the M1, isn't it?'

'Yes it is but we can't go there now.'

Rib grabbed her arm. 'Listen, you don't seem to understand. I have to get there, Slakterghast or not!'

She removed his hand firmly from her wrist.

He emitted an unmanly little yelp as she bent his forefinger back.

'Ow, that really hurt!'

She laughed. 'You sound like a little husky puppy who is being harnessed for the first time and who gets a welcoming nip from the wheel-dogs.'

'So is that what you are? A wheel-dog?'

She ignored his question.

'They are the two dogs at the back of a harness of huskies. They are the strongest and normally oldest and wisest.'

'Back to the point. Can't we just break though them? Surely they won't be actually camped in the middle of the highway?'

'No!' was her blunt answer. 'Listen to me. I'm deadly serious here. If they take you, they will break you, rape you, slice you, cook you, then eat you. And if they take me, even worse!'

He tried to think of what could be worse, reached his own conclusion and kept quiet on the matter.

'So,' she continued. 'We'll wait until dark, head back north, then make a detour.'

They waited an hour, then headed back to the highway, took a northerly course for some 20K, then steered west into deep forest. Rika seemed to know where she was going, negotiating *Venturer II* down hardly visible trails and tracks. Every now and then they had to get out to remove a fallen branch from their way. Otherwise, their progress was steady and without incident.

No sign of pursuit.

Rib reckoned the detour must have put at least two days on the journey. The thought of falling into the hands of the lawless mob stopped him, however, from raising the matter. She let him take over the driving when they finally reached another highway. Not as wide as the M1 but quite big nonetheless.

'Turn left,' she said.

'Does this go to MK?' he asked.

'Yes, sure does. It used to be a Roman road. Just keep on going straight and it'll take us right there.'

Two hours on and they slowed to negotiate a pile of rubble which she called Toaster.

'Not far now,' she said. 'Let me take over. Why don't you take a nap? You'll want to be bright-eyed and bushy-tailed for the homecoming!'

He smiled.

It sounded nice.

Maybe he would just close his eyes for a minute or two.

31

The zipflash of lasercraft sparking across the sky told her that they were almost there. With the first grey light she saw the triple mass of MK citidome towering above the trees ahead.

The sun's rays grew in strength as they glinted sharply off the cobalt blue. She shook him gently by the arm and said we're there. He awoke and she sensed at once his excitement. He spoke long and deep of MK, pleased to be home. She yearned to share his happiness but could not think of anything to say. All she felt was a dullness, a numbness. She had been here before. What she knew was going to happen ground her heart to dust. It started to rain. Big drops splashed on the windscreen, the recent new dawn returned to blackness. It was very hot. The squall became a storm and they lost sight of the citidome. She stopped and switched off the motor. The rain beat on the roof. They sat in silence waiting for it to pass over, no word between them. The rain stopped and they moved on. They circled the city to find a way in.

They drove left at a roundabout, the city now towering above them to the front and right. The closer they came to MK, the more sparse the trees became. The rainforest ceded to the shadow of the Dome. They skirted along straight streets, passing a petrol station, long since burned out. The pumps were empty. The road was empty. *She* was empty. They crossed a lake by an old bridge which had once carried a four-lane carriageway. Now only a thin strip of tarmac, just strong enough to hold a car weight. They set startled herons into flight, creaking clumsily as they gained height. To her right she saw a temple and wondered how could that be? She studied it, saw its purity and moved on. She did not want to deal with it. The straight lines of old roads between the fallen trees and buildings took them to the edge of the rainforest. It turned into a half-light territory where limbless trees stood surrounded by uncertain undergrowth.

The green gave way to a grey underworld without sound, without life, without belief.

Everything greying away into the murky distance. A plastic bag swaying thinly in the wind, crucified for ever on a crossroad sign.

Trees turning to rows of black rotting stumps.

It was once said to have been a city made out of concrete. There was little left now. Buildings blasted to the ground by tsunami upon tsunami.

Vast metal sheds which once contained tin cans, themselves now twisted open and emptied.

They continued to ascend. Towards the crest of the hill was deep shadow. Cold and grey weighed down by darkness and dank.

At each intersect she saw long stretches of grid road. Some still had their signs. Overgate, Marlborough Street.

Before them now, a five-metre-high wall of debris. Metal, toys, bleached bones. To the left a portway. No more than a man's width.

'This is good,' Rib said. 'We don't have to climb over.'

'This is bad,' she said. 'People have been here before.'

The gap was too narrow for their craft. They followed the wall round a hundred metres or so and left the vehicle. They covered it with rubbish so it couldn't be seen. It was now part of the wall. He took a final farewell, a lump in his throat. She took her bag and turned back to the portway.

They passed through and climbed towards spared structures at the top of a hill in the miserly light of the Underdome. There was no sign of life.

Long boulevards crossed each other like a chessboard. Dead black trees stood in lines along avenues, twisted bare branches lay in funeral pyres at their feet. Mildewed teasel stood stiff and brittle beside the road. She forced him to camp down for breakfast before pressing on. They looked for a place where they would not be seen. They found an underpass with marble edging for a bench. They needed a fire to cook by. It had been hard to find dry wood so she had shaved off the damp bark with her knife and used what leaves and twigs she could find. It splattered fitfully at first. It then took with fiery confidence. She went through the motions of tending the flames to an ember glow. She cooked, with no appetite, a breakfast of porridge sweetened with cloudberries, without knowing why she was still there. She asked him 'What now?' and he took from his bag a piece of paper, first he read it to her then, trusting, he showed her what was written.

It said, 'Unity'.

She said, 'What does it mean?'

He said, 'I guess it's a clue … It tells us how to get up to the MK citidome.'

She said, 'How does it tell us?'

He said, 'I don't know. It must be the name of a street or a house.'

She didn't answer.

A tear formed in her eye.

32

'We need to find a map,' he said.

'Where can we find a map?'

He said, 'Maybe a bookshop.'

They trudged up towards the centre of the old town. Before them what looked like the remains of a mall. Sheets of glass in thin pillar shards. Debris. Twisted girders.

They went through an entrance which said, 'Acorn Walk'. Everywhere ransacked, ravaged, looted, dark and desolate.

Something slithered through the shadows to their right. They stopped and it fell silent. A centipede the length of a leg scuttled from a doorway.

He shuddered. 'Let's go,' he said. 'There's nothing here.'

They went out onto the boulevard again and crossed towards a large square brick building. There was nothing much about it, other than it was the only one left standing. Suddenly, she threw him to the ground, knocking the breath out of him.

'What is it?' he said, spitting mud.

'People, over there.' They didn't move a muscle. The people didn't move a muscle. The people were not people. They were statues. Two women sitting on a railing. Life-size. Lifeless. But still speaking.

They got up and walked over to them. One was whispering in the other's ear. What was she saying? What had she seen?

He reached up and touched the shoulder of the whisperer. She's cool, he smiled. The woman were guarding a library. A really old library. They went in and found shelves of books wet with mould, now untouched, uncared for, unread.

She picked up a volume of the *Encyclopaedia Britannica*. Its pages stuck together like slabs of despair. She closed it and put it back.

'Look, over here!' he shouted.

He held up a thin brochure.

It was a map book of Milton Keynes. The date read '2025'. Two years before Watershed. They went outside and leafed through the pages until they came to the entries under 'U'.

'Here it is! Unity Court.'

Street E7.

'What now?' she asked.

'We go there.'

'And then what?'

'We search.'

'For what?'

'A key I guess, something.'

'A search for a key in a street,' she said slowly to herself, shaking her head. 'He doesn't have a clue.'

He set off down the boulevard, map book held open as if he knew where he were going. She stood still and looked up at the black belly of the Dome above them. Dark and silent save the sporadic spark of lasercraft from the western end.

'Come on,' he said. 'I think I've found it.' She followed him at some metres' distance. They made their way through the ruins of an old school. No more children, no more laughter in the playground. No more teachers any more. Just dry, brown ivy in a death-clasp along a rusty paint peeled railing. They trudged past a broken terrace of houses. In one garden a dirty white plastic reindeer.

With a string of Christmas lights.

Once pulsing brightly.

Never again.

They crossed what used to be a car park. Three burnt-out

chassis left as sole witnesses.

'Here we are,' he finally said.

A line of brick rubble on a road curving down into dark water.

They searched all day.

To no avail.

They returned exhausted to the underpass at dusk. She made a fire and cooked snowgrouse stew with red cabbage. He licked his plate dry and came back for more. He said, 'This is the best yet. I don't know what I'd do without you.' He touched her arm. She half laughed, stood up and went over to the fire. 'You'd do OK,' she said with her back to him. 'You'd do OK. Coffee?'

She turned.

He was already asleep.

33

The shrill cry of a bird woke him with a start. It was the middle of the night. What had disturbed the bird? It was an alarm shriek, not a song. An animal perhaps? Or worse. He turned to wake Rika, feeling for her form in the sleeping bag beside him.

'Rika!' he whispered. 'Rika!'

No reply.

He strained his eyes to see whether she had moved nearer the embers of the fire. She hadn't.

She was gone.

He sat hunch-shouldered, his arms around his knees, rocking gently to and fro for a full three hours, listening for sound of her return. Every fibre of his being hoping she would come back.

In his heart of hearts he knew that she was gone. Gone for good. A lone thin ray of sunlight shafting into the underpass confirmed his fears. There was no sign of her stuff. It was as if she had never existed. All that was left was the smallest of her billycans and a few packs of dried food. She'd left him a few days' rations to survive on.

Tears welled up. He had wanted to show her MK. Meet his mum. See the refuge. Go to the New Pitz with him. Be his ...

His tears plopped onto his sleeping bag as he folded it and tied it in a roll. He'd noticed a change in her ever since they reached MK.

Quiet.

Moody.

What had upset her? Had he done something to pee her off? He couldn't think of anything. How was he going to find his way up to the citidome now? On his own …

He made one last search of the camp before he sloped out of the underpass onto the boulevard. He had hoped to find a note. It wouldn't be so bad if he knew why she'd left him.

He spent an hour on a half-hearted search of their previous haunts. The library. The school. She wasn't there. He knew she wouldn't be.

He returned to Unity Court and resumed his hunt for the key. It was hopeless. He'd never find his way up to the citi. 200 million dollars in his bag. Worth absolutely nothing down here in this underworld. He'd come so far. Gone through so much. But he was going to fall at the last hurdle. This was payback time. He should never have taken the looty in the first place. It belonged to the old woman. However badly his mum needed it. It wasn't his to give.

And now he was getting what he deserved. For the rest of the day he roamed aimlessly around the Underdome, wondering how he could get out of this mess. Every ten minutes or so his eyes were drawn upwards to the sunzoom-spark of a lasercraft departing from Silbury Terminal, 400 metres above him. Silbury, where it all started. How many weeks, months ago? He tried to figure it out but gave up as it made him even more depressed thinking about it. And now, full circle. Almost.

He wandered into what must once have been a shopping mall. Most of the structure was still intact. Some of the roof had disappeared allowing wan beams of light to play on the marble covered floor. Just inside the entrance was a bench. It didn't look like an ordinary bench, though. It was a book. A bronze book. A ball and chain was attached to one end. Without knowing why Rib tried to lift the ball. It was heavy and he let it drop as soon as he'd raised it a few centimetres. The crusty dent in the floor showed where this had been done a thousand times over. He sat on the bench. It was cold. He felt along the furrowed ridges of the book's pages. His fingers dug into thick green slime. He shuddered and wiped off as much as he could out the back of his legs before moving back to the underpass.

Part of him expected Rika to be waiting there for him. That sweet-sharp sliver of optimism shattered at once into a thousand shards as he found no trace of her on his return. Where had she gone? Surely not all the way back to Middlemedes. But if not, where?

Venturer II! She must have taken *Venturer II*.

He decided to trace his steps back to the debris strip to where they had hidden her. He didn't want to be on the move once night had fallen but he reckoned he had enough time to get there and back before dark.

It took him precisely twenty-two minutes to reach the spot where they had left *Venturer II* the night before.

It wasn't there.

She had taken it.

Tears of anger, then loss, then anger again rolled down his cheeks. He stood with his arms hung limply against his side, not knowing what to do next. Why had she come all this way if she didn't want to be with him?

'Bitch!' he whispered.

'Bitch!' he said.

'Bitch!' he screamed from the very depth of his soul.

A screeching chorus of lorikeets joined his cry of pain. He looked back over to the fringe of the forest to see the orange-and-red flash of the flock making its final sweep in the setting sun before roosting for the night.

He steadied himself. This can't be a Hendrix moment. No. Not with 200 million dollars in the bag.

He instinctively felt for the bag.

The bag that should have been on his back.

But wasn't.

Aaaargh! He screamed as he lurched into a run towards the opening through the strip. He slipped as he turned into the narrow man-width gap and nearly went over. He sprinted up the hill back into the citidome, skidding as he turned corners on the slimy surface underfoot.

He couldn't think when he had last had the bag. Running at full pelt didn't help. He couldn't think. He slowed to a jog. He still couldn't think. He stopped. He still couldn't think. Shit! What was he going to do?

Had he left it in the underpass? If so, he had a chance. He was sure no one had seen them set up camp there. He started to run again. Where else could he have left it?

He skidded to a halt.

The bench!

When he bent over to lift the ball on the end of the chain!

He remembered.

He'd slipped his bag and placed it on the bench. Out in the open …

Shit!

It took him another four minutes to reach the place called Midsummer Place. As he entered the half-light of the mall, he could just make out the dark outline of the bronze book of a seat. He slowed to within 20 metres and stood there, half bent, hands on knees, breathing deeply. He could see the bag. The question was: Had anybody else seen it?

The twenty-six steps he took over to the bench seemed the longest in his life. It was as if he were walking through a minefield towards an abandoned child, a baby, with a thousand onlookers in rows on both sides. Their proud flags now furled in silent respect.

His heart was in his mouth as he reached the bench and took hold of the bag. He loosened the drawstring and closed his eyes as he felt for the velvet bag.

It was there.

The walnuts were there. The coins were there.

He sat down on the bench, his head in his hands. He took ten deep breaths, trying to regain some sort of control. Finally he stood up, swinging the bag over his shoulder and headed back to the underpass cursing himself for having been so stupid. The half-light was fading fast as he got back to their camp.

Their camp ...

He decided there and then that he wouldn't stay. He couldn't stay. He gathered up the food, the bedroll and the billycan. As if on autopilot he retraced his steps to the book bench. A slim dark figure watched Rib from the shadows of the Burger King doorway as he walked into the darkness of the bookstore entrance ...

34

He set up camp on the first floor of the bookstore, sleeping on a bench by the window. It was a strange mix of a store – mostly bookshelves but with an eating area too. Further investigation told him that it had once been a coffee shop. A wall poster of a moustachioed man letting beans from Colombia run slowly through his fat fingers was the clue. The bench was a good vantage point. Through the long-since glass-less window he would be able to see anything or anyone entering the square. He had checked escape routes and had found two fire exits leading to the back of the building. Something still worried him, nagged at him.

The coins.

They didn't belong to him. They belonged to the old woman. The same old guilt phrase repeated itself for the thousandth time as he formed a fist and punched the tired leather of the bench in anger. If it wasn't distressed before, it was now.

But there was something else. He had come so close to losing the looty last night when he'd left his bag on the big book. How stupid was that? He decided there and then to hide the walnuts somewhere safe where no one would think of looking. He finally found the perfect place. A steel profile hung from the ceiling of the shopping mall a few metres from his lookout position. It held a sign which read 'East Walk'. The square end of the profile had been filled in with a block of wood, presumably to stop birds from nesting there.

Rib took the fli-wire from his bag and aimed it at the

metalwork. The grapple bit first time and he secured the other end to a pillar behind the bench. He took the small velvet bag holding the walnuts and wrapped the drawstring round his right wrist. He yanked on the wire twice to make sure it held, fastened the carabiner, then swung out over the square. His nerve held – just – as he glanced down at the book sculpture some 10 metres below him. The small block of wood came out easily and the bag fitted snugly into the square profile of the tubing. Rib carefully replaced the wood before sliding back down the wire. The fli-wire flew back into its holster at the flick of a switch. Rib scanned the square for any sign of movement as he sat back on the bench, his heart still pounding from his exertions.

Closing his eyes as his pulse started to slow, he felt a wave of relief flood over him. It was as if the heaviest weight in the whole world had been lifted from his shoulders. For the first time he felt he could concentrate on the search for the key, unsaddled from the burden of the gold. He could now look properly.

That's what it was. Look properly. When he was home and couldn't find something, he always went to his mum and asked her if she'd seen it. She always said, 'Have you looked in your bedroom?' He always said, 'Yes that's the first place I looked.' Her reply would always be 'Well, look again, and this time, look properly.' She wasn't being sarky, she really did mean look properly. And nine times out of ten, he would return to his room, furrow his brow and find what he had lost.

So he set about his task with renewed energy, taking a systematic approach by ticking off grid squares one by one. There must be another house or dwelling called Unity. Surely the key must be hidden somewhere in the centre of the old city.

For the next two days, he covered the dank and desolate remains of what once had been a buzzing metropolis but to no avail. His early optimism soon gave way to a deep depression. He had eaten his last food. The chewy cubes of reindeer in a rich, thick gravy tasted good but only served to remind him of Rika and flatten him face down in his ditch of despond. He moved without resistance into Hendrix mode and found himself late that afternoon, sat in the middle of an intersect rocking gently to and fro singing to himself the second verse of 'Castles Made of Sand', about a little Indian brave who dreamed one day he would be a fearless warrior chief. It didn't happen. He was killed in his sleep by a surprise attack on the eve of his first battle.

As he finished, a tear rolled down his cheek. He felt so low that he wished a surprise attack would end it all there and then.

Suddenly something flashed.

He started and looked up.

Down the hill to his left, something shone at him. From straight up the road that once had been Witan Gate.

Shone sharp and fierce.

It came from beyond the shadow of the Dome. From beyond the debris strip.

From out where the sun burned bright.

Check it out in the morning, he told himself. He was too tired to explore further now. He returned to base camp bookstore where he spent a restless night, not helped by the growl of his unfed stomach.

His eyes reopened at seven with little enthusiasm for the day ahead. No nearer solving the final piece of the puzzle and the thought of spending another day traipsing across the entrails of a long-since dead city filled him with little joy.

Later that morning he stumbled across an amazing contraption. It was, in fact, only just round the corner from his camp. It was a giant clock with an enormous frog sitting on top. There was a long gantry carrying a large pendulum and wheel and the whole thing seemed to be geared up to delivering a golden ball to the clock cabinet. The clock face was of traditional design but the rest of the weird machine certainly wasn't. The cabinet housing the clock still sported patches of bright blue shining out from its now faded paint-work. Instead of the maker's name, it read 'Milton Keynes, 2002'. A large red wheel rested midway along the gantry, which connected the clock to a smaller box. The wheel had something written on it, in faint gold lettering. Rib could just about make it out: 'ANDREW BEASANT AND SONS, CLOCKMAKERS, ENGLAND'. But the real deal was the big frog itself. It was quite simply magnificent, squatting on top of the clock cabinet, arms folded across its enormous belly. From wherever you looked, the huge bulging eyes seemed to follow you with a surprised stare, as if to say 'Who are you? And what the hell are you doing here?'

I'm here to fettle you up, me old matey, was Rib's silent answer. The question was, could he get it to work? It was too great a challenge for a Nanozoomology star pupil to resist and he went at it with a will.

OK, it was displacement activity, but it was good for the soul to get his hands dirty on a prime piece of primeval engineering. To prove to himself that he was no longer on the run. To prove to himself that he was in control.

Gantry, clockwork, pulleys …

It was hard to believe that things actually used to work like this.

Yet strangely comforting.

It was a welcome distraction from his search for the key. The control panel was easily located, just a single flight up an ossified escalator. He was surprised how well the machine had survived the many lonely years of inactivity. No more than a couple of mechanical repairs were needed to bring it back to life. In less than three hours he had it working, taking care not to trip the final programme phase, which had sound attached. No need to broadcast his whereabouts to the world and his oyster. Was that the right phrase? Maybe not. Anyway ...

He followed the instructions from the plaque screwed to the wall of the control cabinet, setting the programme to run to Phase 3, before leaping down the escalator to watch the show from below. It was wonderful! It was like a big circus act cum magic circle trick played out 10 metres above the thoroughfare of a shopping mall. Rib stood there in total awe wondering what it must have been like to have witnessed the spectacle as part of a crowd of hundreds gathered every Saturday morning.

Waiting for the clock to strike the half-hour.

Waiting for the golden ball to be delivered safely into the clock cabinet.

Waiting for the fan of the golden oak leaves to rise up.

Waiting for the frog to come to life.

Waiting for the music to play.

Waiting for the stream of bubbles for the children to catch.

And that was clearly the most exciting bit.

The bubbles.

The final phase of the programme that was too risky for Rib to run.

He promised himself that he would come back one day, run that risky routine, burst those bubbles and scream out loud. Rib paused, felt in his back pocket, ran back up the escalator and emptied a sachet into the bubble reservoir.

That night he crashed into a deep sleep without dream. He slept soundly through to seven.

He awoke to another dank, dark day beneath the Dome. As soon as he'd finished the first hamstring stretch, he knew that his need was for food.

Now.

He decided his only option was to leave the city and return to the rainforest. Rika had shown him how to dig out the flesh from one of the palm trees. He couldn't remember what it was called but that didn't matter. He was sure he'd be able to recognise it. She had told him that it was perfectly edible, non-toxic and all that. As long as he didn't eat too much of it. Thinking of her again started to take him down. He bit his lower lip, swung out over the plaza on the fli-wire and retrieved the small bag from the East Wing sign.

Rib reckoned it would not be safe to go out of the Underdome the way they had come in. Someone might be watching the narrow passageway through the debris strip. It would be the ideal spot for an ambush. Without giving further thought he set off across the plaza, back down the dead boulevard once called Midsummer, the place which would never feel the fierce heat of midsummer again. He picked up pace down the hill, until he came to the spot he'd reached the day before. Standing at the intersect, his eye was caught again by a flash in the mid-distance from exactly the same place as before. But this time something was different. Seriously different. It took him a few seconds to work out what it was. Looking down the hill out through the domestrut legs, over the top of the debris strip, the scene had changed.

The whole swathe of land between the Underdome and the rainforest was now under water. Yesterday it was a brown stumpy muddy mix of mangrove and dead trees. Now it was a lake. The water must have risen by 10, no maybe 20 metres. Overnight! How could that be? As he stared down the hill at the newly arrived lake in disbelief, his eye was drawn again to a sharp reflection. The rays of the strengthening morning sun were picking out something floating in the middle of the lake. Something small and very, very bright. Was this what he saw yesterday?

For no particular reason he looked behind him up the hill. What he saw made Rib hurl himself to his right in a double forward roll. Difficult enough to do in perfect gymnasium conditions and certainly not the best stunt to pull with a rucksack on your back. Ending up in a heap behind a pile of rubble with his right arm wrenched near to dislocation, he lay still, hearing only the pounding of his heart. He stayed in this contorted state until he could no longer feel the fingers of his right hand. Gently easing himself into a prone position, he wriggled a half-metre to his left to give him sight of the road.

What he had seen was still there. At a distance of some thirty paces. Back up the hill. At a right angle across the road. It was difficult at first to determine the shape. Rib still had the bright light of the reflection from the lake burned on the back of his retina. As his eyes accustomed to the gloom, he slowly picked out the details.

It looked like a big banana. An enormous banana ...

No, that couldn't be right.

Whatever it was, he was absolutely sure it hadn't been there thirty seconds before when he walked down the hill.

He stayed there for a full five minutes listening for any telltale sound.

There was nothing.

He slowly picked himself up and moved in a half-crouch towards the object.

As he neared it, he smiled.

It was big all right. It was yellow all right. It was, however, no banana.

Yes, we have no banana.

We have, instead, a canoe, flat-bottomed and curved up at each end. Just like the ones at Middlemedes, in fact. And placed neatly beside it, a paddle.

There was no way he could have walked past it. He would have tripped over the bloody thing!

He felt dizzy.

He hadn't eaten for over thirty-six hours. Maybe that was it. He wasn't thinking straight. What he needed was food.

Back to Plan A. Return to rainforest. Find edible palm. Chop open with Swiss Army knife. Eat. Think straight.

He set off back down the hill with purposeful stride. He halted in his tracks halfway down to stare at the shimmering expanse of lake which now lay between him and the rainforest.

Shit! How was he going to get across the water?

Rib stood motionless, a picture of despair. Was anything ever going to stack up for him? Why did nothing go his way? Yesterday, he could have strolled down the hill and feasted on the fruits of the forest. Today, 800 metres of water to cross. Probably full of piranhas and leeches and things. How the hell was he going to get across?

From their vantage point on top of a week-old pile of flying fox dung, two earwigs had watched this scene unfold before them. Earwigs normally have little occasion to swear. They go about their lives, eating vegetable matter, dead insects, some live prey, every now and then brandishing their pincers to defend themselves. Nothing to get yourself really worked up about. Certainly nothing to swear about.

But this was too much. They both bellowed at the top of their tiny voices in earwig tongue, 'Use the fucking canoe, you knobhead!' And immediately felt ashamed for using such coarse language.

Suddenly, Rib had an idea. He could use the canoe! He could get across the lake in the canoe! He raced back up the hill, lifted the canoe onto his right shoulder, took the paddle in his left and set off back down the hill in high spirits, basking in the glow of his ingenuity and general brilliance.

Riley would have been proud of him.

His sense of euphoria was short-lived. He had forgotten the debris strip. The two earwigs exchanged knowing glances as he slowed to a stop in front of the wall of waste. He soon found, however, a thin corridor through. Clearly there were a number of entrances into the Underdome through the strip.

It wasn't far to the water's edge. He took out his beanie hat from the bag and put it on. The dark shadow thrown by the MK citidome extended some hundred or so metres into the lake. After that, he would need as much protection on the open water as possible. He slid onto the canoe and pushed off. Feet and knees together, stomach muscles taut, he soon moved into a smooth, powerful stroke as the canoe carved an effortless course across the surface of the water. He had taken lessons and become quite an accomplished canoeist on the Middlemedes leisure lake and it felt good to be doing something physical again. He seemed to have been spending all his time crouching and crawling and hiding of late. It gave him a rush to be in control again. As he glided out of the shadow, he felt the immediate burn of the sun on his forearms and thighs.

He soon reached a quarter of the distance across the lake and stopped paddling to take in his new environment. It was nothing short of liberating to feel the waft of a warm wind playing over the open water after his spending so many days in the depressing dankness of the Underdome. OK, he knew he had to go back there to find his way up to MK, but this was just what the doctor ordered. As he drifted half-sideways, letting the canoe be taken for a moment by the breeze, his eyes focused on something about 200 metres off to his left. He could now clearly see a large silver ball floating on the surface of the water. This is what he must have seen from the hill. It wasn't directly on his route to the far shore, but he felt himself turning the nose of his canoe to pick up speed again towards the ball. It wasn't much of a detour, he thought. And what's more, he was intrigued. There was something strange about it. He couldn't figure out what it was, but it didn't look right …

By the time he'd come to within a distance of 30 or so metres from the silver orb, he had worked out what it was. It was not actually floating. It was sitting too high up in the water. That's why it had seemed strange – it wasn't moving with the breeze. Which is why it was still in exactly the same position as yesterday, when he'd seen it from the Underdome.

Within a matter of seconds, Rib had drawn up the canoe beside the ball.

It was big.

About a metre in diameter, Rib guessed. Maybe even more.

He gingerly gave it a prod with the end of his paddle. A dull, metallic ring responded. Rib put two and two together and came up with metal. He manoeuvred the canoe so that he could reach out and touch it. It was smooth and already heating up from the sun's rays. He pushed it with the tips of his fingers and it was his canoe that moved. The ball was certainly fixed to something below the waterline.

A voice inside him told him to take a look under the surface.

'What?' screamed another voice. 'Only yesterday you were scared of piranhas and leeches and things!'

'Yes I know,' replied the first voice calmly. That was yesterday. Today, I feel different. I feel good about myself. I feel confident. I am in control.'

'In control!' laughed the second voice. 'You're losing your marbles, more like. You haven't eaten for two days, man. Now leave this bloody ball alone, get over to that far shore and get some food inside you! What are you doing? No! Don't do that!

'Put your clothes back on! You're not going to leave the bag in the canoe are you? Rib! Don't. RIB!!!'

'Don't worry,' the first voice assured soothingly. 'I'm just going to take a look. The swim will do me good,' it said as Rib slipped into the water.

And how good it did feel …

The warm water cleansed him in an instant. His body. His spirit. His soul. He lay motionless and star-shaped on his back on the surface of the lake looking up at the sky.

Drifting.

The screech of a parakeet passing overhead pierced his karma and he took a lungful of air and dived to explore what lay beneath the ball.

The water was clear. Surprisingly clear. And deep.

Some 4 metres, he reckoned, although it was difficult to tell.

He saw at once that the ball rested on three huge spider's legs, bent at the knee joints and tapering inwards and down to where they stood on the bottom of the lake. Rib came up for air and checked the canoe for his bag. It was still there waiting for him. He dived again, this time swimming right down to the bottom. The whole area was strewn with broken brick, twisted metal and debris. He spotted amongst the rubble a faded sign which read 'Refectory', a smashed keyboard of some sort, a basket ball hoop. He surfaced for air and dived again immediately. Whatever had demolished the building had made a good job of it. It had been razed to the ground. Nothing left standing.

Apart from the silver ball sitting on top of three rusty legs.

Last man standing.

A bit like him really.

Rib dived again, this time swimming away from the structure only to find the same story. Everything totally flattened.

He breaststroked up to the surface and felt the immediate burn of the sun on his forehead. It was time to go. He had to press on and find food.

Yet something held him back. Something inside him didn't want to leave. He felt an odd affinity with the place. And what exactly was the silver ball perched on spider limbs? A meeting point ? A piece of sculpture? Without really knowing why and against his better instincts, Rib dived again this time down towards the base of the spider ball. Four pulls and he was there. He found the structure to be built on a plinth, which had remained largely intact.

Something caught his eye. Embedded in the plinth was a small rectangular plaque. With words on it. Rib closed in and started to read.

The first word was 'Unity'.

'Unity!' Rib screamed. Not a good thing to do 4 metres down.

The sociable waters of the lake readily accepted his invitation and flooded into his lungs. He pushed off the base with all his might and fought his way up towards the light.

He surfaced and vomited, hanging on to the horizontal of one of the legs. Not food, just warm water. He reached and retched a dozen times until he thought his ribs would ping through his skin.

When he thought he'd finished, his diaphragm said, 'Just one more for the road, shall we?'

Ten minutes later he was still draped over the ball, trying to get it together. The sun scorched his back by the second. He couldn't let go what he had seen 4 metres down.

Unity.

This had to be the place.

35

In his heart of hearts he knew that this was the most important part of his long journey. In his heart of hearts he knew
had to dive again.

This time he took six strokes to reach the bottom. He had
enough air to read the plaque in full …

'UNITY'
By Dominic Walpole
Art Foundation Programme
1992–1993
Unveiled by Allen Duff
Governor of
Milton Keynes College
21 June 1995

… and then digest its meaning on the way to the surface.

Once back up, and sitting on the ball, the revelation hit
home. This was Milton Keynes College! Before Watershed,
before Exodus. This was the college! The original college.
Unity was a sculpture by a student named Dominic in 1993
and it was the only thing in this alien world that was left
shining.

His left foot dangling in the lake felt a change in the water.
It was cooler, a swirling eddy gaining in urgency. Time to
move on, his senses told him.

One last dive.

As he reached the bottom, the refectory sign and basket ball hoop all made sense now. He read the plaque once more, reached out and gently touched it.

Rib imagined it was like this saying goodbye to a friend you knew you would never see again.

He reluctantly pushed off from the plinth, careful not to kick the plaque. Arms flat against his sides, he kicked towards the surface. He was directly beneath the ball, so he looked up to avoid smacking his head.

Something caught his eye.

Something was attached to the bottom of the ball. As he drew close he could see a piece of metal held by a criss-cross of tape. He touched it. It was stuck fast. Out of air, Rib surfaced and climbed up onto the sculpture's leg. He reached down, feeling along the rusty underbelly of Unity. It was a stretch but he could make it, keeping his mouth just above the water.

He slowly peeled off the tape with his right hand, holding its cargo in place with the forefinger of his left. The last thing he wanted to do was let it sink down to the bottom.

Twenty seconds later Rib was sitting on top of the silver orb, staring at the untaped piece of dull grey metal in his cupped hands.

He was trembling with excitement.

It was a key.

It had the number 44 etched onto it. Rib knew immediately it was the key to the door of Domestrut 44. It was the key which would get him back to MK. It was the key he had been looking for.

Still trembling, he allowed himself a wry smile. Why did you have to make it so bloody hard, Kaddie? How the hell was he supposed to have found the key here, taped to the bottom of a silver ball on a sunken college campus? But the only thing that mattered was that he had found it.

He let out a long sigh of relief.

Just as he heard the unmistakeable splash of a canoe paddle.

He was no longer alone on the lake …

He looked up to see a canoe travelling towards him at speed. Some 50 metres away.

36

It was 5.45, the temperature already 32 degrees and rising. His morning ritual completed, Hesperus Besk applied the finishing touches to his shave with two puffs of cologne to the taut tanned skin below his jaw line.

He then took breakfast in the lee of the cruiserwagon and ran through the plan for the day in his head one final time.

He was satisfied with his position. That the girl had now left the boy rendered matters less complex. The boy had moved his base to the bookshop. Besk's associates had been sent to dispose of the ridiculous vehicle in which his quarry had been travelling. He smiled to himself as he pictured the scene. Two of the worst the Slakterghast had to offer carrying a bright-yellow motion simulator the best part of a demi kilometre down to the nearest lake. They were under strict instruction to sink it. Besk smiled again, musing how they would approach the task. The craft's doors were locked and sealed tight. No matter, he thought, as he returned to the day ahead.

He crouched in quiet contemplation, moving only to waft away the occasional early-morning midge. The peace of the moment was broken by the heavy crash of something large approaching.

Without moving a muscle, Besk waited for the two men to emerge from the undergrowth. They stepped into the clearing and stood before him, both shifting uneasily from foot to foot.

Besk glanced up to survey the pair without a trace of

expression on his face. He held them in his gaze.

His two associates.

Olass and Maliss.

Olass and Maliss were senior-ranking officers of the Slakterghast Squad, South East Midlands sub-region. They were hardened criminals, guilty on an habitual basis of rape, murder, cannibalism. And smoking, though normally only after the first three. As Maliss frequently put it, nothing like a cool menthol after a hard day at the office.

They were of similar height, over 2 metres. Sun-scorched, pale-blue eyes glinted from their scarred and crusted faces. They wore the uniform of the Slakterghast, a deep-red bandana stained with blood and sweat. Each held a length of scaffold pipe. Olass had adorned the business end of his with nails; Maliss had gone for razor wire.

They were sadistic thugs of the highest order.

Which was precisely why Besk had enlisted them.

Of course, Besk didn't actually need assistance to carry out his plan. He was more than capable of despatching the boy by himself. What he had been preparing was an exquisite execution involving not only Master Meskitoe but also Messrs Olass and Maliss. An intricate final episode which would ensnare both hunters and hunted in a most delicious denouement. And the added incentive of 2,000 Dead or Alive bonus points for a multiple kill …

Besk broke the silence. 'I trust your mission is accomplished?'

Olass and Maliss blinked back with little trace of comprehension. 'Did you get rid of the yellow machine?' Besk tried.

'Oh yes, Mr Besk. We carried out your command to the letter. Job done, sir,' answered Maliss.

'Did you drive it to the lake?'

The two brigands exchanged a swift glance before Maliss offered: 'Not exactly, sir, we decided to carry it to the lake.'

'Why would you carry a vehicle capable of motorised movement?'

Another snatched glance between the two. 'We couldn't open the doors, sir.'

'Ah, I see. The hermetically sealed doors?'

'Yes, sir.'

'So you carried it all the way down to the lake?'

'Yes, sir.'

'Well done, my good men. Well done.'

The tension visibly drained from their faces at these words of praise.

'Thank you, sir,' smiled Maliss. 'Our pleasure to be of service.'

'And I trust the craft sank without a trace?'

A ferocious fear fart exploded from the crack of Olass. Swiftly followed by another.

'Do I take that as a no?' asked Besk, fixing them with a stare. 'If I go down to the lake this evening and find a yellow machine bobbing on the surface for the whole world to see, you will both suffer. Do I make myself understood?' he hissed.

'Yes, sir!' said Maliss and Olass in unison.

'Go on then, what are you waiting for?' screamed Besk.

The two almost fell over each other as they stumbled from the clearing back onto the track into the rainforest. After sprinting for some 50 metres, Maliss braked hard, causing Olass to slam into his back.

'Wait, wait, wait,' he shouted. 'Why are we running?'

'Because Mr Besk is angry with us,' blurted Olass.

'And why is that?' asked Maliss, turning on his oppo.

Olass did not answer, knowing full well that Maliss knew the answer.

'Because a certain person passed wind when asked a certain question about a certain yellow thingy,' Maliss continued, warming to his theme.

'And if a certain person hadn't cacked his pants when placed under no pressure whatsoever, a certain two people wouldn't be running through the jungle scared shitless, WOULD THEY?!'

'No,' said Olass meekly.

True, they were both seriously bad bandits. True, they both maimed, mutilated and murdered morning, noon and night. But Olass, as he was called, was not all bad. He had a softer side. If things had worked out differently, he might not have ended up on the wrong side of the tracks. If only it hadn't been for the Wilf Rumblestrips incident.

Wilf Rumblestrips …

His best mate at school.

Olass went under another name then, of course. (David Dinkelberg – the switch to Olass was not a difficult one.)

Wilf Rumblestrips was known to his classmates as Speed Bumps.

This rather unkind nickname was acquired through his capacity to develop growths, boils, pustules on his face within seconds. One minute his cheek would be clear, the next a throbbing shagger of a spot would erupt like a boiling bubble from a volcanic mud pool.

An alternative theory behind his nickname was that his mum, Wilma Rumblestrips, had been sleeping with a police-man and Wilf was the result of their happy union. The case was never proven and anyway, no one was brave or stupid enough to ask Wilf. He could dish it out, could Wilf.

David and Wilf were inseparable friends, right from the age of six, when they first sat next to each other knocky-kneed before the stern gaze of Miss Gibbons, Form Tutor of 1C and School Dragon. They mended each other's punctures, flew each other's kites, exercised each other's racing newts and scratched each other's scratch cards.

Utterly inseparable.

Until they were separated.

By a flick.

Who went by the name of Tanya.

Tanya Tinglepipe.

From the instant they first set eyes on her, they were in deep, head-over-heels, ultra-*amore*. Olass remembered it as if it were yesterday. Outside the Vietnamese vegetarian restaurant on Bletchley High Street. They'd just had a dim sum followed by banana fritters. They emerged to see a vision of beauty on the other side of the road. A swaying, hip-rolling walk which turned heads wherever she went. A Cuban cigarillo hanging provocatively from her lips. Green, sultry, make-love-to-me-now eyes.

And that was just her poodle ...

Tanya Tinglepipe was seriously stunning. Also green eyes, but bright and flashing. Her hair waist-length blonde, her complexion pure as porcelain. Always in leather. Red leather.

She came between them and it was never the same again. To be fair to her, she tried to limit the damage by dating them alternately. Strangely enough, this only seemed to make matters worse. Especially when she got the names mixed up.

One night in May 2005, David Dinkelberg staggered out of the Rat and Parrot, having celebrated an incredible victory for Liverpool in the Champions League final by consuming ten pints of Guinness, three double Southern Comforts and a bottle of Babycham. Somebody had once told him that if you finished off the evening with a Babycham, you wouldn't wake up with a hangover in the morning. What they didn't tell him was that he would wake up in a police cell in the morning facing a twenty-year stretch for murdering his best friend.

He had seen them coming out of KFC in the Xscape: Speed Bumps always knew how to give a girl a good time. David had walked up behind them as they headed for a taxi queue and stabbed Bumps in the back with a yellow-handled butcher's boning knife he had picked up at The Bowl car boot sale the week before.

Wilf Rumblestrips, aka Speed Bumps aka Bumps, died in the ambulance on the way to hospital. David Dinkelberg cried in the squad car on the way to the police station. Tanya Tinglepipe cursed 'you bastards' at both of them for leaving her all dressed up and nowhere to go on a Saturday night in CMK.

Wilf Rumblestrips was laid to rest in New Bradwell Cemetery. David Dinkelberg served eighteen years in Woodhill where he completed an Open University degree in Social Sciences and an NVQ Level 2 in Food Preparation and became known as Olass. Tanya Tinglepipe visited him regular as clockwork twice a day and sat until three in the morning writing long letters of love and devotion. Halfway into the second week of his sentence, she got pissed off with the whole thing and bagged off with a street poet named Ossian who was bagging groceries on the checkout at Morrisons, Westcroft.

In the early days Olass visited the prison chapel.

He prayed for forgiveness.

It never came.

So he gave up.

He met Maliss on the wing and they forged an alliance based on power, extortion and control over the other inmates.

So it was the natural thing to do to follow Maliss and join up with Slakterghast Squad when it all went lairy at Watershed time.

Maliss, on the other hand, was pure-bred evil through and through. There was not an ounce of remorse in his soul for the atrocities he had committed.

They feared nothing.

They feared no one.

Except Hesperus Besk.

Which was why they were both up to their chests in stagnant water wading out towards *Venturer II*, bobbing brightly in the middle of Willen Lake.

37

Rib hadn't moved a muscle. Still sitting on top of *Unity*, holding the new-found key in the cup of his hands. As soon as he had seen the speed of the approaching craft he knew that flight would be futile. Fast as he was, the yellow banana boat would be no match. He would have to fight it out here. He shifted slightly and gripped the key in his left hand.

The figure in the kayak stopped paddling and the boat glided to a halt some 10 metres away.

'Hello, Rib.'

This threw him twofold. Firstly the figure knew his name. Secondly it was the voice of a woman.

'How do you know my name?'

'There's a lot I know about you, Rib.'

'Who are you? What do you want?' Rib asked, trying to give the impression of being cool and calm when in fact his pulse was up in the one-twenties. Making every effort not to look at his bag, perched at the back of his canoe.

The woman ignored his question. 'I see you've found *Unity* then,' she went on. He didn't answer, but gripped the key tighter in his hand. She paused, looking at him intently. 'And you will have found the key, then?' Another silence between them, save the lapping of the lake against the side of his canoe.

'Good,' she nodded.

Now he was really confused. He remained on guard, ready to spring if she made a move.

There was something strangely familiar about her voice.

He wished he could see her face.

As if she could read his mind, she unzipped the hood of her body suit and pulled it back over her head.

Rib gasped. He knew who it was immediately. It was the old woman in the lottery queue.

The old woman who had handed him the winning ticket. The old woman whom he had cheated. The old woman whose 200 million dollars sat in the bottom of his bag. Just an arm's width away.

'I guess you've come for your money,' Rib said.

'I have,' she nodded.

'Look, I'm sorry, it wasn't for me ...'

'There will be time for explanations later. Now give me the money,' she said firmly. 'And I advise you not to try anything foolish!'

Rib was in no state to do anything foolish, even if he had wanted.

All he felt now was guilt.

And tired despair.

He slowly leaned forward and pushed his canoe towards her. 'It's in the rucksack in a velvet bag.'

She rested her paddle on her knees and reached to take the bag, keeping her eyes on him all the time as she did so. Having found the velvet bag she loosened the drawstring and felt inside. She fixed Rib with a quizzical stare as she pulled out a walnut.

'There's a million dollar coin in each nut,' Rib said.

She raised her eyebrows.

'Honestly, I promise,' he said.

'Ingenious,' she said, returning the nut into the bag and stowing it on the kayak floor behind her. 'We need to leave this place. We must find cover. We are too exposed here.'

She grasped the paddle and manoeuvred backward with one strong, deft pull before turning the kayak back towards the shore.

Rib sat motionless on *Unity* as he watched her pick up speed in a matter of a few long powerful strokes. She paused and turned. 'Come on, quickly!'

He obeyed without resistance. He felt an empty numbness. He couldn't believe what had just happened. He would have fought tooth and nail against anyone who had tried to take the money.

Anyone except the old woman, that is.

What could he do?

There was nothing to do …

He managed to climb back in to the canoe, buttoned his boots, picked up his paddle and followed slowly in her wake.

He remembered reaching the shore, trying to step out of the canoe. That was all.

38

Before he opened his eyes, Rib heard the sound of a crackling fire. He could feel its heat on his cheek. He could hear the bubbling sound of something simmering in a pot.

Before he opened his eyes, he smelt food. Chicken. It smelled good. He started to salivate.

He opened his eyes. He was lying under a large tree in what looked like a large circular hall. It was night-time and the flames flickered shadows onto the walls around.

'Back in the land of the living, are we?' came a voice from behind him. He lifted himself up on his elbows and looked around to see the old woman emerging from a small tent pitched the other side of the tree. She was no longer in the neoprene all-in-one suit. She wore faded jeans, a kingfisher-blue T-shirt and a pair of black-leather sandals. And she was smiling at him.

'Hello. How are you feeling? I was worried about you back there. Hope you don't mind, but I gave you a revival shot, just to be sure.'

Rib's fingers went to the small swelling on the biceps of his right arm where the needle had gone in.

'What happened?' Rib asked. 'How did I get here?' He tried to remember. He was out on the lake. He found *Unity*. He found the key. He had the money. The old woman found him. He gave her the money. She paddled off ahead. He followed her. He reached the shore. And then … He couldn't remember any more. The next thing was bonfire and chicken smells.

She came over and crouched beside him. 'You got out of your canoe, bent over to pick it up and then keeled over head first into the water. You'd passed out. When did you last eat?'

'I'm not sure, I think it was two days ago.'

'Then it's no wonder. You'll feel a whole lot better with some food inside you.'

'But how did I get here? And where are we?'

'I carried you all the way up the hill. Not bad for a sixty-niner, huh?'

Rib blushed at the thought of being slung over the shoulder of someone old enough to be his grandmother. 'And I'm surprised you don't recognise where you are,' she continued, whilst ladling the contents of the pot into two bowls. Rib took in his surroundings again. Looked vaguely familiar, but he couldn't recall. He shook his head, too tired to speak.

'We're under the big Midsummer Oak. Long since dead, of course. But just round the corner from your bookstore.'

Rib recognised it now. He'd seen it many times in the gloom, but not in the dark. Its black branches seemed to spread upwards for ever. Upwards, thought Rib, is MK.

'The key,' he blurted. 'Where's the key?'

'Don't worry,' she reached into a pocket and handed it to him.

'Thanks,' he said. He was confused. The old woman didn't seem at all friendly on the lake. Understandably. And yet she carries him all the way back, cooks him food, smiles at him and keeps the key safe for him. He was really confused.

'Look,' he said. 'I really need to talk. I want to tell you why I took your Lotto ticket.'

'All in good time,' she said calmly. Then, sensing his anxiety, 'We'll eat first, then talk afterwards, OK?'

'OK.'

The Thai green curry with chicken was of another world.

He demolished two bowlfuls. (Whoever the old woman was, she could certainly cook.) With food inside him, he was feeling more at ease with the world. He still eyed the woman nervously. She was busying herself preparing a mixture in a bowl as if he were not there. How was he going to explain his act of deceit all those weeks ago in the Waste-Rows lottery queue? He decided that the best strategy was honesty. He had once heard that inquisitors could tell if you were lying by making you tell the story backwards. And he could easily do that – find key, walk around MK in a daze, mend frog, lose Rika, find body in clearing, travel down M1, escape from Middlemedes (torches, dogs), stay at Middlemedes (Ruth, duck, fondue, Rika, golf balls), wake up at Middlemedes, Slingshot Terminal, Dick's Bar, face in mud beside rainforest track, jump off Wigan citidome strapped to turquoise kite, flight through the citi at dawn, Kaddie and the coins, the old woman. The Old Woman …

Who was now all of a sudden giving him a piercing look. He shifted uncomfortably as she stood up from her seat by the fire and looked down at him, arms akimbo. For all the kindness she had shown towards him, she was clearly not to be messed with. She was no ordinary old woman, of that Rib was certain. Firstly, she had tracked him across half the land and found him in the middle of a lake. Secondly, he had never seen anyone paddle as fast as her in his whole life. Thirdly, she had carried his sodden, dead weight for what must have been the best part of a kilometre uphill. There was also a fourthly, fifthly and sixthly. However many certainties and half-certainties were circling his frontal lobes, they all added up to the same sum total.

Rib was scared.

Seriously scared.

'Time for an explanation,' the old woman said in a meaning-business tone.

'Yeah, sure,' Rib faltered. 'Do you mind if I have another

bowl of curry before we start?' She fixed him a penetrating stare. 'Are you sure you're still hungry or is this a delaying tactic?'

'No, I'm hungry, honestly,' he lied.

She knew he was lying.

And he knew she knew he was lying.

And if the two earwigs had been there, they would have known that he was lying too. 'Fucking liar,' they would have said, and then felt ashamed at their profanity.

She took his bowl and filled it with the rich sauce from the larger of the two pots, adding a ladleful of rice from the other.

'I'll just go and check the laser tripwires while you eat,' she said.

Rib's spoon stopped halfway to his mouth. 'Tripwires? Are we expecting company?'

'Can't be too careful,' she said over her shoulder as she padded off into the shadows.

As he spooned the spicy dish into his mouth, he rehearsed his lines. Whichever way they came out, they didn't wash themselves behind the ears. 'Look, sorry old lady, but I stole 250 million dollars from you,' was the long and the short of it.

He started as she suddenly emerged from the dark backdrop of the mall.

'Sorry to make you jump. Occupational hazard. Being light on one's feet. Catching people unawares ...'

She saw his bowl was empty.

'Finished?' she asked.

He nodded.

'Explanation time it is then?' she said as she stood before him, again arms akimbo.

Rib took a deep breath. He was on the tip of the six-metre board. Looking down. There was no water in the pool.

'Well, you see, it was like this ...' he began, not daring to look her in the eyes.

'Now let me stop you there, Master Meskitoe.' She knew his second name too. 'I need no explanations from you. I know who you are, where you have been and what you have done.'

Rib felt his toes wriggle. Flee! they said. I can't! his brain replied.

'But I do owe you an explanation,' she continued. Rib raised his eyebrows. He hadn't expected this.

'I should introduce myself. My name is Zeta and I am the High Commodore of CRISP.' The third bowl of Thai green curry decided it wanted to leave his body and the only way was up. An advanced guard of rice, chilli and green pepper hit the roof of Rib's mouth. The scouting party was repelled by a hard swallow, followed by a gagging choke.

'Are you OK?' she asked. He nodded 'yes' but thought 'shit no'. He was sitting in front of the CRISP. He was sitting at the feet of a representative of one of the most feared enforcement agencies in the Protectorate. What did she say she was? High Commodore? That sounds senior. A senior commander from whom he had nicked a matter of 250 million.

Rib Meskitoe had shit his goose, cooked his potful and panicked his idioms into total disarray.

'I owe you an explanation,' she repeated. 'We've had our eye on you for some time.'

'Me?'

'A very bright student. One of Professor Riley's best. Good family too.'

Rib thought he detected a faint smile at those words.

'So we thought we would run a test on you.'

'Run a test? What sort of test?' His mind was racing. Which part of the journey was a test? He didn't remember anything where he had been tested.

As if she could read his mind, she continued. 'Starting

271

with the moment that I gave you the 250 million dollars ...'

'Whoa! Hold on there a minute,' Rib gasped. 'You gave me the money? How do you make that out? I stole your ticket and that's what I've been wanting to explain. It was a moment of madness. I could see a chance to save my mum's refuge, so I ...'

'I am fully aware of what you thought you did and why you did it. Now, if I may continue. Thank you. We engineered a situation where you thought you had stolen the money. We wished to test you under working conditions. Test your values, your ethics, your character, your skills.'

'Hold on, hold on. Look, I'm sorry. I know I keep interrupting you but you're going too fast for me. How did you "engineer" a situation?'

'When you held my Lotto ticket and I asked you if it was the lucky one, I influenced the decision.'

'How?'

'Suggestive hypnosis. The choice of words, their order, the cadence, the body language. I made you take the ticket.'

'So I didn't really steal the money at all then?'

'No.'

'So I've been beating myself up for the last six months for nothing?'

'No, that was the important part of the test. To assess how you would react under pressure.'

'No!' said Rib, shaking his head. 'I can't believe this for one instant. I don't know who you are, or where you come from, but I'm not buying this story. It's bullshit! Now if you'll excuse me, I have something important to do.' He made as if to stand up. The old woman leaned forward and gripped his shoulder, pushing him slowly but firmly back to a sitting position.

'I can understand why you are angry. I can promise you that exactly what I have told you is the truth. Please do me the courtesy of hearing me out.'

Rib didn't answer at first. He could still feel the after-effect of the grip of steel on his shoulder. 'OK, go on then,' he said, without looking at her.

'Thank you. We wanted to see how you would fare under challenge.'

'But why me? OK, I was a good student but no more.'

'You do yourself a disservice, Master Meskitoe. You have a rare blend of sensitivity, creativity and fortitude. Our faith in you has not been misplaced.'

'OK, so you think I've got potential. But for what?'

'CRISP is always on the search for new talent. For obvious reasons we have to be selective and, for reasons of security, secretive.'

'And you chose me?'

'We selected you for assessment.'

'Well, I'm sorry to disappoint you but I don't believe you. Are you for one moment expecting me to believe that everything that's happened to me in the last six months was nothing more than an extended practical assignment?'

'You could put it that way.'

'Well, that's a load of crap and I can tell you why,' said Rib, warming to his theme and forgetting for a moment that he was speaking to a woman who, if she were indeed telling the truth, was one of the most powerful beings in the known universe. 'Because, because the only reason I got off the Wigan citidome in the first place was a daft Welshman who worked with me in the store. It if wasn't for him, I wouldn't have even passed first base on this test of yours. You say you owe me an explanation. How do you explain that?'

She sighed like someone having to repeat something for the third time.

'You are referring to Kaddie Kadwallader?'

Rib's heart missed a beat. He was sure he hadn't mentioned Kaddie by name. In fact, he knew he hadn't.

'Aka Agent 4.'

Rib's jaw dropped.

Kaddie.

An agent.

Bloody hell.

'We could not have expected a fourteen-year-old to set out on the test without the assistance of a facilitator. Yours was Agent 4.'

Rib's memory rewound to his last image of Kaddie being bludgeoned on the head on the platform as he span out of control down to the Underdome. 'Is he OK? The last time I saw him he was in trouble.'

'Yes he's fine. We entrusted one of our best agents to your project ...'

I'm now a project, thought Rib.

'... And he did a good job. Although you remind me, I must make a mental note never to let him play such a role again. His Welsh accent was so outré and his stunts with the large jars of pickled beetroot ...'

Rib had to join in the smile. 'Well, he certainly had me fooled. What's he doing now?'

'Classified information.'

Rib paused long and hard, collecting his thoughts. She allowed him this space before adding: 'And how would an old woman otherwise know how to find a lost boy sitting on a silver ball amongst the ruins of a city which once was Milton Keynes? Please believe me, I'm telling you how it is.'

'But how did you come across the jackpot ticket in the first place?'

'That was simple. We rigged it. We do it with the lottery all the time.'

Rib needed time to allow this all to sink in. 'Every week?'

She paused. 'Most weeks.'

Finally he looked up at her. 'OK, let's say I believe you. But it still doesn't quite add up, does it? If all this test business were true, why did you not let me cross the finish line on my own? Sit the final exam?'

She nodded.

'A good question. There was a complication.'

'Complication?'

'Something went wrong, very wrong. We saw no danger in using the Dead or Alive competition as a template for your project.'

Rib registered the words "danger" and "dead or alive" and retreated to attentive listening mode.

'Dead or Alive, the modern form of blood sport normally confined to ageing males, typically belonging to a brotherhood society. Have you heard of it?'

Rib shook his head.

'It replaced fox hunting, badger baiting and the like after Watershed. It was based on a 1970s novel wherein the prey is a fugitive and is hunted down as part of a game.'

Rib opened his mouth to speak.

'Please do not interrupt. As I was saying, it was confined to pretty pathetic circles and much of the attraction centred on the boasting, the stories and the celebrations, rather than the killings.'

Rib opened his mouth again but thought better of it.

'It developed into a formal competition with a points scoring system, league tables, championships. As I said, it was really quite a pathetic display of grown men acting out their fantasies. But at the same time, it was a convenient measure against which we could judge our candidates.'

'As fugitives?' confirmed Rib.

'Yes, as fugitives. Of course we made absolutely sure that none of our candidates were exposed to serious peril ...'

'I sense a "but" coming on,' said Rib.

'Yes, you're right. Which brings me to the point of all this. We made a mistake.'

'A mistake?'

'Your Dead or Alive game became too deadly for our

liking. Unbeknown to us, a dangerous competitor had thrown his hat into the ring.'

'What ring?'

'Your flight from the Wigandome attracted interest from an unexpected and indeed unwanted quarter. A man by the name of Hesperus Besk. A dangerous man. He has been under surveillance for some months, believed to be behind a network of extortion rackets in the citidome. We know that he has used his seemingly untouchable position in the Establishment to create a web of fear and violence. What we did not know was that he was a player of Dead or Alive. One would have imagined it to be beneath him. On reflection, however, it presented itself as the easy masseuse to his ego. Little effort on his part. Immediate gratification. Immediate affirmation of his control over his world.'

'So he's not a very nice man, then,' said Rib.

'Well put. I admire the art of the understatement. No, not nice at all. Hence my presence here. Hence my intervention. On account of the fact that he is the hunter and you are his prey. Moreover, my intelligence tells me that he is not in the Alive frame of mind. So now you know why I am here.'

Rib nodded. 'I think so. You chose me to be your apprentice. You messed up. You expect me to say OK.'

'One thing you are not understanding,' she broke in. 'The game is still in play.'

'What do you mean, in play?'

'If I have to criticise you for one thing, Master Meskitoe, you constantly turn the statement into a question and expect an answer. Work it out for yourself!'

He snorted out air through his nostrils and summarised to himself the movie so far. Dead or Alive. Rib Meskitoe playing support as fugitive. At the top of the bill, psychopath Hesperus Besk, licensed to kill.

Directed by High Commodore of CRISP, the old woman who could out-paddle a Redgrave, whatever that meant …

And still in his bag, 200 million dollars.

The question was, did he want to sit here in the back row without a bag of popcorn, let alone a flick to hold hands with.

Or did he want to walk out and watch the film on the next screen – the one he thought he'd bought the ticket for.

He held his head in his hands. He felt a mix of anger and relief. It seemed very much as if he had played the unwitting rabbit in some sort of sick apprentice programme. What were his rights in all this? He knew the answer. It wasn't even worth asking her. He had no rights. And that made him angry. Part of him still didn't want to believe it.

There was one part, however, that he was happy to believe. More than happy to believe. That he didn't steal her money.

The old woman's explanation had ripped the guilt monkey off his back, kicked it up the arse and sent it running into the forest never to be seen again. The monkey that had chattered constantly in his ear. The monkey that had dug its claws deep into his conscience every time he had started to feel good about things.

And now, he could start to feel good about things again. He could be himself. He had the key. He could now get back home. And see Mum again.

Then suddenly another thought struck him. Like a runaway trashsucktruck. What about the looty. Was it his? Was it hers? If he went home empty-handed now the whole exercise would have been futile. He would have failed.

He looked up at the old woman.

39

'What happens to the 200 million?'

She paused.

'Well, that depends very much on you. As I said, you have acquitted yourself very well, enough to assure me that you would add value to the patrol. A proportion of the sum would then be paid to you as an advance payment of your first three years salary.

'How much?'

For a split second, she seemed to hesitate. 'Five per cent.'

Jeeez, thought Rib, doing the mental arithmetic.

'So let's get this straight. If I sign up to be an apprentice secret-squirrel space-cadet thingy or whatever you want to call it. I keep a million dollars.'

'Correct. Subject to a medical,' she added.

'And all I have to do is sign on the dotted line?'

'Correct,' she confirmed.

Rib stood up. This time she didn't try to stop him. He looked her in the eye.

'Well thanks, but no thanks. Your line of business does not attract me in the slightest. If what you've put me through is a taster, then I have to say it tastes shit. With respect,' he added. He drew a deep breath. 'But I do think that some of that money is mine, anyway.'

She raised an eyebrow.

'I think I should be recompensed for loss of earnings, injury to feelings, damage to reputation and violation of human rights.'

She smiled at him. 'And how much do you assess your ... damages to be?'

He clearly hadn't thought this through. He hadn't expected her question. He thought she'd laugh him out of town.

'Ermm, a hundred thousand dollars,' he said none too convincingly.

'One hundred thousand dollars,' the old woman repeated to herself thoughtfully. 'You demand so much yet you demand so little.'

She remained deep in thought for what seemed an eternity before looking Rib fully into the eyes.

'I sense your mind is made up. The choice has to be yours.' She then turned away from him and knelt beside the fire. She spoke into the flames. 'I will pay you one hundred thousand dollars in the morning for your troubles.'

The occasional crackle of burning wood was the only sound to break the gulf of silence now between them. It was as if they no longer had anything to say to each other. Rib wanted to explain his reasons for not accepting her offer, but he knew that now was not the time.

He should have been feeling happy with how things had turned out. He hadn't stolen the money. He had made it back to MK. He'd found the key. He was a hundred grand richer.

But he wasn't feeling happy. Something was stopping him. Something about the old woman.

And some unfinished business gnawing at the back of his mind.

Rika.

'Do you know what happened to the girl I was travelling with?' he asked without engaging eye contact.

'Ah yes. The young Lappish woman. A woman of spirit ...'

'What happened to her? Why did she leave?'

The old woman paused before answering. 'She had her reasons.'

It took a few seconds for the words to sink in. 'No, you're wrong! There's no way she was working for Besk!'

'Look, I know it must hurt …' she said.

'You know nothing!' he snapped. 'She would never betray me. Why did she save me in the clearing when we found the dead guy with the wine? Tell me that. Why did she save me?'

The old woman paused again, deep in thought. 'I don't know. I genuinely don't know. You may have a point. Time will tell.' She saw tears well up in his eyes. 'Look,' she said, 'the game is far from finished. Wait for the last throw of the dice. It's the only one that counts. Listen carefully to what I say. The last throw …'

The flames flickered darting shadows on the broken brick-work around them. They sat under the dead branches of the oak tree named Midsummer. Not a word passed between them for a full five minutes.

Suddenly she stood up and turned round to face him.

'I have not been totally honest with you.'

Rib's heart sank.

'This is really difficult for me,' she went on. 'I did not want to have to tell you this way.' She walked over and sat beside him. 'You see, I was hoping you would join my team.'

'So that bit's true then, you really are a High Commodore?'

'Oh yes, of course, all of that is true. Where I have misled you is the 200 million dollars.'

He groaned inwardly. Just when he thought he'd pulled off the deal of his life.

'It's all yours.'

Rib's jaw dropped.

'Mine? All of it?'

'Yes.'

'200 million dollars?'

'Yes.'

'All of it?'

'Yes.'

'But I'm not changing my mind about signing up, you know.'

'I know. You do not need to.'

'Then how is the money mine?'

'I am giving it to you.'

Rib shook his head. 'I don't understand. Why would you give me 200 million dollars?'

The old woman breathed deeply before saying ... 'Rib, the money has your name on it. Under the terms of my will, Master Rib Meskitoe is a named beneficiary to receive the sum of 200 million dollars in the event of my death.'

'But I don't even know you, and you're not dead!'

'No, I am not dead, but I do not have long to live. In my line of business death is a constant companion. And whilst, however, it is indeed true that you do not know me, I know you. That is all that matters.'

Rib flushed with anger. 'And you're expecting me to buy that! You've already lied to me once, you admitted so yourself. And now you're spinning me another yarn about leaving me all your money in your will cos you're about to die. Well, I don't believe a word of it.' He stood up and stomped over to the tree.

She stood up and followed him.

'Please don't be angry with me, Rib. The last thing I want to do is cause you distress. Believe me, I have your best interests at heart.'

'Why should I believe a word you say?' he said, still facing away from her. She placed her hand on his shoulder and gently turned him round.

'Because I am your grandmother.'

She looked him straight in the eye. The same look she had given him in the Waste-Rows Lotto queue six months before. But no suggestive hypnosis this time.

He knew she was telling him the truth.

He was staring at Zeta Meskitoe. His dad's mum. His grandmother.

Zeta Meskitoe.

The name never to be uttered under the roof of H222.

His mum had blamed her for the death of his dad and had made it quite clear to her at his funeral that she never wanted to see her again. Rib was only two at the time, but could somehow remember the animated exchange between the two distressed women as if it were yesterday.

That was the last time he had seen her.

Over twelve years ago.

And now, here she was, standing before him. Her hand on his shoulder. Part of him wanted to wrench it away. Part of it wanted just to touch it.

Finally he said, 'Why no contact for all this time?'

He could see a tear beginning to well up in her left eye. 'It was Alice's wish. I had to respect that. She had lost Mike. We both had. We all had.'

She turned away from him and walked over to the fire.

'But I had no idea you were a High Commodore,' he called after her.

'Again that was Alice's wish. Mike had been lost in action. On a mission. In my team. She probably did not want to see her only son fall under my influence. I can understand that.'

'And yet here you are. How do you think she would feel about this cosy little chat we're having?'

She turned to face him. 'Your challenge shows that you are no longer a boy. I would suggest it is for you to decide with whom you wish to hold a cosy little chat or otherwise.'

His senses were running riot. He sat down at the base of the tree and held his head in his hands. He did not know what to feel. Emotions attacked him from every direction. All conflicting. Riptide and rescue. Rescue and riptide. Out of the stampeding senses, one suddenly stood stock still and spoke.

'You said you didn't have long to live …'

She laughed. 'It's an occupational hazard. It goes with the territory. I exchange pawns with Death on a regular basis.'

'But that's not all, is it?'

She thought long and hard before answering. 'No it isn't. My consultant considers that it would no longer be ethical to take out a loan.'

He sideswiped her attempt at levity.

'How long have you got?'

'Two, maybe three years.'

Her sentence took time to sink in.

'Remember, Rib, I am an old woman and I have lived a full and eventful life. Death holds no fears for me.'

The crackle of the fire took over as silence enveloped them again.

'But 200 million dollars' said Rib, still to her back. 'Why give me all your money and why now?'

She turned to him. 'Firstly, do not flatter yourself. What you have in your bag is not the full extent of my estate. I have other plans, although as I said before, you are the prime beneficiary. Secondly, you have had the money for six months and thought it to be yours. Thirdly, what is the point of letting the money sit on the market when you have use for it now?'

'Do you mean the refuge?'

'For example,' she nodded.

'Then why don't you give the money straight to Mum?'

'The last thing on earth she would do is to accept charity from me. That much you know.'

She was right. 'And why should she accept it via me?'

'She will make the connection only if you make the connection for her.'

'So are you telling me to lie to her?'

Zeta snapped at him. 'I said nothing of the sort. The money is yours. How you came across it is your business. As I said, you are no longer a little boy.'

Rib wrestled with this. As far as he and his mum went, he was still a little boy. 'I'm sorry, I'm not trying to be awkward. But how am I going to explain to her how I have 200 million dollars in my possession?'

She raised her eyebrows. 'What were you going to say before? You stole it from a poor old lady? Your explanation is now much more straightforward. Tell her you won it on the Lotto. End of story. The money is yours, morally and legally. Get over it. Move on. Make her happy.'

She stood up, clearly irritated, and walked round to the other side of the fire. Rib watched her as she poked the embers with a stick.

The fire was dying down now and she made no move to add more wood. It felt late and he felt drained. Physically and emotionally.

Rib knew she was pissed off. Seeing it from her side, it was understandable, when he thought about it. Grandmother denied access to only Grandson, Grandmother finally finds Grandson, Grandmother gives Grandson 200 million dollars, Grandson finds all sort of problems with it, Grandson doesn't even say nice to see you, Grandson doesn't even say thanks.

He walked over to her. She looked up from busying herself with the embers.

'What should I call you?'

'Well now,' she paused. 'Assuming you're not joining me professionally ...'

He shook his head.

'Then I think Gran would be very nice.'

'Gran it is then.' He smiled. 'Oh and one more thing.'

'Yes.'

'Any chance of a cuddle?'

'I think that would be entirely appropriate,' she said as she

284

stood up and embraced him.

They stood swaying ever so slightly from side to side without a word, each deeply immersed in their own version of the experience. The hug ended with them both looking at each other long and hard in the eyes before letting go with a smile.

'You have a hard day ahead of you tomorrow,' she said as she unrolled two sleeping bags.

Rib had almost forgotten. He had the key to Domestrut 44. All he now had to do was find it, climb it, and then he was there.

MK …

Gran had gone to carry out a final check on the lasertrips. There was so much he wanted to tell her, so much he wanted to ask her. When she came back, he said, 'Before we go to sleep, will you tell me about Dad?'

'Are you sure? Haven't you had enough for one day, young man?'

'No, I'm sure,' he said as he wriggled down into his bag.

'Very well then, but only the shortened version. Mike Meskitoe was born son of Nathaniel Meskitoe and Zeta Meskitoe. And before you ask, yes, your grandfather *is* still alive. As we speak he's probably taking a bite out of a chilli pepper and washing it down with a Red Stripe lager.'

'Where?'

'Somewhere on Tycho is all I know. Probably on a beach. Probably with a mongrel at his feet and wearing a disreputable jacket. Him, not the mongrel. As you can guess, we went our separate ways …'

Gran Meskitoe served Rib a story sandwich of his dad's life. She told him of Mike's boyhood, where he went to school, how they spent their holidays.

Rib lay silent all the way though. The only time he spoke was when Gran spoke of her son's love of chess.

'I didn't know he played chess,' he whispered to himself.

She carefully wrapped up the bitter pill of Mike's death in a savoury-sweet mix of memories. How his troop had been ambushed by a group of insurgents, how six had been taken hostage. How Mike had led the rescue assault. How they all came of that hellhole alive. All except Mike.

Zeta blamed herself for his death. And she knew that Alice did. All that Rib could taste on his tongue was the bitter-sharp pill. He swallowed it.

It was inside him.

For ever.

He got out of his sleeping bag and lay down beside his gran. They fell into a deep sleep in each other's arms.

40

He felt the pain before he opened his eyes. The piercing pain from the puncture in the back of his neck. Overlaid by the thick throb of pain pounding around the rest of his head.

He opened his eyes and immediately wanted to be sick. He was hanging upside down, trussed like a turkey, his hands tied behind his back. Suspended from his ankles by a rope. The coarse fibres cutting deeply into his skin.

It was difficult to focus. He was swaying gently from side to side, adding to the overpowering sense of nausea. What had happened? The last thing he remembered was saying goodnight to Gran.

Gran! Where was she? He soon saw the answer, swinging beside him, less than 3 metres away, seemingly lifeless.

'Gran!' he hissed. 'Wake up, Gran!' She opened one eye. She was at least alive, thank God. He tried to work out how they'd got there. Hadn't Gran set lasertrips around the camp? They must have been shot with tranquilisers from a distance.

An enormous upside-down frog stared at him. Rib stared back in disbelief. It was the mechanical clock he'd repaired. The big frog. He was suspended above the mall opposite where the giant frog used to play out his performance however many years ago. The big clock read 6.55.

Rib was now alert, forgetting the pain. He was suddenly aware of activity on the floor below him, or above him as it seemed. Two men, two frightening-looking men were pointing up at them, laughing. Rib recognised them immediately as Slakterghasts. How could he forget that train of terror which thundered past him and Rika beside the M1? The brigands now presented a threat ten times more terrifying because of one thing. He had their attention. No, a hundred times more terrifying. They were brandishing above their heads what appeared to be eating irons. The one on the left a skewer and cleaver, the one on the right carrying a knife and a fondue fork. Fondue fork?

What had Rika said? They'll beat you, rape you and eat you, or something like that. He couldn't remember her exact words, but the message was loud and clear. He was in trouble. His eyes were drawn back to the frog, then the clock.

It read 6.57.

He was sure the minute hand had moved. Had they set it in motion? He straightened his neck to look up at the floor. It was about 7 or 8 metres away. Far down enough to smash his skull to smithereens even if he managed to wriggle free and drop. He'd dabbled in high diving and could perform a passable somersault and double twist. At best, he'd end up with a broken back and shattered pelvis. At worst, well it was a no-brainer. There would be no brain, was his assessment.

6.58.

'Gran!' he hissed. 'The clock. It's working.'

Zeta Meskitoe chose to ignore this important piece of news. She was either feigning dead or she had slipped back into a state of unconsciousness. Either way, she wasn't answering.

Rib cupped his hands behind his head and tensed his stomach muscles, put his knees together, and angled his body out of the perpendicular to survey what was going on above him. The findings were as painful as the act. He was hanging some 5 metres down from a once-white girder, now blistered and paint-cracked. The other end of the rope tied to his ankles was wrapped round the girder fourfold and tied in a ship-shape manner in what could be a running half-hitch or a roaring reefer or a shagging sheepshank.

Knots were not his forte.

The only important thing was that they were holding. And they seemed to be.

He saw for the first time the window behind him. Part shattered, its green-and-yellow stained-glass statement still stood strong. The early, low, sharp rays of the new-day sun bounced off the forest canopy and cut under the unsuspecting belly of the citidome to strike through the glass onto the forehead of the frog. He was mesmerised by the intensity of the moment.

6.59.

Something was going to happen ...

And it did.

A red-feathered crossbow bolt, travelling far too fast for its own good, severed one of the three strands of rope suspending Rib. He almost saw it coming but not quite. The three strands had become two jolting him down with a jerk. Actually and emotionally. Now seriously destabilised, he breathed deeply. Was this how it was going to end? He heard the rope fibre sinews groan in protest as new demands were made of them.

The Slakterghast crew squealed in delight as they shuffled forwards in the queue for their reserved table. Steak tartare. Forget the chopped onions and eggs.

They looked up and behind them in anticipation as if seeking a signal. Rib followed their line of sight and for an instant caught a glimpse of a slim grey-clad figure in the shadows. On the first floor behind the frog, up the frozen escalator and to the right. As soon as he saw him, he was gone. No longer there. A shadow figure sliding into the shadows. Besk, he thought. Was this the man who had been hunting him?

Rib's upside-down eyes then saw something which made them blink, screw themselves up – upside-down-wise – and strain to focus on what they saw. And they were right. A crumpled khaki bag hanging from the end of the barrier rail. A forlorn study of forgotten dreams.

It was unmistakeably his. The question was, had it been left there by mistake? Or was it a trap? A tad too studied? Maybe. Did it still hold his looty? And could he do anything about it anyway, being trussed up as he was, dangling in the air, about to become a Slakterghast feast?

The string of questions scurried through his head without answer.

The clock hand moved to seven. A haunting melody filled the air.

The two Slakterghasts stopped their noise and turned to look at the act unfolding above them. Suddenly they were three. Rib hadn't even seen the slim grey-suited figure slip into their company. Rib immediately looked for his bag. It was still there, on the rail of the first-floor landing.

The mesmeric dance of the big frog held its audience spellbound. Captives and captors alike.

Rib knew the sequence inside out. He was, after all, the person responsible for giving the frog a new life cycle. Only this time no trace of slimy spawn and tadpole. Just pulleys and chains, rods and levers.

Rib held his breath. Something had to happen. Unless this giant circus show was to be nothing more than a stay of execution.

Then it happened. Olass turned to look at the slim man beside him. 'Master Besk,' he pleaded (So it *was* Besk! Rib noted). 'Can we have the bubbles? Please!' he beseeched. 'Please.'

Besk seemed to smile and nodded, sending the Slakterghast henchmen careering over the slippery floor and up the escalator in leaps and bounds.

'Quick!' urged Maliss. 'Or we'll miss it!'

Olass disappeared from view behind the body of the frog.

Rib knew exactly what he was doing. Opening the door of the control panel. Pressing the red switch to the left of the operating instructions plate. Olass rushed back down the frozen escalator to join the others.

'Gran!' Rib hissed. 'Gran!' He knew he had to wake her. And fast. At the third time of asking, she opened a bleary left eye as if emerging from a deep sleep. She opened her mouth to speak but nothing came out.

'Gran, listen. Can you hear me?'

She sort of nodded. Very slowly. 'Good. Don't try to speak but do exactly as I say, when I say – OK. This is really important. Gran, do you understand?'

She nodded again, a little more steadily this time.

Two large fans unfolded like wings from the back of the frog and a stream of bubbles spumed forth from its mouth. Rib noted their trajectory with keen interest: first a strong jet stream outwards from the mouth, and then they floated like parachutes softly down towards the floor of the mall. Olass and Maliss started to dance beneath them, hands held up in eager anticipation.

They were children again.

They joined the tens of thousands of child spirits before them who had done exactly the same thing. Besk joined them. He too became an entranced child.

'Gran!' hissed Rib. 'I want you now to close your eyes tight and hold your breath for thirty seconds. Do it now!'

She obeyed, but Rib didn't do as he had told her. He had to see for his own eyes. To be absolutely sure.

The first bubble landed on the back of Besk's raised hand. His two henchmen had deferred to his power. He would have the first bubble. He balanced it deftly so that it remained intact. Besk held it up towards his hanging captives, as if to show off his trophy.

What happened next seemed to tumble forward slowly frame by frame.

Olass and Maliss leapt into the air, burst a dozen bubbles or so and immediately collapsed unconscious in a crumpled heap on the floor.

Besk reached for his crossbow and aimed it at Rib. He was too late. His bubble had burst. The XL5 nerve gas was searing his eyes and had already entered his lungs. He managed to despatch a loose bolt which pinged against the wall way off to Rib's left, ricocheted against the ceiling before coming to rest on the upside-down Debenhams sign which had long since crashed down onto the marble mall floor.

Uttering an anguished cry he collapsed to the floor as more bubbles burst around him.

The toxic XL5 fumes were already reaching Rib and he knew it was time to take evasive action. The acrid taste at the back of his throat and the stinging sensation in his eyes told him that he might already be too late. He screwed his eyes shut, took a deep breath and started counting to thirty. Holding his breath was no problem. Four-thousand-metre sessions in the pool had given him a powerful set of lungs. His only worry was that some of the gas might have seeped into his system. If it had, then he had no hope.

It was make-or-break time. Anything could happen in the next half-hour.

After ten seconds he knew he was safe. Just a question now of keeping it together. And trusting that Gran would pull through. She hadn't looked in good shape at all.

Twenty-nine, thirty ...

He opened his eyes and surveyed the scene above him. The three bodies were as he last saw them, lying lifeless on the mall floor. He looked across to Zeta Meskitoe, High Commodore. She looked anything but in command as she hung there limply without a sign of movement.

'Are you OK?' he rasped.

No response. Then a faint nod.

One eye, then the other opened.

She tried to speak but couldn't.

Rib knew he had to act fast.

Looking back on it later, he could hardly believe how he had managed to get himself and his gran down safely from their place of execution. The slow motion of the bubble scene moved into fast-forward as he cut his hands free on the jagged edge of the yellow stained glass, climbed up the rope to the beam, then edged cat-like on all fours to where she was hanging, hauled her up and untied her. By this time, Zeta Meskitoe had recovered enough to make their descent at least possible, if not easy. Rib spliced the two lengths of rope together – something he had learned at Middlemedes – climbed down and dropped the final 3 metres to land safely amongst the debris on the mall floor. His gran was clearly still suffering from the knock-out shot and did not make the final jump cleanly. Rib managed, somehow, to break her fall and they ended up entwined in a heap with nothing worse than a few cuts and bruises.

'Are you OK?' were his first words.

Zeta Meskitoe, High Commodore of CRISP, merely nodded and strode over to the three bodies strewn under the frog.

She seems to be making a speedy recovery, thought Rib as he watched her lean over the prostrate form of Besk. She started to remove his trousers.

'Gran! What are you doing?' hissed Rib.

'He used a device to kill the lasertrips. I need to find it. Ahah!' she said as she removed a thin strip of leather covering his manhood and proceeded to strangle him by wrapping it round his neck and gently increasing the pressure.

'Whoa! Stop! What the hell are you doing?' shouted Rib.

Gran looked up with a half-smile on her lips. 'Killing him softly with his thong,' she replied.

He thought at first she was joking but realised she wasn't when she continued to tighten the leather band around Besk's throat.

Rib raced over and grabbed her arm. 'You can't do that.'

She loosened her grip. 'Why not? He was about to execute us. He deserves to die.'

'But it's against the law. It's murder.'

Zeta thought better of telling the boy that she *was* the law. He probably would not see it that way. He probably would not understand the fine line between right and wrong. That fine line which at times like these becomes blurred.

'And anyway,' he continued. 'They're my prisoners, not yours.'

She looked up at him, releasing her hold on the thong. 'And how do you explain that, pray?'

'Quite simple. I put the XL5 in the bubbles.'

The High Commodore looked up at him. 'You put the XL5 in the bubbles? How did you get hold of XL5?'

'A very bright student. You said so yourself. Now you wouldn't expect a very bright student of the MK School of Nanozoomology not to have a trick or two up his sleeve, would you?' Rib had never used a double negative before and was quite pleased with the effect.

Zeta Meskitoe let go of Besk. The back of his head met the marble of the mall floor with a resounding crack. She stared at her grandson with her mouth half open. 'But ...' she faltered. 'How did you get it into the bubbles?'

Rib thought that this was a stupid question coming from someone supposedly as wise and powerful as she.

'When I was fettling up the frog, I thought I'd add a sprinkling to the bubble solution.'

'Why on earth would you do that?' she asked.

'Well, I figured that if I ever got in trouble, maybe I could persuade that trouble to find its way here and maybe I could persuade that trouble to want to see how the big frog worked. And that's what I did. Sort of ...'

Zeta Meskitoe shook her head in disbelief. 'Ingenious,' she said to herself. 'Totally and utterly ingenious. I am seriously impressed, Rib. But tell me one thing. What if a third party had stumbled across the frog and set it in motion? You would have poisoned a perfectly innocent and unsuspecting soul.'

'Yeah, I did give that some thought. Firstly I reckoned on the odds of perfectly innocent souls taking an afternoon stroll in the Underdome as being pretty remote. Secondly, I added only enough XL5 to knock someone out for about half an hour. So the very worst would be a period of unconsciousness followed by symptoms of nausea and one hell of a headache.'

'Did you say half an hour?'

'Yes, about.'

'How long did it take us to get down from the rope?'

'Ooh, about ten minutes, I'd say.'

'And how long have we been happily chatting here?'

'Ooh, about another ten minutes, I'd say.'

'So we have approximately ten minutes before these criminals revive, presumably to take up where they left off. All the more reason to kill them now,' she said as she leaned down to wrap the thong around Besk's throat again.

'No!' said Rib firmly. 'As I said before, if these are anyone's, they're mine. And please don't forget, Gran, who rescued you from the rope. If you go through with this, you won't see me again. Ever. I won't have their blood on my hands!'

The High Commodore relented.

She could have despatched the three without a trace of remorse and look herself in the mirror with no question of doubt. This was her profession, her chosen path. Death was a daily routine. Death had written itself in her work diary for the past twenty-five years.

What had not been in her diary, however, was the young man who now stood defiantly before her.

Her grandson.

It did not take her long to conclude that the stakes were

too high. She would meet these three again. Another time, another place. She could not risk losing him, the son of her son. The loss of Mike still cut into her like a knife and she could not bear to make the same mistake again. So she gave way.

'OK,' she said. 'Let's get you up to MK.' As a parting fond farewell gesture to the nearer of the two unconscious Slakterghasts, she ground her heel into his groin. He would have more than a headache when he awoke. She then neatly folded Besk's trousers and placed them over his exposed private parts as if to bring a degree of dignity to the proceedings.

She turned to address Rib, but he was already halfway up the escalator. She watched as he grabbed the bag hung over the end of the rail, reached into it, took out a small purple velvet bag and held it aloft, more in relief than triumph. He hadn't needed to check the number of nuts, he could feel their weight. 200 million dollars worth.

She'd already set off with purposeful stride down East Walk by the time he got to the bottom of the escalator. So tricky, running down something stationary that your brain tells you is definitely moving. He jogged until he came along-side her just where the mall opened out to the place Rib had made his home. He took in the bronze book bench with the ball and chain. He looked back up at the far-right top window where he had kept lookout, the sign with the wooden block where he had hidden the looty. He would not return in a hurry, he promised himself.

The old woman broke his train of thought. 'Inheritance intact?'

'Absolutely.'

'Then you are back on track now for Domestrut 44. You still have the key?'

'Yep,' he replied without falter. He was still on a high from the high drama played out beneath the giant frog. He had burst Besk's bubble. Boy, would he be bitter.

'Come on, we had better make haste. They may regain consciousness soon.'

She broke into a run, short steps, more of a fast pad than a run, but deceptively fast. Rib had difficulty keeping up at first, but soon got into his long, loping stride and the odd couple ran side by side back down Silbury.

It was going to be another sweltering, sticky day.

41

Rib's shirt was sticking to his back already. He hoped that they would follow the same route he had taken yesterday so that he could take one last look at *Unity*. Gran cut off sharply to the right before the intersect, however, and steered a path through the tangle of brick, steel and glass which were once proud places of industry.

Conversation was kept to the minimum in shared unspoken awareness of the need to put distance between themselves and their former captors. They came to an open boulevard and she immediately picked up the pace. He responded, slowing only to hurdle a fallen tree in their path. They ran straight over a large raised circular area. It must have been some sort of carousel intersect, Rib figured.

Roundabout, he remembered from his local history. The old city had been famous for its roundabouts. And concrete cows. Why not the Frog? If he could rewrite history, he thought, he would have made it famous for the Frog.

He was now sweating profusely, needing to concentrate to keep pace with a woman five times his age. He smiled to himself as he stole a glance at the slight figure beside him rattling out a steady 12K per hour pace. She was impressive, no question about it. The High Commodore of CRISP. His grandmother. How chill was that.

They were heading for the eastern edge of the citidome and the curved line of uprights supporting the whole mass of the structure above them became clearer with each step. They shifted from two-dimensional thick black silhouette lines into towering cylindrical pillars, grey in colour.

'Domestrut 44?' Zeta asked.

'Yes, I think so. Hold on a sec – I'll check.' Rib stopped and took the key out of the zip pocket on the side of his bag.

'Yep, 44 it is.'

'Then that's it, over there,' she pointed. He couldn't see which one she meant.

'Which one?'

'The one with forty-four written at the top.'

And sure enough, as his eyes became accustomed to the brightness of the outside world streaming into the gloom of the Underdome, he could pick out the numbers. Printed in white as if through a giant template:

44

Only now did it start to sink in. He was the marathon runner turning the final corner into the finishing straight. Crowds lined the road cheering. He half tottered and stumbled as the wall of sound hit him. His adrenaline levels soared as he saw the white banner with the large red letters 'FINISH' stretched across the 42.2-kilometre line.

His brain screamed, 'Sprint!'

Every aching muscle and sinew strained to lengthen his stride. The *Chariots of Fire* theme tune rang in his ears as he sped past others who had slowed to a painful limp, running on empty.

Somewhere behind the pounding of his heart he heard a voice. 'Rib! Stop!'

He felt a hand on his shoulder. 'Take it easy. You are almost there. This is no time to lose control,' came the calming words of Zeta Meskitoe.

'Sorry,' he said. They both stopped to catch breath.

He could now clearly make out the door at the base of the strut, some hundred metres away.

'Do you want me to see you to the door?' she asked.

It was the voice of his mother. He was seven. It was his first day at college. Do you want me to see you to the shuttle stop, she had said. The thought of being escorted by his mother for all to see. He was seven, for God's sake!

He answered the same as he had then. 'No thanks.'

But this time for a different reason. Then, it had been a reaction based on embarrassment. Now it was something else. His Year 5 Forskyne-Smythe Assessment Profile had remained imprinted on his memory:

Rib Meskitoe is creative and sensitive to the feelings of others. He works well in teams and is careful to wash behind his ears … His style is to create the perfect piece of work until he is close to the end. He is then prone to move on to the next opus. Rib finds it hard to finish.

Rib finds it hard to finish …

'No thanks. I'll take it on from here.'

He paused.

'Unless you want to come and see Mum?'

'No, Rib, Alice will not wish to see me.'

She paused.

'Are you sure you do not wish to join me? We can contact your mother and release funds for the refuge?'

'No, Gran, I really need to see her. *Be* with her.'

'You are right, absolutely right.' Before he knew what was happening, she had gripped him a vice-like bear hug and held him there.

She released him. 'Right then, off you go, my young man,' she said as she gave him a mock punch to his left shoulder.

He saw a tear in her eye.

'Will I see you again?' he asked.

The answer came slowly. 'Yes, I believe you will.' She unzipped a pocket on her trouser leg and handed him a small

300

paper bag. He opened it. It was a black leather necklace with an aluminium tag.

'It was your father's. Take good care of it.' He held it on his upturned palm and studied it. It was beautiful.

He grasped and held her hard. He kissed her on a tear-stained cheek.

He was now the one who wept as he turned to head towards the strut. He ran a few paces. He couldn't swallow.

He stopped.

He turned.

She was gone.

42

The square dull grey key fitted the door lock perfectly. Rib turned it to the right and pulled. The door did not budge. Tried the key to the left. It wouldn't go. Back to the right, this time with a tug. Something gave. Only by a millimetre or so. But it gave. He tried again with a jerk and the door creaked open just wide enough to let him slip his hand inside. The hinges groaned their annoyance at being disturbed from their long slumber. The handle caught in his dad's ID tag which he'd wrapped around his wrist. He swore and put it in his pocket. Before stepping through the door, he glanced over his shoulder to check whether he'd been followed. He didn't think so.

He felt inside the door and found at once a plastic-covered light button. It responded to his touch and filled the space with a pale, yellow, semi-glow, hardly enough to see your way by. Certainly not enough to see to the top of the strut. A metal staircase with a handrail on either side spiralled up the middle of the featureless column.

He shivered. His bones felt a dry coldness for the first time in months.

400 metres.

That's all it was. 400 metres up to the MK citidome platform. Journey's end. He took a deep breath and began to climb. His footsteps sounded noisily on the metal steps, ringing an echo off the strut walls. If pigeons had been roosting in this dark, sterile place, they would have fluttered skyward in alarm. His mind started to replay the events of the previous four days. He tried to block out the painful thoughts by focusing on the steps, one by one, but they came flooding back. All collecting in one deep pool.

Rika.

A minute passed. Then another. He was making good progress. Rib started to perspire. Then something made him stop, stand upright and grip the handrail hard. What was it? He instinctively reached in his pocket to feel for the tag. It wasn't there.

Jesus Christ! he gasped. The tag wasn't there!

Blind panic.

Where was it? Think back! Think back! Had he dropped it coming up the steps? No.

Had he had it when he started to climb? Not sure ... maybe not ...

He hurtled down the stairs at breakneck speed, smacking his hip against the rail as he did so. He was making enough noise to raise the dead, not that he cared. His dad's tag was the only thing that mattered. He landed in a heap at the foot of the stairs and lay panting for five pants, his eyes transfixed on the door. It was open. Had he left it open? There was no tag to be seen.

He stumbled towards the doorway and pushed through and there it was, lying spread out in the mud.

He slid down the domestrut wall until it came to rest sitting with his knees raised and the tag clasped tightly to its chest.

Eyes closed.

Bathed in sweat.

Fighting for air.

A rustling sound from semi-distance. He opened his eyes, now alert. Had he heard something? The shredded remnants of a white plastic bag tumbled across the street until it became entangled in a gnarled piece of deadwood. It fluttered fitfully, like a torn shroud. Rib slowly moved to his feet, scanning the street for any sign of movement. There was nothing. Just a thirty-year-old plastic bag now trapped in eternal purgatory.

Rib checked his rucksack for the walnuts, put the ID tag beside them, then fastened the rucksack securely, first with the straps over his shoulders, then with the buckle at the front. He pulled it tight one notch extra. Taking one last look behind him, he stepped back into the domestrut.

Inside, the pale-yellow light still shone. Rib took the first three steps of the stairs in one bound, eager to make up the lost time. He then noticed something in his line of sight between the treads, a heap of materials on the domestrut floor. He swung round and jumped down the bottom steps, then padded over to a jumble of plastic, metal and packaging piled against the wall. It looked as if these were the remnants of some repair work carried out on the stair handrail. Rib bent down and picked up a short metal tube, a piece of scaffold pipe, no longer than his forearm. It was smooth at one end and sawn-off sharp at the other. It sat snugly in his grip. Never know, he thought to himself as he started his ascent two steps at a time.

400 metres, he whispered. Just 400 metres and then I'm home. He soon became breathless and steadied his pace, stopping at intervals to look down at the domestrut floor, smaller but still visible, and up towards the domestrut ceiling, not yet visible through the weak yellow glow given off by the bulkhead lights mounted on the walls.

Suddenly, something made him stop. Was it his imagination or was the light fading? It was hard to tell. So he stared directly at the bulb of one of the lights, some 5 metres up and to his left. And as slowly and surely as the auditorium lights fade before the film starts, the bulb weakened, second by second. Mesmerised, Rib watched the filament lose its glow until it reduced to a final ember prick in the darkness which now enveloped him.

The *total* blackness which now enveloped him.

He held up his left hand in front of his face. He couldn't see it. He touched the tip of his nose with the flat of his palm, then drew it back a centimetre.

Nothing, just thick, dense blackness.

What had happened? His first thought was that someone had switched the lights off. He strained to hear any telltale sound. Nothing. He knelt down and placed his ear flat against the step. Nothing. He stayed that way for a full minute before he was satisfied that nobody was climbing the stairs. His heart rate gradually started to come down as he tried to figure out why the lights had gone out. Power failure? Possible, but unlikely. It then dawned on him. The lights were on a time switch. How far up the domestrut had he reached before he turned back? About halfway, yes, about halfway. And then he spent a couple of minutes finding his tag, and then had climbed over halfway up again.

Yes, that must be it, he reasoned. It made sense. Automatic cut-out after the time needed to complete the climb.

Reassured, he took the first tentative step upwards. It was slow-going, but he soon developed a rhythm, his left hand on the hand rail guiding his progress; two feet on one step, left hand sliding up the rail, gripping rail and pulling, left foot onto next step, right foot up to join it, and so on. The only obstacles to his progress were the landings which seemed to occur every two hundred steps or so and which consisted of small platforms no more than 4 metres square, presumably to allow maintenance or repair work to be done.

He negotiated the first landing by crawling on all fours, tackled the second by following the rail all around the platform, and felt confident enough to walk slowly across the third, left hand outstretched, feeling for the rail.

He edged his way upwards for a further couple of minutes until he stopped dead in his tracks.

A sound.

From the bottom of the stairwell. A tiny, tinny clang. He

held his breath and strained hard to listen.

There it was again. And again.

He was no longer alone in the domestrut.

Someone was coming up the stairs.

His heart jumped into his mouth. He could now hear a rhythmic ping-ping of steel boots on metal steps. A regular, quick rhythm. Whoever was following him was moving fast. A droplet of sweat fell from his nose onto his hand. He had a good head start. Must be over 300 metres, so he should be able to outrun his pursuer, he thought as he turned and slid his left hand up along the handrail. He stumbled and nearly fell, only preventing himself from doing so by thrusting out his right hand in front of him. The sharp edge of the step took the skin off his knuckle. His grip held firm on the length of tube as he raised himself to his feet, breathed in deep and set off unsteadily upwards.

'Ping, ping, ping' echoed up the stairwell. Whoever was following was not trying to hide their presence. And they were gaining.

Fast …

It sounded as if they were literally bounding up the stairs. They seemed to be drawing nearer by the second. Rib shuffled on, trying to shut out the sound from his mind. All he had to do was reach the door at the top before them. He must be nearly there by now. Surely …

How could they be travelling so fast? The terrible thought struck him that he might have to turn and fight. Faced with this unwelcome prospect, Rib knew that he now had to reach the door first and he redoubled his efforts to move upwards into the blackness.

But it was no good. By the time he reached the next landing, he could clearly hear steps striding across the landing below. He reckoned he had a minute at the most. Rib gripped the bar in his right hand. He decided to make a stand. On the landing. If he had to fight, he needed room. Or maybe an ambush? Maybe he could spring out on his pursuer on the landing? He couldn't decide what to do. All his powers were focused on feeling his way to the far left side of the landing, where he stood upright, the back of his head touching the wall.

The blackness closed in around him. His heightened sense of hearing picked out a slowing of the steps as his pursuer approached. He was now on the flight of stairs below him. Rib's heart hammered away at a beat of 160 plus. He tried to control the contractions, but without success. He fought hard to sharpen his senses. He detected a faint smell of stale sweat, layered over by new sweat. His own. Rib held his breath. He tightened his grip on the tubing.

The man was now nearly on the landing. Which man? A slimy henchman? Besk himself? It didn't matter. Whoever was chasing him was hell bent on one thing.

His destruction.

The darkness was as thick as black treacle as it swallowed everything. The pursuer stopped. Some four or five steps down from the landing.

He had realised.

He had realised Rib was there.

The treacle held them for what seemed an eternity. Then Rib caught a sound. The slightest, almost imperceptible, grating noise. Then silence …

What had he heard? Tearing plastic, small teeth slowly biting. A zip! He had taken off his boots!

Rib instinctively ducked down to his right as something swished past his left ear and clanged against the wall behind him.

It was a knife.

He must have another. Why would be throw it otherwise?

Rib could not strike back. His right hand holding the bar was pressed to the floor, giving him balance. But he knew he could not stay there. He twisted up and out to the centre of the landing. They stood there, face to face, each holding their breath. The second blow came fast and this time sliced through the skin at the very point of Rib's nose. Like the tip of a chef's knife slitting the skin of a parboiled tomato. At first, he wasn't sure that he was cut until he felt the blood flow across his top lip.

There was a time when Rib Meskitoe would have screamed out loud at having his nose sliced and yes, he had been hurt. But this was nothing serious, not after what he'd been through. Silence enveloped them again. He tried to keep his heart on hold. His hand on the pipe was soaked with sweat. He was scared of letting it slip from his grasp. The blackness engulfed them. He sensed a movement in their air. Was it a breath? An arm raised to strike?

He crouched low as the third blow sliced the air above his head. Rib used his forearm strength to deliver a swinging uppercut with the pipe into the man's ribs. He let out a gasp and Rib sprung up to full height to smash down at where the gasp had come from. He hit bone. He swung again and struck bone again. The man was down.

Silence and inky blackness now resumed its rightful ownership of the space and closed in around both men.

Rib stood trembling as he listened for any sound from the man somewhere at his feet.

There was none. For all he knew, for all he cared, there was no life left in the man who had tried to take his.

He spat out the blood from his mouth and dropped the piece of tubing onto the floor. He felt his way gingerly around the handrail, seeking out the stairs that would take him up. More than ever, he had to get out of this place.

It took him no more than two minutes to climb the final flight of stairs, locate the door to dome level, take out the key from his trousers pocket and unlock it.

He stepped out, his eyes squinting against the brightness of the citidome morning.

He was home.

43

The heavy metal door of Domestrut 44 slammed behind him and he stood, eyes closed, scarcely able to catch his breath. Rib finally opened his eyes and surveyed the cobalt-blue street scene before him.

It was pure-bred MK.

Yes, he was home.

He closed his eyes again and leaned back against the wall, the palms of his hands flattened against the cool carbon steel. The low hum of the climatecon flooded through his every fibre. How long was it since he last heard this every-day, ordinary, *normal* surround sound? How many months? Five, six? He really had no idea. He didn't care.

He replayed the events of his journey. The rainforest, Slingshot Inn, Middlemedes, Rika ... Rib pressed the fast-forward button. The motorway, *Unity*, Gran, the Frog, Besk ...

He shuddered and took off his rucksack, undid the draw-strings and instinctively felt for the velvet bag containing the twenty walnuts and his dad's ID ...

They were there.

Unbelievably, he was here now, back in MK, 200 million dollars richer. He snapped to. He had to move. He was attracting attention.

It must only have been 6.15, but already the citidome was stirring into life and people were on their way to work. A passing white trannivann slowed and Rib knew that he was being watched.

Being clocked.

The fact that he was standing at an emergency evacuation point on the yellow criss-cross paint lines that no one was allowed to stand on ...

The fact that he was wearing torn khaki muddied by extreme sun, forest stain and sweat when everybody else in MK citidome was attired in deodorised greysuit ...

The fact that the end of his nose was split open and the fact that he had 200 million dollars burning away in the bag hanging from his back ...

All this made Rib Meskitoe feel uncomfortable.

And exposed.

Which he was.

So he set off in a leaping gallop under an awning which, some five minutes later, would transform itself into Paulo's Trattoria Espresso. Tables out on the sidewalk, chink of cup and saucer.

Rib knew this place well. He sat in the shade and thought about Uncle Vin. When Rib was five, he was allowed albeit reluctantly by his mum to go on the early-morning trash-sucktruck round with his Uncle Vin. She rationalised that it would widen his perspectives, broaden his horizons, teach him how the other tenth lived. But, as Rib soon realised, that did Vin a serious disservice. His uncle, Rib was to discover in his formative years, could drink in twelve languages and swear in forty-seven. The drinking would begin at 6.45 at Paulo's with a purposeful nip of brandy in the Blue Colombia and the swearing would flow from 6.46 onwards.

He was a marvel of a man. He could, and would, drive a trashsucktruck one-handed and without looking through the front windscreen for a whole session, whilst leaning out of his wound-down window, hurling indiscriminate obscenities at anybody and everybody who happened to be in hearing distance.

The inaugural trip in Uncle Vin's cab at the tender age of

five had increased and enriched Rib Meskitoe's vocabulary tenfold. When he was dropped off home at the end of the day, his mum had raised an acknowledging wave in the direction of the truck, which thumped off back to the depot with a blast of the horn. She had met a flushed and breathless son at the door, almost hyperventilating with the burning question: 'Mum, what is an unadulterated arsehole?'

Unsurprisingly, further excursions with the Vin branch of the family were strictly rationed.

To his credit, Uncle Vin was a loyal public servant. His sickness record was unmatched at the trashsucktruck depot. In fact, he had taken sick leave on only one occasion during the span of his twenty-seven years' service, when he was hospitalised with a hernia having pushed down too hard on the cafetière plunger in the conservatory one summer's evening in late August 2036.

It was 6.25 a.m. The temperature an ambient 19 degrees. Rib sat on a white plastic chair under a blue-and-white striped awning which said Paulo's in red letters and knew he was home. And it felt so good. MK citidome had its critics, but nowhere felt anywhere like it. Nobody wanted to come here, and yet nobody wanted to leave. Rib certainly wouldn't be venturing far for the foreseeable future.

First priority. To get back home before he aroused further suspicion and was pulled by the polizzia. Just imagine his bag being searched and him losing the 200 million now. What was the phrase? Many a drop spilt 'twixt cup and lip' or something like that. Anyhow, spillage was not on the menu.

Spillage.

The word jerked his memory back to Waste-Rows. To Kaddie. 'Look at me, I'm the only grey in the spillage.' That stupid fool who made everybody laugh. That idiot who was really an agent, placed there to help him escape and assess him. Rib felt a mix of emotions. If he were to meet him again, he wasn't sure what he'd do. Give him a big hug or a smack on the nose.

He was snapped out of his thoughts by a passing shuttle. Did it slow as it shooshed by? Certainly a few passenger heads turned to look at the out-of-place figure under the awning. He had to move.

And fast.

Luckily, Domestrut 44 had brought him up only a short distance from his mum's house on the East Side.

H1-222.

'Well, Mum, the cavalry is just about to ride over the hill with its armour shining and its lances pointing sharpy-sharp,' said Rib to himself as he cornered the intersect into H1. It looked just the same. The units and factories on either side of the road deserted, boarded up, ripe and ready for demolition. Some walls bore graffiti tags – unheard of else-where on the Dome. But there it was, number 222, at the end of the road, its yellow-and-green banded security roller shutter shining bright like a homing beacon, as bright as the day he had helped his mum to paint it. As he neared, slowing to a jog, he could see that the front yard was still in good shape. Buckets, wash tubs, old tin baths, bread bins, anything vaguely resembling a container, salvaged, restored and filled with plants. Yellow plants. Only yellow, as his Mum had insisted at his dad's funeral.

Only yellow.

All the containers lovingly painted black and adorned with bright-blue, white, red and yellow designs, in narrowboat style. His mum had once taken him to the perimeter rail after they had fed and watered the animals for the night. 'Just down there,' she said, pointing, 'used to be a waterway which was the longest man-made channel in the country. The Grand Union Canal, they called it.' And she had stood behind him, placed her rough but gentle hands on his shoulders, and told him of barges and cargoes, locks and tunnels.

Oh God, how he was looking forward to seeing her again.

He walked up to the door signed '222' by three white ceramic French-style tiles with blue borders. He pulled on the kitsch bell in the form of the tail on the back end of a rhinoceros embedded into the wall. This set off the usual barks, squawks, grunts, screeches and growls of the refuge. If Mum were out on the perimeter, it would take her a full minute to get to the door. H1-222 was the only residence on the citidome to extend beyond the dome wall. All of the cages and outhouses stood in an area which was outside the controlled atmosphere of MK, hence the relative ease with which Mum had got the planning permission in the first place. Quite simply, nobody else wanted it and nobody else could have created a sustainable micro-climate on the perimeter using tinfoil, fifteen heat exchangers and a deceptive degree of ingenuity.

The cacophony had ebbed, but no familiar footsteps towards the door.

Shit, she's not in, he swore under his breath, suppressing the 'How dare she after all I've been through?' thought. He looked back at the main drag to see the traffic building up. He had to remove himself from the public gaze, but where?

Sammy's!

44

Two birds with one stone. A safe port of call for an hour or two and a thoroughgoing haircut and maybe even a wash. For Sammy's was East Side's best hairdressing establishment by a long chalk. And it was like a second home. When Uncle Vin's star had fallen from the heavens, Sammy's was where Rib had spent his formative years sweeping up, running errands, making endless cups of tea. And learning how to gamble – Chinese style.

Sammy's was on the same grid, H1-251 to be precise. He opened every morning at 6.00 on the dot.

Rib loped back to the intersect and then sprinted across the main road picking out the red-and-white barber's pole in the mid-distance. He slowed to a walk, trying to assess how long the queue would be by the number of mopods parked outside. On entering, he was met with the familiar sound of whirring razors and the commercial radio crackling the latest update on sleaze, travel, sport and more sleaze.

There were four men seated on the leather bench waiting to have their hair cut. The protocol was that the bench served as a queue, everyone shuffling along a bum's width as soon as someone came in the door. It was a time-honoured system which worked well and which had the added bonus of a warm seat for all newcomers. As the bell above the door rang Rib's arrival, the four men looked up as one, and then eased nervously as far as they could towards the end of the bench. A sideways glance in the mirror told him why. He stared at the reflection of a person who looked as if he'd been dragged through a hedge backwards, through the mill, up shit creek without a deodorant and worse. In short, he looked bloody terrible. The sliced nose did not help.

'Mister Rib!' came a cry from behind the till. 'You look bloody terrible. What happen your face?' The diminutive figure of Sammy Chung scuttled the length of the salon to embrace the sprog he had known since his mother had brought him in for his first trim twelve years before.

'You smell bloody terrible, too,' said Sammy, releasing him quickly. 'Where you been? Your mother very worried. She say you no call. Why you no call? Mister Rib? You in trouble? Why you no call your mum?'

'I couldn't,' Rib started to protest but there was no stemming a Sammy in full flow.

'Why you no with her today? Special day – tough day.'

'But I've just been home and no one's there. And what do you mean "tough day"?'

'Today your mother in court. Today the day they try shut her down.'

'Shit!' swore Rib. Was he too late?

He felt everything well up in him – despair, frustration, anger. He turned to leave. Sammy grabbed him by his arm. 'Where you going now?'

'I'm going home.'

'Not looking like that. I need fix that nose. Your mother kill you. You need good wash and brush-up. Your mother kill you anyway but at least you look good. Now go get shower and I give you short, back and sides.'

'Excuse me,' said the man at the far end of the bench. 'I think it's my turn, I've been waiting for over fifteen minutes.'

Sammy produced a cut-throat razor from his breast pocket and deftly flicked it open. 'You want Sammy cut your hair or your want Sammy cut your throat?'

It was a rhetorical type of question, but Sammy didn't deal

in rhetoric. 'Well?'

'I would like you to cut my hair, please,' the man answered meekly – after a pause.

'OK, you shut shitty cakehole then,' said Sammy as he snapped the blade shut and returned it to his pocket.

He took Rib out the back, gave him a towel and pointed him to the shower room.

'Shout when you ready, Mister Rib. I get you new clothes.'

Rib stood under the shower for an age, letting the sharp jet of water wash away the grime and grit from his body and soul. Sammy had laid a greysuit out for him. It felt crisp and fresh against his skin.

Sammy was right. His mum would have died if she'd seen him in the state he was in. He went out into the salon. Sammy was thankfully busy cutting hair not throat and turned to give him a broad smile.

'That better, Mister Rib, much better. You want haircut now?'

'Yeah, that would be great, thanks.' He sat back in the worn leather chair and closed his eyes as Sammy started to comb out his now-long locks.

45

A woman sat three seats from the back on the 8.05 shuttle from Silbury staring impassively out of the window. Her eyes did not see the offices, shops, factories and the stream of rush-hour traffic moving in the opposite direction. She just saw the reflection of her own face.

The face of a beaten woman. A crushed woman.

She had once seen Mike in a dream. She was walking in a cloistered quadrangle of Trinity College, Cambridge. She didn't know how she recognised the weathered slabs, the perfectly clipped lawn. She had, of course, never been there. Never seen the hand-painted sign which read 'Do not walk on the grass'.

She was walking on the grass.

Mike appeared by her side.

'Mike,' she said.

He smiled at her and then started to walk upstairs in mid-air. There were no stairs. He was four steps up when he turned to her and smiled again.

'Mike,' she said. 'Is everything all right?'

'Yes,' he said, 'everything's all right. It really is. Very all right.'

Very all right.

She woke on those words.

She opened her eyes and felt her whole body glowing. A tidal wave of hope, happiness and life force surged through her being. She had to breathe deep and hard, so heady was the emotion.

Alice Meskitoe was in no way a believer. In fact, she avoided churches religiously. But what she had felt that night was without doubt a spiritual experience. It had moved her so deeply. At the same time it had saved her. She had never mentioned it to anyone. Not even Rib.

And every night she ached for its return.

She devoted all her energy to keeping the refuge going, constantly facing obstacles thrown at her by the Citicouncil, who were determined to close it down. Even today, it timed her court hearing at 6.30 in the morning. Not because they thought she might not turn up at so early an hour.

No.

They knew that 6.30 was feeding time at the refuge.

Alice could handle all of this. And more. And did.

The verdict had been given at 7.17 by an elder in a grey-suit with a fluffy wigcurl on the left shoulder. The court found against the MK Animal Rescue Centre and ordered costs of 450,000 dollars against the registered owner, Mrs Alice Meskitoe.

And notice to quit if the payment was not made in full within twenty days.

She could have handled even this one last blow to the body if her son had not been missing for over six months.

She had begun to worry after three days of not hearing from him. She called his i-shield daily, but it was either switched off or the cell had dried. She confirmed with the laserjet office that he had disembarked at the Wigan citidome terminal. She phoned the local polizzia to report him as a missing person but, when she gave her name, detected an edge to the officer's replies. After two weeks, she asked Maggie to look after the refuge for a few days and took the lasercraft to Wigan citidome to hunt for her son herself. She traced where he worked, talked to supervisor Svensson but drew a blank. Managed to persuade a bastard of a landlord to open up Pod 512, where she found her son's clothes piled in a heap, a used towel on the bathroom floor, an unmade bed.

She pressed a brown T-shirt against her chest and sobbed her soul out while the landlord's silhouette darkened the doorway, demanding due rent. She stayed for only a further day, stifled and suffocated by what seemed to be a conspiracy of silence. How could he have disappeared without trace? She returned to MK and tried to throw herself back into her work. But half of her was always standing at the front door, looking for the next shuttle or straining to hear the tuneless whistle out in the cages at feeding time.

She had returned to MK with heavy heart and sense of foreboding at the upcoming court case. Storm clouds were gathering and Alice could sense no shelter.

No shelter. No refuge.

Here she was, a forlorn passenger on a shuttle to nowhere. All other members of this busy commuter community with a role, a purpose, a destination in life. As she neared her stop on Silbury, she came to a stark realisation. All that awaited her was a final twenty days of caring for the animals.

The court's verdict had condemned the MK Animal Refuge Centre to death row. And her lot was to play out the role of warder, pastor and executioner to the animals, all in one. She had absolutely no doubt whatsoever as to their fate. They would suffer the same agony as many before them. They would be thrown over the edge.

The end was inevitable.

Because she no longer had the will to fight.

Something in her subconscious forced her up from her seat to press the stop button as the shuttle approached her station.

The doors swooshed open and she stepped onto the walk-way. She had taken five heavy steps before the doors closed and the shuttle continued its course. She stopped as it shifted soundlessly into the semi-distance, its brake lights sparking into life 300 metres down the drag at H2. Alice moved on, nearing the 222 intersect. She slowed and took in the neighbourhood. Alice had trodden this path a thousand times before. She now saw it for the first time; the letter 'L' missing from the signage of Alf's Electrics; the overturned skip on the forecourt of Divorces R Us, the For Sale sign in the window of Barleystow Leaves, Estate Agents. It was run down, it was tacky. Out of luck, down at heel, on its uppers. As a younger woman, she had chosen this quarter for her home. It had been alternative, vibrant, even bohemian and full of zest. She now saw it for what it was, a sad tale of yesteryear.

She turned into 222, unable to raise her gaze to the refuge at the end of the road. She walked head down, intent on her turquoise toenails. She had been persuaded only the week before to have them done.

Colour on calcium.

Colour so confident.

And chipped, still somehow bright but chipped.

Her eyes welled up with tears. She looked up through a wet mist towards the MK Animal Refuge sign in yellow against the blood-red fascia.

Her heart stopped as she saw him, stretched out in the wheelbarrow, his left leg dangling over the front edge as it always had. Even from where she stood she thought she could make out the clean line of his jaw, the trim brush-cut hairstyle.

'Mike?' she whispered hoarsely as she broke into a run. 'Mike!'

The figure fell out of the barrow as he heard her voice.

She then screamed. 'Oh my God, Rib!' They hurtled towards each other and met with a force of body and emotion that nearly took them off their feet. He held her tight in his arms and whirled her 720 degrees. She let him, limp in his hold.

They stood locked together for an eternity. They tasted the salt of each other's tears.

Alice Meskitoe and her found-again son finally walked across the front yard, arm in arm, exchanging small talk in soft tones, neither yet ready or steady or able to ask or answer the difficult questions. Once inside, they found peaceful refuge in the routines of old: she cooked him his favourite lunch of grilled mustard herring and hash browns and stood watching him in silence as he devoured it in silence. They cleared up and went out to the cages to feed and water the animals, little yelps of recognition greeting Rib as he neared the bandicoot pen.

Then they stood against the perimeter rail, looking out over the vast canopy of rainforest. Each knowing that talk would come later, when their burned senses had recovered. That night they both slept more soundly and deeply than for many a moon.

Rib woke early, stirred by the faint hum of the aircon. Strange that he had become unaccustomed to it. He could hear the clink of cups and bowls from the galley, so he took a quick shower and went down for breakfast. A bowl of honey yoghurt with blueberries and a cup of carrot juice sat waiting for him.

'Thanks, Mum,' he said as he sat down. He started spooning the yoghurt into his mouth and then looked up. He had felt her gaze upon him as she stood leaning against the worktop.

'Love you,' he offered.

'I love you too,' she returned, although he knew that his offer would not be enough.

'So, where have you been, Rib? What on earth's happened to your nose, and how did you get that scar?'

'Oh that,' he said. 'Well, it's a long story, Mum, and I'm not sure I really feel up to it just yet.'

'Listen, you can't just disappear for six months without talking to me about it.'

'I know Mum, I know, but later, eh?' he said as he stood

up. 'I'm going to college, see if I can catch up with a mate or two.'

She knew better than to protest as he left the galley. Something had clearly happened to him and she had been wrong to force the pace. All in good time, she told herself, all in good time, as she cleared away the dishes. But time was something she knew she didn't have.

46

Rib slowed to a walk as he neared the intersect. He had instinctively broken into a run as soon as he left the yard. He just felt he had to get distance between him and his mum. How stupid was that? He'd spent six months trying to get back, and eighteen hours later he was on the run again. But deep down he knew why. He didn't have his story yet. Firstly about how he first 'relieved' an old woman of 200 million dollars and secondly about how that old woman had turned out to be his gran, whose name was never to be uttered under his mum's roof. And it was really a test. And it wasn't really theft, it was his inheritance. Shit! He needed some breathing space. He needed to rehearse.

He made out the hum of the approaching shuttle. He sprinted hell for leather onto the main drag and just caught it. He sat down in a seat opposite two young flicks. He took a deep breath, feeling pretty impressed with his show of athletic prowess. He certainly wouldn't have been able to do that six months ago. Probably would have collapsed in a wheezing heap 50 metres back. One of the flicks whispered in the other one's ear. They both looked at him. The whisper receiver reddened. Rib hadn't heard the comment. But he could guess the drift. He alighted at Chaffron and walked the short distance from the stop to the college entrance.

'Eeyup, chuck!' came the familiar welcome from Brenda, the receptionist. 'Long time no see. You been doing a gap year or summat?'

'Er, no,' Rib replied. 'I've just … er, been away.'

'Well, it's good to see you back, chuck.' Brenda had worked at the college as long as anyone could remember. She welcomed everyone as if they were special. She used to be on the switchboard but the 'eeyup, chuck' had not gone down well one day when the Chairman of the Board phoned the switchboard from his i-shield to complain that he had been lurching around the car park for fifteen minutes, unable to find a space. Brenda had eeyup-chuck'd him and told him that there was 'nowt' the Principal would be able to do about it and that the Chairman should 'thank his lucky stars' it wasn't Tuesday, as it were 'bleedin' bedlam on Tuesdays, bleedin' bedlam'!

Brenda was switched from switchboard to reception overnight, gaining cult status by securing a pay rise in the process. Principals came, Principals went. Each one to be greeted on their first day by an 'eeyup, chuck'.

'Have you seen the twins, Brenda?' Rib asked.

'I do despair of them lads,' sighed Brenda. 'Why they have to carry on as they do is beyond me. What they need is a good firm hand. I blame the parents. I do.'

'Oh thanks,' said Rib, extricating himself from the yarns of homespun moralising about to unravel. 'I'll take that as a no …'

A quick search of the Chaffron Campus failed to uncover the Deccaheads. He'd catch up with them later at the New Pitz. He spent the rest of the day dropping back into the everyday routines. He signed up for class, took some files from the LRC, grabbed a doughnut from the refectory and ate it on a bench out in the quadrangle, watching the student world go by. All of which he should have been enjoying. A return to the comfort of the everyday.

Yet he wasn't. He was on edge, ill at ease with himself. Gnawing away at his insides was the thought that at some stage he had to go home. He was just painting by numbers, filling in the blues and yellows and greens. The deep crimson red was waiting for him back at the refuge. However hard he tried, he couldn't get his story straight. About how he came into 200 million dollars.

About how he'd won and lost Rika.

About how he'd found Gran, or rather how she'd found him.

He knew she wouldn't understand. She'd go quiet, breathe deeply and then explode. He remembered her doing it only once before when he was much younger, eleven, when he'd promised to feed and water the animals when she went away on an overnight conference. He had forgotten.

It was well into the afternoon before he found himself back at the door of 222. He had left in such a hurry that he hadn't even taken his keys. He pulled the rhinoceros tail and heard the bell ring in the galley.

As he heard his mum's footsteps approach the other side of the door, he steeled himself and repeated the rehearsed explanation in his mind.

What happened next was totally unexpected. The door opened to a smiling Mum, orange parrot on forearm, also seemingly in a good mood as it preened its wing feathers.

47

'Hi, darling.' She reached forward with her free arm and touched his hand. 'Had a good day at college?'

'Yeah …' he replied, unsure of his ground. 'Yeah, I re-enrolled, had a bite to eat, checked out the …'

'Rib, you have a visitor,' she interrupted, turning away from the door to allow him in.

'A visitor? Who?' he asked as he followed her down the corridor.

'It's your friend from Wigan citidome, Mr Kadwallader.'

Rib stopped in his tracks.

'Kaddie! It can't be!'

His mum was still talking over her shoulder at him as he caught up with her. 'He's told me all about you. Where you worked. What you got up to at weekends. I'm really proud of you, darling,' she said as she turned off into the galley. 'I'll just go and put on some muffins. You go and join him. He's out on the platform.'

Rib half ran down the corridor past the reptile cages. His mind was a whirr, a mix of emotions. So pleased that Kaddie was alive and had come all this way to find him. So angry that he had duped him into believing he was a halfwit.

But how good would it be to see him again!

As he passed through the last of the three doors, the heat of the evening hit him. Although the sun was just setting to the west of the dome casting the whole of the platform in shade, the temperature was still registering a humid 34 degrees.

He sprinted round the corner of the snake compound to see a grey-clad figure seated at the patio table with his back towards him.

Rib slowed to a halt some 5 metres behind the man. He could feel the hairs on his neck rise.

'We meet again, Master Meskitoe,' whispered Hesperus Besk, without turning round. He raised his left arm and a bony digit beckoned.

'Pray join me, young man. Your mother really does cook exceptionally good Java.'

'Besk,' snapped Rib. 'How the hell did you find me here?'

'I have … certain connections. Surely you should know that by now. And I was naturally inclined to ensure an early re-acquaintance with you after the unnecessary scene beneath the frog. Please be seated. It's in your interest so to do.'

Rib moved cautiously around Besk and sat down at the other side of the table.

'Thank you. And now if we may proceed to business.'

'Business? With you? I don't think so!'

'Ah, the spirit! Such an admirable trait. The problem is, Master Meskitoe, you have no choice.'

Rib opened his mouth to respond but Besk hissed.

Here he was, face to face again with the man who had pursued him for the past six months. His thin lips parted in a vicious slit of a smile.

'See the table before you. My left hand is visible. My right hand is not. It is under the table and is pointing a crossbow at your crotch.'

Rib froze.

'That's better. Now we can talk business. I sense that you have something that I want.'

Rib tried to act is if he didn't understand. He moved to raise his palms in a sign of non-comprehension.

'Keep your hands flat against the table,' snarled Besk.

'I suggest you remove the rucksack from your back and share its contents with me.'

'I wish you'd make your mind up. Either you want my hands flat on the table or you don't. Now which one is to be, Mr Besk?'

The beads of perspiration which were starting to form on his forehead were due partly to the high humidity but mostly to the fact that he was cacking it. Dancing with death, playing with fire, basking with Besk.

Rib was waist high in shark-infested waters. He took the plunge.

'Tell me, Mr Besk, do I detect a redness around the eyes. How did that come to pass?'

A muscle in the old man's jaw twitched, sending a ripple across the taut brown leathery shin. His right hand appeared from below the table and, sure enough, it did hold a crossbow.

Rib hadn't doubted his word for one moment. And unsurprisingly, the crossbow was loaded. With a ten-centimetre stainless-steel bolt with a bright-red feather flight. Rib started. He had seen one of these before.

'Your bravado verges on the masochistic, Master Meskitoe,' hissed Besk. 'Your self-indulgent impishness fails accurately to assess the severity of your situation. I hold all the cards in this game. I always have. I always will. Your lucky move with the nerve gas to which you refer was but a sideshow. Inventive, I concede, but indecisive. It merely served to delay the inevitable. Which is where we are now.'

Footsteps could be heard approaching.

It was Mum.

'Stay wise, young man,' said Besk. 'I will have no hesitation in killing her.' He returned his right hand to under the table.

'I am aware of your thoughts,' he whispered as the steps came nearer. 'Only one bolt, you are thinking. Let it be understood that if you show any sign, she will sense the full pain of the steel. Does your bravery embrace such a sacrifice?'

His twisted sneer transformed instantly to a smile to greet Rib's mum as she came round the corner. She was bearing a tray laden with muffins, fruit, two beakers of cranberry juice and a cafetière. 'More coffee?'

'Mrs Meskitoe, how could I possibly resist? Your Java is simply to die for.' He looked Rib in the eye as he uttered these words and knew that there would be no resistance. She topped up Besk's cup with the rich aroma'd full roast.

'Sugar?' she offered.

'Thank you, no, I'm sweet enough as I am.'

Sick enough, thought Rib.

'Well, if you'll both excuse me, I'll leave you to it. I know you've got so much to catch up on.'

'Thanks, Mum, that's great,' Rib said, taking a muffin. He breathed a sigh of relief as she left the platform.

'Excellent,' said Besk. 'Sound sense prevails at last.'

The crossbow reappeared.

The cold steel held the boy's gaze.

'Have no doubt that I will use this if you fail to cooperate. The Slayer has already slaked her thirst threefold on this quest and I sense that she is not yet sated.'

It had a name? And it was a female? This geeza was seriously twisty. Twisty and lethal.

Rib suddenly went chill to the marrow. He had already killed *three* people. Kaddie had to be one of them.

'So, er, so who has it, er, *she* quenched her thirst on then?'

'Slaked,' corrected Besk. 'Your question surprises me. I expected you to surmise.'

'Why would I ask if I knew?'

'Very well then.' He settled back in his chair as if he were about to tell his favourite grandchild a fairy story, sucking on a Werther's Original as he did so. This was a very different once-upon-a-time, thought Rib. But at least while he was telling a story, he wasn't unleashing the Slayer. Right now, Rib was short of strategy options, so he too settled back a little in his chair.

'Firstly, the rogue Australian who operated the Slingshot. A bolt to the right temple from 15 metres. A challenging shot in difficult circumstances. Adverse conditions. Electrical storm.'

Rib had not meant to do any of the talking but couldn't help himself. 'You killed that big guy, Cairns? Why?'

'Pour encourager les autres.'

'Eh?'

'My dear boy, you are not familiar with the works of Voltaire?'

A blank look on the dear boy's face.

'As to be expected,' sighed Besk, with a note of disappointment in his voice. He returned to his theme.

'The second was the woman. Her name I knew not. Let's call her the woman with the glass eye. A bolt to the back of the neck, piercing the windpipe. 32 metres. Simple execution.'

'Wait a minute,' interrupted Rib for a second time. 'I once saw a woman with a glass eye in the Slingshot Inn. She wore blue. She looked very drunk.'

'The very same lady,' smiled Besk. And most accommodating she was, in spite of her state of inebriation. A generous soul. To the very end ...'

Rib gasped with sudden realisation. Kaddie was OK! At least *he* hadn't fallen victim to the Slayer. A wave of relief flooded through him. Kaddie was OK. Because Rib now recalled where he had seen the red feather. How could he have forgotten? In the clearing in the rainforest. The table formally laid, the untouched glass of red wine. The fat man in fox-hunting gear with a bolt through his heart. Rika's reaction – 'We must flee. Run! Run!'

Rika.

He had tried so hard to keep her from his thoughts. She stood now before him. Her bright-red spiky hair, the same colour as the feather on the bolt now pointing at his heart. How perfect, he thought bitterly. He shut her from his mind. Too late.

A single tear rolled slowly down his left cheek.

'I see you recall the third episode. Such sweet reminiscences ...'

'Shut it!' snapped Rib.

Besk raised the crossbow and pointed it at Rib's forehead.

'2.7 metres I would assess. Hardly a challenging target. From this distance the bolt will pass through your cranium and out the other side, taking with it a trail of brain tissue.'

Besk paused to let the picture sink in. He clicked his fingers, making Rib jump. Any sudden movement would have made Rib jump with a loaded crossbow pointing at a spot some 7 centimetres above his eyes; the last thing he wanted was sudden movement.

'The rucksack. Unbuckle it, place it on the table. I advise you not to try anything, for the Slayer remains ready.'

Rib did as he was told, all the time looking at the sharp point of the bolt held unwaveringly before his eyes. He was now drenched with sweat. Droplets forming at the end of his nose before falling at decreasing intervals. Every twenty seconds, seventeen, fifteen, plot, plop, plop onto the front of his shorts.

'Open it,' hissed Besk. 'Extremely carefully.'

Rib leaned forward and undid the drawstring.

'Now, remove each item. Extremely slowly and place them on the table.'

Rib did as he was told. The Swiss Army knife, the map to Slingshot Inn, the compass, a desiccated banana skin – how did that get there? – two T-shirts, a spare khaki beanie. All the time acutely aware of the twenty walnuts clicking about at the bottom of the bag.

'Is that everything?' asked Besk.

'Well, just about,' said Rib.

'I said each item.'

'There's just a couple of bits of orange peel and nuts and other rubbish in the bottom.'

'Nuts, did I hear you say?'

'Yes, nuts.'

'And would they perchance be walnuts?'

'Er, yes.'

'And would there be twenty of them?'

'There might be, I'm not sure.'

'Well, let's take them out and count them. And then we can be sure, can't we?'

The tip of the crossbow bobbed up and down: a clear instruction to empty the bag. The walnuts rolled out onto the flat wooden surface of the table. Most of them stayed together, herd-like, as if seeking safety in numbers. All bar one intrepid nut, which rolled all the way over to where Besk was sitting. He caught it as it tumbled over the edge of the table, held it to his ear and shook it.

'Mmmm, extremely interesting. It sounds as if something hard is encased within this walnut shell. What do you think it might be, Master Meskitoe?'

'How about a walnut?'

'I think not. Let's see, shall we?' With that he deftly rolled the walnut across the table to rest a finger's width in front of Rib's left hand. 'Crack it open,' came the terse command.

Rib took the nut between the thumb and forefinger of his right hand, adjusted the seam so that it ran 90 degrees to his thumb and squeezed.

It popped open and the two small coracles pinged off to either side, leaving their precious cargo to fall onto the table.

A small but perfectly formed, solid-gold, one-million dollar coin.

'Aah ... just as I suspected. An ingenious hiding place. You are to be congratulated. Now, open the others for me. And beware, the Slayer is ever watchful.'

Rib reached over to the centre of the table and rolled the nuts back towards him. He proceeded to crack them open, each time placing the newly liberated coin on top of the others. Besk looked on amused.

'The games children play. Did you like to stack bricks as an infant? What was your record?'

Thirty-seven, Rib thought to himself, but that's for me to know.

'I am now faced with an exquisite choice,' continued Besk, almost distantly, his eyes intent on the coins piling up before him.

'Do I take you dead or alive? The choice is mine. Do I show mercy? Or no mercy? Irrespective of my decision, my status as champion is secured. The points are mine.'

Coin number twelve chinked onto the pile.

'Yet I must confess, Master Meskitoe, that you have been no customary quest.'

'Nice to know,' Rib said, under his breath as he tackled nut thirteen.

'I have thrice reprieved you in recognition of your ...'

Rib broke off from his walnut-breaking routine.

'Reprieve? Thrice? How do you make that out. Thrice does mean three times, doesn't it?'

Besk nodded.

'Just checking. Where and when did you once let me off the hook? And don't even think of counting the time you killed what's his name, Tally-Ho. We escaped. Three times – no way.'

'Once in the rainforest you lay in the undergrowth behind a rotting tree trunk. The truck that stopped beside you. That was my truck. It would have been simplicity itself to cash in the quest at that instant.'

Rib paused, then cracked open nut thirteen.

'So that was you?'

'Your second reprieve was granted at the Slingshot terminal. After I dispatched Cairns, I opened your capsule. Your cheek was pale with the pain of the sedation.'

Rib shuddered at the thought of Besk leaning over him while he was under.

'But who fired me off into the middle of nowhere? I didn't land anywhere near MK.'

Besk laughed. 'Ah yes, I do confess that I toyed somewhat with your destination. And the third time was indeed in the clearing. I watched the two of you intently. In fact, the Slayer held you in her sight for a full fifteen seconds.'

Rib snapped the nut in his hand so that one-half of the shell splintered.

'No way, I am not accepting that.'

'So be it. Even so, thrice stands.'

'When? When was the third time you … what's the word, reprieved me?'

'Now, young man, now! You are at this very moment suspended in a web of reprieve. I could have terminated you at any time since we have been sitting here together, and I have chosen not to. So if you need your own version of thrice, let the present be your answer!' he spat out, clearly incensed.

Rib retreated to walnut duty.

A thousand screeching lorikeets decided to take the air together. Instinctively both men looked out over the rainforest canopy and marvelled at the bright-orange flash of feather. Their eyes came back to meet a moment later, their attention to matters of life and death resumed.

Nuts fourteen to eighteen were cracked. Coins fourteen to eighteen were stacked in a perfect pile.

Besk had gone quiet. Rib didn't know whether that was a good sign or not. He sensed that he had somehow silenced him and that had to be good.

Didn't it?

The crossbow remained aimed at his head, the slender finger poised on its trigger. However good he felt about Besk's silence, the hard currency on the table was not the coins but the crossbow.

What would Gran have done in this situation? What was it she said that night when the two of them sat round the campfire?

What had she said when he wept over Rika?

Wait for the last throw of the dice. It's the only one that counts. The last throw.

The last throw. Yes, that was it. The last throw.

'So what's stopping you from killing me now? Why don't you do it?' asked Rib.

Besk looked down at the pile of coins on the table.

'That, Master Meskitoe, is the question. To kill or not to kill. Dead or Alive allows me to claim maximum points whether I return you to Wigan citidome as a breathing soul or as a corpse. Of course, there is no requirement for the whole corpse. A heart or head will suffice. This is my twentieth hunt over a span of five years. I have, to date, never ...' He looked up and fixed Rib with an icy stare, '... never elected to take the Alive option.'

Rib shuddered deep inside.

'The choice is mine. Returning to your question, I have to confess that you have represented the most succulent quest of all. Your resilience has surprised me. A part of me whispers that to slaughter you would somehow detract from my pleasure.'

Besk paused, deep in thought.

'And then there is the added dimension of the 200 million dollars,' he continued, 'a not insignificant sum to pour into the equation.'

Rib sensed that somehow he was gaining a fingerhold on

the rock face. He was flattened against a wall of sheer granite, a thousand metres up, just clinging on.

He took the nineteenth nut, cracked it open and placed the shiny piece of gold carefully on the top of the pile. Their eyes met as he looked up.

'In which case, Mr Besk, I propose that we have the basis of a deal.'

Besk smiled.

'A deal? And what do you suggest the basis of a deal be? As I said, I hold all the cards.'

Rib knew this, but was just playing for time.

'Well, it goes like this. We call it quits. It's been a great game. We've both had our fun. You take the coins on the table and walk away 190 million the richer!'

Besk laughed.

'And what of my Dead or Alive points? How do I register my kill if, how do I put this, if I have not killed? Unless, of course, you wish to return to Wigan with me and face the consequences of your crime? Surely not.'

Rib took a deep breath. 'You can take a part of me, a small part. The top joint of a little finger – as proof that you have killed me. You could say that you shot me down by the swamp and then, just as you were about to … er … chop off my head, an enormous crocodile surged out of the water, snatched my body and dragged me back into the swamp. All you managed to sever was the top of my little finger. There, simple,' Rib finished.

Besk shook his head in disbelief.

'Your preposterous proposition leaves me disappointed. I had expected better of you. The sacrifice of a body part is in itself not without interest. The serious flaw in your so-called deal, however, lies in its mathematics.'

'How so?' Rib asked.

'You suggest that I walk away from the deal 190 million dollars richer. The stake is 200 million. I walk away from the deal 200 million dollars richer.'

'But what sort of a deal is that?' protested Rib. 'Where is my cut?'

'Your cut, as you put it, is your life. The 200 million dollars are mine. Unless, of course, you are suggesting that the final nut is empty of gold. Now open it!' he hissed.

Rib took the last intact walnut from the table and slowly rotated it with the fingertips of his left hand.

Before hurling it at Besk's head with all his might.

The last throw.

Besk was ready for him. He ducked instinctively and the nut grazed the top of his right ear before smacking against the metal of the animal pen behind him with a resounding clang.

'Rib, was that you? Is everything all right?' came his mum's voice from the galley.

'Answer her,' hissed Besk.

'Yes, sure. Everything's fine, Mum. I just dropped something,' Rib shouted.

'OK, make sure you clean it up.'

Rib Meskitoe and Hesperus Besk locked eyes across the table, the tension between them now electric.

Besk was the first to speak. 'You little fool. Your greed will cost you dearly. I was seriously considering your gambit. I am no sadist and was prepared to listen to your proposal, however pathetic. Yet you chose to spurn me, your superior. You chose to turn your back on your only survival chance.' Besk was seriously agitated.

'Why could you not have negotiated?' he screamed. 'I would have listened. I would even have left you an allowance, a token of my respect for your fortitude.'

'But Besk ...' began Rib.

'Too late. Your act of defiance is terminal. Our conversation is over. I have nothing more to say to you. The Slayer will prevail. I shall now take your life, move back into the galley, amuse myself with your mother before taking her life too.' Besk raised the crossbow and aimed.

The boy sat motionless before him. A smile spread slowly across his lips.

For a split second, Besk hesitated.

A smile?

48

The python's name was Ainsley and he measured 8.5 metres in length. In his native habitat, he was usually slow-moving and primarily ground-dwelling. He was an amethystine python, so-called because in certain light his otherwise camouflaged body showed a purple or violet sheen, and was by nature primarily active at night, especially during the warmer months of the wet season.

He was not, however, in his native habitat. (He had been cooped up in a small cage for the past 139 days.)

Having been rescued by a shuttle-driver named Dan, he had not been able to gather with other pythons in open valleys to sunbathe and mate. (He had been cooped up in a small cage for the past 139 days.)

He had not been able to bask in the morning sun on rocky ledges, flat out on trees or even floating on vegetation at the edge of lakes. (He had been cooped up in a small cage for the past 139 days.)

And he had certainly not been able to provide his preferred female with twelve fertilised sticky eggs. (He had been cooped up in a small cage for the past 139 days.)

The amethystine python is carnivorous, feeding mostly on mammals such as bandicoots, possums, rats, mice and marcopods including tree-kangaroos and pademelons. Ainsley had not tasted meat for ... 139 days. He had been lovingly cared for, his veggie-eco diet of tofu flying-fox-flavour steaks more than enough to sustain him and yet not quite enough to satisfy him.

The moment the two humans had come out onto the platform, they had attracted Ainsley's attention. He stirred from his afternoon nap and slithered to the front of his pen. His tongue flicked as he pressed up the glass wall towards the aluminium ventilation slits.

He started to writhe against the warmth of the glass, his coils twitching involuntarily. The twitch became a thrash as his tail swept from side to side, disturbing the layer of dry leaves and twigs covering the bottom of his pen.

The scent of one of the humans was driving him crazy. His sensitive glands attempted a swift lab analysis: menthe-arvensis leaf oil, cocamidopropyl butane, tea tree leaf oil, sodium benzoate PPG-20 methyl glucose ether, citric acid – all the usual ingredients humans, for some unknown reason, insist on splashing all over themselves. But there was more.

His tongue flashed across his palate.

He had potoroo ... He had whiptail wallaby ... And, oh my God ... He had quokka!

One hundred and thirty nine days without so much as a sniff of decent meat and then all in one sensory explosion the ultimate python feast wrapped up in a single human. The very thought of quokka prematurely unhinged Ainsley's lower jaw in anticipation. He swallowed hard with nothing between his jaws. He thrashed frustration against the glass. He could not get at his prey. The scent was now so strong it suffocated him.

A shrill, barking sound came from quokka-man. The boy human raised his arm and threw something. It hit the top of the pen door with such force that Ainsley recoiled. He looked up from the floor of the cage. The object had hit the door-release button full on.

The door of the pen slid soundlessly open. The 8.5-metre python slithered smoothly out of the pen and across the platform towards its prey.

49

The python struck hard and fast, its backward-curving teeth sinking deep into the flesh of Besk's neck.

Besk screamed as he arched his back. In shock and pain his finger jerked on the crossbow trigger. Rib felt the bolt rip into his side. He heard the wrench of splintering wood as it then tore through the chair and the metallic cling as it hit the cages behind him and fell to the floor, now blooded and spent.

He breathed deeply. He put his hand to his side and held it palm upwards. There was no surprise, no reprieve. It was covered in warm blood. He felt no pain, just a numbing feeling of nausea. He knew that the pain would follow fast. He sat, transfixed by the scene being played out just 3 metres before him. The python had wasted no time in throwing its muscular body in coils around Besk's upper body. The breath whistled from the man's lungs as the snake exerted pressure each time Besk was forced to exhale.

It was literally squeezing the life out of him.

Rib saw the snake coil itself round Besk's whole body. At first Besk stood stock still. Rib knew what he was doing. He was trying to stay as big as possible, not exhaling, not allowing the snake to tighten its grip. Once it did so, his lungs would not be able to expand. All the time his eyes stared wildly at the pile of coins on the table without blinking.

The looty was the last thing on Rib's mind as he began to lose consciousness.

A hoarse scream dragged him up from the depths.

'Help me!'

It was Besk, now encoiled up to his shoulders.

'Help me, Rib, help me.'

He had somehow managed to walk away from the table by some 5 metres. His skin was grey. Beads of perspiration stood out on his forehead. But he was still on his feet. The python snaked slowly, almost casually around him, tightening its grip with each movement.

Rib tried to stand. He couldn't. He looked down at the pool of blood, dark red, which had dried at the foot of his chair. He tried again. He pulled himself up on the arm of the chair. Halfway out of his seat, his eyes met Besk's.

Besk's eyes asked the question. Rib's eyes answered in the negative.

Rib fell back into the chair with a groan of pain. He closed his eyes, fearing it would be for the last time. He heard, or did he feel, a shuffling sound on the platform. He forced his lids apart with a supreme effort to see Besk making one final effort to free himself of the python. He had somehow teetered over to the edge of the platform and was now smashing himself against the rail. The snake released its grip on his neck and opened its jaw wide enough to give out a death-rattling hiss.

Besk twisted and turned, using every ounce of his ebbing strength to scrape the snake against the rail, back and forwards. And it was working. The python was clearly agitated. It coiled up the 2 metres of tail which to that point had acted as a stabiliser and whipped it up to encircle Besk's entire head. Besk gave out a muffled grunt, tottered two steps away from the edge and then hurled himself back against the rail.

Alice Meskitoe was drying a coffee cup when she heard the scream. It made the blonde hairs on her forearms stand rigid.

'Rib!' she in turn screamed, dropping the cup on the floor.

She rushed down the corridor, causing a commotion amongst the cockatoos, and sprinted out onto the platform.

The sight of her son slumped in a chair, the pool of dried blood on the decking, brought her to a halt.

'Oh my God,' she gasped as she ran over to him. She found a weak pulse in his neck, felt for the wound in his side, took out a paring knife which she always had in her sleeve pocket and gently cut the material of his suit and T-shirt from around the wound. The wound seemed clean but was still bleeding. She needed to stem the flow of blood. Reaching into the inside pocket of her jacket, she found her ID card. She slid it carefully over the wound and pressed it down to make a tight seal.

Rib groaned, his eyes still shut.

'You're going to be all right, darling. You're going to be fine,' she said as she raised 111 on her i-shield. She began to take in the scene around her, noticing for the first time the open snake pen. Her gaze returned to the table, to a crossbow and a pile of shiny, gold coins. Her brain registered somewhere in the distance that she was looking at millions of dollars. She looked behind her at the trail of her son's blood and skin splattered across the platform.

An intense anger welled up inside her. 'Emergency!' she screamed into her i-shield. 'Medics to H222 now!'

She saw the broken rail. There was no sign of Ainsley.

There was no sign of the man who called himself Kadwallader.

Epilogue

It was a Tuesday in October. The early-evening crowd had thinned out, heading off downtown to Zubizuri's.

The New Pitz paused for breath.

A group of students remained, occupying the large round table in the centre of the room. They had been on the lash since late morning and were now in reflective mood. A sombre cloud of indecision hung over them. Should they stay or should they go? They were leaderless and looked like they'd be there for the long haul.

In the far-left corner of the bar sat a slim figure dressed in grey, partly hidden by the fronds of a potted fig palm. A cut-glass tumbler of Southern Comfort with crushed ice sat untouched on the table.

Two boys, totally wrecked, sang and gyrated on the raised platform used by local bands at the weekends.

It was the Deccaheads as Boney M, polluting the Rivers of Babylon. '... When we remembered Brian,' they screeched in rat-arsed refrain.

Brian the Bar Manager shook his head in tired despair and motioned them to leave the stage.

The door opened. A shaft of light cut into the room. The silhouette of a young man exchanged a playful mock punch with the duty door supervisor.

The arrival was welcomed with squeals of delight from Boney M, who rushed over and hugged him, careful at the same time to preserve the integrity of their coiffures. He disentangled himself with a degree of difficulty, aiming a friendly kick in their direction as he did so. He strode over to the entrance to the Cool Room. The New Pitz management had re-introduced the chess theme by popular request. Over the door, a sign flashed in blue 'MK Citidome Chess Championships Final Nite'.

Out of nowhere, a short, stocky man of powerful build blocked his path. He swayed unsteadily, seeming slightly the worse for wear. A cut-throat razor hung from his breast pocket.

'Good luck! Be seeing you, Mister Rib,' he said.

'Thanks, Sammy,' the young man replied as they embraced.

A smile formed on the thin lips of the figure in the corner. 'Yes, indeed. Be seeing you, Mister Rib ...'